TURQUOISE GIRL

Also by Aimée & David Thurlo

Ella Clah Novels

Blackening Song
Death Walker
Bad Medicine
Enemy Way
Shooting Chant
Red Mesa
Changing Woman
Tracking Bear
Wind Spirit
White Thunder
Mourning Dove

Lee Nez Novels

Second Sunrise
Blood Retribution
Pale Death
Surrogate Evil

Sister Agatha Novels

Bad Faith
Thief in Retreat
Prey for a Miracle

Plant Them Deep

TURQUOISE GIRL

✖ ✖ ✖ ✖ ✖

AN ELLA CLAH NOVEL

AIMÉE & DAVID THURLO

A Tom Doherty Associates Book
New York

TURQUOISE GIRL

Copyright © 2007 by Aimée and David Thurlo

This book is printed on acid-free paper.

A Forge Book
Published by Tom Doherty Associates, LLC
175 Fifth Avenue
New York, NY 10010

www.tor.com

Forge® is a registered trademark of Tom Doherty Associates, LLC.

ISBN-13: 978-0-765-31715-5
ISBN-10: 0-765-31715-X

First Edition: April 2007

Printed in the United States of America

0 9 8 7 6 5 4 3 2 1

To Sergio and Lourdes Rodriguez for their friendship and unflagging support. Friends like you two come once in a lifetime. And to Poupée, who watches from a better place.

ACKNOWLEDGMENTS

To those experts and specialists in law enforcement who've helped us with the tools and techniques of their profession, especially Jack and Judy. And to M. K. for her help with the Navajo language and customs of The People. The knowledge shared was given freely and generously, and if any mistakes have been made in translation, they are our own.

TURQUOISE GIRL

ONE

✖ ✖ ✖

Special Investigator Ella Clah of the Navajo Tribal Police ignored the chill of the early April night breeze. Her heart felt too heavy for minor concerns like the vagaries of the weather. She missed her daughter Dawn with all her soul and the circumstances responsible for their separation would not be changing for weeks.

Years ago, the prospect of moving in with two other women—both police officers—would have seemed perfect. No one would complain about the crazy hours or the dreadful toll taken by the pressures of a law enforcement career. But those days were gone. Now, living away from Dawn, her eight-year-old daughter, made her throat tighten up and her chest feel constricted.

Dawn had chosen to stay with her father until the renovations on their home were completed. All in all, it was a very practical arrangement, but she still worried. It was part of being a mom. With luck, the next few weeks would fly by.

There had been a lot of changes in her life this past year. Rose, her mother, was now married to Herman Cloud. Rather than move into Herman's home, the new couple had decided to build an addition to Rose's home so their extended family could stay together. It made sense, but the more they tried to keep things the same, the more pronounced the changes seemed to become for all of them.

At least the situation at work was stable at the moment and there were no planned shifts in personnel. Ella's partner and second cousin, Justine Goodluck, would remain here where she was needed most.

The young, petite officer loved her work as a crime scene investigator and detective as much as Ella did hers. There had been a time when she'd been tempted to join another agency, one that could give her the opportunity to work crime scene investigations exclusively—and with the kind of budget she could only dream about here in Shiprock. Yet, despite the temptations, Justine had remained loyal to the tribe and had stayed on the Rez.

Like Ella herself, many Navajos left the reservation at one point or another, curious to see what life was like outside their borders. Yet the land between the sacred mountains never stopped calling its children. The simple truth of the matter was that this was home—the one place where a Navajo never had to explain what it meant to walk in beauty.

"Yo, partner?" Justine called as she half dragged and half pulled Ella's duffel bag out of the SUV. "What do you have in here—adobes?"

The duffel bag, an army surplus store purchase, was nearly as large as Justine. Emily Marquez, Justine's roommate, laughed. Emily, a San Juan county deputy who worked outside Rez borders, was tall, blonde, and had clear blue eyes. She was trim, and more important, fit. "Let me help you with that. With my build, I have a lot more leverage."

"Go for it." As Justine turned it over to her, Emily's hand and shoulder dropped abruptly. She barely managed to keep it from falling to the ground. "Ugh, Justine's right! You stealing cinder blocks from your mom's construction site?"

"Okay, let's double-team this one," Ella said, laughing as she grabbed hold of one of the handgrips and Emily took the other. The light from the front porch made crossing the flagstone walk a lot easier for them. It was late in the evening, and they'd kept the entrance closed to keep out the cool air. The last frost of the season was still a week or two away. "I've got half a library in there. I've been trying to read up on something."

"Near-death experiences?" Justine asked on a hunch, jogging ahead to open the door for them.

"Mostly," Ella answered as they manhandled the bag into the house. She'd been in a serious accident a few years ago, had died, clinically, and been revived. Her experiences in the world after this one continued to fill her mind with questions even after all this time. It wasn't a subject she liked discussing with anyone, but Justine was Christian and, unlike more traditional Navajos, her cuz didn't consider it dangerous to talk about death.

Before Emily and Justine could ask her more, Ella switched the conversation. "I'm really glad I was able to get you guys together as roommates. Things have worked out pretty good for you these past, what, two years?"

"That's about right," Emily answered with a nod, "and it has been great. I've got a little greenhouse in the back. When you take a break, go in and take a look around. With the days lengthening again, everything is coming into bloom."

"She's got orchids and gardenias, and some other tropical flowers I've never seen. It's really gorgeous," Justine said.

Emily smiled, pleased. "Although water's a luxury out in the desert, I think it's wrong to neglect things that make us happy. I remember my grandmother, who had her everyday china and her *special* china. The really pretty stuff never came out unless it was a holiday. I think she used it only a handful of times during her entire life. Had she treated herself to the fine china every day, she would have enjoyed it a lot more."

"That's not a bad philosophy, Em," Ella said.

Justine led the way to the third of the four bedrooms, the one Ella had used once before, and they set the bag of books down on the floor beneath the window. "I've turned this into a permanent guest room. At the far end of the hall is our office.

We've got our computers and everything else you might think of in there. Feel free to use any or all of it, and, if you want, we can find room for the books on the shelves. There are fresh towels in the bathroom. You get blue, Emily gets green," Justine said.

One of the things that made her cousin so good at crime scene investigations was that she had an eye for details. "Thanks," Ella said and began unpacking the big suitcase she'd placed on the bed. The first thing she set out on the nightstand was Dawn's photo with Wind, her pony.

Emily picked up the photo and smiled at Ella. "She looks very confident on that horse."

"Too much so, almost cocky," Ella agreed. "Horses aren't always dependable. They can spook at the oddest things and without any warning. I worry about her, but I've got to admit, she's a natural."

"She's going to be staying with Kevin until you all move back in, right?" Justine asked.

Ella nodded. "Wind and Chieftain were already over there, away from the noise and confusion, so Dawn naturally wanted to be with them . . . which sorta tells me where I fit in the scheme of things," she added with a rueful smile.

Although it was late, Justine and Ella had kept their pagers clipped onto their belts. As part of the special investigations team, they were usually on call. The department had a shortage of officers again after losing several experienced officers to other agencies. Pay, and the lure of other departments with more logistical support and better equipment, would remain an issue for the foreseeable future.

"Are you sure you only want to stay for two weeks?" Justine asked. "You're welcome to stay until all the construction's finished at your mom's place."

"I appreciate that, but Dawn's and my side of the house— the old part—isn't going to be impacted much longer. So, as soon as they finish the rest of the work, install the new heating and cooling unit, and replace part of the roof, my daughter and

I will be able to move back in without any problems. Boots, our regular sitter, is attending the community college these days, so having Dawn's father watching her when Boots is in class makes it easier on everyone."

"You've sure had the babysitting aspect covered between your mom and Boots," Justine said.

"Yeah, but I've got to admit I miss the days when Mom was the only other person taking care of Dawn. Of course that's pretty selfish of me. Now that she's got her work with the Plant Watchers *and* a new husband, she's the happiest she's been since my father died. I can't believe it's been almost eleven years since . . ."

Justine nodded, but didn't comment, and Emily smiled awkwardly.

Ella let the subject drop. She wasn't a traditionalist, but some subjects were better not discussed. It wasn't that she was worried about calling the *chindi,* the evil in a man that remained earthbound after death. With her, it was more a matter of not calling sadness into her life. Thoughts and words had more power than the *bilagáana* world, the white world, realized.

"It was a sad time but it brought you home," Justine said gently. "Now you're raising your daughter to know the land and The People."

Emily glanced at one, then the other. "You're both pretty lucky to have such a wonderful cultural heritage. People like me, who don't have a definable ethnic background, miss out on a lot."

"You may be right, but there's another side to that," Ella said, realizing how much she sounded like her brother Clifford, the *hataalii,* at the moment. The Navajo Way held that everything in life had two sides—like light and dark, good and evil. It was finding the balance between the two that led to harmony. "At least you didn't have pressure coming at you from two opposite directions when you were trying to find your own niche in life." Ella was about to say more when both Justine's pager and her own went off simultaneously.

"I'll get it." Ella called in, and then after a moment, hung up. "We've got to roll, partner. We've got a 10-72," she said, grabbing her jacket off the bed. Nodding to Emily, who'd already stepped back, Ella headed for the door. Justine followed.

"A road's being illegally blocked? What's the rest of the story?" Justine asked as she slipped behind the wheel of the unmarked tribal vehicle.

Ella gave her the details as they raced toward the highway. "Trouble's going down at the access road to the new power plant construction site. They were scheduled to move in heavy equipment to begin digging foundations for the main reactor building, but there's a group of diehards trying to block access to the site."

"I thought they'd called off all their protest demonstrations after their lawyers lost the legal battle. It's been pretty quiet the past few months," Justine said, not taking her eyes off the road.

"Yeah, it has been. The construction company didn't want to incite anything either, so that's why they waited until nine P.M. to move in their heavy equipment. But someone obviously tipped the group of protestors off."

"What's the sit-rep?" she asked, requesting a situation report. "Any details on what level of protest we're walking into?"

"The workers and their equipment are being blocked by numerous individuals, several pickups, and even a small trailer, according to a security guard's report to Dispatch. Apparently the protestors plan on keeping everyone out—or at least equipment and vehicles. Tempers are running short."

"Is there another way in?"

Ella shook her head. "Not unless the construction company put in another road we don't know about. I also remember from our earlier visits—before the courts threw out those restraining orders—that there's a fence on both sides. The place is pretty easy to seal off."

"Or seal in."

"That's the problem. And what the protestors haven't

blocked with vehicles, they're covering with manpower. The construction crew doesn't have permission to take down the fence and try to drive around the protestors either, so they're stuck."

The small nuclear power plant, first proposed by a mostly Navajo consortium called NEED, had already cleared the years of paperwork and legal hurdles. But now that construction could finally get under way, tensions appeared to be escalating once more.

As they approached the turnoff, Ella saw that a fire had been set in the middle of the graveled road about fifty feet from the eastbound lanes of the highway. Beyond that fire, between the construction workers and their vehicles, were the protestors.

Justine pulled off the highway, emergency lights still flashing. Several construction workers moved aside, letting the SUV proceed down the shoulder of the access road past the construction vehicles to the main gate, which was closed. Beyond the gate was a small bonfire, fueled by firewood, it appeared.

"I don't see that many protestors, Justine," Ella said as they came to a stop. "And there are, what, four pickups and a homemade trailer full of firewood?"

"Not like the demonstrations when the site was first selected, that's for sure," Justine agreed. She turned off the lights and engine and they both stepped out of the unit.

Just beyond the chained and locked metal gate were four warmly dressed Navajo men holding signs whose messages she recognized from earlier incidents. PROTECT OUR HOLY PLACES, read one, and the other held big letters, NO NEED, which referred to the Navajos Opposed to the Navajo Electrical Energy Development project. Outside the gate were a half dozen workers, standing beside a loader, two dump trucks, and a big bladed Caterpillar atop its transport semi and trailer. Closest to the gate was a white pickup belonging to the construction firm, and beside it, a small Jeep that had the name of a security service on the door.

Ella immediately heard, as well as felt, the deep-throated pounding of drums somewhere up ahead. She saw two more protesters on their knees beside the fire, beating on the drums in a steady tattoo.

"Think I should take the shotgun?" Justine asked.

"No. It might just escalate things. Bring your nightstick and keep the Mace handy. This looks to be just a shadow of what we've seen before, but don't get complacent."

"You come at night like cowards," one of the protestors yelled. He was standing just out of reach, beyond the gate, moving back and forth and shouting through a bullhorn.

"That's Benjamin Harvey. He was arrested last time for disorderly conduct. He's trying to goad someone into starting a fight," Ella said quietly. "Call for backup. It'll make it easier on everyone if we can outnumber them."

Ella walked up to the heavy metal gate, her eyes alert for possible weapons among those across the fence. Standing at the edge of the glow from the fire, away from the other protesters, was a seventh Navajo in a low-billed cap aiming a camera, filming everything. She didn't recognize him as being from one of the local news services, and his camera wasn't high-end, but maybe he was freelance or working the propaganda angle for the demonstrators. When she reached the gate, he aimed the camera directly at her and Justine and continued filming, but didn't move any closer.

Ignoring him for now, Ella turned as someone from the construction company, wearing a gray company shirt, walked up to join her. The man, his name tag identified him as Stover, was a tall, light-skinned Anglo. His expression suggested he was barely restraining his temper. Ella moved back her jacket, showing him her badge, which was clipped to her belt. Her pistol was also there, holstered. "I'm Investigator Clah. My partner is Officer Goodluck."

"Sending in the big guns, huh? It's about time. We called the tribal police over a half hour ago. Security around here is a joke." He motioned with his thumb toward an overweight nineteen-year-old redhead in a brown security guard's uniform. The boy had a flashlight, a small can of pepper spray on the belt of his ill-fitting uniform, and a two-way radio in his pudgy hand. He looked more relieved than concerned at the moment.

"Bring me up to speed on what's gone down here so far," Ella said, not responding to his criticism.

"I chose this time to bring in our equipment because it would avoid traffic tie-ups on the main highway. I had also hoped to avoid any more protesters. With actual construction about to begin, I figured—"

Another tribal police unit pulled up, emergency lights on. Ella knew from the number on the patrol cruiser that it was Officer Michael Cloud, one of Herman Cloud's twin nephews. Her new stepfather was related to two of the best patrol officers in the department. Michael Cloud was an excellent officer with a cool head, just the person she wanted as backup.

As Michael got out of his unit, one of the construction workers used a pair of bolt cutters to snap the chain the protestors had used to lock the gate. The second it opened, another employee slipped through with a fire extinguisher and ran toward the fire. The drums stopped as the drummers hurried to block the way, but the man with the bolt cutters joined his ally, waving the heavy tool at the closest protestor, snapping the jaws. The workers outside the fence shouted their encouragement, and began moving toward the gate to join their more adventurous colleagues.

Ella knew she had to intervene before the two groups met or the situation would spiral out of control. "Keep them outside the fence," she yelled to Michael as she and Justine passed through the gate.

When the man with the fire extinguisher tried to douse the fire, one of the protestors, a tall but fit-looking Navajo man, broke the stick holding his sign over the worker's hard hat, then tore the extinguisher away from the worker's hands. Without skipping a beat, he ran to the gate and tossed the extinguisher into the windshield of the company's pickup.

Ella took advantage of the distraction to grab the bolt cutters from the other worker's hands, then motioned toward the vandal, who was about to bolt. "Detain him, Officer Goodluck."

The protestor ran into the darkness, Justine on his tail.

Ella whirled around, checking to see what the construction workers were doing.

Officer Cloud had closed the gate, and was blocking the way with his body now. "Touch the gate, and you'll get a eyeful of Mace," he said, the cannister in his hand.

The redheaded security guard now came over to join Michael, a container of pepper spray in his hand. "Ya'll back off!"

"Benjamin Harvey!" Ella shouted, trying to find him among the remaining demonstrators, who'd moved forward to defend their two drummers. He'd been the organizer on the past demonstrations.

"Yeah, I know. We're under arrest!" He stepped forward so she could see him, then held out his hands, palms up. "Cuff me. But the *Diné* will be back!" he announced, turning toward the man with the camera. Unfortunately the guy had disappeared.

Benjamin looked around, obviously upset that his big moment wasn't being recorded for posterity. "Where's the camera?"

"You've made your point, people," Ella said to the demonstrators. "Go home now, or spend the night in jail."

In the distance, she heard the sound of a motorcycle racing off. The perp Justine was chasing must have hidden his transportation elsewhere in the dark.

"What about my windshield?" the Anglo named Stover asked, coming up to the gate, then stopping as Officer Cloud turned in his direction.

"One problem at a time, sir," Ella responded, her eyes searching in the direction Justine had gone. Then her cell phone rang.

Motioning with her head, Ella gestured for the two construction workers to step back outside the gate, and, as the first one passed, she handed him the bolt cutters.

"Yeah?" she said into the mouthpiece of her cell, still looking for Justine.

"One of our officers called in a 10-58, Priority One," the dispatcher said, giving Ella the address and the details. "We've also contacted Agent Blalock of the FBI, but he's in transit down from Colorado. Your Crime Scene Unit and the ME will meet you on-site. Officer Marianna Talk is there now."

Ella took a breath. A 10-58 was a report of a dead body, and Priority One designated it as a murder victim.

It was going to be one of those nights. Seeing Justine finally returning, alone, Ella glanced around once more, trying to locate the man who'd been filming. If he was trying to get a story, or record the incident, why had he left as soon as the action started? It didn't make sense.

"The vandal got away. Had a motorcycle stashed in an arroyo. I suppose you heard?" Justine said, shrugging. "I was able to ID the plate, though. I also called in a description of the perp, and they're running down the tag already."

Ella turned to Michael. "I just received a 10-58 call. Once you get some backup, we're leaving."

"It looks like we've got things covered here. Go ahead." Michael pointed with his lips toward the highway.

Ella looked past him to see that Officer Philip Cloud, Michael's twin, had just stepped out of his unit and was walking toward the crowd. Sergeant Joe Neskahi was with him.

As the officers approached the fence the protestors began to walk toward their own vehicles.

Ella surveyed the scene. The gate was all the way open now, and two of the construction workers were shoveling sand onto the burning logs while the young security guard watched. Other workers were already climbing into their vehicles, knowing they'd have to move off the road to let the protesters leave. "The crisis here is over. It's time for us to move on," Ella said.

Stover came up to join them. "If you catch the guy who busted my windshield, my company will be pressing charges."

"We've got a lead on him," Ella answered. "One of our officers will get your statement, and you'll be contacted."

Ella and Justine were on their way a short time later. Yet, knowing what lay ahead, Ella remained tense as they raced to downtown Shiprock.

"Where did they find the body?" Justine asked, her eyes on the scant traffic. With a four-lane highway and the divider between east- and westbound lanes, they could make good time this time of night.

"In the apartment just behind the Morning Stop," Ella said. "Are you familiar with that café?"

Justine nodded. "They fix a decent breakfast burrito. Stan Brewster, an Anglo, runs it these days. His wife is Navajo, and she actually owns the place." Justine checked her watch. "But the place has been closed for hours. Brewster only caters to the breakfast and lunch crowd. I think they close at two or three P.M."

"We don't have an ID on the victim, but the first officer on the scene was the rookie Marianna Talk," Ella said. "She comes from a traditionalist family so she won't want names mentioned if at all possible," Ella said. "Just a heads-up." Although tribal police officers adapted to the demands of the job, some habits were too deeply ingrained. "Apparently Marianna responded to an anonymous tip."

"Will Agent Blalock meet us there?" Justine asked.

Ella shook her head. "He's in transit from Colorado, so we'll be working the scene on our own."

The relationship between the FBI and the tribal police had been very strained at one time. The law dictated that the FBI had to be involved in felony investigations because if prosecution followed, the case would be handled in federal court. Yet the Bureau's presence had served to antagonize more than help. Special Agent Dwayne Blalock and she went way back and, after a few rocky years, they'd finally learned to work well together.

Justine raced down the road with lights flashing. No need

for sirens, they were too late to do anything for the victim. But crime scenes were fragile things, and they had no way of knowing what vital evidence might remain outside, exposed to the elements. Crucial evidence could already have blown away.

"Has Ralph been called yet?" Justine said. These days their Crime Scene Unit was comprised of only three regulars—Ella, Justine, and their photographer, Officer Ralph Tache. Sergeant Joseph Neskahi often came in on special assignments, but the rest of the time he was involved in routine patrol duty.

Ella nodded. "Dispatch made the call. He'll be there. And so will Carolyn," she said, referring to the tribe's ME. Dr. Carolyn Roanhorse was one of a kind—a Navajo woman who was a forensic pathologist. The tribe had paid for her education and though that debt had been paid many times over, Carolyn had chosen to remain on the reservation, using her skills on behalf of the tribe. Dr. Carolyn Roanhorse served above and beyond New Mexico's centralized OMI system, and was a valuable asset to the Navajo Nation. Yet fear of the *chindi* had made her a virtual pariah around many Navajos. Few wanted to be around someone who worked with the dead.

Justine pulled into the small parking lot in front of the Morning Stop Café, located just east of the downtown junction with Highway 491. The officer at the scene had cordoned off the area with police tape, so they had to park about fifty feet away from the front entrance.

Ella got out first, and went directly to meet Officer Talk, who was standing just outside the tape perimeter. The rookie officer had to look much younger than she was, since the department didn't take sixteen-year-olds. Officer Talk was barely five foot two, and that height was enhanced by the boots she was wearing. Although she was standing guard like a professional, protecting the crime scene, Ella saw the slight tremor in her hands as she raised up the yellow tape to let Ella pass beneath.

"I don't have much to give you, Investigator," she said,

turning to speak across the barrier but avoiding using Ella's name. "I responded to an anonymous tip that came through Dispatch at twenty-two-fifteen. A man who wouldn't give his name reported a break-in at this location and claimed he'd heard a woman screaming. The call has already been traced to the pay phone just down the highway at the Quick Stop. I was dispatched Code Three Priority One, and was promised backup as soon as possible."

Ella sensed the struggle going on inside Marianna Talk, who was fighting hard to keep a tight lid on her emotions. The jargon helped neutralize the reality sometimes, but Ella was willing to bet this had been her first Code Three—emergency—and Priority One—homicide—call. Although as an officer for the tribal police, Marianna must have known she'd quite possibly be the only one at the scene for some time, the reality of it must have hit her hard. Her upbringing as a Navajo told her that staying near a corpse was dangerous, yet her duty as an officer demanded the opposite.

"When I arrived on scene, it was quiet," she said in an unnatural but steady voice, as Justine passed by. "Nothing seemed out of order, and there were no individuals in the area. I checked out the doors and windows of the café, but there was no sign of entry, forced or otherwise. So I went around back to the other building, the apartment, I guess it is. That's when I saw that the door had been forced. Inside it's a mess and the body . . . well, once you go inside, the sounds reported by the witness who made the call will make a lot of sense."

"Did you touch anything?"

"No, ma'am. I left everything as it was then came out here to secure the scene."

"Excellent. You've done a good job, Officer."

Officer Talk nodded, then glanced down the highway watching for additional units. "Unless you need me, I'll remain outside the perimeter and provide security while your team works."

Ella stepped carefully into the apartment, what might have

been called a cottage in other regions, pulling on latex gloves—
two pairs—as she did. The extra set of gloves would insure she
didn't touch anything that had come into contact with the
dead. Not that she was a traditionalist, but some teachings
went too deep to ignore. The practice of wearing two sets of
gloves was one followed by most of the officers in the force
and, in particular, those in her Crime Scene Unit.

Justine, who'd been taking photos around the entrance,
followed Ella inside, evidence kit in hand. Ella paused, taking
in the small, simply furnished three-room apartment at a
glance. The place had been tossed and, judging from the blood
splattered all around including the floral patterned wallpaper,
Ella suspected the victim had been beaten, and probably
hadn't gone down easily.

After doing a preliminary walk-through, she called back to
Justine. "Body's in the bedroom. From the wounds and the
blood splatter it appears the vic was either knocked into the
wall mirror or she fell into it during the fight."

Ella focused on the victim, her concentration total as she
studied the way the killer had posed the body. He'd arranged
her in a kneeling position against the side of the bed, as if in
prayer. Her hair was still a bit damp, and had been dripping
water discolored by blood at one time. A *jish*, a medicine bundle filled with pollen and soil, had been tied to one of her
wrists and a closed Bible was on the bed in front of her, a handwritten note on top of it. Ella acknowledged the other evidence, but continued to concentrate on the victim.

"Bathtub's full," Justine said, "the water is bloody, and
there is a lot of spillage on the floor. Maybe a forced baptism—
after at least some of the cuts were inflicted?"

Ella focused on the immediate area around the body. It
had been cleaned up . . . staged. Paper towels had been used to
wipe away some of the spilled blood and water from the carpet. The wastebasket against the wall was full of bloody paper
towels. Streaks on the carpet made it clear it hadn't just been
the perp's intention to clean the blood off himself. Her initial

impression that it had been a simple burglary gone bad faded as she took in the facts.

Ella moved to the side of the bed to take a better look at the victim's face. "I know—knew her," she said, feeling as if someone had just knocked the wind out of her.

Though her nose had been broken, and possibly some facial bones as well, Ella recognized Valerie Tso. Her daughter Boots—Jennifer—was Dawn's babysitter. Deep cuts and bruises covered her naked arms, but she'd been dressed in her Sunday best. Her clothes were clean and undamaged and the absence of blood around her facial cuts told Ella that Valerie had been dressed after her death—once her body had finished bleeding out.

Blocking the emotions running through her, Ella looked for defensive wounds on the body—torn fingernails and bruises on her hands. She was surprised to find only a few cuts on her palms and fingers, ones she might have easily inflicted on herself as she tried to rise off a floor littered with broken glass. Finally, she examined the note that had been left on top of the Bible.

" 'The Lord has made all things for himself: yea, even the wicked for the day of evil. Proverbs 16:4,' " Ella read out loud without touching it. "If you've got enough photos now, bag and tag this, partner. Maybe the killer left us more than he intended."

Justine had already returned her camera to its storage bag. She placed the note in a transparent evidence pouch, then held it up and studied it for a moment. "What the heck is it supposed to mean? God made the wicked for a reason?"

"I'm sure there are numerous interpretations. Maybe the perp was using Scripture to justify his own actions." The scriptural passage teased her memory, but she couldn't quite get a handle on where she'd heard it before. From her father? He'd been a preacher. . . . Yet she was sure it hadn't been one of his favorite or often mentioned quotes. Her father had preferred to emphasize hope, faith, and good works rather than punishment and retribution.

Pushing those thoughts from her mind for now, Ella looked around. "I don't see any paper or pens around that might have been used to write the note, do you?" Ella asked, searching.

"No, not in the bedroom," Justine answered, bringing out the camera again to take more photos of the cleaned-up sections on the worn carpet. "It's interesting that the killer didn't just pose the body, he also tried to clean the immediate area up a bit, too. The only part of this room that's not a mess is within four or five feet of the victim."

Ella saw the dried blood on the broken mirror and on the pieces of glass that lay scattered on the floor. Streaks showed where the killer had pushed some of the pieces out of the clean zone, probably with his foot. There was even some blood splattered on the ceiling. "Maybe the blood's not all hers. She may have taken a chunk out of her killer," Ella said, then took a deep, steadying breath.

"Hey, you okay?" Justine asked.

Ella nodded. "According to what I've heard, mostly from my mother, the victim worked here at the diner and got free rent. She was just starting to get her life together again and was hoping to patch things up with her daughter."

"Your mother's best friend is the victim's mother, isn't she?" Justine asked.

Ella nodded. "And my mother will be right beside the victim's family, demanding answers, when she finds out what happened. This won't be just another case. It hit too close to home. This one's personal." Valerie Tso's life had ended, but Ella's work was just beginning.

TWO

✖ ✖ ✖

Ella waited as Dr. Carolyn Roanhorse studied the body, then began the task of bagging the victim's hands. "She's been dead for about four hours, give or take—a wide range. The body's muscles are starting to stiffen a bit now, suggesting the onset of rigor mortis. But the amount of work the muscles did before death can throw that off. The body temperature is in a range that supports my general estimate, too, but that reading would be affected by the amount of time the body remained in cold water. The perp must have worked hard to put her in this position, though. Notice that the bed itself is propping her up. And take a look at this."

Carolyn lifted the body up a few inches, and Ella could see a shoestring attached to the victim's collar, then to the mattress frame.

"Kept her from falling back, or to the side," Ella observed.

"The lividity, the discoloration of the body—pink as you can see in areas where her clothes are still wet—means the perpetrator didn't bother drying her off before dressing her. That cooled her body, too, as well. So the time of death is still shaky, thought I'd say anywhere from two to maybe five hours ago is a fair estimate. I'll try to narrow it down a bit more for you when I do the autopsy."

"The bathtub's full. She may have been drowned. . . ." Ella said.

"If she was alive when she was put in the tub, I'll know when I examine the body back at the morgue. But considering the punctures on her hands and slashes on her wrists, with pieces of glass still imbedded there, I would have expected to see more blood in the tub. I took a look."

"There's still a lot of blood around, but not on her. . . ." Ella observed.

"He may have changed her clothing, or dressed her, after the body bled out," Carolyn answered.

"That never ceases to amaze me. You can be dead and still bleed for a while," Ella said.

"Thirty to sixty minutes after death, the blood becomes incoagulable. Fibrinolysins do the job." Carolyn's gaze was focused solely on the body. "I'll have a cause of death to you by tomorrow."

Before Ella could move away, Carolyn spoke again. "Neskahi around?"

Ella nodded. "He's in one of the other rooms. We needed a full team on this one."

"Get him."

Ella sighed. Joe had made an unthinking remark about Carolyn's weight about two years ago and since that time, Carolyn had made it her mission to see that he continued to pay the price. He was now her body-mover of choice. Knowing the futility of arguing with her about this, Ella nodded. "I'll go get him."

As Ella passed by the living room, Justine glanced up from where she was crouched gathering fibers and hair. "I found the victim's purse on the floor in the kitchenette," she told Ella. "All her money is gone—including any change she might have had. I sent Joe to check and see if the diner had also had a break-in, but Joe found no signs of forced entry."

"This may have started as a burglary or home invasion before it escalated to murder. But how either of those fit in with the biblical quote is beyond me at the moment," Ella said.

"I still haven't found any paper that matches the type used for the note, nor have I seen a pen lying around anywhere. There's a pencil on the kitchen counter, but that's it, so far."

Ella looked around. "Where's Joe?"

Justine gestured toward the door. "Outside, checking the victim's car, the trash, and the grounds for evidence."

Ella stepped outside and, seeing her, Sergeant Neskahi nodded glumly and went inside. No explanation had been necessary.

Ella's phone rang just then. One look at the caller ID told her it was Agent Blalock. Ella greeted the Bureau man, then gave him a thumbnail sketch of their initial findings.

"As soon as I get back, in about five hours give or take, I'll access databases and see if there's a similar MO on file somewhere. In the meantime, if you get any leads, call me. I'll be out of range at times, but leave a message and I'll get back to you as soon as I can."

"See you in a few hours then."

Ella helped her team collect evidence a while longer, then turned things over to Justine. Aware of how quickly news traveled on the reservation, it was imperative she go see Lena Clani and tell her about her daughter's murder before anyone else did. On the way, for purely practical reasons, she'd stop and break the news to her mom. Her mother's presence at Lena's home would help while Ella questioned Lena.

These days Rose was staying at Herman's house, ten minutes east of Shiprock. After telling Justine how to get hold of her, Ella set out, glad that the short drive would give her time to think.

The facts were a chaotic blend of information points that had yet to make sense. But it was her job to find the pattern to restore order and harmony.

There'd been a time when she would have seen the case as just a matter of doing her job—of giving the taxpayers their money's worth. But her work here on the reservation was far more than that. She genuinely loved the land between the sacred mountains and wanted to protect it. This was her daughter's legacy.

Ella arrived at Herman's, or *Bizaadii's* as her mother had nicknamed him. It meant "the gabby one." It had been her mother's way of teasing, since Herman was a man of few words.

Herman's house, down in the former floodplain of the river, had been more carefully planned and constructed than many Navajo homes. It was set on higher ground in the middle of two fenced-in acres of fine sediment and sand. In the moonlight, Ella could see a dozen sheep grazing peacefully in one of the far corners where the vegetation was tallest.

When Herman left, his nephew Philip was going to move in. Philip Cloud was engaged to a young traditionalist woman who was already a talented weaver. The sheep would supply most of the wool needed.

Ella was just getting out of the tribal unit when she noticed her mother and Two, her shaggy old dog, returning from a walk down by the river. Sometimes when Rose couldn't sleep, she'd go out and enjoy the evening air, wandering far from the house. It was a practice Ella had never liked, and that was especially so in this more populated area closer to town. It just wasn't safe, not with active gangs and crime on the rise on the Rez.

Rose, who'd obviously seen her headlights, came over immediately. "I just finished my evening walk. I know you don't like my wandering around like this, but I'm safe," she added, reaching down to pet her faithful companion.

Ella started to argue then shook her head. That would wait for another time. Right now there was a more pressing matter. Ella searched her mind for the best way to begin but there didn't seem to be any right words.

"Something's happened, daughter," Rose said quickly. "I can see it on your face. Is it your daughter, or your brother, or his family?"

"No, they're all safe," Ella reassured her quickly. "But I

need your help passing along some really bad news to a friend."

Hearing an owl's mournful cry somewhere nearby, Rose shuddered. "Let's go inside the house. Owls are spies for evil spirits. We can sit in the kitchen and have some tea while we talk."

Tea, her mother's special blend, was a mellow tasting mixture of orange and spices that soothed and warmed at the same time. On a night like this one, it was exactly what they both needed.

Herman's home was sparsely decorated. Only one couch and a chair provided seating in the living area and both had been placed near the wood-burning stove. There was a shelf full of books, a floor lamp, and that was pretty much it. Ella followed her mother into the small kitchen, glancing around for Herman.

While Rose poured water into the tea kettle, Ella paused, wondering how to begin.

"My husband's asleep, so speak softly," Rose said, quietly moving about the kitchen, reaching for the tea, cups, and napkins. "Now tell me what's wrong."

Ella knew that her mother preferred to be given bad news while she was busy. It was her way of coping, of relying on the comfort of familiar routines to offset the disharmony that bad news brought.

"The daughter of your best friend is dead," she said, avoiding the use of names in front of her traditionalist mother. Though Ella's message had been cryptic, no further explanation had been needed. Lena and Rose were as close as sisters. They'd shared a lifetime of friendship, of births and deaths, and everything in between.

Rose paused for a second as she poured the tea but then continued. "That one has been dead to her mother for a long time," she answered in a sorrowful voice. "Her drinking, all the men . . ." Rose shook her head. "She broke her mother's heart."

"What can you tell me about her?" Ella took an offered cup of tea.

"She was married at least three times, no, four, I think, and she pretty much abandoned her only child. She had a very serious alcohol problem for most of her life, then a year ago, it almost killed her. She was ordered by the courts to go into a rehab program and, after that, it looked like she was finally changing her life around. She went back to school, received some business training, then got a job at the Morning Stop Café working behind the counter and keeping the books. She wanted to use that employment experience to lead to a better job soon, maybe at one of the Farmington restaurants."

"How do you know all this?" Ella asked. "I thought you said her mother had given up on her?"

"She did. We never spoke about her. It was Boots who'd often tell me about her mother, mostly in bits and pieces. Boots never stopped loving her mother, though she's never really understood the woman. Being raised by her grandmother, Boots has had an orderly life—walking in beauty. But her mother . . ." Rose sighed and shrugged. "So tell me. What happened to cause her death? Since you're here, I'm assuming there's a crime involved and it wasn't just a car accident?"

Ella nodded. "She was murdered at her home, the apartment behind the café."

Rose sat down across from her, and they both drank their tea in silence for a while. "Was it one of her men friends? She saw many, if the gossip can be believed." Rose looked into Ella's eyes, then added, "But there's a lot more you're not saying, isn't there?"

Ella was very good at keeping a poker face. It was part of being in law enforcement. But she'd never been able to put anything over on Rose. Ella gave her a sanitized version of what they'd discovered, leaving out the gory parts and specifics.

Rose paled, then with an unsteady hand took a sip of her tea. "You made the right decision coming to tell me first. My friend is up in years, daughter, and she has problems with her heart. It wouldn't be good to give her this kind of news while she's alone. Boots isn't at home, she's sitting with your daughter, so I'll go with you. Just give me a minute to leave a note for my husband in case he wakes up."

As Rose went into the next room, Ella set down her empty cup. Learning that Kevin was working late again annoyed her, but the only thing she could do was hope he wouldn't make a habit of it while Dawn was there.

"I'll follow you in my truck," Rose said, hurrying to the front door with her. "That way I'll have a ride back and can stay for as long as I need to." She paused for a moment, then added, "Boots will have to be told, too," she sighed. "But maybe we should take things one step at a time."

"You'll have your hands full tonight, Mom. I'll send one of my officers to tell Boots."

It was late by the time they were seated in Lena Clani's living room, Rose by her friend's side. As she broke the news, Ella watched Lena's face register shock, then sorrow, and finally, rage.

"Who did this to my daughter?" she asked, her voice strangled. "He's in jail, right?"

"No, not yet. We've barely had time to process the scene," Ella said gently. "But we're not going to let up until we track the person down.

"Was your daughter seeing anyone special, maybe someone with strong religious ties?"

"Not that I know of. But what is it you're implying? Was my daughter murdered by some religious nut? Is that it?" She looked at Ella as if struggling to understand the incomprehensible. "Why would anyone like that pass judgement on my daughter now? She was finally getting her life back!"

Lena wiped the tears from her face impatiently, then ran a hand through her hair. Then, as if with great force of will, she took a deep unsteady breath and, to Ella's surprise, met her gaze. Navajos seldom looked directly at anyone. It was considered a sign of disrespect. But all she could see in Lena's eyes now was anger and, beyond that, the emptiness that came from utter and complete devastation.

"I want justice for my daughter. I respect what you do for the tribe, so I'll give you a few days to find the man who did this. But I won't wait long, and if you fail, there are others who still respect the old ways and will help me."

Ella didn't have to ask what she meant. Lena was talking about the Fierce Ones, a vigilante group who believed Anglo law enforcement had no place on Navajo land. The Fierce Ones often got in the way of legitimate law enforcement efforts, and although their brutal methods often achieved results, their tactics of intimidation were the antithesis of everything Ella stood for.

"Your family is very much part of my own. I'll find whoever did this to your daughter. But I don't react well to threats," Ella said.

"Don't ask me to turn the other cheek. That's not our way," Lena answered.

Lena's voice was quiet now and more controlled, and maybe that's what made it even more disturbing. Ella knew that having a vigilante group breathing down her neck would just slow down her investigation.

Ella started to respond when she saw Rose shake her head. Her mother stood and urged Ella to the door. They stepped outside.

"Daughter, she can't really hear you, not now," Rose whispered. "Her heart is broken and she's in too much pain. Let me take care of her while you return to work. The quicker you solve this matter, the easier it'll be for everyone."

Ella looked at her mother and saw something in her eyes that disturbed her. "You don't really disapprove of her threat to call in the Fierce Ones, do you?"

She hesitated for a heartbeat. "*Bilagáana* law doesn't always exact justice. Whether you like it or not, you know that's true."

"That may be, but do your best to keep her out of trouble, Mom. I'd really hate having to arrest her," Ella said, then added, "but I will if I have no other choice."

"That's to be expected," Rose answered stiffly.

As she walked back inside, Ella returned to her unit. This case was like a pebble tossed out into a pond. The ripples would travel far and wide. Worried, she drove back to the crime scene.

Despite the late hour, the crime scene team was still hard at work. Ella joined her partner, who was inside processing evidence along with Officer Tache. Officer Talk, not part of the team, had been sent to give Boots the bad news about her mother. The young women were about the same age, and Ella hoped it might make it a bit easier, especially because both had traditionalist backgrounds. Marianna was also going to ask if Boots could provide any additional information on Valerie.

Joe Neskahi was still outside, going over every inch of ground around the building and in the parking lot. Floodlights powered by a generator made his work a little easier but, clearly, it was going to be a long night.

"I spoke to the diner's owner," Justine said from the kitchenette, standing beside a cardboard box already full of collected evidence. "He'll be here shortly. Wanna help me out in the bedroom? I'm still going over the area where the body was left."

They'd worked for a half an hour searching for trace evidence that might have been overlooked when Ella heard the sound of a vehicle pulling up outside. "That's probably the owner. I'll go meet him," she said.

Sergeant Neskahi directed the big pickup to an adjacent parking spot, then pointed at Ella when she exited the building. A tall man in his early fifties climbed down from the oversize cab and went to meet her. The Anglo, who looked as if he worked out regularly, was dressed in a fitted Western style shirt and a turquoise and silver bolo tie. New-looking blue jeans and snakeskin boots suggested he might have just come from an upscale country and Western bar.

He didn't offer his hand, maybe knowing Navajos as a people weren't big on handshakes. "Sorry it took me so long to get here. I've been having trouble with my truck and it refused to start. I'm the owner of this place. My name's Stan Brewster. I understand one of my employees, Valerie Tso, was killed here tonight."

"In her apartment, we believe," Ella responded, nodding and noting that the man appeared nervous, behavior typical of people called to a murder site by the police. If he'd been too cool or collected, then she would have been suspicious. "What I need you to do first is check out the café and make sure that nothing was taken, or is out of place. We need to start ruling out some of our theories."

"Let's go," he said, leading the way.

He unlocked the door and looked around the dining area carefully, but it was clear, even at first glance, that no one had come in. He checked the cash register next and showed her the bills inside. "There's not much here, but that's the way it should be. Every afternoon we make a deposit at the bank. There's never any substantial amount left in the drawer overnight, only enough to begin the next business day."

Ella had taken a good look at the man's hands while he'd operated the cash register. He had no obvious bruises or cuts. Of course, even if Brewster had been the killer, he could have easily worn gloves. The man looked strong and healthy and she wasn't even close to ruling anyone out at the moment. "Do you have any idea who might have wanted Valerie Tso dead?" Ella asked, studying his reaction.

Stan stared across the room, lost in thought. He didn't seemed to be particularly emotional about Valerie's death, but then she didn't know a thing about Brewster's relationships with his employees.

"Valerie had a drinking problem at one time, and several marriages behind her. She didn't hold back her history when she applied for a job but, after that, she kept her private life private, at least to me, her boss. The only thing I know for sure is that she was working hard to turn things around for herself. Valerie really wanted a second chance at life. That's why I hired her."

"Do you know if she was currently seeing anyone in particular? A boyfriend?"

"I'm not sure about that, but I can tell you this. She went to school and she worked here forty hours a week. That pretty much took up all her time on weekdays."

"And on weekends? Did she go to church or have any other regular activities?" Ella knew that this would have been the wrong question to have asked Valerie's mother, Lena, who was a traditionalist. But right now she needed a full profile as quickly as possible.

"I think she mentioned attending the church up on the mesa, east side of the highway. The Good Shepherd, it's called."

She nodded. It was where her friend Reverend Bilford Tome, Ford for short, preached. Life for her had taken some strange detours lately. If anyone had told her a few years ago that she was going to be involved with a Christian minister she would have laughed. She made a mental note to speak to Ford later. He'd be able to tell her if Valerie had been a regular.

"Come to think of it, I overheard Valerie talking to one of our patrons here at the café recently. Valerie mentioned she was having problems with one of her ex-husbands. Does that help?" Stan added.

"Which husband? Do you have a name?"

" 'Fraid not. She never mentioned it to me, and I never asked."

"Okay, Mr. Brewster. We're probably going to have other questions for you as the investigation progresses so if you decide to leave the area, please let us know in advance. We'll want to be able to contact you if something new comes up." Ella handed the man her card.

"I understand. Just catch whoever did this to Valerie, okay?"

"We will," she nodded, wondering from his offhand tone just how sincere the man was, or if he was just saying that for effect. "There's really no reason for you to have to stick around anymore, Mr. Brewster. But if you can leave us a key to the café, we'd appreciate it—just in case we need to get back in here tonight."

He took two keys off a metal ring and handed them to her. "I have another set at home. Should I even try to open the café tomorrow? I honestly don't know how my regular customers are going to react to this."

Ella knew Navajos didn't like going anywhere someone had died. The old ceremonial grounds, just across the river on the west side, had been relocated years ago after an old man had died there during a Sing. Maybe Brewster's café would survive if people didn't mind that someone had died right *next door,* and not exactly inside the business.

"We might still have some officers around in the morning, so I'd wait a day. You'll get a call when we release the scene."

"Okay then. Good night." Brewster walked back to his truck. It faltered at first, then finally started. A second later he drove away, heading east.

Justine came out to join her. "Still no pen anywhere, inside or out, and no paper except a little memo pad by the refrigerator. Whoever killed her brought his own writing material, or took what was here with him. There's a bank deposit slip on the floor. We'll check with the bank in the morning and see who made the transaction."

"Do you still attend the Good Shepherd church?"

"Yeah, why?" Justine answered.

"The victim supposedly attended that church. Do you recall ever seeing her at the Sunday services?" Ella asked.

Justine thought about it for a long moment. "No, I don't, but I may have missed her, or maybe she just attended the Sunday evening service or the one on Wednesday night. Reverend Campbell and Reverend Tome always greet the congregation and guests at the main entrance, so you might ask them. She may also be on the members list."

"Okay, thanks. I'll check first thing."

While Justine went back to work, Ella approached Joe

Neskahi, who was collecting blood samples discovered out on the paved parking area.

"You're with us on this case until we're through," she said.

"I'd like a permanent transfer, if one can be arranged," he said.

Ella hesitated. "I'm not sure I can swing that as long as someone else controls our budget, but I'll make the request to Big Ed and see what happens."

"Thanks."

It was three in the morning by the time they wrapped things up and had stored away all the evidence in the crime scene van. Ella helped Tache stow away the portable lights while Justine locked and sealed the apartment.

"We've got quite a bit of evidence," Tache said. "Let's hope it leads us to the killer. I hate to think of a sicko like this running around the Rez."

"Me, too," Ella answered.

Justine placed the last of her gear into the unit, then glanced at Ella. "Back to the station?"

"No. Let's pack it in for now. We'll have to get an early start tomorrow."

Justine glanced at her watch. "We may be able to get about three hours of sleep, if we're lucky."

Ella smiled wryly. At least she wouldn't have to tiptoe back into the house. Rooming with two other officers who kept long hours had its advantages, but the bottom line was that she missed Dawn terribly. It didn't seem right to go to bed without making sure that Dawn hadn't kicked off her covers, and brushing a light kiss on her forehead. Ella even missed watching her sleep.

That was the thing about motherhood. Whether Dawn was eight or thirty-eight, she'd always worry about her. The love she felt for her daughter would never diminish nor fade away. It was the one constant they could both count on. And for some reason that fact gave her immense comfort.

THREE
—— ✖ ✖ ✖ ——

Justine handed Ella a cup of coffee as she entered the kitchen the following morning. "Get any sleep?"

Ella smiled. "As much as you did," she said, looking at the circles under Justine's eyes.

Justine nodded somberly. "I was so tired, yet I kept seeing her. It was the way the killer positioned her . . . kneeling in prayer. It seemed . . . well, obscene."

Ella nodded, understanding. "That form of prayer is supposed to bring peace and comfort. I can see why you might feel that way about it."

"I ran a check on her ex-husbands this morning while you were getting ready," Justine said, putting on her jacket as Ella sipped coffee.

"Any of them Christians, active or not?"

"That I can't tell you yet. But here's what I've got. One's in the military and overseas, so he's out. The second one died a few years ago in an auto accident. The third one lives over by Gallup with his girlfriend and their three kids. His name is Andrew Pettigrew, and he works at an auto shop in downtown Gallup. The fourth is Gilbert Tso, who lives east of Shiprock not far from Herman Cloud's place. Tso is currently unemployed and attending a mandatory outpatient alcohol program after his last DWI arrest. I tried his number, but the phone's been disconnected."

"Good work," Ella said, finishing off her coffee. "Let's get going. I'd like to stop by the church and see Ford first. While we're there, we can talk to Reverend Campbell, too. Then, afterward, we'll go drop by the Tso residence." Ella grabbed her own jacket, attached her holster to her belt, then took a final glance around the kitchen. "Where's Emily?"

"Working in her greenhouse. When she's done she'll have a fast breakfast—meaning one of those inedible breakfast bars—and then head off to work. I tried to tell her about the Barela family's breakfast burritos. They sell them on the road to Farmington, so I figured she could treat herself to one on the way to work. Their *naniscaada* sandwiches are to die for, too."

"But she wouldn't give up the breakfast bar?"

Justine nodded as they walked to the car. "Amazing, don't you think? I mean I've tasted her breakfast bars. *Peeeuuu!* It even *looks* like the sweet feed you give horses. It's some kind of oatmeal granola thing with fat-free something or another."

"If there's any justice in this world, someday you'll know what it's like to have to worry about your weight," Ella said, climbing into the passenger side and putting on her seat belt.

Justine burst out laughing. "Oh, yeah, like *you* do, Miss Skinny-Tall? You've never watched calories in your life."

"No, but they find me anyway . . . particularly if I don't take time to run at least three times a week."

With Justine driving, they reached the highway and headed toward the community of Shiprock, which, like many New Mexico towns, had nearly all of its major businesses alongside the main road.

"There's the Barelas' stand," Ella said, gesturing ahead to a wide spot beside the road where a pickup was parked, the tailgate down. That was where the breakfast fare was displayed and served. "You've made me hungry, and not for grazing at roughage. What do you say we pick up a quality breakfast?"

Two other vehicles were parked alongside Barelas', and Ella could see three men wearing hard hats, carrying bulging paper sacks. They were walking toward a big, extended-cab pickup with a local oil company sign on the door. From their slow pace, she got the idea they were coming off the midnight shift at a drilling site instead of heading out. Mrs. Barela stood beside her old folding chair, already anticipating her and Justine, who were semiregulars.

A fourth man in a cap and sunglasses sat on the running board of his own pickup, just the other side of the vendor's vehicle, finishing off a big sandwich. He stood and came over to the tailgate. "I'll have another. I've missed this kind of chow," he said, glancing at Ella and Justine as they came up.

"Ladies first," he said, nodding to them. He stepped back, eyeing them behind dark glasses and obviously noticing their weapons. "Police officers, huh?"

"You must be from out of town, *hosteen*," Mrs. Barela said, chuckling as she used the Navajo term for "mister." "Everyone around here knows our most famous women detectives." She smiled at Ella and Justine. "Right, ladies?"

Ella glanced curiously at the man, trying not to make her interest obvious. In his late forties or early fifties, he wore jeans and a flannel shirt, which was typical dress for the Four Corners. He looked hard and a little dangerous—your standard romance novel fodder. Assuming he had charm to go with his looks, he probably had his pick of women. He was definitely the type of man mothers would warn their daughters about, she decided immediately.

On his forearm was an elaborate yet crude handmade tattoo of a cross, an instant turnoff for Ella that broke any potential attraction. It wasn't the cross—she was dating a Christian minister. Going back to her years in the FBI, she'd learned to associate homemade tattoos with convicts. And the sunglasses were for "beach Navajos"—a name her mother used to refer to members of the tribe who'd lived in California, then returned.

Ella herself had been one of those at one time. Her nickname when she'd returned to the Rez had been L.A. Woman though. Fortunately, she'd lost the title after finally earning the respect of those who mattered in her life. These days the habit of wearing sunglasses was just a holdover from her Bureau days.

Ella didn't stare at Mr. Beach Navajo, a glance or two was enough after her years of training and experience. Far too many men interpreted obvious attention as a come-on, including Navajos not raised to avoid eye contact with adults. She and Justine ordered their food, paid, then left immediately.

They ate as they drove to the church on the north side of Shiprock. All throughout Ella remained quiet and pensive.

"What's bugging you?" Justine said at last.

"It's this case. I've got a strong feeling that I'm missing something important. The scene was carefully staged, but to what end? What exactly is the killer trying to tell us? And the other thought that worries me is the possibility that this may only be the first victim, that there are others on the killer's death list. If that's the case, we have a serious problem because the Fierce Ones *will* get involved," Ella said, then added, "Just as a precaution, start keeping an eye out for a possible tail. Lena Clani might have talked to someone already about looking into the murder."

"You think they'd use us to bird-dog suspects?"

"Absolutely. Their MO isn't to investigate, it's to even the score, though they'd see it as restoring the balance."

Justine glanced over at her, then back at the road. "I understand the satisfaction their type of justice gives the *Diné*, The People. You can't tell me there haven't been times when you wished you could blow a suspect straight to hell."

"Sure, but the difference is that we have rules, and we follow them. Civilization needs rules, partner, limitations we place on ourselves instead of letting our emotions rule us. Without them, there's only chaos, and more crime."

"I know," Justine replied with a sigh. "But pulling a Dirty Harry now and then would sure be satisfying."

Ella laughed. "What have you been watching at night?" Before Justine could respond, Ella's cell phone rang. She answered it immediately. It was Special Agent Blalock, and he wasn't a morning person, obviously. Before his third cup of coffee, he always sounded as if he'd been gargling with lye.

"I'm in my office, Ella. Got your reports and I'm currently checking VICAP to see if this crime matches the MO of any of the violent offenders on file. If VICAP finds any similarities, it'll suggest possible suspects and produce fingerprints. Then we can compare those to any you might have found at the scene."

"Those databases are worth their weight in gold," Ella said, updating him. The thought that Valerie's death hadn't been the first was almost as scary as the possibility of more to come.

"I'll catch up to you later," Blalock said, then hung up.

As they parked beside the side entrance to the church, Ella spotted Ford on a tall stepladder setting up a surveillance camera underneath the roof overhang. She smiled, thinking it was probably right up his alley, or close to it. Although his past remained shrouded in mystery, she knew that the preacher had a very high government security clearance and he'd had a background in cryptography.

On a previous case, he'd been able to access databases that had eluded the best efforts of even her favorite hacker, Teeny, or as he was more formally known, Bruce Little. Then, when they'd tried to learn more about Bilford Tome, the computers had locked up and phone calls had come down the chain of command ordering them to cease inquires immediately. For all intents and purposes, Ella still didn't know who Ford was or—more to the point—who Ford had been. The man continued to be an unanswered question, one that never failed to intrigue her.

Justine winked at Ella. "You're really hooked on our reverend, aren't you?"

"He's just a friend, partner."

"For now."

Ella scowled at her. As her second cousin, Justine felt free to get much more personal than a mere colleague. Getting out of the car, Ella glanced across at her partner. "Let's split up and save time. You take Reverend Campbell, and we'll compare notes later on our way to see Tso."

As Justine entered the church, Ella joined Ford as he stepped off the ladder. He was tall, probably six one to her five ten, broad shouldered, and classically handsome. Yet what attracted her most was his gentle spirit and high degree of intelligence.

"It's good to see you, Ella," Ford greeted. He shortened the ladder and set it flat on the ground, then walked back to the church with her.

"How come you're setting up a surveillance camera?" Ella asked as he opened the door for her.

"Someone's been getting into the cars during our Sunday services, and I've about had it," he answered. "It's a nuisance, that's all. Nothing is ever taken, there's just the obvious invasion of privacy. But tell me, what brings you here?"

"I need to ask you some questions about one of your parishioners."

He grew somber and nodded. "The woman who was murdered?"

"Yes, but how did you know? I don't think the press had it yet."

"Press? I got this from Stan Brewster, the Anglo who runs the Morning Stop. He comes by every so often to make a donation and today was one of those days. He used to belong to this church when he first got married, I've been told, but he's not much of a churchgoer these days. His wife, Donna, a Navajo, apparently joined a congregation in Farmington. Brewster doesn't get along with Reverend Campbell, but he still makes donations to our youth ministry and sponsors the church softball team. I think he only does it to maintain a positive image in the community," he said, then added. "Stan didn't know any of the details, but he mentioned having to meet with you and answer questions about his employee. What happened?"

"I can't discuss the specifics yet, but I'd appreciate it if you could tell me what you know about the victim, Valerie Tso. I understand she attended church here."

"Yes, but only for a short time. She'd been raised with the traditional Navajo beliefs, so I'm not really sure what drew her to Christianity, or our church, but the Lord calls whomever He will."

Ella said nothing as they entered Ford's office. It was simply furnished, nothing more than a desk, two file cabinets, and a large, carved wooden cross made of what looked like cottonwood. Despite the simplicity, or maybe because of it, the place exuded a sense of peace and tranquility. Ford sat behind his desk and waited for her to make herself comfortable.

"Was Valerie ever interested in becoming an official church member?" Ella pressed.

"She did stay after services one Sunday and asked me some questions about our members. She pointed out that most of our congregation had newer model cars and wanted to know if banks sometimes gave preferential treatment to churchgoers." He chuckled softly. "I assured her that wasn't the case—at least in my experience."

Ella laughed, remembering Ford still drove a 1971 VW bus. "So do you think she had an angle?"

"Maybe she was just trying to make conversation, or hinting that she needed a recommendation or cosigner on a loan. I honestly don't know. But after we took up a collection for one of our members who'd been in an accident, Valerie saw how supportive we are of each other. That really touched her. I think that was something she wanted very badly in her own life."

"Did she make friends among the members?"

Ford considered it. "I only recall greeting her on the steps a few times and seeing her during the service. I think Reverend Campbell mentioned later that she'd decided to join another church here on the Rez."

"Think back. Did Valerie ever say or allude to anything that might give me a lead to her killer, or maybe just something that seemed odd or out of place?"

He considered it for a long time. "No, not that I remember. All I can tell you is that she was a person looking for more than what she had in her life, and that's what can lead a person to God."

"Thanks. I appreciate the information."

"Changing the subject—I suppose dinner anytime soon is out?" he asked quietly.

She nodded. "Sorry. When I'm working a case, my personal life basically goes into the trash," she answered.

"But your work is what makes you, you," he observed with a smile and a shrug.

It was right on target. "You know me better than some people who've known me all my life, Ford." But it was more than that. He understood because he'd given his life to his work as well. His duty to God would always come first.

"That's part of why we get along so well, you know," he said. "In many ways, our work is as necessary to us as breathing."

"Common ground," she answered with an easy smile, then said a quick good-bye.

A few minutes later Ella joined Justine at their unmarked unit. "I don't like the expression on your face, partner," Ella said. "What did Reverend Campbell have to say?"

"You got diddly, right?" Justine asked her as they got underway.

"Pretty much. I gather from your tone you got more?"

"Valerie liked talking to Reverend Campbell more than to Reverend Tome. She knew you had a relationship with Tome, and didn't feel comfortable confiding in anyone with a link to her family. Everyone knows that Boots is Dawn's sitter, and that Rose and Lena are friends for life."

Ella nodded silently. Ford and she had deliberately encouraged others to think they were an item, and it had obviously worked well, maybe too much so. Their original plan had just been their way of getting other people to stop trying to fix them up with just about anyone who came along. And things had worked out . . . better than either of them had anticipated.

"Go on," Ella urged.

"According to Reverend Campbell, Valerie worried about Lena's influence over Boots. She really didn't like the fact that her daughter had become a traditionalist. She felt that would hold Boots back. Valerie was interested in Christianity because she felt that it could help break her own mother's hold on Boots. She knew Christianity had a strong foothold here and that it was the only force that could hold its own, even against the staunchest traditionalist. Valerie was hoping to convert and eventually talk her daughter into joining the church as well."

"That's really some manipulative thinking, partner, I mean Valerie's wanting to use Christianity to turn her daughter against traditional tribal beliefs."

"All I can tell you is that it obviously made sense to Valerie. And she *did* have a point. Christianity—had she been able to get Boots interested—would have been the antithesis of everything Lena holds dear. That would have driven a big wedge between them."

"True enough," Ella answered. "According to what I've learned over the years, Lena barely tolerated my father, a Christian evangelist, and she never approved of my mother marrying him." Ella fell quiet for several moments. "But Lena *did* respect my father. I remember realizing that back when I was working my way through that age of confusion and contradiction called my childhood. Maybe that's what Valerie was *really* after. Recapturing her child's respect."

"How would *you* feel if Dawn took to the old ways and became a traditionalist?"

Ella sighed. "She's certainly been exposed to traditionalist beliefs, with Mom, Boots, and Clifford—and I've even allowed her to go to church a few times with friends. I think exposure to other cultures and religions is very important. So does Kevin, though he doesn't seem to feel that strongly about religion in any form. But we both want Dawn to get a good education. What she chooses as her lifestyle after that is her own business. I won't care as long as she gives herself all the options she can—and with that freedom comes the ability to change her mind."

"That makes sense."

"But if she becomes a member of the Fierce Ones, I'll strangle her," Ella added, and they both burst out laughing.

A few minutes passed, then Ella brought out her cell phone. She punched out Officer Talk's home number. Marianna was off duty now, but the discussion of Boots had reminded her she hadn't checked yet to see how Jennifer had taken the death of her mother. Marianna hadn't called in, so Ella had already concluded Boots hadn't been able to help in narrowing the suspects. Still, Ella needed to follow up on this.

Unfortunately, just as Ella had feared, Marianna hadn't been able to get much information. Boots had broken down at first, then later explained that, although she and her mother had been in contact lately, not much information had passed between them, only emotions, regrets, and apologies. According to Marianna, Boots had no idea who Valerie had been associating with outside her work. Ella, hearing that Marianna had a written report waiting at the station, ended the call and advised Justine of the news, or lack of it.

"I've often wondered what my life would be like right now if I hadn't had such a close family, Ella," Justine commented. "For Boots, it must have been devastating, growing up knowing that her own mother didn't want her in her life."

"At least Boots had Lena. The woman is annoying and headstrong, but she did a good job raising her granddaughter," Ella replied. "My mom has been so good with Dawn. You know, I can't wait until we're all back together again."

"There have been times, cuz, you'd have cut out your tongue before admitting that," Justine said, chuckling.

Ella shrugged. "Yeah, well . . ."

As they drove into Shiprock's east side, Ella noted that, as it often was in poor communities, the number of abandoned vehicles left to gather dust behind a house seemed to increase almost daily. They were usually scavenged for parts until only the outer shell remained.

Driving past the small, cheaply made government houses built in the late Sixties, they entered a helter-skelter residential area littered with mobile homes and shacks in all stages of disrepair. Although most of the land leases were for one-acre lots, there were no fences to differentiate them and animals roamed freely.

"It's that one," Justine said, gesturing ahead by pursing her lips, Navajo style. "The pale green one with the small black dog on the porch. His truck's there, and it's not on cinder blocks, so maybe he's home."

As they turned up the dirt road a man came out to the porch to feed the dog, saw them approaching, and suddenly bolted for the truck.

"He's making a run for it." Ella said, watching him speed away in a trail of dust, heading north, away from the main highway. "Try to stay with him, but watch out for kids and animals." Ella adjusted her seat belt and called it in.

The road was rough and clouded with dust, but Justine's pursuit training paid off and she slowly gained ground. "He's weaving all over the place. Either he's trying to lose us in the dust, or he's still drunk from last night," Ella said.

"Maybe he had leftovers for breakfast," Justine said.

Tso took a right at the next intersection, then another right at the corner after that, completely reversing his direction. As soon as he reached the highway, Tso shot across the median, barely missing a semi, and swung around into the eastbound lanes. He was now heading toward Hogback and the eastern edge of the Rez. The man quickly picked up speed on the good road, and his driving became much more controlled. This time he only weaved when he raced around slower vehicles in his way.

"Maybe he's hoping we'll give up once he gets into county jurisdiction," Ella said. "But no way that's going to happen, not when we're in pursuit of a possible murder suspect."

She picked up the mike and called for county backup. Before long Sergeant Emily Marquez, who patrolled the near Rez areas of San Juan County, responded.

"I'm in Fruitland, SI One, proceeding west. I'll lay down a spike belt when I see him coming. He'll either have to stop or blow out all his tires."

"Ten-four," Ella said, racking the mike.

"We've got him now," Justine added. "Let's see what he does."

Sirens wailing, the pursuit continued east around the curve at the south end of Hogback and off reservation land. Most of the vehicles in the way managed to pull over to the shoulder, a good thing considering the trap Emily was setting just ahead. The two lanes were wide at this point, and the shoulders level, so the perp picked up the pace.

Then they saw the emergency lights of Emily's unit in the median. "Here we come," Ella said into the mike. Justine slowed, not wanting to be close to their quarry when he encountered Emily's surprise.

"She's laying the belt," Ella said, seeing Emily dart across the two lanes, dragging the array of hollow metal spikes into position. "Now get out of the way," Ella added under her breath.

The driver braked hard, nearly losing control as the pickup started to crab a little. "He's going to roll it!" Justine shouted.

Somehow Tso managed to straighten out the pickup, but as the vehicle squealed, sliding down the pavement on locked brakes, there was a blue puff of smoke and flying rubber.

"He blew out a tire. Looks like he's not going to make it to

Emily's belt," Ella said, watching the truck bed swing to the right from the drag of the blown tire on the left rear.

The pickup slid sideways another ten feet, then stopped. The driver jumped out of the cab and shot across the median and two lanes of highway. He raced down the shoulder, hurtled a fence, and headed north across a field.

"Next stop, Colorado," Ella said. "Pull over into the median. I'll get him, and you help Emily clear the highway."

Ella was a good runner, one of the best high school cross country competitors ever in the Four Corners, in fact. She'd won State her senior year. But it took her a few seconds to get across the highway without getting hit by oncoming traffic, and by then, the man they believed to be Gilbert Tso had a two-hundred-yard lead on her. Even semi-intoxicated, he was making good speed across the dry alfalfa. Twice he stumbled and nearly fell, but somehow he managed to stay on his feet and continue.

Ella kept pace with him, not letting him get any farther away, knowing he'd tire out sooner or later and maybe start falling. She'd have him then.

Suddenly, out of the corner of her eye, she saw Emily's county vehicle paralleling the chase on a dirt road at the east edge of the field. Justine, in their unmarked SUV, was right behind her. They had to go fairly slow, but they were matching Tso's pace easily.

"Tribal PD. Give it up," she called out to the man. "You're not going anywhere."

The man didn't respond. If anything, he picked up the pace, angling toward the corner of the field, which ended at a big arroyo.

Ella wished she hadn't eaten such a large breakfast on the go, it was making her sluggish, and the stubble of plants that remained after the last cutting made it hard to maintain solid footing. She poured it on, but had only halved the distance between them when the perp reached the arroyo. He jumped down inside. Assuming he wouldn't head in the direction of the vehicles, to his right, Ella angled toward the left, hoping to head him off.

She came to a stop when she reached the rim of the ten-foot-deep wash just as the man ducked into a big metal culvert. Here, the wash had been filled where another dirt road lined the western margin of the field.

She ran across, expecting to see her quarry racing away. But the arroyo was empty, and there were no tracks in the bottom. He was still in the culvert.

"He's trapped," she whispered into her handheld radio. "He's hiding in the big culvert beneath this road. I'll block the west end, and you two take the east."

Emily and Justine acknowledged immediately. They left their units on the parallel road to the east, and came toward the culvert along both edges of the arroyo. Tso, or whoever it turned out to be, would have to pass between them.

It didn't take long before they were ready. Ella and Emily jumped down into the arroyo at opposite ends of the earthen bridge, while Justine stood on the top, Taser in hand, ready to jump down and back up whomever needed her.

Ella stepped forward, her hand on the butt of her weapon, then stopped right outside the four-foot-diameter metal pipe and looked in. She could see someone near the middle, crouched low, and at the other end of the fifteen-foot metal culvert was Emily.

"Hey, tumbleweed. Come out slowly and we won't have to use the Taser. Standing on all that metal you're going to glow like a spark plug if we have to shock you," Ella said.

Less than five seconds later the suspect bolted, knocking Emily down as he erupted from her end of the big metal pipe. Ella sprinted forward through the culvert as fast as she could, hunkered down. But by the time she cleared the east end, Justine had already jumped right behind the fleeing man and fired the Taser. The contacts struck him in the back like wire-guided hornets and he flopped forward onto the sand.

Justine cut the power and Emily cuffed the stunned suspect. Fifteen minutes later, the suspect was in the back of Ella and Justine's unit. Emily had given him a field sobriety test, and he'd failed the Breathalyzer as well. Gilbert Tso, verified from his driver's licence, was still a bit dazed and in no condition to go anywhere now, even if he'd been able to remove the handcuffs.

Emily had already called in the all-clear to other sheriff department units when she came up to say good-bye to Justine and Ella. "I'm going to make sure our prisoner didn't try to stash anything inside the culvert. Then I'll examine the prisoner's vehicle and, after that, it'll end up in the impound yard. I called in a wrecker."

"Good work. Let us know if you find anything. Otherwise, see you later tonight," Ella said. "And thanks for your help."

"Not a problem. By the way, I've never seen anyone keep up such a fast pace in stubby ground like this—except a jackrabbit, maybe. What do you have, little wings on those shoes of yours?"

Ella laughed. "Actually, no one can run fast through a field like this one. But when you're chasing a drunk he usually makes you look good."

Emily walked away, and Ella turned to her partner. "The county will handle the situation at this end. In the meantime, we'll take the prisoner back to the station and see what he can tell us," Ella said.

Once they arrived, twenty minutes later, Justine went directly to booking with Tso. Ella, a few steps behind, only got as far as the front desk before Big Ed came out and signaled her into his office.

Big Ed Atcitty, their chief of police, was aptly named. The veteran officer was shaped like a rain barrel with arms. However, it would have been a big mistake to assume his bulk was simply flab. He was as solid as they came and, to date, he enjoyed the fact that no perp had ever knocked him off his feet, though many had tried during his years in the field.

"Take a seat, Shorty," he said, gesturing to a chair in his office. He'd given her that nickname to tease her since Ella was actually taller than he was.

"I just heard that the Fierce Ones are planning on looking into your homicide case. What do you know about that?" Big Ed asked.

"So far I don't think they're directly involved, but that could change, depending on how fast we get results," she said and explained the circumstances and her conversation with Lena Clani.

"You think the suspect you hauled in could be the killer?"

"It's too early to know for sure, but why else run from the police? Maybe we'll get lucky and close this one fast," she said, hoping it would be true. Yet, even as she said it, a part of her knew it wouldn't be so easy. Nothing on the Rez was ever that simple.

FOUR

—— ✖ ✖ ✖ ——

Ella sat in the stark interrogation room across the table from their suspect, saying nothing, letting him sweat. Justine had already tried to question him but he hadn't said a word, not even to ask for a lawyer, which, generally, was one of the first things out of a suspect's mouth. Justine had left to write up the initial report.

"You realize that we've already got you on a variety of counts, reckless driving, DWI, resisting arrest ... I could go on, but I think you get the idea. We'll be looking into all your activities, so if you've got any secrets, they won't remain that way for long."

For the first time he glanced up.

Ella waited for the man to say something. She could sense him trying to make up his mind.

"I'll tell you what," Ella finally said. "Let's start with murder. We found your ex-wife dead, and it looks like someone used her for a punching bag before they finally killed her." She made a point of letting him see her staring at his bruised knuckles.

Gilbert shifted in his chair nervously and took his hands off the table. "You can't pin that on me. No way."

"Why not?" Ella pressed.

"Look, I haven't even seen my ex for a month or maybe

two. I didn't know she was dead until I heard it on the radio this morning."

"Then how do you explain your bruised knuckles and the cuts on your face?"

"What else? A bar fight."

"You playing games with me, Gilbert?" she asked, deliberately using his name. He clearly wasn't a traditionalist, but even most modernists on the Rez avoided the use of names whenever possible. Names had power, and using them stripped the bearer of that source of help.

"Give me a break, will ya? I can't even remember what I did last night," he grumbled.

"Bad answer. You need to stop drinking, Gilbert. That's at the bottom of all your problems."

"I've complied with the courts," he said in a weary voice. "I'm in the program—for all the good it does me."

Something about the way he'd dropped his voice alerted her. "Maybe we should go speak to your supervisor or counselor over at the drug and alcohol rehab center," Ella said, playing a hunch.

His shoulders sagged. "I'm telling you right now. I didn't take it."

"Take what?" Ella pressed. She'd had a gut feeling that he'd been hiding something.

"The money from the cash box. I thought that was what you were after me for, not killing my ex-wife."

Ella tried to stay on track. "But others think you did—steal the money?"

He shrugged. "Yeah, I guess."

"Will we find it when we search your home?"

He swallowed hard. "You can't do that, not without a warrant. I want a lawyer."

"One can be provided for you. We told you that in the arroyo when you were read your rights," Ella said. "But let's get back to the money. Are you a betting man, Gilbert, 'cause I'm willing to bet we get lucky at your house."

Ella knew that Officer Tache and Sergeant Neskahi were there now. They'd been able to get a warrant based on the suspect's behavior and the physical evidence, including the bruises and injuries that must have been inflicted during a struggle—or a beating.

"When you search my place . . . well, it may look like I took that cash, but I'm not a killer. And you can't prove I did that, 'cause I didn't."

"Things look bad for you." She pointed to his skinned knuckles. "And your memory seems to be improving now that the stakes have gone up. How about some truth, now? You didn't get those while raiding a cash box, did you?"

"I *told* you I was in a fight. I got into it at the Double Play Sports Bar over in Kirtland. Some white boy called me a name I didn't like, so we threw some punches. But I got the best of him."

She knew about the Double Play. It was one of the roughest bars around, and in a community full of hard drinkers that was saying something. She and Justine had been there before on business and had barely managed to avoid having to fight their way out.

"I *will* check on your story. Count on it."

"Then that's that. I'm not saying another word until my lawyer gets here."

A moment later there was a knock at the door, and a man she recognized was let in by an officer. Lee Yazzie was the tribe's latest public defender. He was all of twenty-five, if that, but she'd heard he was very good and was acquiring a reputation for getting his clients off on the slightest technicality.

"I'll give you some privacy," Ella said, standing up. "Have you been apprised of the situation?" she asked Yazzie.

He nodded once. "I saw the paperwork. Now I need a few minutes in private to confer with my client. Once we're done, I'll call you back."

Ella knocked on the door, and the officer on duty outside let her out. Rather than return to her office, she walked down the lobby and got herself a cup of coffee from the machine. The coffee that flowed into the foam cup was syrupy thick. She grimaced as she picked it up, wondering if it would eat right through the foam cup.

"I wouldn't touch that if I were you," Justine cautioned, coming up the hall. "I had a sip of that stuff a while ago and nearly heaved. Either the machine's out of whack, or the coffee grounds went sour."

"Can coffee go sour?" Ella dropped the cup into the trash. "Thanks for the warning."

She was about to put two quarters in the Coke machine when Yazzie came out into the lobby.

Seeing Ella, he motioned to her. "We're ready now, Investigator Clah."

Ella went back inside the room with the attorney and sat across from Yazzie, who was seated beside his client.

"Mr. Tso has something to say to you," Yazzie said.

Gilbert squirmed in his chair and stared at a corner of the table. "You're going to find the cash box that's missing from the rehab center over at my place. I couldn't get it open, so I just grabbed the whole thing. It's a little dented up, but all the money's still in there. We can just give it back, okay?"

Ella glanced at Yazzie, whose expression remained neutral. "If the center presses charges, you'll have to go to court. From there, it'll be up to the system. But I've got to tell you, Gilbert, stealing a cash box should be the least of your worries. I need to know about you and your ex-wife, Valerie."

"Look, I didn't tell you anything before because I thought you'd just twist my words around. But Mr. Yazzie has advised me to tell you what I know." He looked over at his attorney, who nodded.

"Please note that my client is volunteering information of his own free will," Yazzie added.

"Noted, counselor." She looked back at Gilbert and waited.

"I hadn't seen Valerie in a long time, don't really know how long—weeks, or months maybe. But I ended up in a jam last week 'cause my rent was due and I was tapped out. I'd heard she had a good paying job these days, so I dropped by where she worked and hit her up for a loan. She was glad to see me. That same night she came by and gave me all the cash she had. It wasn't that much, but I scraped the rest together."

Something didn't sound right. "Why would she help you, Gilbert? You two were history."

He gave her a cocky grin. "She never got over me, I guess."

"What were you doing yesterday, say between about four and nine P.M.?"

He shifted in his chair, then looked at his attorney, who nodded. "Answer her," Yazzie said.

"I was at my place. Alone, unfortunately."

"Did anyone see you, neighbors, maybe? Anyone at all?"

He shook his head. "If they saw me, I didn't see them. I was mainly inside the house, watching TV and . . . just relaxing, you know?"

"What were you watching?"

He hesitated. "Reruns, probably. I can't remember. I was a little drunk at the time," he muttered.

"Investigator Clah, we've already established that my client has a drinking problem, and he's willing to admit he fell off the wagon yesterday. That's not a healthy situation, but it's also not a crime."

"No, but the rest of it—like stealing, driving while intoxicated, and resisting arrest—is a crime."

"My client has cooperated and told you all he knows. So how about cutting him loose? You know where he lives, and he has no plans to leave town."

"He's not leaving our custody until we finish searching his home. For now, he remains here."

"You don't have much to hold him on. I mean, resisting arrest? I can argue that you didn't identify yourself properly, that my client was on his way out and saw someone chasing him. He'd been in a fight recently, and was afraid of retribution."

"So two Navajo women were coming to kick his ass? I don't think so." Ella stood up and knocked on the door. "Sorry, counselor. For the time being, your client remains in a cell."

The officer outside opened the door and let her out into the hall. Justine was just coming in her direction. "I've been going over his records and checking with other agencies. Gilbert Tso has a long rap sheet for violence and petty crimes. He likes to use his fists, especially. I think he's a strong suspect."

"But we need solid evidence to prove he killed Valerie, and we have nothing so far. We can't even prove that he ever went inside her home, unless some of the fingerprints we've recovered end up being a match. How are Tache and Neskahi doing over at Tso's house? Have they found anything that ties him to the murder?"

"Not so far. I'm heading over there now."

"Any news from the ME?"

"Not yet."

"What about our anonymous caller? Any ideas who that could be?"

"No, but I haven't had time to follow it up."

"All right," Ella said with a nod. "Go give Tache and Neskahi a hand. I don't want to let our suspect out on bail until I'm sure, but the clock's ticking. In the meantime, I'll try to get a lead on our anonymous caller. We already know that the call came from the Quick Stop down the street, so maybe the clerk will remember who was at the phone."

"Benny and Jane Joe run it these days. Jane said that she and Benny needed breathing room, so he takes the late shift and she the early one. They're open until midnight."

"Then I better go by their home and wake Benny up. After that, I'll stop by the morgue. I wonder what the holdup is? I expected Carolyn to have her preliminary report by now."

As Justine left, Ella looked up Benny Joe's home address. It wasn't far from the station, in an area of new family housing. Houses were sprouting up everywhere these days, it seemed, though it was anything but easy to legally build on reservation land. The first thing that had to be done was a thorough search for antiquities and that usually took months of digging. That phase

Margaret opened the screen door and waved her inside. "He's in the kitchen," she said. "And he's a mess this morning, so go easy on him, okay?"

"What happened?"

"I'll let you ask him yourself," Margaret answered.

When Ella entered the kitchen, she saw Benny sitting at the center island, staring forlornly at the mug of coffee he held between his hands.

"I knew you'd track me down," he said glumly.

As Ella sat across from him, she noticed that Margaret hadn't followed her into the kitchen. Margaret knew the drill too well to want to stick around when police officers were asking questions.

"Just tell me what I need to know," Ella said flatly.

"Okay, I admit it. I was the one who called the police about the trouble, and I didn't leave my name. So what else do you need to know?"

"Your store is a block away, so how did you find out what was going on? Start from there, and tell me everything you saw and heard."

He nodded, took a deep breath, then began. "There's a shoe game every evening at Joe Curley's house, down the street. So, every once in a while, I close up shop for an hour or so at around eight, and walk down to check out the action."

The shoe game, a popular way for Navajos to gamble, didn't require any special playing pieces, like dice or cards. A team of players gathered up a pile of shoes, and hid something simple, like maybe a pebble, inside one. Then the others would try and guess which shoe it was in. The game required the ability to read faces and note even the smallest of reactions. And, of course, every attempt possible was made to mislead the players. Bets would then be placed on the likely shoes. It was a bit like poker, but in a more down-to-earth way.

"Everyone's seen the shoe game sign that sits on his front porch, but your officers never bother us. There're never any fights or trouble of any kind. We just play."

Benny fell silent, and Ella waited, knowing he needed time to gather his thoughts. On the Rez, patience was not only a courtesy, it was a sign of respect for their culture.

"I left early 'cause I'd already lost a bunch of cash and I knew I'd need some time alone to come up with a way to cover for that, or Jane'd kill me. Then, as I went by the café, I heard a woman screaming her head off from somewhere close by, and then there was this big crash, like furniture smashing or something. Everything went quiet after that.

"I walked over and peeked into the café window, but it was empty and closed. Wondering if the noise had come from the little house in back where Valerie Tso lived, I stepped over there, but just as I got close, her TV came on. Once I heard that, I breathed again. Her car was there, and it was the only vehicle I could see, so I figured she was okay, and I should get the heck out of there. Valerie . . . well, she has a reputation with men. If anyone saw me there they'd think the wrong thing and I'd catch hell from my wife."

"So why did you call us at all? What am I missing here?" Ella asked.

"Later, I was half watching the cable news at the store when they ran that story about the lady in Rhode Island who'd died and none of her neighbors noticed. Her body had been on her kitchen floor for weeks before they found her. Anyway, I started feeling guilty after that, so I decided to call the station and have them check on Valerie. I was hoping to keep my name out of it. Otherwise, I knew I'd have a lot of explaining to do. If Jane ever found out, I'd be screwed in more ways than one."

"Did you see anyone on your way to the game or when you were coming back?" Ella asked, keeping Benny on track. "Or any vehicle other than the victim's?"

He paused, considering her question. "On the way to the game I heard a coyote howl and I remembered my mother's words. She'd taught me that First Man gave Coyote the name First-to-get-angry. Trouble always follows him. He brings bad luck. And death sometimes. I should have gone straight home then and forgotten all about the shoe game. Instead, I ended up losing my entire roll on the first bet. After that, I figured I should head back to the store before Coyote brought me even worse luck. But then Coyote really let me have it. First there was that scream, then the awful silence. It was as if everything that hides in the darkness was suddenly holding its breath," he said and shuddered.

"Think hard. You were walking home. Did you see any cars drive past you?"

"Yeah, later, when I was farther down the block, two or three went by. But I didn't really pay any attention to them."

"Who was at the shoe game?"

He listed several names and Ella wrote them down.

"But they all live in that neighborhood. I bet they walked to the game, like me."

Ella waited, hoping that he'd remember something useful, but he just stared at the cup of coffee as if it contained the secrets of the universe.

"I want you to think back," Ella pressed. "Did you have any customers at the Quick Stop before you left, or maybe right after you came back?"

"Reverend Campbell pulled up just as I was unlocking the door. He came in to get some coffee and a loaf of bread. And right before I left, one person showed up to get gas at the pump outside. A glonnie, nobody important."

Navajos often referred to the drunks as glonnies. It was an Anglicized version of the Navajo word. But the word could fit a lot of people. "I'll need a name."

"Marco Pete. You've seen him. He takes his half of the road out of the middle. It's a wonder he's still alive."

Ella knew whom he meant. But it was doubtful that Marco had been the perp. His hand-to-eye coordination was nothing more than a distant memory, even when sober. She still remembered the comment he'd made last time Joe Neskahi had arrested him for DWI. In olden days the only time a man would cut his hair was after a long illness. Seeing Joe's short military buzz, he'd asked very sympathetically how long Joe had been sick.

"Was he drunk?"

"Not at the time. When he comes in I always watch him. If he has trouble finding the hose on the pump, I won't let him fill up his tank."

"Any idea where I might find him?"

He nodded slowly. "Yeah, as a matter of fact, I do. He drove off the road and ended up in an arroyo. He's at the hospital in bad shape, last I heard."

"Getting back to Reverend Campbell. Did you notice anything unusual about his behavior when he came in and you spoke to him?"

"He didn't have blood on his hands, or look like he'd been in a fight or anything, if that's what you're really asking."

"No. Just looking for other potential witnesses." Ella slipped a card out of her wallet and placed it on the table in front of him. "If you remember anything else, call me."

He nodded. "You telling Jane?"

"I came to interview a witness. What you choose to tell your wife is your business."

He suddenly looked more hopeful than he had since she'd walked in.

"I'll think hard on this. Maybe I can remember something else," he said in a hopeful voice.

Ella was almost out of the kitchen when he stopped her.

"Wait. Something else about Reverend Campbell. He's been trying hard to get new converts for his church, stopping by to see people at their homes at night and asking them to come to church and be saved. And if you're polite to him, he keeps coming back. I think that's half the reason he's always stopping by the store for this and that—and what he might have been doing last night. Me and Jane are on his radar, and there have to be others along the street. Does that help?"

"Maybe. Thanks for letting me know."

FIVE

✖ ✖ ✖

Ella headed to the hospital. She needed to meet with Carolyn and, if Marco Pete was in any condition to answer questions, she'd need to talk to him as well. Ella had just reached the tribal vehicle when her cell phone rang. It was Justine.

"We've processed Tso's home. We found the cash box from the center, still locked, and a handful of expensive-looking watches and rings that are definitely not his style."

"Anything at all that might link him to the murder?"

"We found a letter from Valerie on his kitchen table. No date. It looks like a match to her handwriting and, in it, she wrote that she wanted to get back together with him and that he still meant a lot to her. It's signed 'Val.'"

"That supports Gilbert's claim that she'd loaned him money," Ella said. "Okay, let's follow that up. Interview Gilbert again when you get back to the station and see what he has to say. He might have overreacted if she was pressuring him, and something like that could have led to a fatal confrontation."

As Ella drove to the hospital, she was glad to see that the haze blanketing the river valley, pollution mostly from the coal power plant, had cleared out because of the breeze. The pollution that came from the smokestacks was believed to be responsible for many birth defects in the area, though no one had ever been able to prove it. The plant itself had been built in the early 1970s so it wasn't required to meet the modern-day standards set by the EPA. Most of the electricity it provided, ironically, supplied customers hundreds of miles west in Arizona.

The second the new, modern hospital came into view, her thoughts shifted back to the business at hand. Valerie Tso's killer needed to be found and soon. The first twenty-four hours were critical, and that time had passed already. Maybe Carolyn could give her some information that would point her in the right direction.

Ella went downstairs to the basement of the hospital where Carolyn worked. The doctor and she had become friends over the years. Neither had a lot of time to socialize because of the demands of their work, but they still managed to get together now and then.

As she entered the outer office of the morgue, Ella glanced around. Carolyn had no receptionist, secretary, or assistant. First, the budget didn't allow it, and, more important, few people beside the police ever came down here anyway unless they'd gotten lost. All too often, bodies brought into the facility remained unclaimed. On the Navajo reservation, it was who the person had been in life that mattered. What was left behind after death was better avoided.

Ella opened the big door to the work area and saw Carolyn in her pale green scrubs at the autopsy table, still working on the naked figure before her and speaking softly into the mike. Ella didn't interrupt, knowing that Carolyn had looked up and seen her, and would come out when she could.

Carolyn joined her ten minutes later. "I have a preliminary report ready, and there's a very interesting detail you should look into. The victim didn't drown, she bled to death, probably while unconscious. The lacerations on her hands, and particularly the deep one on her right wrist, were enough. I found a lot of glass from the mirror in those wounds. There was no water at all in her lungs, and only a small amount in the mouth and throat. She'd already stopped breathing when her head was dunked in the tub."

"She was beaten, ripped to shreds in a collision with the mirror, then allowed to bleed to death. Then the killer dressed the body in her Sunday best and her head was immersed. . . ." Ella said thoughtfully. "Like a baptism . . ."

"Yeah, maybe," Carolyn said. "But I don't think those are usually done in bathtubs to dead people."

Ella smiled grimly, then studied the report Carolyn handed her. The time of death Carolyn had originally estimated had been narrowed a bit more. The victim had died between eight and ten in the evening. Because Valerie's hair had almost dried, it was probably closer to 9 P.M.

"The victim's connection to Boots . . . and your family . . . is really getting to you, isn't it?" Carolyn observed in a quiet voice.

"It's more than that. There's something else that's just out of reach in my mind . . . something I should be seeing. . . ." she said, then shook her head slowly.

Carolyn poured herself a cup of coffee, and without asking handed Ella one, too. "Take a step back and stop trying to force the answers," she advised. When Ella didn't reply, Carolyn changed the subject. "I hear that the construction company working at the new power plant site found some artifacts this morning—not long after that trouble last night. The newspapers and media got wind of that, and now all hell's breaking loose."

"This is the first I've heard of this. When did you find out?" Ella asked, surprised.

"I went upstairs for lunch and heard it from some staffers while in the cafeteria line. Apparently it made the noon news on the radio stations."

She shook her head slowly. "I've been concentrating on this case and haven't had time to check in on the rest of the world. I'll have to dig into it."

"Security has been beefed up again. The real bottom line

here is that a lot of people are opposed to this new power plant. They think a nuclear reactor is just like a time bomb waiting to go off."

"I think they should take another long look at the choking smoke coming out of the old stacks then."

"Yeah, I agree with you."

Ella stared at Carolyn's report for several moments longer, lost in thought. Reverend Campbell had been in the area, he knew Valerie, and there was a religious connection to the crime. His church baptized through immersion, she suspected, remembering the riverside baptisms her father had performed. Campbell's church was probably similar, though she didn't know that for sure. But the idea of Campbell being responsible for Valerie's death was just too pat. Then again, sometimes the simplest answer was the best one.

As Ella stood, Carolyn glanced up at her. "We need to get together soon, Ella. I've found a chocolate cake recipe that's to die for."

Carolyn was a large woman who tipped the scale at around two hundred pounds, but she never worried about her weight. Unlike most of the women Ella knew, Carolyn never gave it a thought.

"Your baking is second to none," Ella admitted. "But I've got to trim down a little. Yesterday I had to chase down a suspect and, for a while there, I nearly pooped out. It was a rude awakening, believe me. I used to be able to run for miles without a problem."

"It's called getting older," Carolyn said after a loud guffaw. "You know, old friend, I think half of the women in this country have a problem because they try to look like anorexic runway models. Mind you, as an M.D., I can't recommend being overweight, but the truth is that each of us has to find a weight we're comfortable with. I'm happy the way I am, and that's half the reason I've never had high blood pressure. Stress is the real killer. Now I agree that you need to stay fit, but portion control might work better than denial."

"You've convinced me. When this case is closed, I'm coming over."

"It's a slow-cooker recipe. That might sound odd, but it tastes like chocolate souffle when it's finished."

"That, I've got to try."

Leaving Carolyn to her work, Ella went upstairs to the main desk and inquired about Marco Pete.

The nurse made a quick call, then glanced up at her. "The attending physician says he can't be questioned. He's in ICU."

"Is he expected to make it?" Ella asked.

"His chances are good. He's in critical but stable condition."

Ella left the hospital, considering everything she'd learned. It was possible that Valerie's killer had run Marco off the road in his eagerness to get away from the crime scene, especially if he thought Benny Joe might report the scream. According to Benny, Marco hadn't been drunk. But it could also have been just an unrelated accident. Ella called Dispatch and got the directions to the site of Marco's accident. She'd head there at the same time she checked in with Justine.

"Gilbert Tso's lawyer is working overtime to get him released," Justine warned her immediately.

"If Gilbert bolts we may never find him again," Ella said quietly. "Just in case he's released before we're ready, see if we can assign someone to keep an eye on him for at least the first twenty-four hours. Maybe an officer looking for overtime."

As Ella continued down the highway, her gaze swept over the colorful wildflowers at the edge of the road, everything from bindweed with its purple blossoms to low growing pinks. Supplied mostly by runoff from the rare thunderstorms, the flowers came and went, just like the Navajos who came from the Earth Mother and returned to her someday.

Realizing the turn her thoughts had taken, she shook her head and smiled. She was starting to think like her mother. Who'd have ever thought it?

Pulling off to the side of the road at the site of the accident, easily located from the bright paint used by the investigating officers, Ella studied the skid marks on the asphalt and the furrows left by the tires as Marco descended down into the shallow arroyo. He'd tried to brake hard at the last minute, that was clear.

Ella walked down the road, looking for other skid marks that might indicate another vehicle taking evasive maneuvers. But there was nothing—not a tread mark, or even a shard of glass—just the normal asphalt surface.

Maybe she'd get more by studying the condition of Marco's car. Had he been sideswiped? Were there paint traces there? Ella headed over to their impound yard.

There was still the matter of Reverend Campbell to be considered, too. Justine had interviewed him, and couldn't recall if Campbell had told her about his visit to the area around the time of the crime or not. Of course, when that interview had taken place, they hadn't conclusively established the time of death and they'd been asking about Valerie, not what Campbell had been doing at the time. Campbell had been in the area, apparently, so it was possible he'd seen someone . . . or maybe he *was* the someone they were searching for. Questions rolled around in her head in an endless loop that yielded no answers.

Ella pulled into the impound lot a short time later. Gene Begay, in charge of their motor pool, was sitting in a folding chair by the gate, sipping a cup of coffee. He stood and waved as he saw her pull up.

"Thought I'd have company," he said, coming over to meet her and unlock the gate. "That pickup brought in last night was a mess."

"Where's it at?"

He pursed his lips and pointed Navajo style to the far corner of the lot. "I heard about the murder. Happened about the same time this accident did, maybe," he said, walking with her to what was left of the pickup.

"Were you friends with the victim or maybe the driver?" Ella asked.

"The victim. But it was a while back," he answered and looked away. "Long before I took this job."

"What can you tell me about her?" Ella asked.

"Telling you about her will be telling you about myself," he answered slowly. "Don't know how much good that'll do either of us. As I said, it was a long, long time ago."

"I'm listening," she insisted.

"Back then, she was always hard up for cash 'cause she spent every dime on booze. So she . . . entertained."

"You mean she was turning tricks?" Ella countered, getting directly to the point.

"Well, it was more personal than that," he said. "She would choose one man and make herself available to him—for a price. I saw her as often as I could after my divorce. It was a no-strings-attached thing, and, except for all the drinking, it helped me with some problems I had after my wife left."

"How long ago was this?" she asked.

"Maybe three years ago. But since then I heard she got sober, went to school, and got a regular job," he said, then added, "Just don't seem right, her murdered now and all. No justice . . . no balance."

Ella nodded. The possibility that an old client of Valerie's had sought her out and been rejected gave the case an entirely new perspective. "Who else was she entertaining back then?"

"I don't know."

Ella gave him a hard look.

"It's the truth. She never spoke about any other men. For all I know, I was the only one . . . but I doubt it." Gene pointed to the pickup ahead. "That's the vehicle."

Ella walked over alone and examined the old Ford. It was covered with dust, and a few sturdy weeds from the trip into the arroyo were still wedged in between the crumpled bumper and the front grille. There were plenty of dents and scrapes, most of them new and shiny, but a lot had obviously been part of the vehicle for decades.

Searching for characteristic scrapes from a recent collision with another vehicle, Ella studied the driver's side, especially the front fender and door, but there was nothing there. Either he'd been forced off the road by someone very aware of what he was doing, or Marco had simply had an accident.

Ella forced the door open and looked inside. Several bottles lay on the floor, all of them empties of the high-alcohol-content cheap wines found everywhere on the Rez, though it was illegal to sell booze on the reservation. As she looked around the back seat, Ella found a small crumpled piece of paper with a phone number scrawled on it.

Placing it inside an evidence pouch, Ella headed toward the gate, where Gene was standing, watching. "My crime scene people will be here later today, so don't move the Ford without letting us know first," Ella said. "We need to search it for evidence."

"It'll remain untouched," he said, with a nod.

Ella studied Gene for a moment. At one time he'd been one of the best tribal officers around—dependable and with a cool head. But four years ago he'd shot a twelve-year-old who'd attacked him with a knife. He hadn't been the same since. He'd started drinking, his marriage had fallen apart, and, after a year of desk duty and AA, he had requested a transfer and ended up here.

Ella's radio crackled and she heard a patrolman requesting immediate backup at the construction site for the nuclear power plant. Using the unit-to-unit frequency, she called the officer, Marianna Talk.

"I'm fifteen minutes away. What's your situation?"

"About twenty demonstrators have hiked in to the work site, and are getting in the way of the construction. Some pot shards turned up this morning in the area being excavated, and word got out. The protestors are claiming the workers are desecrating holy ground, so they're trying to put an immediate stop to the work. There are three security guards present, but they haven't been able to catch any of the trespassers. The real problem is that the work crew is getting fed up and are about to take things into their own hands. I could really use some backup."

"Do the artifacts look like the real deal? Supposedly, the site was already checked out by the anthropologists and cleared."

"The ones I saw didn't look old to me, but I'm no expert on Navajo pottery."

"Hang tight. I'll be there."

Ella switched on her sirens and raced down the highway to the same turnoff she'd taken the other day. The gate was closed, and an anxious-looking security guard stood behind the fence, a two-way radio at his ear.

The actual construction site was a mile farther down the road, and when Ella finally arrived, she spotted Officer Talk standing among a group of five men in white hard hats. The contractor's vehicles, mostly bulldozers, graders, scrapers, and a few big machines with knobby rollers, were parked together, their engines turned off. She could see operators or drivers in each of the cabs or seats.

At least the workers were cooperating, Ella noted as she got out of her vehicle, Mace and baton in hand. The protestors were standing in a group about fifty feet away, down in a depression where several feet of earth had already been removed. Three men in dirty security guard uniforms were about halfway between the groups, standing beside a seated, chubby, handcuffed Navajo man in equally dusty street clothes.

Ella walked over to Officer Talk. "Looks like you've managed to keep tempers from flaring so far."

"Just barely. When I got here, the demonstrators were running around in groups of two, getting in the way and forcing the machinery operators to stop or change direction to avoid hitting them. According to the foreman"—Marianna gestured toward Stover, the man Ella had seen the other night—"they showed up on foot in pairs, coming in from the direction of the highway."

"What about those artifacts?" Ella asked.

Stover took a step forward, then pointed toward a white company pickup in the middle of the parked vehicles. "Got them locked in my toolbox. I think somebody sneaked them in early this morning and stuck the pieces just below the surface. They don't look authentic. We saw some real tribal pottery at the meetings we had months ago with the experts. You know, so we've be able to protect any authentic sites."

"Did you pick up everything?" Ella asked. As she turned her head toward the group of demonstrators, she saw someone with a camcorder, maybe the same guy as before, filming them. He looked familiar, only this time he was wearing sunglasses in addition to the cap. Since none of the other demonstrators had anything but regular glasses on, the cameraman stood out.

Cameraman tapped a huge guy in a gray sweatshirt and baggy jeans standing beside him on the shoulder, and the big Navajo stepped forward. She recognized the man, Albert Manus—a former tackle for the Kirtland Central Broncos football team. Now in his thirties, Manus worked as a bouncer at a Farmington bar. She knew this because Manus had a reputation for getting into fights, on the job or off, especially when encountering Shiprock High alumni. The rivalry between schools had been going on since the late Sixties, and word had it that Teeny had been the only one who'd ever kicked Albert's butt.

Manus began to walk, actually it was more of an attitude-enhanced waddle, headed directly toward where she and Officer Talk were standing.

Marianne brought out her Taser. "Hope this thing is packing a full charge."

Ella touched the young officer's arm. "Let me have first crack at him. If he gets by me, light him up like a Christmas tree."

"It's your . . ." Marianne said without thinking.

"Decision? Funeral? Ass?" Ella mumbled, stepping forward. She planned on meeting Albert halfway. If things got violent and the big guy got past her, it would give Officer Talk room to maneuver.

Unfortunately, shooting him wasn't an option at the moment, and she didn't really want this to escalate into a full-out confrontation if it could be avoided by using her baton. Maybe Manus was just pulling a bluff. But she was a Shiprock High alumni, and that was a strike against her already.

"Counting on me not hitting a woman, Clah? Even one who used to play hoops for the Cretans."

The shot against the Chieftains was pure Albert, so she ignored it. "Nobody needs to get hit today, Mr. Manus. Your people have already made the point. Now it's time to go home. Don't make me have to lock you up. Inciting a riot can get people hurt." Ella stopped on hard-packed ground, wanting to be sure of her footing. She thumbed the safety of her pistol on, then turned so the weapon wasn't within easy reach. Then she waited for the two-hundred-fifty-pound man to close the distance.

Manus, broad shouldered and barrel shaped, with short legs that looked like stumps, changed his direction slightly, but kept on coming. He pretended to pass her by, then suddenly turned, grabbing at her waist.

She'd seen it coming a mile away and was ready to respond. She kicked him right in the groin. The loud groans Ella heard came from the two groups of men, not Albert, unfortunately. He rocked back, staying on his feet, and laughed, shaking his head and wagging his finger at her.

She staggered back; kicking him had almost knocked her to the ground. "A jock wearing a jock," she said. "Should have known your priority would be protecting your brains."

"Behind that cup is every woman's dream, Clah. Better be careful or you'll get me all excited." He held out his hands in a big welcoming gesture. "Too late. Let's start with a *big* hug."

Albert reached out, trying to grab her again. He was slow, and she evaded him once more, ducking past his defenses and slapping him hard on the face.

She then faked a right jab, and slapped him on the left cheek. Messing with his pride was part of her strategy. Albert was used to shaking off punches.

His face was turning red already. "Don't bitch-slap me!" Manus reached out, trying to grab her wrist.

It was what she'd been waiting for. She grabbed his wrist instead and took hold of his hand, pinching the nerve behind his fingers with her finger and thumb. She then applied all the pressure she could muster.

"Damn!" Albert squealed, stumbling to his knees. Cursing, he swept out with his other arm, trying to knock her down. She kicked him in the elbow and stepped up the pinch hold.

By then Albert was in agony. "Stop! I give! I give!" He moaned, his face contorted.

Ella backed off on the pressure just a little, having noticed Marianna standing close. "Cuff his left wrist to his left ankle, Officer Talk," she ordered.

"If it'll fit," Marianna said, reaching for the cuffs at her belt. Albert tried to turn away.

Ella applied more pressure. "Hold still, and this'll be over in a minute."

Albert yelled, then stopped moving. "Okay, okay. I'm . . . cool."

Ten seconds later, Albert was lying on his right side, his left arm fastened to his left leg.

"Now what? Ma'am," Marianna asked.

"If he gets an attitude, rap him on the shin with your baton," Ella ordered. She turned to verify that the construction workers hadn't moved during the confrontation. All were still there except for one.

A tall Navajo in a company hard hat with the name "Morgan" written in permanent marker on the front decided to join them. He was maybe six foot two in his boots, and obviously in a foul mood. Dusty sweat ran down his face, and there was a racoon effect around his eyes that told her he'd been wearing protective goggles. "Okay, you've got the big guy. You gonna get rid of these other jerks, too, so we can finally get some work done?"

"If we move in, they're going to scatter like before. It'll take hours to round them up with the manpower we have," Marianna said, looking at Ella for confirmation.

"Just keep your people here another five minutes," Ella said to Stover, ignoring Morgan. "I'm going to go talk to them, and maybe we can find a way to resolve this."

Ella knew that with their manpower shortage they weren't going to get more officers on the scene for quite a while. Taking Manus out of the picture was a good beginning, but she had to find a way to diffuse the situation now before it turned nasty— as in a riot.

Ella started toward the demonstrators. As she passed by the security guards, she gave them a nod, and added, "Just stay here, and remain calm, okay?"

The oldest guard, who appeared to be in his sixties and looked as if he would have much rather been playing checkers or walking a mall, smiled weakly. "You've got it, officer."

Making sure the demonstrators she was approaching could see clearly, Ella brought out her handgun. Holding it barrel down, she slipped out the clip and placed it in her pocket. Ejecting the shell in the chamber into her hand, she stowed away the round in the same pocket.

At least this way, if the demonstrators turned on her, they wouldn't get her loaded weapon. Ella holstered her pistol and brought out her baton, holding it in front of her. She would play a bluff, then make a deal, but the baton would let her protect herself if things went wrong.

"Benjamin Harvey!" Ella yelled.

"Here," came a familiar voice. The man took a step forward but just then, an object flew out from the back of the group. Ella blocked it with her baton, and a large clod of dirt shattered in a cloud of dust and sand.

"Who threw that?" Benjamin turned, along with half the others around him. Ella saw a man running off, the same guy with the camera—and sunglasses.

"Ella?" Marianne yelled.

"Let him go," Ella yelled back. "We're not here looking for trouble, we're here for the truth, right?" She looked straight at Benjamin, trying to ignore the sand the shattered dirt clod had sprayed into her face and eyes.

"Yeah. The truth," Benjamin responded. Several men around him nodded in agreement.

"Then listen to what I have to say," Ella replied, placing the baton back into the loop on her belt as she stepped within ten feet of the group. They all looked as hot and dirty as the security guards, and were probably as eager to find a way out of a violent confrontation as she was, especially now that Albert was no longer there to cover their backs. The realization gave her confidence. Her plan *would* work.

"How about you and I go check out these so-called artifacts?" Ella asked Benjamin. "After examining them, if you still think they might be authentic, we'll have the experts come back, along with a *hataalii*, my brother. You *know* he can be trusted to tell you the truth."

Ten minutes later, the crisis had past. Benjamin studied the shards of pottery in Stover's truck and their examination revealed the pottery to be unfired and quite recently made. Signs also indicated that all three of the pots had been broken before being unearthed, probably by being dropped. Benjamin himself had made the final discovery that irrevocably revealed the true nature of the pot shards. On one piece he'd discovered the gummy remnants of what had obviously been a price tag.

Ella spoke to Benjamin briefly about the protestors. "Is the guy with the camera one of your regulars?"

"No, I've only seen him twice," he said. "He's a real puzzle, that one," he said, and gave Ella details she hadn't known, like his first name, Leroy, and where Benjamin thought the man lived.

"Thanks," Ella said, digesting what he'd told her. She'd talk to Justine and the others about this as soon as possible.

Lost in thought, Ella watched Benjamin hurry off. For now peace had been restored. The protestors were dispersing, moving out in twos toward the locations off-site where they'd hidden their vehicles.

Albert Manus had been questioned, but was unable to tell her anything about the cameraman except his first name, Leroy, and that Leroy had dared him to take on the tall lady cop. Manus was released after that, and he walked off quickly without comment.

Ella stood with Marianna as the workers began to start up their equipment again. "I think we're okay here now."

"Someone's determined to keep trouble brewing, though," Marianna warned.

Ella thought about the instigator with the camera and what she'd learned. They were either up against someone determined to get a hot story, or with another agenda she'd yet to discover. The only thing she knew for sure is that they hadn't seen the last of "Leroy."

SIX

✖ ✖ ✖

Justine arrived minutes later just as Ella was walking to her vehicle. Work was beginning again, and they had to shout to hear each other over the roar of heavy equipment. Ella gave her a quick summary of events, then brought up the question that had been bothering her.

"That camera guy . . . it's a weird thing. He wasn't at any of the demonstrations held while the power plant was going through the approval process. We never saw him at all until the other night. Then, today, he shows up, tries to provoke a riot by throwing the closest thing he could find, and runs off rather than face the people he's supposed to be working with."

"So who is he, Ella? Shouldn't somebody among the protestors know the guy?"

"I asked Benjamin, and he said he thought the guy lived near him in one of those squatter houses. Calls himself Leroy, no last name. This Leroy offered to film the demonstrations so they'd have a record of the truth that neither the tribe nor the construction workers could twist around."

"So he's not connected to any of the media or press," Justine said thoughtfully. "He's just a troublemaker out to stir things up, like siccing Albert Manus on you. I'll ask around and see if I can get a lead on him."

"I wonder if he's the one who planted the phoney relics?

Benjamin's pretty ticked off about the whole thing. He assured me he's going to find out if it was one of his own group. He's worried that he's going to look like a fool and lose all credibility once the story gets out," Ella said.

"Officer Talk kept her cool today," Justine commented. "But you took some serious chances."

"I gambled that Benjamin's allies would turn out to be reasonable people who'd recognize the truth when they saw it."

"It was a good call," Justine said.

"Anything new on our case from your end?" Ella asked, trying to focus back on the murder investigation.

"Nothing yet."

"I've got to fill you in on a few things then," Ella said and updated Justine on what she'd learned about Marco's accident and Valerie's "call girl" activities of a few years ago. Then she showed her the piece of paper found in Marco's wrecked pickup. "Can you follow up on this telephone number?"

"It looks familiar." Justine stared at it for a moment. "I think it's the victim's, but let me check." She made a cell phone call to Tache, then read it off. A moment later she had her answer. "It's Valerie's," Justine said. "Do you think Marco killed her? But that note with the biblical passage doesn't fit in with him at all. Marco's not Christian. He's not anything, if you follow. Modernist, maybe. But I think booze rules his life."

A high rate of alcoholism was one of the Rez's less flattering statistics. Right up there with teen suicide. Low self-esteem and poverty took its toll in many different ways. "Unfortunately, we can't question Marco. He's in ICU," Ella said. "But have Tache find out everything he can about Valerie. That's his priority for now." Everyone did double duty these days. Being the crime scene photographer didn't mean he wasn't expected to take part in other aspects of the investigation, too.

For a brief moment Ella felt a touch of nostalgia as she remembered how it had been when she'd worked for the FBI. They'd had the resources and a decent budget. She then thought of her old partner . . . and a case they'd worked on in

L.A. It had been many years ago, over a decade in fact, but she was almost sure there were distinct similarities between this case and that one. She made a mental note to call Blalock and see about his search through VICAP, the Violent Criminal Apprehension Program database. She'd be calling Dennis Anderson, too, as soon as possible. Her ex-partner was now serving out of the Denver office.

"You have a photo of the victim with you, Justine?"

"Nope. Everything is on my desk. When I heard you needed backup . . ."

"That's okay. We'll return to the station, pick up a photo, then visit the Double Play Sports Bar in Kirtland."

As they headed to the bar, Ella updated Justine on Reverend Campbell's visit to the Quick Stop the night of the murder, then added, "I'd like you to talk to Reverend Campbell and see if you can figure out what he was doing in the area."

"I can tell you where he was that night, at least for a while," Justine said. "But it's far from an airtight alibi."

"What do you mean?"

"He teaches a Bible class and that evening's session was held at Ramona Willie's home, scheduled to begin at eight. I was there, too. He was late, and didn't show up until eight-thirty or so. He'd stopped to buy some coffee for the gathering. But he was at Ramona's for less than ten minutes when he got sicker than a dog. I mean the man was green. He excused himself at one point, and was gone for so long Ramona went to see if he was okay. He was in the bathroom for maybe a half hour."

"And you all stuck around?"

"We went over the lesson ourselves, then everyone but me went home. Ramona and I were ready to take him to the hospital, if needed, but he came out close to nine-thirty or so, shaky, but feeling better. From what he said yesterday, I think it was a really bad case of food poisoning."

"From what?"

"He said he'd picked up one of the homemade sausages Jane Joe made for the Quick Stop, and scarfed it down on the way to Bible class."

Ella cringed. Jane was one of the worst cooks around, and sometimes the Quick Stop had problems with outdated food items. "I wouldn't have touched them with a ten-foot pole. But tell me, are you sure that the bad food wasn't just an excuse? People who've just killed someone often get sick to their stomachs. I've seen it with cops more than once."

"I suppose, but Reverend Campbell isn't the kind of person to do something like that," Justine said firmly.

Ella considered this latest piece of information. Traditionalists believed that all things were interrelated but she'd yet to find any connecting threads in this case.

"I don't like this, Ella. You're not seriously considering Reverend Campbell as a suspect, are you?"

"He is until we can rule him out."

"He wouldn't hurt a fly. And I mean that literally. I was in his office one day and instead of swatting it, he shooshed it out a window."

"Believe me, Justine, the last thing I want to do is go after the reverend. If we do, we'll have trouble from all sides. But we can't ignore the fact that the victim was drowned in what might have been a forced baptism. Then there's also the biblical quote and the fact that we can't prove where Reverend Campbell was during a critical time, except that he was in the right neighborhood."

"He practically staggered to the bathroom that night, Ella. Something besides fear and anxiety was at work here. He could barely stand up."

Ella let it go, for now. "I'm going to call Emily. The Double Play is in her jurisdiction and we'll need her department's cooperation to go there for answers."

It took less than ten minutes to get what Ella needed. The county often worked closely with tribal PD and both sides had learned the advantages of cooperation.

Emily was waiting for them as they pulled up at the bar. There were only a few cars in the parking lot, all as close to the entrance as possible, under outside lamps.

Emily joined Ella and Justine at the door. "This place is the pits at night. We get calls three or four times a week. The county has even tried to get it shut down."

"Were any arrests made here last night? In particular did county haul in a Navajo man by the name of Gilbert Tso?"

"There *was* a fight here last night but, by the time the patrolman arrived it was mostly over. The owner handles thing pretty well, considering the knuckle-draggers this place attracts."

"I know—she's ex-military, right?" Ella asked.

"Yeah, and she's tough as nails," Emily said. "An exsergeant in the Marines. She keeps a baseball bat behind the bar and she looks like Bruce Lee with that thing. I've seen her in action."

It took a few minutes for their eyes to adjust to the dim lighting inside, so they stood at the end of the bar closest to the door. Ella heard the dull thud of a game of darts over to her right, and the sound of some kind of sports event on the TVs in the back. The smell of sweat, tobacco, and booze was so strong it flooded her senses for a moment. As her vision cleared, Ella saw the large, muscular woman behind one of the beer taps, watching them as she topped off a tall glass of draught.

"On or off duty?" the woman asked, cutting the tap just as the head threatened to overflow the glass.

Ella, whose badge was beneath her jacket, glanced at the others with her. There was no outward sign that she or Julie were law enforcement. "Good eye, ma'am. You the owner of this place?"

The woman smiled. "That's me. I'm Chris Vasquez, bartender, bouncer, and badass. What can I do for you and your backups?"

Ella had to smile. "We're not here to arrest anyone," she answered, hoping to put Ms. Vasquez at ease. "I just needed some information. There was a Navajo man here last night, one of your regulars, I believe, and he got involved in a fight. Do you remember the incident?"

She laughed. "Good old Gilbert! Wait, don't tell me. He sent you to arrest me because I thumped him with my bat before he could break up the place."

"No, it's nothing like that," Ella said. "I just needed to verify he was here. I don't suppose you remember the time this fight took place, do you?"

"Yeah, he came in early, around six-thirty. He was in a surly mood, too. Probably 'cause he didn't have a woman with him who would pay his tab. The fight started about seven-thirty, I guess. Lasted, what, thirty seconds before I clocked him and that cowboy."

Ella nodded to Justine, who showed the bartender Valerie's DMV photo. "Did you ever see Gilbert with this woman?" Ella asked her.

She looked at it a moment. "Yeah. I think so, but he had several women, one young enough to be his daughter. Last night he was with the young, uptight girl. It was the first time I'd seen her. She sat ramrod straight and never ordered a thing. Didn't even want a Coke. When she finally left, she refused to pay his tab, too. Smart girl."

Ella's luck was working today so she decided to play a hunch. "Was the young woman about five foot two, maybe one hundred and thirty pounds, really long hair, and wearing traditional Navajo clothes, like with a long skirt and all?"

"That's a good description. And no makeup, or very little."

Ella had no doubt now that the woman with Gilbert had been Boots, Valerie's daughter. It was natural that she would have wanted to know the man her mother cared about, but why a staunch traditionalist like Boots had agreed to come to a bar with Gilbert was beyond her. Even more troubling was that the investigative circle kept coming closer to home all the time. Boots had helped take care of Ella's daughter for years and was practically family.

The ex-Marine spoke again after a moment. "In case it

helps, I recall that they didn't come in together. He showed up first, then about fifteen minutes later she came in and sat down with him at a table. After about a half hour, she left—alone. And if you ask me, she'd never been at a bar in her life. She hardly ever looked up, and when she did, her eyes were as wide as saucers."

Ella nodded slowly. "So she left, and Gilbert stayed?"

"Yeah, but I stopped serving him right after that because he'd run out of money. He stayed nursing the last of his beer for a bit, feeling sorry for himself, then someone made a smart-ass comment about the young woman who'd been with him earlier. Gilbert flew out of his chair swinging. My backup bartender tried to break it up, but when I realized it wasn't working, I grabbed the Pacifier," she said, pointing to the massive bat propped up behind the counter. "When I bring that out, people know it's going to be thumping time unless they walk away."

She looked at Ella, then at the others, and shrugged. "Anyway, as far as fights go, it was a quickie. A few punches, a little blood—that's all."

With the interview over, Emily headed back east on patrol and Ella and Justine hit the road in the opposite direction.

"The bartender was referring to Boots—Jennifer Clani—wasn't she?"

Ella nodded. "It had to be her. That means we'll have to question her next. She's always at Kevin's, so head on over there." Seeing Justine nod, she continued. "Tache is following up on the names of the people at the shoe game, right?" Ella asked her as they passed through the rural community above Kirtland—Fruitland—and continued west toward the reservation.

"Yeah, but last I heard he'd come up with nothing. The guys all live in the area and are regulars. They're night people and the Morning Stop Café isn't one of their haunts. They also operate on Indian time. Not many of them even carry a watch. Getting the precise time of Benny's visit and other events that they may or may not have seen is difficult, as you can imagine."

Ella nodded, her thoughts racing. "Tell me, what's this I've heard about Reverend Campbell going around trying to convert people on the Rez?"

Justine said nothing for a moment. "He's not a fanatic about it, Ella. Really. The rev is low-key except during the high points of his sermons. But there *is* a membership drive going on at the church right now."

"I got a different take from Benny Joe. He claims that Campbell is bugging a lot of people in the neighborhood."

Justine nodded slowly. "Okay, now your interest in him makes more sense. Reverend Campbell *is* on a mission but, Ella, he stays away from the traditionalists and New Traditionalists. People in those groups already have something they can hold on to, a belief system that grounds them. I'd be surprised to hear that any of them are griping about him. Reverend Campbell says he's hoping to connect with the Navajos who've lost track of the old ways and haven't replaced them with anything else. Those are the ones he says need us. They're vulnerable to things like alcoholism because they have nothing to hold on to. A moral vacuum, he calls it. Reverend Campbell wants to give them an alternative—a way out and a way in—by opening our doors to them."

"By converting them, you mean."

"Yeah, I guess, but it's not a hard sell. He tells us he's just offering an outstretched hand in the name of Jesus Christ. It's up to them whether they take it or not."

"Think hard, Justine. Are you sure it's all that low-key? How does he sound when he goes one-on-one with someone? My father used to bring out the ole fire and brimstone speech whenever he felt he wasn't making headway."

"He's nothing like your father used to be, I've heard them both. True, I've never seen Campbell in action outside church, but, Ella, you've met the man and spoken with him several times. Does he strike you as the type to thump people on the head with a Bible?"

The mental picture made Ella laugh. "That's the most colorful description I've ever heard of a Bible-thumper. Okay. Point taken." Reverend Campbell looked more like a kewpie doll than a preacher.

Ella fell silent during the rest of the drive. Dawn's father, Kevin, and she were still friends but the fact that Dawn had chosen to stay with him for now still stung. She understood the reason for it—Dawn and her horse were inseparable—but she missed her daughter terribly.

"How do you want to handle this with Boots? Go easy?" Justine asked, interrupting her thoughts.

Ella took a deep breath then let it out slowly. "No. We'll treat her the same as anyone else." There were no personal considerations when it came to a murder case.

They arrived at Kevin's home twenty minutes later. The house itself was less than ten years old, and Kevin had recently added a corral and had stalls built for Chieftain, Ella's horse, and Wind, Dawn's pony. To her surprise, there was a third stall there, too. As she watched, a large dapple gray gelding, like the ones Dawn had always favored, came out prancing.

"If he bought her a horse without my permission, I may shoot him," Ella grumbled. "Or at the very least Taser his butt."

Ella strode up to the door so quickly Justine had a hard time keeping up. Just as they stepped up onto the wooden porch, Kevin came out, dressed in an expensive oxford dress shirt and chino pants that screamed old money. Of course his five-hundred-dollar watch added to that image, as did his Italian loafers. Even as a tribal lawyer, Kevin did well for himself financially.

"It's good to see you, Ella. And Justine, hi," he said, then glanced back at Ella. "You've got great timing, mother of my daughter. I was just about to call you."

Kevin was trying too hard to be smooth, and it annoyed Ella. "Let me guess. You wanted to talk to me about that horse I just saw out there," she said.

"Yes, but I can see you're jumping to the wrong conclusion. The new horse is mine."

It took Ella less than five seconds to go from a smile to outright laughter. Kevin was the type to ride in a Porsche, not a horse, and his current selection of clothing served to support that lifestyle. As far as she knew, Kevin had never even been on a horse.

"I bought him from Mercedes Manuelito. She assured me he was a beginner's horse," he added, irately. "Boots has already offered to teach me to ride, but give me a break, how hard can it be? I mean you saddle the thing, sit down, and hold on the reins so you can control the animal. The horse is the one doing the work, right?" He looked at Ella, then at Justine.

"All things considered I'd strongly advise you not to take that horse out of the corral until you've had time to get to know him under the saddle. Horses are very unpredictable," Ella said.

"Yeah, like that idiot pony," he muttered. "The danged thing *bit* me. No joke."

Ella's sympathies were with the pony. "Don't ever let him get away with that."

"I didn't. Well, actually Boots straightened him out. But this new horse is gentle. Boots looked him over before I put my money down."

"Good. That was smart. Boots knows horses. But speaking of Boots, we need to talk to her. Is she around?"

He nodded. "She just gave Dawn her riding lesson and they're putting the pony away now. Do you want me to keep Dawn occupied while you interview Boots? I'm guessing this is related to the murder."

"Yeah, it is, so please keep Dawn away while we talk," Ella said, then added, "Just to make sure we're on the same page— our daughter *won't* be riding the horse you just bought, right?"

Kevin hesitated.

"Kevin, she's okay on her pony, but she's not ready for

more than that. You and I had an agreement and I expect you to honor it." Ella noticed out of the corner of her eye that Justine was trying to distance herself, sensing an argument coming on.

"Dawn doesn't know that eventually the horse will be hers. Nobody does," Kevin said in a whisper-soft voice. "It'll be our secret. Of course I'll be the one riding him at first. Then, after Boots feels she's ready, maybe we can let Dawn ride Willy, too, from time to time. She'll be moving up to a competition horse soon enough anyway."

"And if I say no, then I'm the bad guy. Nice going, counselor. You knew *exactly* what you were doing."

"Look, what's the harm? The horse can stay here for as many months or years that it takes, and I'll be footing the bills. Later this year, maybe we can finally give her what she wants most for her birthday—going for a trail ride with both of us."

Ella smiled slowly. Trail rides with Dawn took all day. That was why Ella usually scheduled them way in advance. Just the thought of Kevin trying to stay on a horse all day long improved her mood. If anyone deserved a pain in the butt, it was him. No way he'd make it—even if the horse didn't unseat him on the way.

"Fortunately for you, we're going to have to take up this conversation again some other time. Right now, Justine and I need to talk to Boots alone."

Spotting Ella, Dawn ran over, taking off her riding helmet along the way. Ella roughed up her daughter's long black hair playfully, then gave her a quick hug. "Having fun?"

"I took Wind over some small jumps today! It was so much fun! A lot better than just stepping over logs."

Boots came up behind Dawn. "We've moved to the next phase of her training. She's got a very good seat, but I'm going to insist that she always wears a helmet."

"Good," Ella said.

As soon as Kevin called Dawn away to help him brush the new horse, Ella and Justine accompanied Boots inside the house where they wouldn't be overheard. "We're here on business, Boots," Ella said, waving for Boots to have a seat. "I understand that you were at the Double Play last night."

Boots stared at the floor. "It was a horrible place," she whispered. "I'm not going back again, ever."

"Why were you there?" Ella pressed.

Boots hesitated. "It was family business . . . personal."

"I know this is going to be awkward, but I need you to tell me everything you know. This isn't the time to hold back. Your mother's ex-husband, the man you met there, is in custody right now. He's a suspect in her murder."

SEVEN
✖ ✖ ✖

Boots gave her an agonized stare, her eyes filling with tears. "All I wanted was for him to stop seeing my mother. That's why I went there."

"Start at the beginning," Ella said softly.

Tears spilled freely down Boot's face. "My mother was trying very hard to put her life together again and he wasn't . . . a good influence. But he didn't want to talk about him and Mom. That's why he insisted on meeting in that awful place. He thought I wouldn't go."

Boots cried silently for a while and Ella resisted the impulse to give her a hug. Even though she'd known Jennifer for years, touching another was not something that came easily to a Navajo, and it would have felt even more awkward to a traditionalist.

Finally Boots took a deep unsteady breath and looked up, though she continued to avoid eye contact with either Ella or Justine. In the Anglo world, the refusal to make eye contact would have been seen with suspicion, but it was the way things were done here on the reservation. To look Ella straight in the eyes would have been a sign of disrespect— and of confrontation.

"Did her ex-husband agree not to see her?" Ella asked gently.

"He said that it was my mother who kept coming to see him, not the other way around. He told me I shouldn't be talking to him, that I should talk to her."

"Did you?"

"I'd tried several times already, and I was going to do so again, but I never had the chance," Boots answered, her voice fading to a whisper.

"Did you and your mother see each other often?" Ella asked.

"No, not really. She and I . . . didn't agree on many things. But Mom asked me to meet her at her place, behind that café, a few weeks ago. She was going to church again, and wanted me to go with her. I told her I wouldn't feel comfortable being there. Mom said I didn't have to believe or anything, she just wanted to do something good together. I told her that there were a lot of other good things we could do together that didn't involve her religion," Boots said flatly.

"Did your mother mention anyone giving her a hard time?"

"No, but there was something going on. While I was there, her phone rang. She got angry and told whoever it was that she didn't have time for all that nonsense. She told the person to leave her and everyone else alone."

"Thanks for telling me all this. I know it was hard for you and I appreciate it," Ella said.

"The Fierce Ones—my grandmother has them looking for my mom's killer, doesn't she?" Boots asked.

"Yes. How do you feel about that?"

"I understand what they're trying to do, but I've heard about their tactics. . . ."

"We'll get to the person responsible first, Boots," Ella responded, hoping she would be able to back up her words.

"Find him soon, please." Jennifer replied. "I'm afraid my grandmother will get arrested or something. She can be difficult when she gets upset."

"I know." Ella didn't need to elaborate further.

Justine nodded to Boots, then left with Ella. Once out on the back porch, Ella waved to Kevin, who was trying to show Dawn how to rope a fence post with a lasso and failing miserably, judging from Dawn's laughter.

Seeing her, Dawn hurried up. "Mom, you aren't going yet, are you? You just got here!"

Ella felt the sting of Dawn's words. "I'm working on an important case right now and I've got to go back to work."

"Once you've done with that, can we go on another trail ride?" Dawn's brown eyes looked at Ella imploringly. "It's been *weeks*."

Dawn had mastered The Look, and Ella knew a ploy when she saw one. She glanced at Kevin, who smiled innocently, and Ella suddenly had the distinct feeling that he'd already promised Dawn one. "Let's let your father decide when, because he's going with us, of course," she said, working hard not to grin. Kevin would be in traction after an hour.

After saying good-bye to her daughter, Ella walked back with Justine to the SUV. "We need to stop by Blalock's office first. He's been checking VICAP, and I need to know what, if anything, he's found. After that, we need to interview the other employees at the Morning Stop Café. They worked with Valerie, and may know something helpful."

Ella lapsed into a long silence as she gathered her thoughts. "This case has too many loose ends," she said at last. "Why would the killer clean up the body and arrange it the way he did? What message was he trying to send? And, most important of all, was Valerie chosen randomly? If so, then she could be the first of many."

"A serial killer," Justine said, nodding in agreement.

As they reached the parking lot outside of Blalock's office, Ella got out but Justine remained seated.

"While you talk to Blalock, I'll get the addresses of the waitresses and any other employees from the café," Justine said, bringing out her cell phone. "And Joe's supposed to be interviewing one of the victim's ex-husbands, the one who lives near Gallup. I'll give him a call and see what he's turned up."

"Good. You know where I'll be if you need me."

Ella entered the old brick and stone building and hurried down the long hallway, an idea in mind. As she was passing by Bruce Little's office, he stepped out into the hall to meet her. These days, the ex-police officer hired out his services to the tribal police and others, maintaining and repairing computer networks. Craving more action than that provided, he also handled security for area concerts and events.

"I heard about the murder. Are you okay? I understand this one hit kinda close to home for you," he said, his voice gentle.

Ella stopped, though she was in a hurry. Bruce Little and she went way back. Ella was one of the few people who could call him Teeny and not end up needing a new set of teeth. The tall and muscular, pro football player–size ex-cop had always had a sweet spot for her.

"Thank's for caring, Teeny. This one's practically in my own backyard, but I'm handling it. I'm working the case now, in fact. That's why I'm here, to see Blalock."

"Don't let me stop you, then. Just remember if you need anything, call me."

"Thanks. I'll keep that in mind." Big Ed and Teeny were from the same clan, and that cultural connection carried a lot of weight on the Rez. No one ever complained when Ella, normally shorthanded, brought Teeny in on a case.

Ella eased past him carefully. Teeny could block the narrow hallway all by himself.

Special Agent Dwayne Blalock's office, last door down at the end of the hall, was smaller than the others she'd been in and hopelessly cluttered. The two metal desks inside were usually stacked high with files. As recently as a few years ago, two agents had been assigned to the Four Corners area, but Blalock was the only one who'd managed to stick around for long. The younger agents could never get out fast enough because there was no opportunity for career advancement as long as they stayed here. In fact, this was the type of assignment young agents went out of their way to avoid.

"About time you got here, Clah. I've been digging through VICAP and I uncovered something interesting. It was a case you and your old partner, Dennis Anderson, worked on at one point."

"Anything you can tell me?" she asked, trying to recall the specifics. Only bits and pieces, like the fact the murder scene had included biblical quotes teased her memory. It had been over fourteen years ago.

"No details, just the category of the crime, dates, and the names of the investigating officers. It's a cold case, with no arrests and no suspects. The specifics are in another California agency database I can't get into directly. I've put in a request, so I'll have more for you soon."

"Can you access my old Bureau files and maybe cross-reference? That'll at least give us part of the picture."

He tried for a few minutes, then looked over at her. "Come back in a while. I can't work with you sitting there staring at me."

Leaving Blalock at the keyboard, Ella walked back outside and joined Justine, who was still on the phone. As Ella slipped inside the patrol vehicle and fastened her seat belt, Justine hung up and glanced over.

"The Morning Stop Café has two waitresses, Ella. Lea Garner was part-time until a few days ago when she got fired. Lynn Bidtah's full-time. She also helps Stan Brewster with the cooking. Since Lea was just fired, she might be willing to give us more dirt on Brewster than Lynn. So, what do you say we go see her first?"

"Good idea," Ella said.

They drove to an area of scattered homes, site-built houses provided by the NHA. These structures were nicer than most

Navajo homes, and many had late-model vehicles parked out-side. "Lea's parents are professionals?" Ella asked, seeing the address where they were headed. The house was spacious for a reservation residence.

Justine nodded. "Her dad, Arnold, is a mining engineer. Her mother, Vina, is a nurse."

"Any idea why Lea got fired?"

"Not really, but I guess we're about to find out."

As they pulled up into the graveled driveway, a middle-aged woman wearing slacks and a long-sleeved red sweater came out of the house, cell phone pressed to her ear with one hand and keys and a purse in the other. Seeing them, she ended the call and went over to meet them just as Ella stepped out of the SUV.

"I'm Vina Garner. Do you need to talk to me?" she asked quickly as Ella flashed her badge. "I was on my way to the store."

"Don't let us slow you down then, Mrs. Garner. We only need to speak to your daughter, Lea," Ella said.

"I heard about the death of that woman. My girl isn't some kind of suspect, is she?" the woman asked.

"Not at all," Ella said calmly. "We just need to ask her a few questions." Ella noticed someone standing at the open door, listening.

"Well, you might have wasted a trip. Lea was home that day and won't know a thing."

A young woman around nineteen, wearing a tight sweater and even tighter, low-cut jeans, came out onto the porch. Her hair was long and pulled back into one long, loose braid that fell halfway down her back. "*Mom,* they said they wanted to talk to *me,*" she said and rolled her mascara-lined eyes. "I'll be fine, now go on and do your shopping."

As Mrs. Garner got into her vehicle, her daughter waved to Ella and Justine, inviting them inside.

"Sorry about that, officers. I wish I didn't have to live at home, but until I get out of school, I'm stuck here," she said, plopping down onto the couch and inviting Ella and Justine to take a seat. "You want me to tell you about Valerie, right?"

"As a matter of fact, yes," Ella said.

"For a woman old enough to be my mom, she was all right. She started off as a waitress at the café, went to school at the same time, and ended up doing Brewster's books. She was a superhard worker. And street-smart, too. Valerie could say no and still get what she wanted," she added, in a barely audible voice.

"What do you mean by that?" Ella asked.

Lea shrugged. "Brewster's a dirty old man. He liked hiring waitresses who looked like me. With curves, you know? And if you played along with his games, then you'd get extra."

"What games?" Ella pressed.

"After we closed for the day, he'd catch one of us alone and ask us to strip for him, to music, like at a strip club. He'd tell us what to take off next. He kept his clothes on, so nothing was going to happen. It wasn't a big deal, at first, and he'd pay us for it. Then one day he told me he wanted to give me a bath—lather me up and make me feel good all over. That just creeped me out. Him touching me. I told him I wasn't interested. Two days later, he fired me. He said I was being rude to the customers."

Ella and Justine exchanged glances. "Did Valerie play his games?" Ella asked.

Lea nodded. "I think she did at the beginning. But Valerie had serious clout these days. She kept his books and made his daily deposits so I think he was afraid to push it. He'd still come on to her, making little suggestions, but she'd just laugh and walk away."

"Do you think it's possible that Brewster killed her?"

Lea considered it for a long time before finally answering. "I don't think so. He liked Valerie . . . and I think he respected her, too. He told me once that he admired the way she'd pulled herself out of the gutter."

"Is Brewster a Christian?"

She laughed. "Naw, he's a real hypocrite. He's looking out for himself—for old number one. See what I'm saying?"

Ella nodded. "Is there anything else you can tell me about Brewster?"

"He's doing his thing with Lynn now, last I heard. She's hoping he'll eventually leave his wife and marry her. But who in their right mind would want a pervert like Stan?"

Ella stood, and Justine followed suit. After thanking Lea and giving her Ella's business card, they returned to their unit.

"I want to go talk to Lynn, but first we're going to pay Brewster a little visit," Ella said as they were driving away. Before they got to the highway, Dispatch came through on the radio.

"SI One, see the minister at Good Shepherd church. Reverend Campbell needs you to take a look at a message someone left for him."

Justine spun the vehicle around, and was racing up the mesa even before Ella racked the mike. They arrived at the church less than five minutes later. Coming up the road, it was obvious why Campbell had called. The large, carved sign that had stood beside the steps of the main entrance was now flat on the ground. The wooden post that had held it upright had been snapped in half. A long length of heavy rope was still tied around the sign.

"Did you see this happen?" Ella asked, joining Reverend Campbell.

"I was alone working when I heard the commotion. I rushed out from my office just in time to see them driving away, going north," Campbell said in an unsteady voice. "It was two people in a big gold or bronze Ford pickup. I didn't notice the license plate. They must have attached the rope to a bumper or trailer hitch."

"Anything else?" Ella asked.

"They left a note. It was stuck to the entrance door with a knife."

"Did you touch any part of it?" Ella asked.

Reverend Campbell nodded, looking disgusted with himself. "I should have known better, I know. But I came rushing out sure that there'd been an accident. When I saw what had happened, I could hardly believe it. I was on my way back in to call the police when I saw the note and the knife stuck on the door . . . of God's house. It was an offense—do you understand? That's why I reacted without even thinking. I pulled the knife out and grabbed the note."

"Where are the knife and the note now?" Ella asked.

"In my office. I bent the tip of the knife blade prying it out, I'm afraid."

Ella tried not to groan. That meant he'd probably wiped all usable prints from it in the process—providing the vandals had been dumb enough to leave any. "Let's go take a look," she suggested.

Moments later Justine placed the blade, an inexpensive hunting knife with a handle made from deer antlers, into a cardboard express mail envelope provided by Campbell. Ella slipped the note into a clear glassine envelope, then studied the message a while longer. Unless she missed her guess, this was also a warning that the worst was yet to come.

"What's it say?" Justine asked.

" 'Our land, our justice,' " Ella answered.

EIGHT

——— ✖ ✖ ✖ ———

Ford, who'd just returned from visiting a sick parishioner, came in with freshly brewed cups of coffee for everyone. "This incident must have something to do with our membership drive. It's the only explanation that even comes close to making sense."

Ella could think of other reasons, but didn't comment. If there had been a leak at the station or one of her people had inadvertently let the Fierce Ones know how the victim had died or about the biblical quote found at the scene . . .

"But we've had membership drives before," Reverend Campbell protested. "We're simply opening our doors, inviting people to come join us. But maybe I've been overzealous and have offended someone. I suppose that's possible," Reverend Campbell added sorrowfully.

"It would probably be a good idea for you to ease up for a while," Ella said, looking closely at Campbell's hand as he held the coffee cup. There were no cuts or bruises. "But in all fairness there are other factors at play here that I'm not at liberty to discuss at the moment."

"Could any of our parishioners also be in danger of retaliation?" Ford asked.

"I don't have any reason to believe that at the moment, but both of you may be targets," Ella said slowly.

Reverend Campbell nodded and took a sip of his coffee trying to calm himself. "I can't for the life of me think of anyone I've offended," he said, then paused. "Well, I did have a serious discussion with Stan Brewster not long ago, but it was church business, not related to any of this."

"I'd like to know more."

"It was about the example he should set for the community since he sponsors our team," he said with a shrug. "As I said, unrelated to this."

Justine caught Ella's eye. They both had a good idea what Campbell had talked to Brewster about.

Then Ella looked at Ford. He was Navajo and she doubted the people who'd pulled down the sign would have had him in mind as a target, but she couldn't guarantee anything at this point. "I'll do my best to find out who's responsible for this, and to make sure it doesn't happen again."

As they left the church, Ella realized how quiet Justine had become. That usually meant she was nothing short of furious. "Okay, spill it, partner. What's bugging you?" Ella asked.

"I think we have a leak in the department. I'd be willing to bet that this attack ties into the fact that the victim was 'baptized.' If word got out that the note contained Scripture, it might have easily caused the Fierce Ones to jump the gun and react. I'm sure Lena Clani has gone to them already for help."

"That occurred to me as well. We should increase patrols in this area," Ella said, then called it in. As soon as she was finished, she added, "What do you say we go lean on Jimmy Levaldo?" Ella suggested. "Word is that he's calling the shots now for the Fierce Ones."

"Great idea."

They arrived at an old crumbling gray stucco-coated house southwest of the San Juan River about a half hour later. The road, really not more than two ruts, was in terrible shape and the trip had felt like a motorcycle ride down the center of a railroad track.

"Jimmy's a traditionalist. Do we wait?" Justine asked, parking.

"Let's give him that. We know he's here. That's his pickup over there," Ella said, pointing to the side of the house.

They were there less than a minute before a beefy Navajo man appeared in the doorway and waved, motioning for them to enter.

Ella led the way, letting Justine watch her back. If anyone else was there, they wouldn't be surprised from behind, at least. Neither of them liked dealing with vigilante groups, but a line had been crossed and Ella intended to make sure that it didn't happen again.

"I've already heard what happened at the church," he said, preempting them. "It wasn't our doing, though the two people responsible were hoping you'd think it was. In any case, I've handled the matter. It won't happen again."

The statement surprised her. "You certainly didn't waste any time. Who was responsible?"

Jimmy said nothing, staring off at a corner of the room, and Ella guessed from his expression that he was trying to decide if he should tell her or not. It took several long moments before he finally spoke. "We have a younger generation. They're more . . . impatient," he hedged.

"Maybe you should muzzle them," Justine said sharply.

He looked at her, then nodded. "Ah. You go to that church, don't you? The Good Shepherd, is it?"

"Yeah, and . . . ?"

"It was just a statement of fact," Levaldo said calmly.

"If you have knowledge of a crime and are keeping it from us, *that's* a crime," Ella pressed, deliberately getting in his face and staring into his eyes.

"I have no knowledge of anything," he said smoothly, looking away. "I hear things, that's all. I was at the Quarters Laundromat earlier. I was nowhere near that church."

On the Rez, where water was a precious commodity and

septic systems were poorly maintained or nonexistent, people regularly used Laundromats. Ella had learned that you could find out just about anything you wanted to know if you hung out in one long enough. Laundromats were a legendary source of gossip—a gathering place on weekends for many.

"Do *not* let this happen again," Ella said in a hard voice. "This is *our* case and we won't tolerate interference."

"Understood. But perhaps you should spend more time investigating the death of that woman than running down petty crimes like church vandalism. Unless you've already made an arrest in the murder case?" His expression was one of faint amusement.

"Now who's being impatient?" Justine replied.

He walked to the door and held it open for them. "I would like you to leave now. You bring disharmony to my home."

Justine was muttering all the way back to the vehicle. "Can you believe that?" she said, slamming the car door. "*We* bring disharmony."

"To people like Jimmy, we're just an arm of Anglo law," Ella said, wishing things were different.

Justine said nothing at first, then finally added, "Maybe we are, but we're still needed here."

"Yes, we are."

When they reached the main highway, Justine glanced over at her. "Where to now, Ella?"

She was about to answer when her cell phone rang. It was Blalock.

"Hey, Ella. I finally got a copy of your old files. I think you should get over here."

"To Blalock's," Ella told Justine as she hung up. "It sounds like we're finally about to get some answers."

Ella sat across from Blalock's desk, looking through the printout, which included copies of her own handwritten notes. "It's coming back to me now. I remember a lot of this. Dennis still has possession of his old notes, maybe he'll have something to add. Feelings and impressions can make a difference beyond what was written down at the time."

Blalock punched the speaker button on his phone. "Dennis, you hear me? I'm here with Ella and her partner, Officer Goodluck."

"Hello, Officer Goodluck. You have my sympathies. Not to take anything from Officer Goodluck, I heard from Agent Blalock that you're lost without me, Ella," her old partner quipped.

Ella laughed. "Don't you wish." After exchanging a few friendly words, they quickly got down to business. "It's the same scriptural quote that was left at the crime scene way back then. That can't be coincidental."

"I dug into my files and finally found my own notes, then spoke to a friend in the L.A. Bureau. There's been no repeat of that MO there, not since our time," Anderson replied. Blalock nodded in agreement.

Ella took a deep breath. "Okay, if you've got your old notes in front of you, let's go over the details, at least those we have concerning *our* involvement in the case. Correct me if I remember something wrong," she said.

She continued. "We'd been called in to consult because the victim was a Navajo woman from the Four Corners area, my home turf. The crime scene had been staged—like the one here—except that the victim in L.A. hadn't been robbed and, unlike Valerie, she'd been drowned in her tub. We were barely past the preliminaries when we were pulled off the case and reassigned to a high-priority op."

"That's pretty much the way I remember it," Dennis said. "And that's where my notes end."

"But if we assume we're dealing with the same killer—and the MO is too similar for me to believe in mere coincidence, why did he wait all this time to strike again?"

"Good question," Blalock said.

"Maybe he's been biding his time. Or maybe he was just passing through, needed cash, and decided to have some fun at the same time," Dennis suggested. "Only he's older now and the vic decided to really put up a fight. That ticked him off and, before he knew it, he'd beaten the woman to death—before he could immerse her in the tub."

"That's one of the things that breaks the MO. But, just in case it *is* the same guy, we need to find out who the suspects were back then," Ella said. "We need to look at what happened to the investigation after we were pulled."

"I agree, and that's where VICAP or the L.A. cops are going to have to help you out. It's out of my hands," Dennis said. "But I wish you the best of luck. And if you're ever in Denver, Ella . . ."

Once Agent Anderson was off the line, Blalock glanced over at Ella. "I have a problem with coincidences as well, but the victim in the L.A. case was a Navajo woman. Do you think the local newspaper ran the story? If so, then its at least remotely possible that we're dealing with a copycat."

"Which we have to rule out. Access the newspaper database," Ella said, giving him her password.

After several minutes, Blalock glanced up, then gestured toward his printer, where an image was starting to appear. "Looks like the story got picked up by the wire services first, and then it was run here, a day or two later. I'll put in a request for information on the case from LAPD right now, okay?"

Ella nodded, and as Blalock worked she scanned the printout of the newspaper article, which gave most of the details of the crime, including the drowning in the tub and a reference to the biblical quote. "There's a lot of information here. Our suspect may not have been linked to what happened in L.A.," Ella said, handing the paper to Justine next.

Ella then filled Blalock in on what she'd learned about Brewster and his relationship with the women employees at the café.

"Have you spoken to the other waitress yet?"

"No, but there's also Marco Pete, who may be connected . . . or not. We can't question him until he's out of ICU, but he was in the area at the right time. He might have seen something, or been part of what went down."

"Is an Anglo doctor handling his case?" Blalock asked.

Ella nodded. "I believe so."

"Then I'll visit the hospital tomorrow," Blalock said. "If Marco's recovered consciousness, maybe I can persuade the doctor to let me ask his patient a few questions."

"Good idea," Ella said. Anglo doctors were sometimes more responsive to requests that came directly from the FBI.

Blalock stood. "It's getting late, and it'll take hours for LAPD to dig up the information on the L.A. murder. Apparently it's in their old system, and was never transferred because the case was cold. So let's go talk to that waitress. If we wake her up and she's half asleep and groggy, we might get more out of her."

Lynn Bidtah's place was in the foothills of the Chuskas, a forty-five-minute drive from Shiprock. The road to the house was a joke interrupted by rocks and an occasional deposit of soft sand.

"I'm getting way too old for this, ladies. Maybe I should retire," he muttered, after either bouncing or fishtailing for fifteen minutes.

Dwayne Blalock had been threatening to do that for the past five years. At first, Ella had thought he really meant it, but she'd grown to realize that he actually dreaded the fact that someday he *would* be forced to leave the Bureau. Being an agent had defined him for too long and, like most people who loved their work, he'd be lost without it. Of course he could open a PI firm, many former law enforcement people did, but that just wasn't his style. Blalock and the Bureau were one and the same, even if he liked to gripe.

"Do you want me to drive back? I realize that it's almost ten, past your bedtime," Ella said, teasing him.

"Stuff it, Clah," he growled, braking to a stop in front of the cinder block home nestled by a rocky slope. Here, the boulders were actually the size of large kitchen appliances, and the junipers were tall and full, unlike their stubby relatives closer to town.

They remained several feet apart from each other as they walked to the house, with Ella in the center—a good defensive strategy when approaching a strange house at night.

Ella knocked hard, standing to one side of the door as she'd been trained to do. There was the sound of an inner door being opened, then a porch light came on. Ella could hear someone's slow, plodding steps inside.

"Tribal police, Miss Bidtah," Ella called out, identifying them. "Open up, please. We need to speak to you."

A moment later the door opened and a Navajo woman in her early thirties met them, wearing a dark green floor-length robe and thick blue socks. Her long black hair draped over her shoulders and hung down to her waist. As she stepped out onto the concrete slab of a porch, Ella saw the bruise that started at Lynn's neck and went downward toward her breast and disappeared beneath her robe.

"I'm Investigator Clah with the tribal police," Ella said, flashing her badge, "and this is Officer Goodluck and Special Agent Blalock."

Justine held out her gold shield and Blalock stepped up, towering over Justine, who was almost a foot shorter, and displayed his own badge. "FBI," he said.

"What do you all want from me? It's late and I have to be at work really early," she said, blinking against the glare of the porch light.

"We need to ask you some important questions," Blalock said, pushing the door open and stepping inside instead of waiting for an invitation.

"If this is about Valerie's murder, I don't know anything about it. When I left for the day, she was locking up. Then yesterday when I drove to the café, I saw the yellow crime scene tape and found out we were going to be closed for the day. That's all I know, except for what I hear on the radio."

"We still need to talk to you," Ella insisted, then pointed to the bruise. "That looks painful."

"Bruises always look worse after they quit hurting."

"How did it happen?"

She shrugged.

"Brewster? Did he do that to you?"

Lynn's eyes narrowed. "You've been talking to that little whore, Lea, haven't you?" she spat out. "She hates Stan, so she twists things around. You might as well know it right now. Lea's a liar."

"Then why don't *you* tell us about Stanley Brewster?" Ella said.

"Is that what you're after? You've all decided he had something to do with Valerie's murder?" She sat down and tucked her legs beneath her.

"We're just looking into all the possibilities. But if you think we shouldn't waste our time with him, convince us," Ella said.

"He's a good man, but his wife just doesn't understand him. He has certain . . . needs," she said, then in a more resolute tone, added, "It's good you came to me, 'cause I can set you straight."

Ella nodded, resisting the urge to groan in disgust.

"I *love* Stan, and I have from the first time we hooked up. He's a very virile man with a great fantasy life and very unique tastes in women. He likes games but he needs to be in control. The thing you have to remember is that he never forces a woman to do anything," she said firmly, then added, "On the other hand, he appreciates a woman who's willing to do what it takes to please him."

"Did pleasing him involve that bruise you've got?"

She waved a hand dismissively. "I bruise easily. Besides, we both like to play a little rough. It's consensual."

Ella noted that she'd glanced away, perhaps embarrassed or because she'd lied. "Does he normally leave bruises like that on his women?"

"I'm the only one who really understands him, which is why we're so free with each other. Stan and I can play rough, but Valerie wasn't into that. If what you're thinking is that they were playing games and it got out of hand, you're wrong. Valerie didn't go for stuff like that, and Stan does *not* force anyone."

"Are you so sure about that?" Ella pressed.

"Yeah, I am. You're really going off in the wrong direction. Stan and Valerie were never on the same wavelength, even before she went all holy on him. That's why he dumped her. Then we hooked up. He never talks about her now. She's old news."

"All right," Ella said. Lynn believed what she'd told them, Ella was sure of that. But it didn't necessarily mean it was the truth. If Stan cheated on his wife, he probably cheated on Lynn, too. "If he ever gets too rough with you, call me—if you're still conscious and able to pick up a phone," Ella said, handing her card to Lynn.

"Won't happen," Lynn said. But she still took the card.

Ella noticed how slowly Lynn rose from the couch, as if there were other injuries she wasn't talking about.

"You're playing with your life. Watch out for yourself around an animal like Brewster," Ella said.

Lynn showed them to the door. "Stan isn't a killer. We both get turned on when we play around like that."

"Hurting women for pleasure can slide into something more deadly," Blalock said. "In this case, it may already have happened, and you don't know it yet."

She shook her head. "He tells me how he wants things done, and disciplines me when I get it wrong. He likes ordering his woman around but it's just a game."

"And you're okay, knowing there've been others just like you in his life before?" Blalock asked.

"No one can please him like I can. And pretty soon he's going to leave his wife. He just has to figure out a way to get his share of their investments. She's the one who really owns the café, you know."

Once they were outside, Justine glanced at Ella then at Blalock. "I may throw up. How can that woman be so stupid?" she said, getting into the car. "The man's a cheat and a sadist. He may or may not be a murderer, but there's no way she enjoys getting slapped around like that."

"Some men and women get off on abuse," Blalock said quietly. "I've never understood that, mind you, but there are probably a million or so of them out there."

"Personally, the whole thing just makes me want to puke," Ella said flatly. "But they *are* consenting adults, so there's nothing we can do about it unless one of them lodges a complaint, or ends up in the hospital."

"Let's call it a night," Blalock said, swerving to avoid a big rock in the road.

"Yeah. I think we all need to turn in," Ella said. "First thing tomorrow, I'll get the names of all Navajo men who began long-term jail sentences right after that murder in L.A., particularly any cons who've been released and may be in our area. I'll concentrate on anyone with a connection to the Four Corners, then and/or now. Perhaps our killer was jailed for another crime, and is now finally free to drift back into old habits."

"I'll see what LAPD was able to dig up on the old murder, then search the databases for you and let you know what I turn up," Blalock said. "And tomorrow I'll see if I can drop by the hospital and question Marco Pete. If he's able to talk, that is."

Blalock returned them to the parking lot outside his office, where they changed vehicles and said their good-byes to the federal agent.

"Do you think our problems with the Fierce Ones are really over for now, like Jimmy Levaldo said?" Justine asked as she slipped behind the wheel and fastened her seat belt.

Ella shook her head slowly. "What they want most is power, and to get it, they need to make their mark. I think our problems with them are just beginning."

NINE

×   ×   ×

Ella woke up shortly after daybreak. She could hear one of her roommates in the kitchen already, and the other one was in the shower. As she got dressed, her thoughts drifted to Dawn and Rose. She dearly missed the morning mayhem at home. Brushing aside the now familiar ache inside her, she focused on the day ahead.

Ella walked into the kitchen moments later. "What's cooking?" she asked, sniffing the air.

"Well, I *was* making oatmeal for you guys, but when I went to add a dash of cinnamon, I opened the spoon side instead of the one with the sprinkle holes and dumped about a tablespoon into the stuff," Emily said. "Did you know too much cinnamon makes your lips pucker? Anyway, I decided to make breakfast burritos instead."

"Those burritos smell . . . interesting. Must be the spices you're using in the sausage," Ella said, noting the peculiar expression on Justine's face as she stepped into the kitchen and peered into the frying pan.

Emily worked quickly, then brought several large, steaming hot burritos to the table. Ella was the first to take a bite. The dry texture and odd taste made her reach for a glass of water. "I think the sausage went bad, Em. Or maybe the tortilla picked up some mold," she added, looking at the burrito critically.

"This tortilla has a green pattern to it," Justine said.

"That's because it's made out of organic blue corn and humus. The filling is poy, not sausage. Vegan."

"Poh?" Ella asked, confused. "Vegan what?"

"Poy. It's pork-flavored soy. All pure vegetarian. Very healthy."

Justine gave Ella a horrified look. "I gave up healthy last week. This stuff is disgusting—no offense."

"Guys, upgrade your diet. This is *good* for you," Emily said, taking a large mouthful, "and you can really keep off the weight."

"Probably because you can't eat it," Justine mumbled.

Ella tried valiantly to swallow another bite, and managed to get the sawdust-flavored mix down her throat with a swig of coffee. Finally she put the burrito back onto her plate. "Sorry, Em, I'm allergic to health food. My body doesn't know what to do without meat and cholesterol."

"It's okay. I guess it's an acquired taste. I made these for a friend once and he never came back."

Ella burst out laughing. "Okay, ladies, time to get to work." Just then her phone rang. Ella identified herself and heard Blalock's voice.

"I got a reply on the Los Angeles murder of that Navajo woman. According to the files, the investigating officers reached a dead end a week after you and Anderson were taken off the case, and their people couldn't come up with a suspect. So they were forced to drop it and move on."

Blalock continued. "Basically, we got zip, as far as any more info is concerned, so I was thinking we should pay Brewster a visit this morning—all of us. After what we found out last night, I'd really like a chance to put him in the hot seat."

"You're on. How about we meet at the Morning Stop Café in twenty? He should be there."

"See you then."

Ella filled Justine in on the bad news from LAPD, then told her of Blalock's plans. "Any idea where I can get some cutting-edge stuff on Brewster? The seedier, the better."

"My sister Jayne, naturally. She feeds on gossip, and she knows everyone. It'll just be rumor, mind you, but it'll probably be on target," Justine said, dialing as she spoke.

Ella and Justine arrived at the Morning Stop right on time, parking around the side of the building, closer to the apartment than the café. Business appeared to be good, considering the recent murder.

Ella had driven because Justine was still on the phone, and they were just stepping out of their vehicle when Blalock pulled in to their left, on the driver's side.

"I ran a background," he said, coming around to meet Ella at the tailgate of the SUV. "No charges for battery or spousal abuse. Nothing except one DWI. He's been married for thirty years to one Donna Largo, a Navajo woman from Waterflow, originally. Donna took over this café from her parents when they died in a car accident about ten years ago. Mrs. Brewster has no record whatsoever. That's all I've got."

Justine hung up as she walked around the vehicle and joined Ella and Blalock. "From what my sister Jayne said, Brewster's wife has no taste for kinky sex. She knows he messes around, but she's okay with it as long as he's discreet and leaves her alone. The thing is, he doesn't—leave her alone, I mean. Word is, he's a mean drunk, particularly with her."

"Cowardly bastard," Blalock said.

"We know who we're dealing with. Let's go," Ella said, her tone firm, her jaw set.

They went inside the small café. Every seat at the counter was filled as were the six booths lining the wall. The scent of well-cooked real breakfast fare made Ella's mouth water, and she looked at the diners stuffing their faces. Few looked up, but those who did watched for a second, realizing that the three newcomers were all armed law enforcement officers.

Brewster, wearing a white uniform shirt and jeans, had his side to them, talking to a customer at the register. "I'm telling you," he was saying, "I'm really shorthanded now. I can take care of the books, but unless I find a new cook and waitress, I'm going to go nuts." Glancing over at them, he smiled. "Unless you've come for takeout, it'll be a few moments before I can seat you. Sorry."

"We didn't come for breakfast, Mr. Brewster. Is there a place where we can speak in private?" Ella asked.

Half the patrons looked up from their plates, Ella noticed, and it suddenly got very quiet. Brewster smiled innocently around the room. "Sure. Give me a moment, officers." He turned and looked into the kitchen, just beyond the half-height café doors. "Lynn, can you cover the front for a few minutes?"

Lynn came over, glared at them, then gave Stan a big smile. "Sure thing, boss. We're caught up at the moment anyway." She came out and walked to the coffee brewer, picking up a carafe.

Brewster led them through the café doors, across the kitchen, and into a back room. As he closed the door behind them, Ella took in the small storeroom/office at a glance. This was where Valerie had worked, apparently. On the desk was a small photo of Boots, obviously taken at one of the tribal fairs, based on the display booths in the background. It was a recent picture, and the reminder made Ella's stomach clench.

"Sit down, please," Brewster invited. There was only one chair and a step stool, and nobody took the offer.

"Seems you withheld quite a few details when we spoke with you the other night," Ella said. "It's time to tell us everything about your relationship with Valerie Tso."

"I answered all of your questions," Brewster said, all friendliness gone from his voice. "I don't know what else there is to tell."

"Yeah, you do. Word is that you get off on slapping women around," Blalock challenged, stepping within punching distance of the man, who had two inches on FB-Eyes. "Valerie was a lot smaller and lighter than Lynn, wasn't she, and she just couldn't take punches like the big girls. You got carried away, hit her too hard, and she fell into the mirror. She was all cut up, bleeding everywhere, and maybe she even lost consciousness. You could have called for help, Stanley, but you froze up and let her die. Tell us the truth, man. It was an accident, right? And you tried to cover it up by making it look like a robbery gone south. Isn't that how it went down?"

Brewster looked at Blalock with complete disgust, clenching his fists for a second, then relaxing. "You're delusional. I didn't hit her, and I didn't kill her. How could I? I wasn't even here," he spat out. "I liked Valerie. She was a valued employee and we had a good working relationship—balanced, as they say around here."

"There's nothing balanced about your relationship with women," Ella said. "Or are you too warped to realize that any more?"

"I don't take advantage of anyone," he said flatly. "And I don't have sex with my employees. Just ask them."

"I'm going to be asking all the women you've been with, starting with your wife," Ella said, getting in his face.

Brewster snorted in disgust. "My wife already knows I'm into harmless little role-playing games with the ladies."

"More than a little, and certainly not harmless. Give me a reason why I shouldn't haul you into jail for the murder of Valerie Tso," Blalock demanded.

"Because you need evidence to make charges stick, that's why. And you won't find any against me, because I didn't kill her." He took a deep breath, then continued slowly. "Valerie did my books. I'll admit that there was more to our relationship when she first started working for me, but it didn't go on very long. She got hooked on church, religion, the whole nine yards, and I'm not out to corrupt anyone."

"You lost me," Ella said.

"I respect God-fearing women," he said simply.

Justine groaned, shaking her head. "A man of character."

Ella studied Brewster's face, wondering if he was joking. To her amazement, he seemed to be completely and utterly serious.

"Sure, I like to mess around," Brewster continued. "Big deal, most men like a little strange stuff now and then. I have my fun, and my ladies make some extra bucks when they keep me happy. It all works out. But there are some lines I won't cross," he added sharply. "If the woman doesn't want to, or if she's got religion, she's off-limits."

"How about giving us a DNA sample?" Ella asked.

"Let us rule you out, clear you of suspicion," Justine added.

"No way, officers. Evidence can be manipulated and planted anywhere. You're out of suspects and looking for a scapegoat to pin this on so you won't get jack from me without a warrant."

"You said you weren't here when she died, so where were you between six and ten two nights ago?" Ella asked.

"I was having a drink with a friend, and watching a game at the Double Play on their big-screen TV. After that, I went to my cabin up near Navajo Lake. That's where I was when one of your people called me."

"What's your friend's name?" Ella asked. "The one you were with at the bar."

"Jerry Montoya. He owns the Big Wheel Tire Company in Farmington. Now is there anything else? Lynn's going to need help fixing breakfast for our paying customers."

"I have another question. If you didn't kill Valerie, do you have any idea who did?" Blalock asked.

"No, but the moron obviously didn't plan it very well. Valerie goes to the bank every afternoon. Had the killer broken into her place around three P.M., he could have scored the day's receipts instead of whatever chump change he picked up from Valerie's purse. She *was* robbed, wasn't she?"

"Don't leave the area, Brewster. You'll be seeing us again,"

Blalock said. The three officers walked back through the kitchen, and Brewster followed at a distance, stopping behind the grill to take over for Lynn.

As Blalock and Ella headed for the door, Justine slowed down and went to talk to a woman sitting at one of the booths. A few minutes later, she joined Ella and Blalock outside by the cars. "I just spoke to Vera Aspass. Jayne had mentioned earlier that Vera was a friend of Donna Brewster. Vera said that Donna doesn't come around this place anymore, even though she's the real owner. According to Vera, Donna's got an arrangement with Stan. He operates the café and makes sure it stays in the black, and she keeps her distance from the operation. Lately, Donna's kept herself busy taking trips to visit her sisters, but she's home now. The Brewsters live just west of Farmington, north of the highway in one of those newer neighborhoods."

"Got an address?"

Justine handed Ella a slip of paper. "And Joe Neskahi telephoned as I left Vera's booth. He'd spoken to Andrew Pettigrew, one of Valerie's ex-husbands. This is the guy who lives near Gallup. Pettigrew says he was working on his car with his brother all afternoon and evening, and his brother corroborated his alibi. Joe's back in town now, helping Tache interview the people at the shoe game and, so far, they've got nothing. But they've still got names to run."

"Why don't you give them a hand and Blalock and I will go talk to Donna?" Ella turned to get Blalock's reaction. He nodded.

"My guess is that Brewster has already warned his wife to keep her mouth shut," Blalock said as he and Ella walked to his car. "She puts up with all the crap Brewster dishes out, so he's obviously got her under his thumb."

"Could be. Let's see how it plays out," Ella said. "While we're in Farmington, we can also track down Jerry Montoya and see what he has to say."

"Brewster used to go to church, so the verse from the Bible

isn't necessarily a stretch," Blalock said, thinking out loud. "And it could have gone down the way I handed it to him at the café. But if he's not a churchgoer these days, why come up with a quote from Scripture? It doesn't fit the guy he appears to be."

"I know," Ella answered as soon as they were underway. "And that verse at the crime scene also matches the one left by the killer in L.A. If it's a coincidence, it certainly is a big one. Do we know if Brewster was there at the time? That would help us narrow things down, maybe."

"Two big coincidences would be one too many. We need to find out," Blalock said.

Ella raised Justine on the radio. "It's important to find out where Brewster was living fourteen years ago when the first murder with this MO was committed. And if he was living on the Rez, can we find out where he might have traveled?"

"Like Los Angeles? I'll get back to you," Justine said.

"Let's stop by Montoya's place first. We'll be able to catch him there before he takes his lunch," Blalock said.

Ten minutes later, Blalock pulled into a parking space by the tire shop out on west Main Street. They walked inside and found Jerry Montoya behind the counter, processing a customer who'd come in to pick up his car. A name tag pinned to his uniform shirt also identified Jerry as Owner and Manager.

As soon as the customer left the office-showroom, keys and bill in hand, Blalock flashed his badge. "We need to ask you a few questions."

"Yeah, I just heard from Stan. He said you'd probably be stopping by today." Montoya, a chubby man in his early forties who looked almost inflated in his ill-fitting shirt, gestured for them to follow him into the adjacent office. "Stan said you'd be checking on his location the night that waitress of his was killed. I met him about four-thirty at the Double Play. There was a Boston–New York game going on, their first matchup of the season. The Double has a great flat-screen TV. It's like you're right behind home plate."

"Anyone else see you there?" Blalock asked.

"The place was crowded, but hey, the season has just started. Everyone was watching the game. We were toward the back, so I doubt anyone paid any particular attention to us. One of the waitresses, maybe."

"What did you do after the game?"

"It went into extra innings, so it was nearly nine by the time I got home. I'm not sure what Stan did. He was having some coffee before going out on the road. Lots of drunks that close to the . . ."

Ella knew he was about to say "reservation." Unfortunately, Montoya was right. She focused. "Did you ever hear Stan talk about Valerie Tso?"

"I know she was his bookkeeper, good-looking for a woman who'd been through a lot, I recall him saying. But that's all I remember. We get together to escape from work, not to talk about it."

A young couple entered the showroom and walked immediately over to a tire on display. "Be right with you, folks," Montoya said, then turned back to Ella and Blalock. "I'm a man short today, so let's wrap this up so I can tend to my customers."

Blalock handed Montoya a card. "If you think of anything that might be helpful, call me," he said.

"Well, there's one thing you should know," he said, lowering his voice. "I read about the murder in the paper, and for the record, there's no way Stan could have done something like that. The article said that the woman bled to death from her wounds, and Stan has a real phobia about blood. He'd probably rearrange my face if he knew I told you, but one time on a fishing trip I cut my thumb while gutting a fish. I bled like a stuck pig, and Stan nearly fainted. No joke. He's a tough, macho guy, but he can't even serve liver in the café because of all the blood around it. Truth."

Ella stared, trying to figure out if Jerry was on the level.

"Yeah, I know. Sounds like I'm selling you a bill of goods, doesn't it? But it's the truth."

"One more thing. Do you happen to know how long Brewster's lived in this area?" Ella asked.

"Practically all his life. I think he was born in Kirtland. That's where he met Donna, I believe. They both graduated from Central."

"Did he ever vacation in California, that you recall?" Ella asked.

Montoya thought about it. "He's never mentioned California, but I know he used to go to Vegas a lot before we got our own casinos here in the state."

As they returned to Blalock's car, Ella remained silent—and frustrated. Nothing seemed to be fitting together or really making much sense. "This case bugs me. The facts never add up quite right."

"We're just not seeing the whole picture. Let's go talk to Brewster's wife and see what we can get out of her," Blalock said.

They arrived at a large home just northwest of the city of Farmington, which had expanded in several directions and was now incorporating former rural areas. Several acres surrounded the Brewster home, and a large barn stood in the back. Ella could see six horses out in the paddock area.

"They're not exactly hurting for money," Blalock said.

"Hardly. You couldn't afford to feed that many horses if you were," Ella replied, knowing how difficult it was keeping just two horses in tack, shoes, hay, sweet feed, and mineral blocks—not to mention an occasional vet bill. Sometimes she found herself hoping that Dawn's interests would change and she'd discover a passion for basketball instead. Horses were an expensive and often dangerous proposition.

Blalock knocked on the tall, hand-carved door, and a few minutes later a small Navajo woman wearing designer jeans and a loose flannel shirt came to the door. Blalock showed her his ID and Ella did the same.

"Are you Donna Brewster?" Blalock asked. Seeing her nod, he added, "We need to ask you a few questions. May we come in?"

She nodded. "I was told you'd be stopping by."

Ella studied her delicately featured face. There were no bruises that she could see beneath the carefully applied makeup. Yet the woman held herself at an odd angle, as if favoring her right side. Maybe it was from a riding accident, but she was putting her money on Stan.

"Stan said you'd be by to ask me about our employee, the woman who was killed. But, believe me, Stan would know far more about that than I would. I never stop by the café anymore."

"We're more interested in what you know about their relationship, actually," Ella said, her gaze never leaving her face.

Donna expelled her breath slowly. "I know as little as possible. But I can tell you that he hasn't been involved with her recently. Stan moves on."

"Are you all right?" Ella asked, seeing her shift and wince.

"That big buckskin mare out there threw me yesterday. It happens. If you think Stan hurt me, you're wrong," she said firmly.

Ella and Blalock exchanged glances. "I know he's a violent man," Ella said softly.

"Not with me. My husband and I have an arrangement. He doesn't touch me, and I stay out of his way. He can run our business anyway he likes," she said, then added. "Everything has two sides. Isn't that what our people always say?"

"I know about Stan's women," Donna added, then shrugged. "If I wanted to restore the balance by taking a lover of my own, he'd probably understand. He knows its part of the Navajo way. It's just something I've chosen not to do. But there have been positive things about our marriage. I've never known financial hardships, not like many of our people. I have everything I'll ever need or want."

"You don't love him?" Blalock asked.

"That's an Anglo way of thinking and why half of all marriages fail. The wives all expect too much and don't know how to make what they have better."

It was a rehearsed speech, Ella suddenly realized. "It sounds to me like you're afraid of him. But you don't have to be, you know. There are laws that can protect you."

"Everyone makes compromises to get the things they want," Donna said, not meeting Ella's gaze. "My husband knows when to back off. That's why I'm sure he didn't kill Valerie Tso."

Ella suppressed a shudder. The whole situation was making her skin crawl. "Think back, if you will. Did you and your husband spend any time in California about fourteen years ago? Or maybe just Stan?"

Donna gave Ella a puzzled look. "California? No. Too many people, too many cars. Stan loves Nevada, though. The gambling, and the shows."

"One last thing. We need to know where you were three days ago—between six to ten o'clock at night," Blalock said.

"Out of town. I was at the hospital in Albuquerque with my aunt. The nurse and the doctors on duty can verify that for you if you want. I talked to them about getting long-term care for her."

After saying good-bye, Ella hurried to the car, anxious to put as much distance between her and Donna as possible. The woman's attitude and the situation made her sick to her stomach. "I will *never* understand women like her," Ella muttered as they got underway. "They just take it."

"She's like a zombie," Blalock said. "Who knows what kind of hold he really has over her? In a situation like that, all kinds of things can come into play."

"She *could* just walk away. The café is in her name," Ella said.

"Donna may not know beans about running a business."

"She could learn," Ella shot back. "Or hire somebody."

"That's *you*, Clah. The woman is obviously very passive, and has a comfortable life. Brewster has his women, and she's learned to stay away from him as much as she can and not make waves. She made her deal with that devil a long time ago."

"Someday she'll explode and fight back."

"Or not," Blalock said calmly.

They drove west back to Shiprock and Ella had Blalock drop her off at the station. A minute later Ella found Justine at the crime lab, working.

"I need a copy of the Bible quote we found at the scene," Ella said. "I'm going to see Ford and find out if it has any special relevance or interpretation. You got any thoughts on this?"

"I've had it on my mind, actually." Justine read the quote aloud, slowly and thoughtfully. " 'The Lord has made all things for himself; yea, even the wicked for the day of evil.' " She paused for several long moments. "To me, it sounds like we've got a killer with an agenda, partner," Justine added. "He believes he's serving the Lord."

"That's what's worrying me. I think the dying's just begun."

TEN
✖ ✖ ✖

Ella sat across from Ford in his office as he studied the Bible passage. "In our ministry, we usually focus on the teachings in the New Testament, Ella. This is from Proverbs."

"I understand but can you tell me if this particular verse has a special meaning to Christians, beyond the obvious?"

"There are almost as many interpretations of the Bible as there are religions but, to me, it's simply a way of saying that God made all and He will mete out justice in the end." He paused to think about it a moment longer, then continued. "Or maybe, getting inside the killer's head for a moment, he's thinking that even the wicked have a part in God's plan and he's God's instrument of justice." He looked up at her and added, "If that's the case, you've got a huge problem on your hands."

She nodded slowly. "Do you know if any of the other churches in the area like to focus their sermons on Proverbs?"

"So much of that depends on the minister and the community, Ella. Your father's church, for example, is very conservative—old-school Bible Belt—scaring Navajos with retribution and damnation—hoping to save their souls that way. We, on the other hand, look to God as our loving parent, our salvation, too, but we offer hope of heaven, instead of fear of hell."

"That different, huh?"

"Oh, yeah." He gave her a long look. "So tell me, are you any closer to finding the killer?"

"It's my job. I'll find him," she said, not answering him directly.

"This crime practically landed on your back door. That must make it even tougher for you," he said gently.

She nodded. "But, to be honest, I'm always in crisis mode when I'm working. Crime on the Rez is a fact of life, but it needs to be brought under control. All things are interconnected, and everything affects something else. Evil, under control, ceases to be a threat and that's why law enforcement is so important to the big picture. That's really what my job's all about."

"Do you think you're becoming a New Traditionalist?" Ford asked. "Accepting the new world but wrapping it as much as possible in the old values and traditions?"

"No, not strictly speaking. I'll never walk a simple road, or one that neatly fits any label. But I've made my peace with that. The contradictions are all a part of who I am."

"We have two very different jobs, Ella, but what we try to accomplish is remarkably similar. You find order and grounding through law enforcement. I find it through my faith and my love for God. I'd be just as lost without my work as you'd be without yours."

"Order . . . and faith. Do you think there's really common ground there?" Ella asked.

"Yes, I do. Faith brings order . . . and a need for order is one of the many paths leading to faith."

"I may not agree completely with you, Reverend, but I still like the way you think," Ella answered, enjoying his gentle smile.

Ella drove west down the hill and across the mesa to Blalock's office. The agent was on the phone as she walked in. He waved her to a seat and, a moment later, hung up. "I've got some interesting news for you, Ella. The quote left at our crime scene not only matches the one found in L.A. fourteen years ago, it's also identical to one left at a crime scene in Kayenta, Arizona. That murder took place only a year ago."

"Three murders, one unique verse of Scripture. That's no coincidence. Is there any thread that connects all three victims?" Ella asked quickly, hoping they hadn't been randomly selected.

"They were all Navajo," Blalock said.

"Were they all Christian churchgoers?" Ella asked, playing a hunch. "And did they all live around here at one time?"

"It doesn't say," Blalock said.

"Then that's the next thing we follow up on," she said. "Maybe all three were members of one of the churches here," she said, thinking of Valerie. "The church where Ford works was established less than ten years ago, so I don't think his membership roster will be of any immediate help. His congregation probably consists of new converts and people who used to attend elsewhere. But my father's church has been around for thirty or more years. And there are others as well," she added.

"We need to start checking those places out."

"It'll probably be easier to take a different route first. The churches will probably not want to give us access to their membership lists. And, even if they did, they probably have regulars who've never become official members. I suggest we start by digging into the victims backgrounds and find out if they had a church in common. After that, we'll have a better idea how to proceed."

"Sounds good, but how do we do that?"

"We start with Jayne, Justine's sister. The woman has a phenomenal memory, and knows just about everyone in the Shiprock area. Are you game?"

"Sure. Let's go."

"Brewster has to remain at the top of our list," Ella said as they went out to the parking lot. "But he doesn't attend church anymore and doesn't really fit the MO of a serial killer inclined to leave Bible passages behind. We've also yet to place him in two different states at the right times, or find a link between him and the other victims."

"The case is young yet," Blalock muttered.

They left in Ella's borrowed, marked car, knowing that it would give them an edge when they approached people on the Rez. Blalock's Bureau car was well known and Navajos tended to avoid him.

Ella tracked down Jayne via Justine and, shortly afterward, met with her partner's older sister at her workplace, the new motel just inside the Rez borders. Jayne, vivacious and charming as always, was working the front desk. Seeing Ella, she waved and called out from behind the counter.

"I need to talk to you," Ella said, going over to meet her. "Can you leave the front desk for a minute?"

"Sure. I've been expecting you. 'Tine called a little while ago." Jayne checked her watch. "It's close to lunch. Are you guys hungry?"

Ella glanced at Blalock, who nodded. "Yeah, but we really don't have time for a sit-down lunch right now." She looked toward the motel's restaurant dining room just beyond a wide, open doorway. The tables were about half occupied at the moment with tourists, judging from the fact that the majority appeared to be Anglos with cameras.

"Not a problem. I like to eat with the kitchen staff anyway, so let's go find the chef. His specialty is Navajo tacos, and he can put yours in Styrofoam takeout containers."

The thought of Navajo tacos was too much of a temptation on an empty stomach. Ella glanced at Blalock, who was almost pleading with his eyes. "You've got a deal."

Jayne led them though an employees-only door and seated them on folding metal chairs at a stainless-steel table in the kitchen. Beside them was a tall Rube Goldberg–type mixer that looked more like a post hole digger in a bowl. Within five minutes Jayne returned with three big Styrofoam containers and three sets of silverware wrapped in cloth napkins.

Inside each was a dinner plate–size piece of fry bread topped with a layer of pinto beans, lettuce, cheese, tomatoes, and salsa. "This looks great," Ella said taking a bite. "My fry bread always comes out looking like fried matzo. Just can't seem to get it to swell up like this."

Blalock nodded, his mouth full. "Clah, you gotta roll out the dough real thin, then make sure the oil is good and hot."

"You cook, Dwayne?" Ella said, moving a loaded fork to her lips."

"Live alone, love to eat. What can I say? But this food is way better than anything I can whip up," Blalock added.

The three ate for a few minutes, then Ella took the page containing the names of the three victims out of her pocket and slid it across the small table so Jayne could read it. "Sorry to get back to business, but do you happen to know any of these people?"

Jayne studied it for a moment as she ate. "Valerie, naturally. And I remember Dorothy Yabeny. Wait, are these other two women dead, too?"

Ella nodded. "Sorry."

"Yeah, well, I'm no traditionalist, so as long as none of the staff hear us, I don't mind. About Dorothy. She's . . . would have been about your age, Ella, give or take a year, but she went to Mission, not Shiprock High, because her mother wanted her to have a Christian education. They lived about halfway to Hogback. I lost a boyfriend to her the summer of our junior year. Wanted to scratch her eyes out for a few weeks, but we made up. Then Dorothy moved to Kayenta a few years out of high school and I never heard from her after that. Phyllis Begay was three years older than me, but we hung out sometimes and were friends until she moved to L.A. She wanted to be an actress. We exchanged a few letters at first because she was homesick, but then we lost track of each other. That was fourteen or fifteen years ago, at least."

"Did she go to one of the local churches?" Ella asked.

"She went to church, but it was mostly for the social part of it. That way she could go out on Sundays and Wednesday nights even when she was grounded. She met a lot of boys that way, too, when churches from different towns had special youth rallies and retreats. Phyllis and I did some wild things together, I remember." Jayne laughed. "Her mother was different though, really devout. She's buried in the church's cemetery. I remember going to her house. There were so many crucifixes in there it was spooky," she said and shuddered.

Ella understood. Even modernists weren't immune to the teachings they'd lived with all their lives. Navajo beliefs held that death was a subject best avoided. To have something inside a home that depicted a death, showed the body, and commemorated someone who'd risen from the dead seemed just plain dangerous.

"Do you remember which church they belonged to?"

Jayne looked at her in surprise. "Your father's, of course, the Divine Word. I guess you don't remember because you stopped going when you were young, but your dad was really popular back then—for a preacher. If you were Navajo and wanted to convert, or you were unhappy with your own church, that's where you ended up. Your father was a force to be reckoned with," Jayne said, then added, "That should tell you how strong a woman your mom is, because she never converted. She remained a traditionalist."

"She's a force all on her own," Ella agreed. The news that the victims had all been associated with her father's church wasn't unexpected because it had been *the* Protestant church in the community for many years. But it wasn't welcome news. Ella had too many memories of the Divine Word, and only a few of them were pleasant. It had been years since she'd stepped foot in that church.

Finishing lunch quickly, Blalock and Ella said good-bye to Jayne and went back outside. "I saw your reaction when she mentioned your father's church, Clah. You want me to handle that part on my own?"

"No, but it's only fair to give you a heads-up. I'm not sure how we'll be greeted there. There's another Navajo minister there now, Reverend Leroy Curtis, and I heard he doesn't appreciate my family's adherence to traditional Navajo beliefs."

"If Curtis drags his feet, we can always threaten to subpoena their records," Blalock said.

"That may not get us the results we want. And, if word gets out we pressured a minister, you can count on a backlash that'll go all the way back to the Bureau. Let's play nice, at least at first. Maybe we'll get lucky and he'll let us have a look at the old records."

They drove west down the main highway, over the river, then northeast. Her father's old church stood about halfway between the river and the highway, atop a weathered mesa. She'd always hated the view from there, but not nearly as much as the constant pressure she'd been under during her teens to attend services.

For her, that place would always echo with memories of being torn between her mother's and her father's beliefs, the people she'd loved most, and of feeling like she'd never belong anywhere. Of course the end result had been that she'd rejected everything, married as soon as she got out of high school, then moved away.

Ella set all those memories aside and concentrated on what they were here to do. As she pulled up in front of the main church building, partially remodeled into a stylized hogan, a distinguished-looking Navajo man in his late thirties and wearing a white shirt and tie came out.

"Is that Reverend Curtis? And how the heck did he know to expect us?" Blalock asked Ella. "Did he get a sign?"

Ella groaned. Obviously, Blalock was trying to lighten up the moment just a little. "From his office he can see us coming up the road. Maybe he's just affording us the courtesy of coming out to meet us—Navajo style."

Ella got out first and approached the reverend. He knew who she was. They'd met years ago during some public event.

Blalock, a few steps behind, introduced himself and displayed his ID. The Navajo cleric didn't offer to shake hands with him and, Blalock, used to tribal ways, hadn't expected it.

"I'm Reverend Leroy Curtis," he said for Blalock's benefit. "Would you two like to come inside? We can sit down in my office and talk comfortably there."

Ella stiffened. The last place she wanted to see again was her father's old office, no matter who was sitting behind the desk.

Blalock accepted before she had a chance to reply, and Ella followed them in, aware of how little had actually changed on the inside over the years. The walls were still stark white and simple wooden crucifixes hung over each doorway. She suppressed a shudder as Reverend Curtis stopped at the familiar door, with the old, hand-carved wooden sign—PASTOR—and waved them in.

"I believe this was your father's office at one time, Inspector Clah," he said casually.

Ella nodded, trying to push back the uneasiness that gripped her and grateful that at least the furniture and personal mementos on the walls were different.

"So tell me, what can I do for you two officers?" he asked, taking a seat behind the desk.

"We'd like to ask you a few questions," Ella said, her voice steadier than she felt in these still familiar surroundings. Handing him the list of the three murder victims, she added, "Were any of these women members of this church, going back maybe fourteen or fifteen years?"

He glanced at it, then shrugged. "I'm afraid I couldn't tell you. These names don't sound particularly familiar, and our computer records don't go that far back, so it's not just a matter of taking a quick look. I'd have to sort through records stored in the basement and, to be perfectly honest, I wouldn't even know where to begin searching. I've only been here seven years myself."

"We'd be happy to help, or conduct the search for you," Ella said.

"I can't give you access to our records, not without the board's permission. *You* should know that," he replied coldly.

"Then we'd like you to approach them as quickly as possible," Ella said. "We wouldn't be asking unless it was important, Reverend Curtis, believe me. Lives could be at stake."

He nodded slowly. "We wouldn't want that on our consciences. So, all right. The fact that you have personal ties to this church might make things move along a little easier. Your father was very well thought of by everyone here, and his photograph still hangs beside the entrance to the chapel."

"If the church is worried about respecting the privacy of the individuals on that list, rest assured there's no need for concern," Blalock said. "The women in question are deceased."

Ella had to force herself not to wince as she saw Reverend Curtis's expression darken. Blalock, trying to be accommodating, had given out too much information.

"It sounds to me like you're trying to involve our church in a scandal. *That* is unacceptable." Reverend Curtis glared at Ella. "Miss Clah, you never fail to surprise me. You dishonor your father's memory by not joining our congregation, then, adding insult to injury, you form a close relationship with that liberal church up on the hill. Their latest membership drive is focused on poaching away our congregation with a promise of instant salvation and their 'believe what you want' doctrine. Trying to lead God's children astray is Satan's work. Your father always warned his flock of the dangers of failing to follow the literal translation of the Lord's Holy Bible."

He sounded so much like her father that Ella felt like getting up and walking out right then. "We're investigating a crime that has ties to the reservation, Reverend—to the people you claim to care about. If you're a true shepherd of the *Diné* then please take the action needed to protect your flock from a very real, physical danger."

He said nothing for several long moments, his gaze resting on the crucifix across the room. Finally, he looked back at her. "You believe that these two other women are connected somehow to Valerie Tso . . . that maybe all three women went to church here . . . and perhaps the killer as well?"

"I can't verify or deny that, Reverend," Ella said. "I've already told you more than I should have in hopes of getting your cooperation."

Reverend Curtis stood and gazed out the window. "You've placed me in a very difficult position," he said slowly. "Sacrificing privacy in exchange for safety and protection is a mixed blessing, especially if it turns out to be a false alarm."

"Maybe if we spoke to the board president ourselves . . ." Ella suggested.

"No, it should come from me," he said flatly. "It's my responsibility. Give me the rest of the afternoon to track down and speak to the people who need to approve of this."

"Time is of the essence, Reverend," she said quietly. Reverend Curtis led them out, and moments later they were headed down the church road toward the highway. Ella hadn't said a word since they'd left the church.

"Yeah, Clah, I know. Interviewing skills 101. Never show your hand or volunteer information. I blew it back there."

"Just a little," she said with a trace of a smile. They'd just reached the stop sign at the end of the drive when Justine called on the cell phone.

"I've got something for you, Ella," she said. "It seems Brewster hired a new waitress, Barbara Tom. She barely made it through her first shift before walking out and going straight to the legal center to file sexual harassment charges. But there's more. The Fierce Ones know all about this."

"How, so soon?" Ella asked quickly.

"They were in on it from the beginning. Lea Garner's mom arranged the whole thing. When she found out about Lea and Brewster, she had a meltdown. The Garners aren't traditionalists, but they know about the Fierce Ones and were able to get their advice. So Mrs. Garner ended up getting together with Barbara Tom's mom and they set Brewster up. They actually have him on tape now."

Ella cursed, guessing what the Fierce Ones's next move would be. "Okay, I'm going to try and nip this in the bud before we have a disaster," she said. "Brewster will undoubtedly be getting a visit from the vigilantes real soon. Subtlety isn't their style. But there's something else I need you to do right now. Make a list of all the known felons who might have been in the community at the time my father was preaching here and who subsequently went to prison. Concentrate on those with a propensity for violence."

"I'm on it."

Ella hung up, glanced at Blalock, and gave him the short version. "We're going to have to protect that scumbag at least long enough for us to either arrest him for murder or clear him. What do you say we go pay Jimmy Levaldo a visit."

"The only way you're going to muzzle that group is to give Levaldo some serious reasonable doubt. We'll need to convince him that there are other strong suspects—without giving him names," he said. "That's the only way we'll get them to hold off."

"Yeah, but let's make sure they also know that we'll throw their butts in jail if they interfere," Ella said.

Less than thirty seconds later, Ella's cell phone rang again. It was Justine.

"I have an update, Ella. Several of the Fierce Ones have shown up at Jimmy's place. Michael Cloud patrols that area, and he got a tip. When he went to check it out, Michael heard loud, angry voices coming from the ceremonial hogan in the back of Levaldo's property."

"How many people are there?" Ella asked.

"Michael can't say for sure, but he counted six pickups. Big Ed already knows about the Barbara Tom incident and told me to give you whatever support you needed."

"Have Michael keep his distance until we join him. If there are any other officers who can reach the location within a half hour, have them meet us there," Ella said, then hung up.

Before she could update Blalock, she heard her radio call

sign and picked up the mike. Dispatch instructed Ella to switch to the tactical frequency Big Ed was using.

"I'm in on this one," the police chief said. "Don't make a move until I arrive. I know this group."

"Big Ed Atcitty wants to be involved?" Blalock asked as the transmission ended. "I don't remember the last time he went out into the field."

"With luck his presence will keep things from getting out of hand. I believe that Jimmy belongs to Clare Atcitty's clan. That connection, via Big Ed's wife, means a great deal to traditionalists like the Fierce Ones."

Ella and Blalock raced to the site, each lost in their own thoughts. The last time there'd been a confrontation between law enforcement and members of the vigilante group, weapons had been plentiful on both sides. Experience told her that it would only take one misstep by a hothead for things to escalate into violence and bloodshed.

In the grip of that certainty, Ella listened for the whispers of Wind, but this time Wind was keeping its secrets.

ELEVEN

✖ ✖ ✖

Ella stood with Big Ed at the base of the low hill that hid Jimmy Levaldo's home. The residence, a quarter mile away, was northeast of Shiprock among rolling hills and junipers, which afforded plenty of cover for the officers, but also for anyone outside and around the gray stucco house.

Her boss had studied the scene through his binoculars, and had now returned to discuss the situation with the other officers standing by.

"Someone obviously called for an emergency meeting. Most of these guys have full-time jobs, so they usually get together on weekends or late at night. Billy Eltsosie works alone at the gas station, so the fact he's here should be a reminder of how much punch the Fierce Ones carry with the small business owners in this area."

Big Ed looked at Blalock and the handful of tribal officers who'd been close enough to take the call, but said nothing else.

Ella remained silent, knowing Big Ed would often lapse into long silences as he gathered his thoughts.

"Investigator Clah and I will approach first," he said at last. "Everyone else stay out of sight, but be ready to move in instantly if necessary. Agent Blalock will make that call," he said, looking at the FBI agent, who nodded.

"I suggest that Justine move in close and keep us under surveillance," Ella said. "She can report to Blalock."

"Absolutely," Big Ed said. "You and I will drive over to the hogan in my vehicle. It runs quiet and is unmarked. I don't want to give them any advance notice. If we catch them cold they won't have time to prepare a response."

"Good idea," Ella said, then turned to work out last-minute logistics with the other officers, while Justine slipped away on foot to scout ahead. Once Justine was well on her way, Ella joined the chief, who was waiting beside his vehicle. "Ready when you are," she said.

"Climb in. You have your Taser?" Big Ed asked.

Ella nodded. "It's covered by my Windbreaker, but it's on my belt."

"Good." Big Ed was wearing a leather jacket that accentuated his bulk and effectively hid his sidearm and Taser. He drove, and because the road wasn't visible until it passed over a hill, they weren't spotted until they were a hundred yards from the hogan.

Two men were outside, standing guard. When Big Ed stepped out of the car, the men keeping watch quickly conferred and one ran inside. Jimmy appeared less than ten seconds later.

Big Ed chose to remain where he was and extend Jimmy the courtesy of not approaching the hogan uninvited. Her boss had been determined to keep it low-key, and Ella had followed his lead, getting out of the car, but remaining by the door.

Jimmy approached Big Ed. *"Yáat'ééh,"* he greeted.

Big Ed responded in kind. "Nephew, we need to talk."

The term, Ella knew, didn't imply kinship, it was a customary way for an older man to speak to a younger one. It also reminded Jimmy that Big Ed merited his respect.

"We can talk freely here. We're Navajo brothers."

"What separates us is the law," Big Ed said in a firm voice.

"You're speaking of Anglo laws, not ours. We've always looked after our own."

Big Ed said nothing for a long time. "You want the tribe to walk in beauty," he said at last. "That's our common ground. But if you take justice into your own hands, and work around the laws that the tribal council has asked us to uphold, costly mistakes will continue to be made."

Ella saw Jimmy wince, though he covered it almost instantly. "You don't share your information with us so what can be done? We can't depend on the white man's courts. You know as well as I do that justice all too often slips right through their fingers."

"With information comes responsibility. I can't allow my officers to share information with those who refuse to accept responsibility for *their* own mistakes. Is justice served when you go after the wrong person? What of the damage *that* does, not only to the person, but to their family and their clans?"

Jimmy stared off into the distance, his expression thoughtful. "We have a very bad Anglo among us, but you and your people have done nothing to stop him."

"That's not true. We *are* handling the matter."

"You *say* that but nothing gets done."

At that moment Lena Clani stepped out of the hogan. "Everyone talks about justice, but my daughter is dead and no one has been arrested for her murder." Anger made her words resonate, giving them a peculiar power over the ones there.

"Finding the person who killed your daughter requires gathering evidence and that takes time," Big Ed said.

He glanced at Jimmy and continued. "Our men, when they go off to war, understand that battles aren't won overnight. Corn takes time to grow, rugs to weave, prayers to sing."

Big Ed looked straight at Lena and spoke softly but clearly as he continued. "Yet you would have us rush right out and arrest the first likely suspect mostly because you want to believe he's guilty. Without real justice, you can't walk in beauty."

"Talk, talk, and more talk," Lena said, her entire body was shaking with rage and pain. "That's all that ever happens around here. Your time is up. Now it's our turn to find this justice you say is so important."

Joe Jackson, who was barely twenty, came out of the hogan and stood beside the seventy-year-old woman. "She's right. Every day we lose more control over what happens on our land," he said. "We have our own way of finding the truth. Our land—our justice."

Robert Todacheene come out of the hogan next, a Winchester carbine in his hands.

"Don't let this get ugly," Ella said, turning to Lena for help.

"Sniper! In the trees!" Todacheene shouted, swinging the barrel of his carbine toward Ella.

"Shorty!" Big Ed warned.

"No!" Lena shouted, too late.

Ella dove to the side, reaching for her own weapon and Justine fired from somewhere behind them. Robert flinched, dropping the rifle, and fell to his knees, grabbing his left side.

Jackson tried to grab Ella's gun, still in its holster, but the catch was fastened and all he got was her sharp backhand across his face. Before she could take a breath, somebody else came running out of the hogan. He took a swing at her, and she caught a glancing blow to her cheek as she tried to slip the punch. As she stepped to one side, Jimmy flew by her, head first, and crashed into whoever had punched her. The two men tumbled to the ground in a thrashing heap.

She was just getting her bearings when Big Ed grabbed Ella's wrist and hauled her to her feet. He had a grim smile on his face that told her he'd been the one to throw Jimmy.

"Back to back, Shorty," he yelled. Ella got the message, standing so that they literally covered each other's backs.

Lena had disappeared, along with Robert, but several more men had emerged from the hogan and were circling, along with Jimmy and Joe, searching for an opening. Ella glanced down and noted gratefully that the rifle on the ground was within kicking distance. Anyone making a grab for it would catch a boot in the chin.

They were outnumbered, but their assailants' confidence had been shaken. No one was eager to try and tackle Big Ed and they knew Ella still had her pistol. She didn't have to draw her weapon—one man had already been shot. They just needed to hold their own for another minute or so. As the wail of sirens rose in the air, some of the men took off running for their trucks. Others, realizing that they'd never make it, just ran for the tree line.

"Down on the ground!" Justine yelled from somewhere behind the hogan. She looked around the side. "You both okay?"

"Yes," Ella called back. It was over. As she moved in to help round up their assailants, she saw that Jimmy and three of the older members of the Fierce Ones were already in handcuffs or tough plastic restraints.

Jimmy glared at her and Big Ed as Blalock brought him over, none too gently. "This isn't over," Jimmy said. "You won't be able to hold us for long. We were having a meeting—a lawful assembly, I think the lawyers call it. There was a shot, and Robert thought we were under attack from a sniper. You had all those guns and we only had one. There are going to be many sides to this story before it's all said and done."

Ella knew his argument had more than an even chance of standing up in court. The Fierce Ones, except for maybe Jimmy, would probably just spend the night in jail and be released in the morning.

Ella nodded to Blalock, then took Jimmy aside. "You were here, and you saw who's not thinking clearly. We didn't lose our cool, it was your people, overreacting to our backup. And that poor woman is so grief stricken she can't tell right from wrong anymore. But we can't continue to fight each other. If we do, we'll all lose."

"You're right about that," he muttered, glancing around to make sure she was the only one who'd heard him. "But the

Fierce Ones won't forget who was in the crosshairs today, and how this all started. Your tactics may come back to haunt you. After today it's going to be even harder to keep things under control."

"I won't apologize when my officers have their lives threatened. But we didn't come here to create problems, we came here to address our mutual concerns. With that in mind, what can we do to help?" Big Ed asked, coming over to join them.

"First of all, you'll need to control your officers. We have our share of hotheads, too, men who need to be kept on a short leash. If we're going to maintain order, and focus on the problem, I need the chance to track down and talk to the right people. But I have to act fast and with me in jail . . ." He shrugged.

Big Ed glanced at Ella. "Release him," he said.

He was right. There were times when someone had to make a controversial call, and in this case, bending the rules was worth the risk. Ella looked down and saw that Jimmy had those single-use nylon restraints. She brought out her pocketknife and freed his wrists.

"Go do what you said, and remember today, nephew," Big Ed said.

Jimmy nodded once, then quickly went into the main house.

Lena drew back the blanket covering the entrance to the hogan, tied it out of the way with a leather thong, then walked over. Ella could see Robert Todacheene inside the hogan being tended by Michael Cloud and another officer. From the blood still drying on her hands, it was obvious that Lena had been tending the wounded man.

"Some people will do anything to avoid trouble," Lena said, obviously having overheard part of their conversation with Jimmy. "But who'll speak for my daughter?"

"Give us a chance to find out who did this to her, to prove it without a shadow of a doubt," Ella said gently, pushing back her anger. "That's the only way to restore order."

Lena stared at her, tears in her eyes. "I didn't mean for any-one to get hurt today, but I will *not* rest until my daughter's killer is caught."

"As a mother, I understand. I'd do the same thing," Ella said quietly, walking Lena to her pickup. "You've been through a lot here today. Would you like me to find someone to drive you home?"

"No. I'm not helpless," she said, her voice stronger now.

As Ella looked at Lena, she realized that there was more than one meaning woven into her words. "You're my mother's friend, and I sympathize deeply with your loss," Ella said. "But please don't make me choose between my sworn duty and my love for you and your family."

Lena regarded her for several seconds. "Will you give me your word that you'll get justice for my daughter?"

"I won't give up until we catch her killer," Ella said mea-suring her words carefully.

"That's not a yes, and that's why you and I will continue to have a problem."

As Lena drove away, Big Ed joined Ella. "I can't blame that woman for being upset," Big Ed said, "but she's gone over-board. You'll have to watch her. She's not through stirring things up yet."

"I know."

Justine came up to Ella as the other officers started to drive away. "Sorry I gave myself away. The guy must have seen a flash from my scope."

"I'm not blaming you, Justine. We needed your backup, it turned out."

"You paid the price, though. You're going to be black-and-blue all over tomorrow," she said.

Ella looked down at herself. She had tiny drops of blood splattered on her shirt. At least they weren't hers. "I'll ride with you back to the station. I'd like to wash up and change clothes. After that, we can decide what to do next."

"You sure you're okay?" Justine asked.

"Yeah, and thanks for watching my back. I don't know if he'd have shot me, but he had me cold when you took him down."

"You've covered my back more times than I can remember. And the good news is Robert will be healthy enough to face charges. My bullet was deflected by the receiver on the rifle and missed his lungs. It nicked him in the ribs."

"Good work, partner," Ella said. "Now let's get out of here."

They reached the station in Shiprock twenty-five minutes later, and Ella went directly to her office. Justine stopped by the lab first, then joined Ella. "I've got the list of felons you asked for. Good news, it's short," she said, holding out the one name she'd scribbled on a sheet for Ella to see.

"Wilbert Bruce is a bad seed," Ella said, reading it. "It was before my time on the force, but I remember hearing that he killed a clerk at a convenience store for ten bucks and change. So he's out now?"

"Yeah and he's clean. I understand that he credits your father for that, too. Your dad went to visit him in prison often and counseled him. That's what I heard anyway."

"I suppose you've got an address?" Ella asked.

"Yep. Ready to go?"

They were underway minutes later, Justine at the wheel. "Tell me more about Wilbert Bruce," Ella said. "What's he do for a living these days?"

"Your father opened some doors for him and he apprenticed with a Mexican craftsman in Waterflow after he was released. These days, Wilbert's a skilled saddle maker in his own right and very much in demand. He has a huge waiting list."

"Saddles are expensive. I'm surprised he's that successful. Around here people mostly buy secondhand saddles through one of the feed stores or have ones that have been passed down through the family."

"He cut a deal with some shops in Albuquerque and Santa

Fe and I understand most of his high-end business comes from there. Especially Santa Fe, I'd imagine."

"Any arrests since he served time?"

"Not a one, not even a moving violation. Wilbert's as clean as a whistle. Your father must have been a tremendous influence on him."

Ella remembered her dad as a multifaceted man. People who spoke of him tended to do so in absolutes—all good or all bad. Her father never did things halfway and people tended to see him in that same light. Yet, to her, he'd just been Dad—human, and a man who'd tried to be too many things to too many people. She couldn't help but wonder if Dawn would remember her in the same light someday.

When they arrived at Wilbert's residence, a simple stucco building with a pitched metal roof and a small shop attached to the side, the first thing Ella noted was how well maintained everything was. Except for a few native plants in the front of the house there was no landscaping to speak of, yet there were no tumbleweeds or trash or old cars anywhere. Even the small sign above the shop door that read WB SADDLES AND TACK was freshly painted.

"He's a neat freak, like you," Justine said with a grin.

Before Ella could answer, a short, portly Navajo man with long, graying hair tied in a ponytail appeared in the doorway of the shop. "Can I help you ladies?" he asked, then as his gaze fell on Ella, he added, "I recognize you."

Ella held out her badge. "Are you Wilbert Bruce?" she asked.

Wilbert nodded. "Do you need a saddle for your daughter? I'll make you a real good deal, and I'll move you to the top of the list. A courtesy, in memory of your father."

"Thanks, but not at this time. I'm here on police business."

"Then you've wasted a trip. I'm clean now, thanks to your father," he said firmly.

Ella studied his expression. He had The Look. She'd seen it on many of her father's followers. It was that unqualified devon to a God she neither understood nor trusted. If He was all-powerful, then why was there so much misery in the world? Her father had had a dozen answers, but none satisfied her.

"Is this about the death of the fallen woman? She found Our Lord and she's in Paradise now and at peace."

Ella stared at him. For a moment she could practically hear her father speaking those very same words. "Tell me what you know about Valerie Tso."

Wilbert led them into his workshop, a small, well-lit room with the rich smell of leather, oils, and saddle soap. "I'll work as we talk." Sitting on a wooden stool beside a big bench, he picked up a mallet and metal embossing tool and began creating a design along the surface of a leather bridle. Seeing two more stools on the other side of the bench, Ella and Justine took a seat.

"That poor woman was just like me in a lot of ways. A lost soul. When she hit bottom she reached out to the Lord, as I did, and that's what saved her. Her body may be dead, but her spirit lives."

Ella studied the fervor in his face. How well acquainted she was with such enthusiasm. "Was she really that devout? That wasn't the impression I got."

"Valerie was going in the right direction. Sometimes, particularly at first, all you can take are baby steps."

"What else do you know about her, Mr. Bruce? Were you two friends?"

"Just acquaintances. We talked sometimes after Sunday church or our Wednesday night service."

"Do you know if Valerie was afraid of anyone?" Ella pressed. "Maybe an old enemy . . . or a new one."

He continued his careful work for a while, then finally answered. "Valerie was no stranger to fear. That's usually what forces a person to change—fear that you'll self-destruct, fear that you'll never know what being happy is, fear of death and what might await you there." He paused for a while, surveying his work, then added, "But if there was someone specifically she was frightened of . . . well, I wouldn't know about that."

"Do you know any of these women?" Ella reached into her pocket and handed him the list of victims she'd also shown Reverend Curtis.

He looked closely at the names, then back at her. "I've met all three a long time ago, before I went to prison."

"What can you tell me about them?"

"The first two on this list were . . . silly women," he said, then shook his head.

Normally, she wouldn't have rushed a witness who was collecting his thoughts but when the silence dragged on, she realized he didn't intend to say anything else, so she pressed him. "Why do you think they were silly?"

He looked at her, then back at the bridle. "I'm not sure you need . . . or should . . . hear this."

"I'm a police detective investigating a crime. Nothing you can say will shock me," Ella said.

He pursed his lips for a moment, then continued in a hesitant voice. "Your father attracted women like bees to honey. It wasn't his fault, and he did his best to ignore it. He was a happily married man by all accounts. But some of the women dogged him, hanging on to his every word, and flirting with him constantly. Like two of those women on your list."

"They were interested in my *dad*?" Ella repeated, trying to come to grips with what he'd said. Thinking back, Ella really couldn't remember her mother ever mentioning that aspect of her father's life.

"Yes, but it was more like the girls who used to try and touch Elvis when he was onstage. All nonsense. Groupies, they call them. Your father didn't encourage that sort of thing, but I suspect he didn't really mind too much since it encouraged some of the young women to keep coming to church," he said, then added, "They all saw him as larger than life. And, in a way, he was. Reverend Destea had charisma with a capital *C*."

"One last thing, Wilbert. Where were you three days ago between six and ten in the evening?"

He shrugged. "Right here. Working. Alone, except for the Lord."

Ella went back silently to the car with Justine. This new bit of information about her father had taken her by surprise.

"The common denominator seems to be your father," Justine said, still trying to process the information in her own mind. "I was just a little kid when I first heard the stories. Women did have a thing for him. But those of us who had other plans for Sunday always gave him a wide berth. He was a very . . . enthusiastic . . . preacher."

"You mean he'd try to convert everyone? *That* I remember. But the pressure was more subtle at home because of Mom, I guess."

Ella thought about what she'd learned. It opened the road to a new set of possibilities. Maybe the killer was one of the congregation, perhaps a man who was jealous of what her father had accomplished. Unable to save souls by rhetoric, like her dad had done, he was now using violence to accomplish the same—at least in his own mind.

"Let's go find my mother. I need to talk her."

TWELVE

— ✖ ✖ ✖ —

It was a little past 6 P.M. by the time they arrived at Herman's place. He'd seen them coming—the road winded downhill from the highway into the river-shaped valley—and gone inside to get Rose. A few seconds later, she stepped out onto the porch.

"Have either of you had dinner?" Rose glanced at Justine and then back at Ella as they came to meet her.

"No. But I don't think we have time—"

"You'll make time, daughter," she said firmly. "You've had a very busy and hazardous day, judging from that bruise on your face. Now come in."

Herman stepped into the living room from the kitchen, a coffee cup in hand. "Welcome to our home, ladies. Please excuse me, I don't mean to be rude, but I have animals that require tending." He slipped outside before they could reply, so Ella and Justine went to join Rose.

Ella's mother moved fluidly in the kitchen, which was smaller than the one she'd been using for decades. But this was her domain, and she'd quickly adapted to the layout and appliances in Herman's home. Even over a cooking fire in the mountains, Rose could make delicious meals without so much as looking at a recipe, much less a measuring cup. To her it was instinctive, an ability Ella had yet to master.

Rose brought out bowls of mutton stew, and freshly made *naniscaada*, handmade tortillas that had no equal on the Rez. "My husband and I have just eaten, so you go ahead."

Ella ate quickly and hungrily, as did Justine. They had a long night ahead and some warm food was just what they'd need to stay focused.

Rose cleared her throat. "Before you tell me why you came here tonight, you should know that I don't want to even discuss my former friend. I heard about the trouble today with the Fierce Ones, trouble that she's responsible for causing. Her grief is destroying her common sense. My former friend had no right putting you, my own daughter, in such danger. Such lack of faith and trust is unforgivable, especially after all you've done for her and her family," Rose said, her eyes tearing slightly.

"Mom, she doesn't know what she's doing," Ella said, deeply touched by her mother's words. Rose's friendship with Lena had spanned a half a century. "What she did was wrong, but she'll come to her senses eventually. Thanks for sticking up for me and my team."

Rose nodded, wiping away the tears. "If you're not here to talk about her, then you must have come on that other matter," Rose said, her voice stronger now. "I've heard that you're wanting to take a look at the old membership records from your father's church. Reverend Curtis said he'd help you, but he hasn't been putting too much energy into his efforts."

"Mom, how do you know all this?"

"Elena Marquez is still on the church board, and she called me. Knowing that my former friend is being slowly destroyed by the loss of her daughter, I encouraged Elena to help you in any way possible so you can find whoever's responsible for the crime. Elena promised to make sure you were given access. Your father kept very good records, daughter. It was his way. That church always had his heart. We, his family, came second."

"Mom, I wanted to ask you about something I heard recently. Is it true that some of the younger women had crushes on Dad?"

Rose smiled. "Oh yes, that's very true. Your father would joke about it and tell me that whatever the Lord chose as a tool to gather his sheep and make them listen to His word was fine with him."

"Did anyone at the church resent that?" Ella asked.

"I have no idea," Rose answered. "I had very little to do with your father's business. But people do get jealous."

Ella sat back, lost in thought. That church, her father, his preaching, the victims . . . were all connected. But how did Valerie fit into that picture? "Was Boot's mother ever a member of Dad's church?"

Rose shook her head. "Her mother, my former friend, would have never allowed it. But I know that when Boot's mother was young, she went once or twice to your father's church with a friend. Not to see your father, mind you. It was that other man."

"Other man? Who was he?" Ella asked, seeing Justine, who'd been busy eating, look over in surprise.

"I don't recall his name. I barely knew him. I never went to the services unless your father specifically asked me to go and, even then, I'd never take part. After a while, your father stopped asking. He told me he understood, but I don't think he ever really did."

"Thanks for telling me all this, Mom," Ella said gently. She could see the sorrow and mixed feelings those memories evoked in her mother and regretted having brought the subject up, especially with Rose already so upset about Lena Clani.

"We're going to go to the church and take a look at that membership list. Thanks for clearing the way for me, Mom."

While Justine drove, Ella leaned back in her seat and tried to sort everything she'd learned.

"I know the church seems to be the best lead we've got to the killer, and this other man your mom spoke about is an unknown, but Brewster still gets my vote," Justine said.

"He's certainly number one on the Fierce Ones's list. But let's look at the evidence. Would Brewster even know a Bible passage like the one the killer used, and more to the point, does he strike you as the type to use one for justification?" Ella countered.

"Yes, if he were trying to frame Reverend Campbell," Justine answered. "He could have looked the passage up in a concordance. And there was a Bible right there in the vic's apartment, too."

"Good point. But if it wasn't Brewster, then we're right back to the link all three women shared—my father's church."

"Even if the killer was an official member of the congregation during your father's time, he's only going to be one name in a list that's bound to be miles long. Your father always packed the house."

Ella nodded somberly. "We'll have our work cut out for us." She checked her watch just as her cell phone began to ring. It was Reverend Curtis. His call was short and cold.

"We've got permission to search the records, I take it?" Justine asked when Ella ended the call.

"We'll probably go over tomorrow morning," Ella confirmed, shoving her phone back into her jacket pocket. It rang again, and Ella flinched. Justine chuckled.

"Surprised me, that's all," Ella said, reaching back into her pocket. The caller was Special Agent Dwayne Blalock.

"I interviewed Marco Pete," Blalock began, then updated her on his efforts. "He was still far too weak for me to lean on, but I got the idea that he's holding back on what happened just before the accident. When I mentioned Valerie's name, his eyes got as big as saucers, and keep in mind that there's no way he could have known she'd been murdered. After that, the doctor asked me to leave."

Ella smiled, thinking of the scene at the hospital. Blalock was as subtle as a brick, so "mentioning" could have covered a lot of possibilities.

"Something else. I decided to run down Brewster's alibi anyway, and double-check what the tire dealer had said. So I went to the Double Play and had a one-on-one with the lady Marine. It turns out that the story about the game on the big screen was garbage. Someone took out the plasma TV with a beer bottle the night before the murder, so they'd brought in a couple of big old-timers on carts. That's supposed to keep the customers around until the big one can be fixed."

"How about meeting us at Brewster's place?" Ella suggested.

"You've got it."

"Before you challenge his alibi, let me play a hunch. Just follow my lead," Ella said.

Twenty-five minutes later they sat in Brewster's spacious den when Donna excused herself and went into the kitchen. Justine followed, ostensibly to question her separately.

"What's going on between you and Reverend Campbell," Ella asked, deciding to play a bluff and see where it took her. She recalled Ford telling her that Brewster and Reverend Campbell didn't get along, and from what Reverend Campbell himself had told her, she suspected that the cleric knew all about Brewster's kinky games.

Stan's eyes narrowed and his shoulders tensed. "What did that pious SOB tell you?"

"I need to hear it from you," Ella said harshly, glad to see she'd hit a nerve.

"He's crazy, that's all, probably convinced that I had something to do with Valerie's murder. He comes in from time to time to pick up lunch and the day Valerie died, he happened to overhear an offhand comment I made to her. But the preacher is *way* out on line on this. I should sue his self-righteous butt for slander."

"Talk to the lawyers later. What kind of comment did you make?" Blalock pressed.

"I was feeling crappy that day and snapping at everyone, so I suggested she should help me relax. She kissed me off, said she'd rather risk losing her job."

"Help you relax, how?" Blalock shot back. "Give you a lap dance?"

He shook his head. "Not just that."

Ella took a deep breath. She wanted to lean over and smack him. Instead she sat very still.

"Quit stalling and get to the point. Were you in Valerie's Tso's apartment the night she died?" Blalock demanded.

"No. I wanted to drop by, but she said she had other plans."

"Like what?"

"No idea."

"So what's the deal between you and Reverend Campbell now?" Ella pressed. Gut instinct told her that there was more to the story.

He expelled his breath in a hiss. "Same old. It goes back a ways." He met Ella's stony gaze. "But I suppose you want a walk down memory lane?" Seeing Ella's curt nod, he continued. "When Valerie ended up joining a different church, Campbell asked me to stop by his office for a chat," he said. "I knew he and Valerie had spoken privately several times before she decided to join the Divine Word. That's why I thought I'd better go find out if she'd said anything I should worry about."

Stan walked to the window, then stared at his backyard. "I went in, intending to offer him a check, if that's what it took to keep him from carrying tales. He'd never turned down any of the money I'd given him for their youth programs, that's for sure. But, this time, he wasn't interested in any cash. He wanted to save me from myself—his exact words. I told him I was fine, and then he said he'd heard some disturbing rumors about the way I treated women, tales he might have had to report to the authorities to keep someone from getting hurt."

"And you thought that the stories came from Valerie?"

"Yeah, of course I did."

"So then what?" Blalock asked.

"Then nothing. I went my way and I haven't spoken to him since."

"Your alibi's crap, buddy," Blalock said, walking over to confront him. "Care to rethink things? According to the owner, that big-screen TV at the Double Play was out of commission the night you claimed to have been watching."

"Did I say we watched the game on the big screen?" he said with a shrug. "Habit, I guess."

"Or a lie. How'd the game turn out?"

"Eight to five, Boston."

"Could have read that in the paper. Winning pitcher?"

"Don't recall. Both teams used several. Johnson started for Boston. One of his relievers obviously got the win."

Blalock stepped right up into the man's face. "So where'd you get your gas that night?" he pressed.

"What gas?" Brewster took a step back, confused.

"I thought you said you drove up to Navajo Lake after the game. Where'd you stop for gas? Use a credit card?" Blalock pressed, inches from Brewster's face. "Where'd you stop?"

Brewster's cheeks were glowing, but his eyes had narrowed. He brought up his hands.

"Make a fist and I'll drop you, dumb ass," Blalock said, his voice low and hard.

Brewster was shaking, but he lowered his arms and sat down, refusing to make eye contact.

"Where *did* you stop for gas, Stan?" Ella asked. "You need more of an alibi than we're seeing so far."

"Didn't need to stop. Filled up earlier in the day. I pay cash, though, usually at Gasco over on Orchard Street. Doubt they'd remember, though."

"Why am I surprised? Don't leave town," Ella said, standing up. "You'll be hearing from us again."

"Sooner than you think," Blalock added, pointing a finger at Brewster. Stan responded with a sneer, but didn't speak or stand.

As Ella started toward the door, Justine came out of the kitchen. Ella nodded and they left together without talking. Once they were all outside on the sidewalk, Ella glanced at Blalock. "Looked like you were bringing him to a boil for a moment, Dwayne."

"There's a monster behind that face. He'll crack one of these times, then we'll see what he's really made of."

"Looking forward to being there," Justine said.

Blalock chuckled.

"Wanna follow us, Dwayne?" Ella asked when they reached the street. "We need to pay Reverend Campbell another visit."

They were en route moments later and as Ella glanced at her partner, she noticed that Justine's hands were gripping the wheel so tightly her knuckles were pearly white.

"I'm not after Reverend Campbell," Ella said, "but we have to follow this up. You know that."

"Brewster is scum, Ella, plain and simple, and I'm sorry FB-Eyes didn't push him hard enough. I wouldn't believe that slug if he told me there was sand in the desert."

"I agree completely, but there's bad blood between Brewster and the reverend. If Brewster did kill Valerie, and we now have another possible motive for him doing so—to keep her from pressing any abuse charges—then he left that biblical quote at the crime scene to implicate Reverend Campbell. Which leads me to another question. What else does Reverend Campbell know that he hasn't shared with us?"

Justine called during the trip back to the reservation and found out that Reverend Campbell was still at the church rectory and would meet with them in his office.

"What did you get from Donna Brewster when you questioned her?" Ella asked as Justine drove.

"Not much that we didn't already know. She was actually making excuses for the sleazebag."

"I just don't get her," Ella said.

"Me neither," Justine replied. "But she fits the bill. Abused women are often their husband's biggest defenders, even after a trip to the hospital."

Less than a half hour later, they were all seated in Reverend Campbell's office, down the hall from the chapel at Good Shepherd Church. Ella felt a wave of disappointment as she learned that Ford was away, visiting a parishioner. Annoyed with herself for getting sidetracked, she focused on the business at hand.

"Reverend Campbell, I'm going to be blunt. What do you know about Valerie Tso's death?"

"Nothing. I would have told you if I did," he said flatly.

"We've just come from our third interview with Stanley Brewster. I understand you and he had words not too long ago."

He nodded slowly. "Okay, I get where you're coming from now. But I haven't been holding back any evidence. What I could offer you is, at best, hearsay."

"Let us sort out what's evidence and what isn't," Blalock said.

Campbell hesitated. "You're asking me to walk a very fine line here, though you may not realize it. One of our ten commandments is specific about not bearing false witness."

"This is a murder case," Ella said sternly. "I believe you have a commandment about that, too."

"You're right, but what I've got to tell you is far from reliable information," he said, then, taking a deep breath, continued. "About a week prior to Valerie's murder, I happened to overhear two girls talking just outside my window after our Wednesday evening service. I don't know who was speaking since it was dark outside, but they were discussing Stan Brewster's . . . sexual activities. I called out to them, but all I heard was the sound of running footsteps. I went outside to find them as soon as I could, but by then they were long gone. A week later Valerie was murdered. The conversation I'd overheard stayed in my mind, so I asked Stan to stop by. I already knew he'd had a relationship with Valerie so putting two and two together . . ."

"And you confronted him with what you knew?" Blalock asked.

"Yes, but I didn't attribute the source. He immediately assumed Valerie had complained to me about him, and that I was out to destroy his reputation now that she was dead. He called me a hypocritical SOB and suggested that I was probably a repressed pervert, undressing women with my eyes. You get the drift."

Seeing them nod, he continued. "But it was his temper that got to me. It's there, and it's nasty. Before he left, he told me that if I ever mentioned what I'd found out to anyone, he'd get even. He threw a punch that stopped just a few inches from my nose, then laughed and stormed out. That's the last I saw him."

"We already knew he liked to get rough," Ella said, thinking out loud.

"Yes but that doesn't mean he's the killer. A man with problems, yes. A murderer? God only knows, I sure don't."

Ella showed him a copy of the quote the killer had left behind. "Does this have any special meaning to you?"

He read it over. "It's from Proverbs. I use Proverbs in my sermons sometimes. That particular chapter, in fact, has many lessons I draw on, like 'Commit thy works unto the Lord and thy thoughts shall be established.'" He pointed to the plaque on the wall above the file cabinet. "I had that made," he said. "But I've never used this particular verse," he added, handing it back to her.

Outside the church moments later, Blalock stopped them at the foot of the steps. "We need to sort all this out. What do you say we go get a coffee at the Totah?"

"Good idea," Ella said. "I could use something to prop my eyes open a little longer."

Blalock led the way in his Bureau sedan. Ella stared out at

the night, tired, wrung out emotionally, her thoughts jumbled.

When they arrived at the Totah a short while later, they were seated in the corner booth the waitress knew Ella preferred.

"Are you ladies thinking that Brewster left that quote to implicate Campbell?" Blalock asked, then seeing Ella nod, continued. "Unfortunately, we have nothing to back that theory up. There are other problems with it, too."

"Like the fact that we haven't established a match between Brewster's handwriting and the note, or his alleged squeamishness around blood," Justine said.

"Montoya lied to substantiate Brewster's alibi, so he may have lied about the blood thing, too," Blalock said. "Since they both mentioned the big-screen TV that indicates that they rehearsed their story. But all that aside, I'm more concerned about the similarities between this case and the deaths in Kayenta and L.A. We've got nothing that ties Brewster to those."

"But there's still a pattern here. The problem is we can't see what's tying all the elements together yet," Ella said.

"Too many people are lying and covering up," Blalock added. "That's bound to complicate things."

Ella was about to reply when her cell phone rang. It was Rose, and her voice was shaky. "You better come over quickly."

"Where are you and what's happened?" Ella asked, her heart suddenly hammering against her rib cage.

"At my husband's home," she said, her voice cracking. "*Bizaadii*'s sheep have been slaughtered. We heard their cries, but five were already dead by the time he got his rifle and went outside," she said, sobbing openly now. "And, daughter, the person who did this left a note for you."

THIRTEEN

— ✖ ✖ ✖ —

Ella called for backup, anger coiling so tightly around her she could barely draw a breath. "This is no coincidence. We just left Brewster's. He had enough time to make it to my mother's."

"How would he even know where she lives, particularly now that she's moved?" Justine countered.

"But what else makes sense?"

"You managed to get the church records we needed despite opposition," Blalock said. "You've put pressure on the ministers and the boards of two different churches."

"And don't forget the Fierce Ones, or those demonstrators at the power plant site," Justine added. "Frankly, the list is pretty long, Ella."

"When I catch whoever did this—and I will—I'm going to take him apart," Ella said.

As they got underway, Blalock in the vehicle behind them, Ella called Kevin and alerted him to keep a close eye on Dawn. If someone was out to punish her, Dawn could become a target next. Then she sent a patrol officer to make sure her brother Clifford and his family remained safe. Yet those precautions gave her little comfort. She knew that she and anyone close to her were now in the line of fire.

It was well past midnight when they arrived and, by then, Ella's stomach was tied into knots. She took a deep breath and forced herself to calm down. Her mother would be upset enough over the senseless slaughter of the sheep. She wouldn't add to the problem.

Ella saw *Bizaadii* standing on the porch, rifle leaning against the rail, and noted her mother had stayed inside. "How's Mom doing?" Ella asked, joining him.

"Not well. It's the waste and pointlessness of the act that bothers her most, I think. She's trying to calm down, but she couldn't even hold a cup of tea in her hands, so she's repotting one of her houseplants.

"I'm so sorry this had to happen," she said.

Herman nodded but said nothing.

"Tell me what you heard," Ella asked quietly.

"The sheep were bleating but not like normal. It was . . . a peculiar sound. I don't think I'll ever forget it," he added, then shuddered. "Your mother's dog started barking and your mother said she'd heard a truck, but I didn't see one when I went outside."

"No gunshots, so I'm assuming the sheep weren't shot?"

"Whoever did this used a knife to slit their throats." He swallowed hard. "There was no gain, no purpose. This person didn't need the food they could provide—or the wool. The sheep are a gift from Mother Earth, and to kill them like this dishonors her."

"I'm sorry, uncle," she said respectfully.

He looked at her. "Your enemy just became ours," he said softly.

"I'll catch whoever did this."

He nodded but didn't comment.

"Did you leave everything the way you found it?" Ella asked. It was a still night, so with luck, they might be able to find footprints.

"All except the note. I'd already picked it up when your

mother told me not to touch anything. Your mother will tell you more, but I need to salvage what I can from the slaughtered sheep. . . ."

Ella nodded, understanding. To waste a kill would anger the gods who sent the animals for the *Diné*, the Navajo people. Sheepskins could be used to sit upon in front of the fire and the meat would become part of a nourishing stew. The intestines would need to be thrown in the general direction of the house according to custom, because it was said that way they'd become sheep again.

Ella glanced back at Justine. "What's Tache and Neskahi's ETA?"

"They'll be here in less than ten minutes. I just checked. But Blalock's got a lantern and I'd like to get started. Okay by you if we get a jump on things or do you need me for something else?"

"Go ahead. I'm going to talk to Mom," Ella said.

Ella found Rose repotting a small plant on top of a card table she'd set up in *Bizaadii*'s living room. There was a fire in the woodstove and the room was pleasantly warm. Two, her old mutt, was lying on a small rug, asleep. He was kept inside at night, which explained why he hadn't barked earlier.

"The note is on the back step, weighed down with a rock. The knife that kept it pinned to the sheep is there, too," Rose said, her voice drained of emotion.

"I'll take care of it," Ella said, not at all surprised that her mother had refused to have it in the house.

Rose continued to work the soil mixture with her hands, feeling the dirt slip through her fingers, finding comfort in what she knew.

"Mom, are you all right?" Ella asked.

"The grass feeds the sheep, the sheep feed us, and eventually we all go back to Mother Earth and become one with her. That, in turn, provides for new life. To know and accept that is to walk in beauty. But slaughter of this kind . . ." She dug her fingers into the moist soil and stared at it pensively. "This person didn't need our animals. He killed them for the sake of killing and that imbalance affects us all. Every action creates a ripple that goes out and affects other things. Without harmony nothing good can come to anyone."

"Mom, I give you my word, I'll find whoever did this."

Rose nodded, then spoke. "I heard a truck . . . an old truck like mine, but out of tune. And Two started barking. Then I heard the cries of the sheep so I looked out the back window. I saw a shape out there that didn't belong but, I thought maybe it was a trick of the light. My eyes don't work too good at night anymore."

"It's okay, Mom," Ella said, placing her hand over her mother's arm. Rose looked tired, but Ella knew it wasn't the late hour that was getting to her.

"People kill without thinking," Rose said. "What if they decide they want *Bizaadii*, next time?"

Ella took a deep breath. "Mom, that's *not* going to happen. I'll have people looking over you."

"Stop whoever did this before he does more harm, daughter." Rose looked down at the plant she was working on. "I'll be up early tomorrow. The Holy People said that there's beauty in the darkness before the dawn. I need to find that, to see it, to honor Sun with pollen."

Leaving her mother to her work, Ella patted the dog, whose tail had started wagging, then slipped out the back door. On the step, just as Rose had said, she found the note and the bloodied knife, an inexpensive lock-back model like many construction workers carried nowadays.

Putting on a pair of disposable gloves, Ella picked up the note. The center of the paper, where the knifepoint had gone through, was stained with blood.

"For many was the blood of one shed." Ella read aloud, hearing Justine coming up behind her. "Is this Biblical?"

"Maybe paraphrased. I'm not sure of the exact wording," Justine said. "Sure sounds Biblical to me though," she added.

"Process the note and the knife and compare the handwriting to the last note. Find something that'll lead me to the walking piece of garbage who did this."

"You've got it."

"What did you find out there?" Ella asked, gesturing to the corral.

"Traces of footprints. I think whoever it was wore moccasins, because there are only flat impressions—no heels or patterns. Whoever killed the sheep was being careful, but I believe it was one person, a man, based on the size of the footprints."

Ella bit her bottom lip, lost in thought. "There's a message to this, and not just what was in the note. But I don't get it."

"Neither do I," Blalock said, coming up.

Ella walked back out with him and surveyed the half dozen lambs that had survived the butcher. They were all huddled together, watchful, spooked. Even in the muted light of Justine's lantern, beside the shapes of the dead animals, she could see the blood staining the ground. A sense of outrage filled her as she contemplated the attack that had been meant to terrorize her family.

It took her a moment to swallow back her rage and stop shaking. "If Herman can lead the uninjured animals out of this corral, we may uncover even more evidence," she said.

Blalock nodded. "Clah, let me work the scene this time. You're too close to this."

She didn't answer, and Blalock continued.

"You don't want the evidence compromised in any way. A smart attorney might use your link to Rose and *Bizaadii* to discredit whatever we may find."

"You may be right about that," Ella nodded slowly. "I'll take the tribal cruiser if you can give Justine a ride back."

"Not a problem. Where will you be?"

"I'm going to track Ford down and ask him about the wording on this note."

"Don't you trust Reverend Campbell?" Justine asked from where she was working.

"Don't get defensive, Justine. Ford is better at this type of thing. He was a cryptographer and he's used to breaking codes and reading between the lines. He may be able to help me figure out the real message the perp was leaving for us."

Ella went inside and found Herman in the kitchen, preparing the knives and other items he needed for the grim task still ahead. "Once my people finish going over the area, we'll need you to separate the uninjured sheep from the others so we can take another look inside the pen," Ella said.

"Just tell them to let me know when. The sooner, the better. The animals that haven't been harmed are very frightened, and there are ritual steps that need to be taken with the others."

"I know, and we'll do our best to work as quickly as possible. My team knows their business, so just do whatever they ask."

"You're leaving?"

She nodded. "I'll check with Mom again, then I'm heading out. There's someone I need to speak to right away."

"Are we in danger?" Herman asked.

Ella saw Herman had carried his 30-30 rifle into the kitchen with him. "I've had your home placed under surveillance, but I'm his real target, not you," she said. "I think the reason you were hit tonight was to keep me and my team preoccupied and away from our other work."

Ella stepped into the living room and saw her mother sitting on the chair, the potted plant now on her lap. "Mom?"

She looked up. "I was just trying to figure out where to put it," she said, looking a little lost.

Ella placed it near the window. "How about here? It looks pretty," she said.

Rose nodded absently. "I suppose that'll be all right."

"Mom, don't let this keep you down. I *will* find the person who did it. That's what I do, and I'm good at it." Ella saw the first glimmer of hope in her mother's eyes.

"An act like this puts things out of balance, and bad luck

always follows," she said. "The one who killed our sheep doesn't realize that yet. But he will."

"*I'm* going to be his bad luck, Mom, count on it."

"Maybe I should have my son do a *Hozonji* for us, a Song of Blessing . . . or maybe a Blessing Way, if he has time."

"I'm sure my brother would be happy to do either of those for you," Ella said. A Blessing Way was a purification ceremony, a way to start anew and stop looking back in fear. It would do her mother a world of good. "Call him, Mom."

Ella had already arranged for an officer to check on Clifford and warn him to stay on his guard. Later, she'd call Clifford herself. As she walked outside, Ella remembered the words of restoration sung during the Blessing Way ceremony, *Hózhone háaz'dlíí*, "it is beautiful all around me." It was just what her mother needed now.

Ella called Ford's cell number and waited. Reception on the Navajo Nation was iffy at best on a cell phone. But there was good coverage the entire distance between Shiprock and Farmington, and though the battery on her own phone was getting low, the call went through.

Ford answered on the first ring. "I've been hoping you'd call," he said. "I've been worried about you. I've heard all kinds of stories about things going on today. . . ."

"No doubt," she said, aware of how quickly gossip traveled. "I need to see you now about the case. Where are you?"

"Home."

"I'll be there in ten minutes."

Ford lived just off the reservation in the community of Waterflow, located north of the old coal power plant. He'd lived in the parsonage behind the church for some time, but had eventually opted to buy his own place rather than share a home with Reverend Campbell, also unmarried. Since no one could actually "own" land on the Rez, he'd ended up here, a stone's throw—literally—from the reservation borders.

His modest two-bedroom home was on an acre of what

had once been an old alfalfa field. There were parcels of residential property all around him where agriculture had slowly given way to the developers. Ella walked up the flagstone path from the driveway and knocked. Ford answered a second later, his giant dog, Abednego, beside him. The dog, a cross between a giant schnauzer and something of indeterminate background, stood calmly next to Ford, a toy monkey clenched in his mouth. He was Ford's constant companion, and Ella knew that Ford loved the mutt he'd found as a puppy beside an irrigation ditch and hand raised.

Ella was tall, but on all fours Abednego nearly reached her waist. "I think he's grown," Ella said.

"You're not wearing your boots, so you're shorter tonight," Ford answered with a chuckle.

Ella bent down to pet him, and the dog wagged its stubby tail. "At least I know you've got a great guard dog."

"You're right about that. Strangers take one look and back away."

Ford led the way into the kitchen though a living room so crowded with bookshelves that it looked more like a library. "I just made a pot of chamomile tea. Would you like a cup? It won't keep you awake."

"That's the least of my worries. I don't think I'll be sleeping much tonight, if you want the truth, not well anyway." She described the scene she'd left behind at her mother's house.

Ford's face hardened. "Your mother and her husband weren't hurt?"

"If anyone would have tried to hurt my mother, Herman would have pulled the trigger without hesitation. He's not at all helpless."

Ford watched her for a moment. "But that isn't why you wanted to talk to me at this hour, right? Let me guess. The butcher left something for you? Another note?"

"A message." She handed him the copy of the note she'd made. "Is this from the Bible?"

He read it quickly. "It's not an exact quote, no. A juxtaposition of the real text, maybe. Or maybe just something he's adapted to justify whatever mission he's on."

"Funny you should put it that way. I think he's on a mission, too. I'm just not getting a handle on what it could be. It's been a long time since I've tried to get into the head of a killer like the one committing these crimes."

"Do you think it's someone affiliated in some way to your father's church?"

Ella took a deep breath, looking down and seeing that Abednego had dropped the toy monkey at her feet. The big dog was sitting in front of her, waiting to play.

She was too tired to take the bait. "I'm thinking it could be a parishioner who was there at the time my father preached and that narrows it down—to several hundred. But maybe we can at least verify that two of the three victims were members. We've got the search for that membership list scheduled for tomorrow morning."

"I've found someone who may be able to give you some useful background information. She was a member of the Divine Word at the time your father was there. She attends Good Shepherd now but, as she tells me every time we get a new member, she likes to know the people she worships with," he said, handing her a slip of paper with a name, Lori Neathery, and an address.

"The lady is quite elderly," he added, "but she's as sharp as a tack and has a great memory. Well, let me amend that. She may not remember what she ate for breakfast, but she can describe with uncanny accuracy events that happened twenty years ago. But be aware that, depending on her mood, she may give you some problems. She didn't like your father, and she doesn't like the Navajo police either. Mrs. Neathery admires the efforts of the Fierce Ones, too."

"Thanks, and if you come up with anything that might give me some insights into the message or the person who left the note, call me anytime—day or night."

"Of course. You're staying at Justine's house, right?"

"Yeah, for now." Seeing the dog was still patiently waiting, hoping she'd play, Ella reached down, grabbed the toy monkey for Abednego, and threw it across the room. He retrieved it then dropped it back on her lap. She threw it again. "Okay, boy, enough for now," she said, standing. "I better get going. I've got to get some sleep tonight."

Ford snapped his fingers and the dog came over, sitting at heel. "The guy you're after is playing you, Ella. He knew where to hit to make you lose perspective. Looking back, he may have done it before, and you just haven't made the connection yet. But don't let him get to you or divert your course. If you do, he wins."

"My turn's coming," she said flatly. "Believe it."

Ella drove slowly, careful not to let her weariness affect her driving. Thirty minutes later, she slipped inside the house as quietly as possible, not wanting to wake Emily if she was already asleep. As she entered the living room, she found Emily and Justine sitting by the fireplace.

"You might try some of this herbal mix," Justine said, and yawned. "I got it from your mother. She said it would help us get some rest."

Ella picked up the pot and poured some of the amber liquid into a mug. She knew her mother's teas did as she predicted and, somehow, she had to get some sleep tonight.

Emily glanced at both of them. "You two look like you've been to Hell and back."

Ella looked at her thoughtfully and nodded. "You know, Em, I think we have."

FOURTEEN
——— ✖ ✖ ✖ ———

Ella and Justine arrived at the station around seven-thirty in the morning. Despite the tea, dark images had crowded Ella's dreams, often jarring her awake. Although they hadn't compared notes, based on Justine's mood, Ella had a feeling it had been the same for her partner.

"I'm going to the crime lab and process evidence," Justine said. "Tache has photo evidence from last night he needs to work on."

Ella nodded once. "I'll be at Reverend Curtis's church looking for that old list of church members. Blalock will probably join me there," she said. "Call if you find anything we can use."

As Justine walked down the hall, Ella dialed Blalock's number and he answered on the first ring.

"You must have ESP, Clah," he said. "I was about to call you. Ride with me this morning. Marco Pete is out of ICU so I'm going to interview him again. This time the gloves will be off."

"Okay and, after that, we need to go over to the church and look at their membership records. There's someone else we should go see today, too," she added, telling him about Lori Neathery. "She may remember someone who isn't on the list."

"Sounds like we've got another busy day," Blalock said.

Ella met with Blalock twenty minutes later and, at her suggestion they took her loaner tribal cruiser instead of the Bureau car.

"By the way, I ran into Bruce Little this morning," Blalock said. "He told me to tell you he's on the job and no one's getting anywhere near your mother's place again. And he's got your daughter's place covered, too."

Ella smiled. She didn't doubt Teeny for a moment. "He's a good friend."

When they arrived at the hospital, Blalock went to the desk and paged Marco Pete's doctor. Dr. Steinberg, according to his name tag, came to meet with them several minutes later.

"We need to question your patient again, Doctor. I'm assuming we have free rein now that he's out of ICU?" Blalock asked.

Steinberg, in his late twenties and prematurely balding—an affliction rare among Navajos—nodded. "We've done all we can for him and he's recovering quickly, but if he doesn't stop drinking, his future's an early grave."

Blalock thanked Steinberg, and as the doctor walked away Ella considered how many people on the Rez would qualify for the same prognosis. She didn't recall a time when alcoholism wasn't on the rise. It seemed to go hand in hand with poverty, which the Rez also had in abundance.

Ella followed Blalock into the semiprivate room, which Marco had to himself at the moment, and found him in the bed beside the window, gazing outside. From his records Ella knew Marco was only in his fifties, but his hard drinking made him look much older.

He turned when they'd knocked and once Ella had flashed her badge, Marco had exhaled loudly in resignation. "I wasn't drinking that much. The blood tests were wrong."

"Then what happened? Did someone run you off the road?" Ella asked.

He shook his head. "It was my fault. I lost control of the

pickup. Headlights were coming up fast behind me, like I was being chased. So I drove faster. But then I hit a piece of firewood or something on the road and the wheel jerked out of my hand. I hit the brakes, but I went right down into a ditch or something."

"Did the person behind stop to help you?"

"Yeah. It was a kid. Don't know who. He tried to get me out, but the door was pinned shut. He moved some brush and rocks, but it still wouldn't open. He hightailed it out of there after that. I had a lot of blood on my face, and I think he thought I was dying. Didn't want to be around for that, you know?"

"What gave you the idea you were being chased?" Ella asked. Intuition told her that there was a connection.

Marco looked away from her, then stared at his hands. Ella heard Blalock shift from foot to foot, restless. FB-Eyes was a graduate of the "lean on 'em" interrogation school at Quantico.

"Things just kept going wrong for me that day," he said slowly. "It all started when I decided to pay an old friend a visit. She and I . . . well, we'd had good times once. I was hoping to take her out to dinner, maybe a movie, then spend the night with her if I could."

"Who are you talking about?" Blalock pressured. "A woman with a jealous husband?"

He looked around, then whispered the name. "Valerie Tso," he said. "I'd heard stories that she'd found religion and wasn't partying anymore, but I thought it couldn't hurt to ask. But when I got to her apartment something just didn't feel right. It was . . . too quiet. No radio, no TV, no nothing. I walked over and peeked in the bedroom window. There was broken glass and blood everywhere. I ran back to my truck and got out of there fast."

"Did you see the killer, or the body?" Blalock asked.

"I didn't see anyone—dead or alive. But I wasn't going to stick around. Valerie's place hadn't gotten that way by itself."

"Why didn't you go call the police?" Ella asked.

"Are you crazy? I'm the glonnie, the drunk who gets

blamed for everything. Once I saw all that blood I knew someone in there was probably either dead or close to it. I wasn't
about to stick around."

"So you drove off," Ella said.

"Yeah, but then I looked down and saw the gas tank was on
empty. So I spent some of the money I'd earned cleaning up the
Double Play after hours, my date money, filling up the tank. I
was thinking about maybe going to Albuquerque and staying a
while. I knew that whatever had happened back there was going to be in the news one way or another, and I wanted to be
long gone by the time you all started investigating."

"After you left the gas station, those headlights came up
fast from behind, right?" Blalock asked, keeping him on track.

"Yeah, but I didn't know it was just a kid. I thought maybe
someone at Valerie's had seen me driving away and decided I
had to be stopped. Face it, if someone had forced me off the
road, everyone would have just assumed it was my fault—just
another drunk Navajo getting in a wreck."

"I need you to think back. What exactly did you see when
you peered in the window?" Ella asked.

"Her stuff, clothes and things, were scattered all over the
place and there was blood everywhere. I'd never seen that
much blood in my life. It scared me spitless."

"Did you *hear* anything?" Ella pressed.

He thought about it for a long time then finally spoke. "I
thought I heard a man crying but I'm not sure. It wasn't the
TV, because that hit show was on, the one where kids try out to
be a rock star. Someone was singing."

Ella and Blalock exchanged quick glances, then Ella looked
back at Marco. "One last question. Did you happen to see a red
Ford truck by the diner that night?"

"The one that belongs to the owner of the Morning Stop
Café?" Seeing her nod, he added. "Maybe, or else it was another night I'm thinking about. Valerie's car was there for sure.
But I'm getting things mixed up in my mind again. Dr. Stein-
something said that the bump on my head might cause me to

lose my memory about things. Or maybe it's because I drink too much."

"Okay, thanks," Ella said. "We'll be in touch."

Blalock walked down the hall with Ella, but didn't comment until they were outside in the parking lot. "Do I have to remind you that Brewster doesn't have a solid alibi?"

"If her death was accidental, I can see him trashing the place to make it look like a robbery. But the rest just doesn't make sense. I mean why clean up the area around the vic, change her clothes, and write that note? That doesn't fit Stan Brewster."

"Unless he decided after the fact to try and frame Reverend Campbell."

"It still doesn't sound right to me," Ella said flatly.

"Let's go lean on Brewster again and point out that we have a witness who can put him there at the right time."

"We'll have to hope he reacts the way we want him to. As far as witnesses go, Marco's just not reliable," Ella said. "But first let's go by the Divine Word Church, talk to Reverend Curtis, and check out those membership records," Ella added. "If Stan Brewster's on one of the lists, that'll give us even more to discuss when we see him again."

When they arrived at the church Reverend Curtis was watering the plants near the front entrance. Seeing them, he turned off the faucet and went to meet them.

"I hope you're ready for a little dust," he said. "Actually, it could be more than a little. We have a cleaning woman but the attic isn't her responsibility, and it's been a long time since anyone's poked around up there except to put something in storage. The records are inside metal file cabinets so the mice can't get to them."

He looked at Ella and continued. "By the way, there's a nest of mice up there somewhere. I didn't have the heart to put out the live traps and relocate them because it's still pretty cold at night. They run around everywhere up there so I hope mice don't bother you."

"Not unless they're armed," Ella replied with a tiny smile. "People are capable of far more damage."

His expression didn't change.

"We've been hearing a lot of stories about the church when my father was the preacher," Ella continued. "By any chance, were you a member of this congregation when he was the minister?"

"I've been a member of this church since I could walk."

"Then maybe you can clarify something we heard from several other sources."

His expression was guarded. "Looking to stir up trouble?"

"Not even close. Understand, Reverend Curtis, that neither you nor this church is our priority. All we want is to catch whoever killed Valerie Tso, and maybe two other Navajo women as well."

He exhaled loudly. "I'm probably being oversensitive. I *am* very protective of this church. It's my calling and my love, if you can understand that."

The glimmer of humanity in the otherwise annoying man surprised her. "I've heard that some of the women attended the service only to see my dad, and he didn't mind because at least they were coming to church."

He smiled. "That was probably true—or at least half true. Your father was very charismatic, but the younger women had another reason for attending our services. We had a real *natzee* in the midst of us at the time. Do you know that term?"

"Cancer . . . or more literally something that's rotting," Ella answered.

"Yes. A Romeo who was, in the words of my nephew, a babe magnet. He was nothing but trouble, mind you, but that didn't stop the young ladies from being drawn to him like moths to a flame. It's often that way, I've noticed," he said, leading them down the church corridor. "That was years ago so I don't remember his name, but I do recall that he was a constant source of aggravation for Reverend Destea—your father."

"Was this ladies man about your age?" Ella asked.

"Ten years older or so, which would put him in his early fifties now. I'm told I look young for my age," he added.

"What else do you remember about him?" Blalock asked.

"He was devout, but I don't think he was completely stable. He also knew a great deal about Jesus and the Bible and he loved quoting from the Old Testament."

Reverend Curtis pulled down the folding steps, then invited them to climb up while he went to answer a ringing phone.

Ella went upstairs first, and flipped the light switch on a metal box once she was close enough to reach it. A single, bare bulb in a fixture attached to an overhead beam was the only light. Ella stepped onto the bare plywood floor and looked around. Blalock, a few steps behind her, started coughing.

The attic was almost full. Stacked in several places were a dozen or more old wooden folding chairs, cardboard boxes of old hymnals, and two large boxes labeled VACATION BIBLE SCHOOL. Each of the five dusty gray filing cabinets was placed in a different spot, apparently to distribute the weight so the ceiling didn't sag. Unfortunately there were no tags to label the cabinets or drawers, and a roof leak sometime in the past had created a rusty spot atop the closest cabinet where the water had pooled.

"I'll be down here if you need me," Reverend Curtis called out to them, now that he was off the phone.

"Which cabinet has the records?" Ella asked.

"You'll have to look around. I have no idea," came his reply. "They used to be in order when they were in the old storeroom, but when they were hauled up into the attic, they were put anywhere there was room."

Ella saw footprints on the dusty floor, and noted that the little slots that had held labels were clear of dust. "Looks like somebody came up here and pulled out the labels, just to make our job a little harder," she whispered.

"Wonder who that could have been?" Blalock responded, pointing down with his thumb.

They went to check different cabinets. Ella saw the mouse nest in a corner where old crepe paper had been piled up and shredded. A tiny creature on one of the ceiling beams came out of the shadows, stopped to look, then ran to the corner and disappeared into the nest. She had a flashlight, but there was no sense in shining it in that direction and stirring things up. "The nest's in that corner," she said and pointed. "They'll stay out of our way."

"Cripes, Clah. What about the Hantavirus?"

"Wrong vector. I got a look, and that's not a deer mouse. Ears are too small. Just a regular house mouse."

"Thank you, Madam Science," he muttered.

Ella laughed. "Just keep looking." She opened a cabinet and searched through the open file drawer. "I've got them," she said after a moment. "This filing cabinet has records from 1990 to 1992." She stepped over to another cabinet to her right and checked there, too. "This one has the files 1993 to 1995. Those are the dates my father was sole minister here."

"Okay, we pull the contents and go," Blalock answered.

They found several empty paper boxes, loaded everything into four of them, then working together, carried the heavy boxes down the stairs one at a time. "What do you say we get your team to search these?" Blalock suggested, looking at the containers resting on the hall floor.

"They've got their hands full. We're here, we should do it ourselves, now."

Blalock nodded. "Maybe Reverend Curtis will let us use his office."

They were able to use one of the Sunday School classrooms, which had long, cafeteria-style tables. It took over an hour, but they finally managed to find the membership records they needed. Except for those who'd left the reservation and a few others who'd dropped out for various reasons, the names had remained fairly consistent from year to year. The total number of members, however, had increased slightly over time, consistent with the community population growth.

"The two women who were killed out of state were members in 1994 and left the church when they both moved away in 1995," Ella said. "We have a common denominator now."

"What about Valerie? She wasn't a member," Blalock said.

"Not officially, but we already know she was one of the girls who came to church to check out the bad boy."

"If we can run the names of the men and find out who was the right age, maybe we can ID that bad boy—that is, providing he was an official member of the church. The problem I'm betting we'll run into is that most of the men won't be on police data files. We need someone who can do DMV searches and whatever else is necessary to get the information we need."

"Teeny," Ella replied. "Bruce Little."

"Good thinking. If anyone can do this quickly, he can," Blalock glanced at Reverend Curtis as he came into the meeting room. "We'll need to take the lists covering years 1994 and 1995 with us. They'll be returned as soon as possible, undamaged and intact."

"I was told to give you access, but taking anything with you is another matter altogether. I don't have the authority to okay something like that."

"Then make the phone calls, Reverend Curtis," Ella said. "I believe you'll find out this isn't a problem."

When Curtis left the room to make the call from his office, Blalock glanced down at his hands. "I've got a year's worth of dirt here. I'm going to wash up in the bathroom across the hall."

Ella nodded and coughed as she dusted herself off. "I could use some fresh air myself. I'm going to step outside for a minute or two. When you're done, I'll take my turn washing off."

Passing Reverend Curtis's office, Ella walked down the hallway and stepped out the back door. She inhaled deeply, enjoying the fresh air. As she strolled out onto the church grounds, Ella glimpsed a figure darting behind the cover of some trees on the far side of the irrigation canal.

Immediately on her guard, she moved closer to the tall cottonwood and placed the trunk between the person across the way and herself. It could have easily been a big kid playing along the ditch bank, but her instincts warned her otherwise and she knew to trust them. They'd saved her on more than one occasion.

Ella watched for a moment longer and saw flashes of a man walking through the tall brush along the far side of the canal. He didn't seem to be looking her way or acting in any threatening manner. Ella relaxed slightly, telling herself that she was getting way too jumpy.

Suddenly, the man stepped out into the open. Though he stood on the far side of the ditch, she could see him plainly, and he looked familiar. He was wearing a T-shirt and jeans and was unarmed from what she could see. He appeared to be his late forties or early fifties and had a wide scar that ran across his forehead right above his eyebrows. The Navajo man, taller than most at five foot ten or eleven, was on the thin side and looked to be in fairly good physical shape.

"We've met, you and I," Ella said coming out of cover. "Refresh my memory. Who are you?"

"Isn't that something? You're a cop, yet I know who you are and you don't know me. Not much of a balance there."

She recognized the voice and finally made the connection. It was the man she and Justine had seen patronizing Mrs. Barela's roadside sandwich operation a few days ago. There'd been the oil field workers and then this guy, who'd been wearing the sunglasses. He was Mr. Beach Navajo, and his sunglasses had hidden that scar. "You're the man with the sunglasses who'd missed the roadside chow, the one who didn't know I was a police officer. So enlighten me and identify yourself."

He laughed. "Good memory, Officer Clah. But it'll take

more than changing your name to keep the sins of your father from catching up to you. Unless you also change your ways, you're going straight to hell. Listen and understand—before it's too late."

"I've got plenty of time—unless you know something I don't," Ella countered, wanting to keep him talking while she figured out how to get across the ditch. She wasn't sure she'd make it if she tried to jump across. Maybe with a running start from farther back . . .

"Luck's been on your side so far, but that won't last. By interfering at the construction site, you ruined a really good slugfest, you know. But you can't avoid the Lord's instrument of justice for ever . . . remember your mother's sheep," he added, grinning.

Ella's skin went cold and her senses became so acutely alert she actually *felt* Reverend Curtis coming up behind her before she even heard him.

"Is this man bothering you, Investigator Clah?"

"Don't get involved in what doesn't concern you, Reverend," the man called back at them, his grin now replaced by an angry scowl.

Ella suddenly rushed forward at a full run, intending on jumping the canal. The desire to find out what the man knew about her mother's sheep drove her, and she leaped, putting her heart and everything she had into it.

Ella reached the other side—almost. She could touch the top of the embankment with her fingertips, but her feet were only inches above the water level. Fighting to firm up her hold so she could climb up, she dug her fingers into the dirt. She was just about to pull herself up, when a chunk of the embankment broke away and she plummeted downward into the swirling water.

FIFTEEN

—— ✖ ✖ ✖ ——

Ella gasped from the shock of contact with the freezing water, but managed to keep her wits. Letting the current pull her downstream, she grabbed hold of an irrigation pipe and its small gate valve. Her grip firm, she stood atop the pipe, grabbed onto the wheel that controlled the gate, and pulled herself out of the canal.

By then Blalock was there. "There's a footbridge right past those trees, Ella. Didn't even get my feet wet. You okay?"

"Cold, but fine. Go after him. And call for backup," she added, checking her gear to make sure she had everything.

Working together, Ella and Blalock thoroughly searched the far side of the ditch, but they found nothing, not even tracks on the hard-packed earth.

"What made you suddenly enter the long-jump competition, Clah? You thought you'd sprouted angel wings or something?"

"Fifteen years ago I would have done that for fun—and I would have made it over without even straining myself," she muttered.

"Yeah, well, get over it. None of us are as good as we used to be."

"Speak for yourself," Ella shot back.

Blalock smiled. "Seriously, what made you think he was worth the risk of trying to make the jump."

"The guy knew about the incident that nearly turned the demonstration at the plant into a violent confrontation. He also mentioned the attack on my mother's sheep. Who would have known that besides the perp, or someone who was with him? The guy has a big cross tattooed on his arm, and he was talking like some die-hard religious nut. We should pull out all the stops to find him."

Blalock went to load the boxes of files, and Ella ran back to her cruiser. While she checked on the alert FB-Eyes had put out, she turned on the heater and tried to dry off. Taking a dry pair of socks and boots she kept in the back, she slipped both on, and then went back inside to talk to Reverend Curtis.

"Did you recognize him?" Ella asked the preacher.

"I know all of our parishioners, and he's not one of them. But he did mention your father, so based on some of what he said, I assume he has a Christian background."

"Could he be the bad boy we're looking for? He was around the right age."

He considered it for a moment, then finally shrugged. "The person I remember was heavier, I think, and less . . . scarred."

"Visualize the man we saw without that big scar, and fifteen years younger."

He tried, then shook his head. "I wish I could help you, but I can't. I barely remember the days when your father was the preacher here and I can't visualize someone in the congregation who didn't really interest me back then. At that age I spent most of my time watching the girls. Church was more a social place to meet my friends. It was before God became so important to my life." He paused then added, "I'm sorry."

"All right, but call me if you think of anything later on. Memory works that way sometimes."

He nodded. "By the way, the board president said that you're free to take whatever files and records you need. Agent Blalock is loading them onto a dolly right now."

"Good."

Ella went to meet Blalock who was coming out of the front entrance, pushing a two-wheeled dolly with all four boxes. As they loaded the boxes into her vehicle, Blalock gave her the once-over. "Clah, I know you're tough as nails, but are you sure you're okay?"

"My underwear's soaked, I smell like a swamp, and I'm still pissed, but I'll live. I'm going to stop by Justine's and change, then we'll continue to Lori Neathery's place. Brewster can wait a bit."

"Why don't you drop me off at my office since it's on the way? I'll run the names through NCIC and VICAP, then take the membership records to Bruce Little and let him have a go at them."

Ella dropped Dwayne Blalock off ten minutes later, then continued on to Justine's. She changed quickly, and had about reached the door when she ran into her partner, who was coming in.

"I heard some of what happened, Ella. Are you okay?"

"Sure. Pissed off, but okay. Do you have anything new on the knife or anything else that was left at my mother's, like the note, or vehicle tracks?"

"No, the perp was really careful," she said, then after a beat, added, "If we could find out why someone wanted Valerie dead, then I think the rest of it would fall into place."

Ella nodded lost in thought. "Gilbert Tso is a liar and thief. He has an alibi, but he might have hired someone else to do the job. Then there's Brewster, who's slime and has already admitted he likes to slap women around. There's this new guy—a troublemaker who apparently knew my father. We have no shortage of suspects. But what we still lack is a clear motive. So we have to keep digging. Why don't you come talk to Lori Neathery with me?" Ella asked.

"I'd love to—anything that'll buy me some time away from the lab. I'm getting cross-eyed looking through that microscope."

Ella was in the car with Justine when her cell phone rang.

It was Clifford. He came right to the point. "We need to talk, sister. I know what happened to Mom's sheep. The officer who came by gave me the details. But there's something you need to know. The motive may not necessarily be connected to you. It appears I'm making some enemies, too."

Ella felt her muscles tighten. "What do you mean? What's going on?"

"It's this business with the power plant. I'll explain when I see you."

Ella glanced at Justine and filled her in. "My brother thinks the attack at Mom's place may have something to do with his stand on the power plant issue. But I don't think the two things are related. After what that guy at my dad's old church said, I still think I'm at the center of what's happened."

Justine considered it for a while. "Let's look at this from a slightly different angle. What if the person with the scar originally had a beef with your father? Now that your father is out of his reach, that anger is being transferred to his family—you, your mother, and particularly your brother. In that light Clifford, in particular, becomes a target. He's a practitioner of a pagan religion. As such, he may be more vulnerable than either of you."

"That's a possibility," Ella said, nodding slowly. "Clifford's on his guard and he also has police protection, so maybe we'll get lucky and this guy'll come after me next. I'd sure love another shot at him."

"Maybe we'll all get lucky and he'll come after you at my place," Justine said. "I know three *armed* officers who would love to be there personally to greet him. Shall we send him an engraved invitation?"

Ella smiled. That had been Justine's way of reminding her that she wasn't alone, and Ella appreciated it. "Thanks, partner. Now let's get cracking. We have business at Lori Neathery's."

Lori's home took over an hour to reach, not because it was so far from Shiprock, but because the roads were all but impassable once they left the main highway. The collection of dirt tracks southwest of Shiprock led through alternating sections of sandy arroyos and tipped beds of sandstone in uneven layers. The ride jolted every bone in their bodies even at the lowest speed.

En route they passed three abandoned hogans, two with holes punched on the sides to signify a death had occurred there.

"I don't get it," Justine said, after maneuvering around a gash in the dirt track that was deep enough to conceal a horse. "Why does anyone live out here?"

"Loneliness doesn't factor for many of our people. You know that."

"It's not about loneliness, Ella, just the basics. If anything happened to you out here, who would you call? I mean assuming you had a cell phone that actually worked in this area."

"The older *Diné* live from day to day. If there's a problem, someone walks or rides their horse to a *hataalii*, and arranges for a Sing. Then you can walk in beauty again. To be honest, Justine, I wish I were more like that. No worries, just take things as they come and do the work the day demands."

"I like amenities. I like TV. I like recording my favorite shows. I like hot water," she answered with a smile. "Guess I'm part of the spoiled generation."

"We all are. The gods gave us the land between the sacred mountains and for generations that was enough. But now even the most traditional Navajo needs way more than that," she added pensively.

As they reached a single dwelling in the sloping terrain leading to the Chuska foothills, Justine reduced their speed to an even slower crawl. They could see an elderly woman they assumed was Lori Neathery up ahead. Her white hair was topped by a cloth scarf tied under her chin, and she was wearing a long, shapeless cotton dress, white socks, and comfortable-looking sneakers. Lori was carrying a metal bucket into a corral containing five *churro* sheep. The enclosure had been formed by blocking off the lower end of a blind canyon with a log fence. There was a rifle propped up against the gate.

They waited in the car until she turned around, waved, and signaled them to approach. "Been having trouble with coyotes who want my sheep," she said, then added, "I'm Lori Neathery. Reverend Tome said you might come by and talk to me."

Ella noticed how she rested her hand on the head of one sheep who'd pushed her neck out between the logs of the fence. These were pets who provided wool.

"Do you weave?" Ella asked, noticing that all the animals had been sheared recently.

Lori nodded. "That's what I do. I make small rugs to sell to the tourists. The money provides for me and for them, too."

Ella noticed that the sheep were being fed grain, something not everyone could afford.

Following her gaze, she added, "When I was a girl we'd take the sheep up to the Lukachukai Mountains in the summer to graze, and in winter they'd have grasses here. But not much rain has come lately, and the land's tired," she said. "So am I. But we both keep going."

She led them inside the sturdy cut stone house, and Ella noted that the woodstove had a fire. With the heat retaining ability of the stone walls, it was warm and comfortable inside.

"I can guess what brought you here," she said with a knowing grin. "I'm old, and I know many secrets. Perhaps you'd like me to share some of those with you."

"Yes, we would." Ella was having a problem guessing her age but she didn't think mid-eighties would be out of line.

"People don't remember nothin' these days, not even the old stories. But maybe their mothers didn't teach them what was important."

Ella had a feeling the comment had been meant as criticism for Rose, but she didn't take the bait. "I understand that you went to the Divine Word Church when my father was there preaching."

She nodded. "I didn't like him very much, your father, that is, just so you know. Didn't like the way he'd try to scare people when they missed Sunday services. But I didn't give him problems, not like some others."

"Like who, for example?" Ella asked.

Lori looked at Ella for a long time before answering. "You and our new preacher, Reverend Tome . . . you getting married?"

Ella blinked in surprise and for a moment, she just stared at Lori. "Not that I know of," she answered at last. "We're friends, that's all. At least for now."

"That's not what your eyes are telling me," she said, laughing. "But this is a good thing. I wouldn't want the gossip to take away his position in our church."

"Is his job in danger?" Ella asked, curious now.

She laughed again. "See? You care. That's *very* good," she added, nodding. "Okay, you told me something and now I tell you something. It's balanced that way. I believe in all that, you know. I guess you can call me a Christian traditionalist."

Ella smiled, and out of the corner of her eye, she could see Justine almost beaming.

"There's always a first for everything," Lori said.

Ella nodded. "I was wondering if you could tell me about my father and his church back then."

She grew serious and her expression, thoughtful. "Your father liked things just so. Many, mostly the gossips, claimed he was such a dictator at church because at home he couldn't control his own family. I don't know about that, but I do know he didn't like anyone to challenge his authority, and few ever did. Your father could squash any opposition with just a few well-chosen words. But one man went head to head with your father. I remember it because, at first, we all thought the young man was more of a son to him than his own son was. They were that alike. Then things changed."

"Do you remember the man's name?"

She thought about it. "Carson? No, wait. I think it may have been Cain . . . or Calvin?" She shook her head, then continued. "Can't be sure about that. The only reason I remember him at all is because he tried to date my niece. I put a stop to it, of course. I knew he wasn't what he seemed to be at all."

"What do you mean?" Ella asked, leaning forward in her chair.

"I overheard him talking to my niece one day. He was telling her that God had a great plan for him and that she could be part of it, if she'd spend a night with him. That's when I knew he was corrupt. He was handsome and the women just loved him, but there was something evil in him. Like with Coyote, lying came too easy for him."

Ella didn't really understand the comparison, but she waited, sensing Lori had more to share.

"When Coyote met Porcupine, Porcupine lived in a small hut make out of bark. Coyote was hungry but Porcupine had no food to share with him. Knowing that his guest was hungry, Porcupine tore a piece of bark off his hut, pricked his nose using one of his quills, and allowed the blood to drip onto the bark. After that, he placed it on the fire. When Coyote looked back at it, he saw that the bark had turned into a roast. Coyote ate and had his fill. Then he went to build himself a hut of bark. Then he tried the same method Porcupine used, pricking his nose until it bled, but nothing happened. That was because we're all different inside and what you expect isn't always what you get."

"Who were his other women?" Ella asked, bringing Lori back on track.

"There were many. I don't remember their names."

"And your niece's name?"

The elderly Navajo woman crossed herself. "Barbara Henderson. She passed on many years ago. She was riding her horse one afternoon and it threw her. The horse came home alone and we all searched but, by the time we found her, it was too late. Now my sister is also gone. But I remain." She was quiet for several moments. "If you're searching for the man I remember, then you should know that you have an advantage over him."

"What's that?" Ella asked her.

"Do you know the story of Coyote and Badger?"

Ella searched her mind, but there were as many stories about Coyote as there were stars in the night sky.

Lori's voice became soft and her eyes misty as she recalled stories she'd learned as a girl. "Coyote and Badger wanted the same woman, so they set out to compete for her. Whoever brought back the most rabbits would win her in marriage. Badger was ahead, so Coyote tricked him. He told Badger about a rabbit he'd seen going down into a hole. Badger went after the rabbit, but as soon as he was out of sight, Coyote rolled a rock over the opening of the hole. Coyote returned with his kills first, but the people insisted on waiting for Badger. Badger finally dug his way out and told everyone what Coyote had done. People knew Coyote lied a lot, so they believed Badger. The next day while Badger and the people went hunting, Coyote tried to steal the woman. But it didn't work so Coyote ended up going his way alone." She paused then continued with a smile. "You have the Badger fetish around your neck. Like him, you have a good heart and honesty on your side, and you're willing to work for what you get, too. All Coyote has is lies. So, whether you know it or not, the advantage *is* yours," Lori concluded.

Ella smiled. "Thank you for sharing that story with me," she said.

Lori nodded once.

Ella stood. "We have to be going now but if you remember the man's name, send word to me."

As they left, Ella remained silent. Nothing was coming together. Frustrated, she tried to mentally sort through all the information they'd gathered on the case so far, but before she could get far, her phone rang.

It was Dwayne Blalock. "We've found something interesting among the records, Ella. Apparently your father kept a daily log of church-related business, and in the entries we found someone he called the heretic. That man betrayed your father, according to what your father wrote."

"Any idea who he was or what he did to my dad?" Ella asked.

"We haven't found any reference that identifies him by name but we're still looking. As far as what he might have done to your father, that remains unclear," Blalock said, then added, "What we did find are some personal notes about you and your brother. His reaction to your Bureau career and how he felt about your brother becoming a medicine man, things like that. I thought you might like to read through those."

Ella hesitated. To read her father's personal notes in reference to the case was one thing, but to read through his personal journal out of curiosity was another matter entirely. She wasn't at all sure about that.

"Is Teeny still doing a search on the names?" she asked, temporarily changing the subject.

"Yeah, and the man is frightening. He gets quicker access to the databases than I do. But so far we haven't had much luck on anything."

"Look for a first name with a C . . . Calvin, Cain, anything on that order."

"Last name?

"Don't have one," Ella replied.

"All right. We'll see what we can do."

"What about Stan Brewster? Was he a member of my father's church?"

"We haven't found his name listed, but what we have learned so far doesn't clear him either," Blalock added. "He had a job in California years back, but he came back here frequently to court Donna. When he married her, he took over her business operations and they've been on solid financial ground ever since."

"California . . ." she said. "So he's still a viable suspect," Ella said, lost in thought.

"One of many, Clah. We need to start narrowing things down."

"Yeah, I get you." Ella telephoned her brother next, but he didn't answer. Loretta worked in town, and their son, Julian, would be in school, and they didn't have an answering machine. When it rang and rang, that usually meant he was out in his ceremonial hogan or with a patient. "I need to talk to Clifford. Let's stop by his place and see if he's around," Ella told Justine.

Deep in thought, Ella allowed the silence between them to stretch out as they headed south down former Highway 666.

"You looked spaced out, cuz. Share?"

"I was looking over at Navajo Mountain, and remembered a story about Monster Slayer. When his enemies made weapons out of spruce and juniper and fired them at him, Monster Slayer planted them, and that's how the mountain became a place of protection for the *Diné*. Our people hid there when Kit Carson and the soldiers came looking for us. Now my brother goes up there to do Protectionways for our soldiers who go off to war," she said thoughtfully. "His link to the past and to our land is at the heart of everything he is and I think that makes him stronger, inside, than either my father or me."

"Just because you don't see Clifford bleed, doesn't mean he can't. Anyone can be hurt."

Ella stared at Justine for a long moment, her words sinking in. She hadn't been looking at this in the right light. Like her brother and her father, she took pride in what she did because she knew she was good at it. A betrayal that had touched her father personally could have only been the result of his having trusted the person first. Lori had pointed her in the right direction, but, until now, Ella hadn't realized how on the mark Lori had been.

"Stop and turn around. We need to go back to Blalock's office. I need some information."

They arrived at the small office complex soon thereafter. They found Blalock in Teeny's office, seated in front of what looked like a state-of-the-art computer.

"Anything?" she asked.

"No known felons on the lists—so far," Blalock said.

"Did my father's log mention anyone he was training—a deacon or preacher?"

"There are no names," Blalock answered. "Just letters sometimes, or nicknames he uses," Blalock said, gesturing toward the side table.

Ella nodded. That had been the Navajo in her dad. Despite his religion, her father had hated using names. Ella picked up her dad's daily log. The leather had cracked and the pages were wrinkled and weathered, but she knew her father's writing.

"Your father *did* mention a person he was forced to ask to leave the congregation. He called him *biyooch'idi*, if I'm pronouncing it correctly."

"Close enough. It means 'liar,' " Ella said.

As she stared at an indeterminate spot across the room lost in thought, Ella's skin began to prickle and the badger fetish at her neck became uncomfortably warm. Clifford had given her the badger fetish years ago. To date, she'd never managed to figure out how or what made it work, but the irrefutable fact was that the hotter the fetish became, the closer and more elevated the danger was.

Ella stepped out into the hall and looked around. Nobody was there. As she came back into the office, she heard a truck revving up outside in the parking lot. Yet that was scarcely reason for alarm.

Teeny glanced over at her. "You okay?"

"No," she replied in a taut voice. "Something's not right." The truck outside was racing now, getting closer.

Suddenly the entire building shook violently. Ella was knocked off her feet as the outside wall gave way with an ear-shattering crunch. Debris flew everywhere as the front end of a truck smashed into the room. Choking dust filled the air. Something heavy had fallen onto her legs, and she groaned in pain. Loud pops like the sound of glass breaking followed, and she covered her eyes instinctively.

Dazed, Ella tried to sit up and realized that the object pinning her to the floor was Blalock, who was flat on his back. "Blalock, get off me!" she yelled at him.

"I'm trying, woman!" He rolled over, and she struggled painfully to her knees. The room was in shambles, with overturned tables, shattered monitors, and sparks flying around.

"Can everyone move?" Teeny yelled, reaching down and helping Ella to her feet.

"Something's burning!" Ella yelled, pointing to the debris around the smashed truck. Black smoke was rising rapidly and filling the room.

Blalock, bleeding from his forehead, looked around the littered floor, then stooped to pick up some papers. "No time, FB-Eyes," Teeny yelled. "That truck's loaded with fuel. Haul ass, *now!*"

Blalock jumped over a collapsed table, stepped around a smashed computer, and lunged toward Justine, who'd managed to stand up. "Go!" He pushed her out into the hall.

Teeny reached for Ella, but she was already moving. As she stumbled through the doorway, he followed, close at her heels. Justine and Blalock were already at the far end of the hall, and Ella was sprinting to catch up when a clap of thunder and a wave of hot air swatted her in the back like a giant hand. She flew horizontally for a dozen feet, then slid on her belly across the waxed tile floor. Teeny, who'd been a step behind her, slammed into her legs, spinning her around completely.

Teeny's doorway—what was left of it—was a dragon's breath of flames and oily smoke from top to bottom, and the high-pitched wail of smoke alarms seemed to come at them from everywhere.

Blalock and Justine poked their heads around the corner. "Get up," Justine yelled, glancing back at them. "We have to get out of the building!"

Ella and Teeny untangled, and the four of them raced together to the entrance, and outside past the covered porch.

"Anyone else in there?" Ella asked, turning to Teeny, who was still trying to catch his breath.

He turned back toward the door, but Blalock stopped him before he could even take a step.

"Stay put!" Blalock shouted, pointing to three other people who'd left the building after them. They were huddled together staring at the burning truck, half in and half out of Teeny's office. "That's the rest of the tenants."

Ella studied the truck that had been used as a battering ram and realized it was an oil service truck. "Find cover!" she yelled to the office workers. "The truck's going to go!"

The trio ran, diving or ducking behind a van just as one of the fuel tanks on the back exploded. The tank arched across the blue sky like a rocket and landed in an open field a hundred yards from the highway, setting fire to some brush.

Ella groped for her cell phone, but Justine already had hers out, calling the fire department. Moving even farther from the building, they decided to join the people who were using the van for cover. Behind them, the building rumbled and groaned as the fire spread from office to office, engulfing everything in its path.

"No sprinkler system?" Justine asked.

Blalock, a handkerchief pressed against the cut on his head, cursed softly.

Teeny shook his head. "This is a pile of crap. I just upgraded every piece of hardware in my office. Now it's nothing but slag."

SIXTEEN

——— ✖ ✖ ✖ ———

It was close to 6 P.M. by the time the fire was finally put out. They were all battered and bruised and covered with soot, but Ella was determined to go back in as soon as they got the all-clear. They'd had irreplaceable evidence in there—the church records—and she needed to salvage whatever she could.

Teeny's massive fists curled and uncurled, his face contorted with rage. "When I catch the *shicho* who did this, I'm going to tear off his limbs and stick them where the sun don't shine."

Ella smiled. Like it was with most Navajo words, pronunciation was everything. By not accentuating the *o* or the last syllable, the meaning changed drastically. It went from the word "my" to the one for male genitalia. "He's ours, Teeny," she said quietly. "I want him in prison."

"You can have what's left. I'm not greedy," he answered.

Blalock joined them. The wound on his forehead had required stitches, but with the hospital not far away, he'd quickly been treated and released. "Think the tribal PD will let me set up temporary quarters at the station?"

"Sure," Ella answered. "You won't have an office to yourself, but you'll get a desk. Just ask Big Ed."

Justine stood by Ella's side. "Do you think we can salvage anything in there?"

"I doubt any of my hard drives survived that, and your paperwork is going to be toast," Teeny said. "With the intense heat . . . But I have a good safe with backups of my business files, and I save data to an online site, so it's not a total loss."

"I've got backups of my case files in my safe, too," Blalock said, "and nearly everything is backed on a Bureau server."

The fire marshal came up, interrupting Blalock. "I can let you all inside now, but watch your step and try to stay out of the way of my people. We're both going to have to work the scene at the same time."

Ella nodded, looking at his name tag. Thomas Denetsosie. He'd worked the fire with the crews, and was looking at them through weary eyes. "We'll be here till late sifting through everything. It looks like everyone got out in time, so hopefully we won't find any bodies," he said.

"It's a weekend," Blalock said. "I don't think anyone else was around."

"One person was. The custodian. We found . . . what was left of him," Denetsosie said. "It looks like he'd been climbing into the truck, trying to stop it, when it hit the wall."

There was nothing Ella could say. Hopefully, the tribe would be able to take care of the man's family. He'd died while trying to save lives and that made him a real hero in her eyes. "Let's get started," she said, heading back into the partially gutted building.

"Just keep your eyes open for anything that's still smoldering. We think we caught most of it, but you never know," Denetsosie said.

A half hour later they were still searching Teeny's gutted office using battery powered lanterns. Whatever was left of the papers or her father's journal had disappeared in the two-inch-deep watery residue on the floor, or been pasted like confetti on the seared walls.

"I don't think I can reconstruct any of the paperwork, Ella," Justine said. "There's just not enough of it left. And we'd have to be real lucky for the right information to have survived intact."

"The guy hot-wired the truck and jammed a board into the accelerator pedal," Blalock said in a tight voice. "He did his job well."

"Yeah, but we're going to do ours even better," Ella answered, determination weaving through every syllable.

"Count me in all the way on this one," Teeny said. "My services are on the house."

She nodded, then looked at Justine. "I'm going to leave you to work this scene. With luck, the truck itself will give us some answers. Right now, there's someone I need to see . . . after I get a clean change of clothes, that is."

It was already dark by the time she arrived at Clifford's home. As she switched off the engine, Clifford came out of the main house. "Don't come in," he said, walking up as she climbed out of her vehicle. "You've been around a death."

"How'd you know?" she asked, surprised. This had to be a new record.

"One of the firemen is from the same clan as my wife," he answered. "So am I right in assuming that the fire—and the attack on our mother—is connected to your work?"

"That would be my guess. That's why I've arranged for extra patrols around *Bizaadii*'s house."

"Good. The Fierce Ones have also offered their help. That's partly out of embarrassment over what happened the other day when one of them almost shot you," he said, then added, "I've heard that they're already trying to figure out what happened to Mom's sheep, too."

Ella groaned. "Just what I need. Help from a group who acts without information . . . or patience."

"Don't dismiss them so quickly. They might be able to restore harmony in ways your department never could."

Ella glared at her brother. "Are you taking the side of Boot's grandmother now, saying I'm just an arm of *bilagáana* law and what they do is somehow more justifiable?"

"That's *not* what I said," he answered. "There's good and there's harmony in what you do, but sometimes it isn't enough. All I'm telling you is that if you can find a way to work things out with them, you may discover they're useful allies."

"I choose allies I can count on, not ones who're as changeable as the weather."

He nodded slowly. "You have a point there."

"I can't give you any details, but I believe that the incident with Mom's sheep is connected to the murder case we're working on—the same one that led to that incident with the Fierce Ones."

"I've heard gossip that our father's church is somehow involved in what's happening, too."

"Involved . . ." Ella repeated thoughtfully. "I don't know if that's the right word, but they do feature in it," Ella said. "That's all I can tell you at this point."

Clifford insisted on doing a blessing over her, then gave her a new *jish* a medicine pouch, for her to carry. Ella didn't argue. She'd take any help she could get now.

After leaving her brother's, Ella drove to Herman and her mother's place over by Hogback, thirty minutes away by road. It was nearly nine now. Rose, who'd apparently heard her drive up, hurried out to meet her, a worried look on her face. "Are you okay?" she asked quickly, ushering Ella inside. "I heard all about what happened in Shiprock." She looked at the *jish* Ella had attached to her belt. "I'm glad you went to see your brother."

"This *jish* will help set a lot of people at ease," Ella explained, then took the cup of tea her mother offered. "Mom, I need you to think back. Did Dad ever try to train a successor? Another preacher to take over for him some day?"

"It's strange that you should ask me that," she said, wiping the kitchen counter before joining Ella at the table. "That passage of Scripture left with the sheep started me thinking."

Ella waited, knowing that the most important news often came while sitting around the kitchen table.

"Your father knew early on that his own son would never follow his ways. That's when he made the decision to bring in another Navajo minister who understood The People. He said it would be his legacy. But it wasn't an easy process. It took years for him to find someone he trusted enough, someone he thought would care about that church as much as he did."

"Who did he choose?"

"I haven't been able to remember his Anglo name . . . something biblical. But I do remember the name some Navajos gave him. It was *ha'asídí*. It means 'the watchman.' He got that because he was always watching people. That made *everyone* uncomfortable, even the Christians. *Ha'asídí* tried to explain it away saying that he liked to study people because there was always more to them than their words revealed. But I think he enjoyed making people uncomfortable. I told your father that once, but he said I was being too judgmental. I never said anything to him about it again."

"This *ha'asídí*. Is he still living around here?" Ella asked.

"I don't think so. Your dad and he had a falling out. Stories got back to us that *Ha'asídí* was telling parishioners that your father had dishonored the Christian God by marrying a heathen. Your father had a long talk with him, but it didn't do much good. Then the two began to disagree on almost every church issue. Not long after that, *Ha'asídí* started using Scripture to justify whatever he wanted to do. Your father lived by his beliefs, and that was a great offense to him."

"What happened?"

"Your father got the church elders together at a meeting and they voted *Ha'asídí* out of the church. I believe he left Shiprock soon afterward, but I'm not sure."

"Did he misuse any particular passages? Something you might remember?"

Rose thought back. "This man claimed that sinners had to

be punished here and now in order to save their souls. Your father disagreed, saying it was anti-Christian. Then your father learned *Ha'asídí* had beaten up a boy he'd caught writing graffiti on the outside wall of his print shop. Your father was furious then, on top of that, he found out that the man had been going around quoting a Bible passage that said whoever killed a man should be punished by man—or something like that. Your father just couldn't let that go and accused him publicly of promoting violence and undermining the church's reputation. He was stripped of his office and was never allowed to attend services again."

"Think back, Mom. Do you know of anyone who might remember *Ha'asídí*'s Anglo name?"

She shrugged. "No. But do you think he's returned, and is making trouble? What's here that he could possibly want?"

"That's a very good question." And an even better one was what all this had to do with Valerie Tso's murder.

"Do you know if *Ha'asídí* ever dated your friend's daughter?" Seeing the anger flash in Rose's eyes, she added, "Make that your former friend's daughter." Ella had deliberately avoided using Valerie's and Lena Clani's name out of respect for her mother's ways.

Rose considered it, then sighed. "I wish I could remember, but I don't. Talk to my former friend, if she's come to her senses and allows you in the door. She'll remember. Mothers do."

Ella left shortly after nine. It would be late by the time she arrived at Lena's, but Ella wasn't worried. Lena would be happy to know Ella was working overtime to find her daughter's killer.

Ella had just reached the main highway near Hogback when her cell phone rang. It was Justine.

"I've confirmed that the truck was rigged to crash into the wall and that a lit flare was thrown between two of the fuel containers. The truck itself belonged to one of the construction companies working at the power plant site. They reported it missing hours earlier. Neskahi talked to their security guard but, according to what he was told, no one saw anything. He'll follow up on that tomorrow."

"What about the truck itself? Any prints we can use?" Ella asked.

"It was scorched so badly there was no hope of finding any prints, but we got lucky anyway. The explosion blew the flare a hundred yards from the wreckage and I found some partial prints on that. We're running what we got now but we need at least eight identification points to really nail down any one individual and we don't have them."

"What about the church records? Did they survive?"

"No, but Teeny managed to remember some of the names on the list and he's checking those out now. That's the best we've got."

"Anything with a C?"

"Not that I remember from the list he made. Hang on and I'll take a look." Justine picked up the phone again a moment later. "No, nothing."

"Where are you? At the station?"

"Yeah, in the lab. I wanted to start processing the evidence immediately and I also needed a change of clothes. I could handle both here."

"How about I stop by and pick you up on the way to Lena Clani's?" Ella asked. "Right now she's unstable, so I'd like someone there as a witness in case things don't go as planned."

"Good idea. Last time, you needed backup, remember? I'll be in the lobby waiting."

Ella stopped by the station—about midway to Lena's—picked up Justine, and soon they were on their way again.

After Ella updated her, they drove in silence, lost in their own thoughts. Finally as they drew near Lena's home, Justine spoke. "Let me make sure I'm on the same track as you, Ella. In addition to this 'ladies' man' we've been trying to ID, you're adding your father's apprentice to our suspect list. You're now looking for a link between him and the victim that'll lead to an evidence trail. Is that the way it stacks up?"

"Exactly. We're missing a vital connection somewhere. Navajo ways say that everything in interrelated. I think that's particularly true in this case. Once we find that link we'll have the answers we need to catch the killer, whether he turns out to be the ladies man, the apprentice, or somebody else entirely."

SEVENTEEN

✖ ✖ ✖

Lena was outside on her small porch sitting on a bench when Ella pulled up. Lena stood, took a close look at their vehicle, then motioned for them to come inside. Nobody said a word.

Ella couldn't help but notice that the woman looked as if she'd aged twenty years since her daughter's murder. Lena had lost all energy in her step, and her back was hunched slightly. As they went into the living room, Ella noticed her reddened, swollen eyes and the dark circles under them.

"What are you doing to catch my daughter's killer?" Lena's tone made the question a half plea and half imperative demand.

After all the trouble Lena had caused, Ella was finding it difficult to be sympathetic. "Working very long hours, obviously. We're here now."

"How can I help you?"

Ella told Lena about the conversation she'd had with her mother. "Do you remember the man my mother mentioned?"

Lena nodded. "He *was* seeing my daughter. I disliked him intensely, which was probably why she insisted on seeing him. Part of growing up, I suppose. The problem, of course, was that he was also very handsome and knew just what words to say. Young women flocked to him and that fed his ego . . . which made him even worse."

"I need a name," Ella said.

"Your mother told you his nickname, right?"

Ella nodded. "I need his Anglo name."

"Calvin . . . no, Caleb . . . Frank, I think. He was a bad seed, that one. I remember he gave my daughter a nickname, one that I found particularly offensive. He called her his Turquoise Girl. I tried to explain to my daughter how disrespectful that was to the *Diné*'s Turquoise Girl. She inhabits Mount Taylor, one of our sacred mountains, and hers isn't a name that should be thrown around so casually," Lena said, then shaking her head, added, "I can tell you this much. I was really glad when his church kicked him out and he moved away."

"Thanks for the information. We appreciate it," Ella said.

"But this can't be the man who killed my daughter. He was as serious about religion as your father. They just had different ways of looking at it. As I said before, I think you should be looking at the Anglo who runs the diner. He was involved with my daughter and no one knows for sure where he was when she was killed. Some believe he was in the neighborhood that night."

"You're very well informed, but you don't have the whole story—and neither do we. Until we see how everything fits together, we won't know anything for sure." Ella gave Lena a physical description of the man she'd seen at the ditch. "Does that sound like Caleb to you?"

"Not really, except for the height. Caleb was handsome and took special pains with his appearance. And he was on the chunky side. But then again, it's been a long time since I last saw him. And scars can drastically change anyone's appearance."

When they reached the car, Ella glanced at Justine. "We have to run Caleb Frank's name through NCIC and VICAP. We should also talk to Reverend Curtis *before* he finds out that the church records went up in smoke. Maybe he can tell us about Caleb Frank now that we have a name."

"Tache is still at the station, I'll bet. He could run Caleb Frank for us while we pay Reverend Curtis a visit at the parsonage."

Ella called Ralph Tache and found him at his desk, still going through the evidence. "Did you get anything from the photos you took at the office complex?" Ella asked.

"Not yet. The building had outside surveillance cameras because of the Bureau office, but those went up with the building and no images survived. I do have some information on the prints Justine found. I ran them against our suspects and there are points matching Stan Brewster's. But before you get too excited, we have matching points that lead us to Reverend Campbell, too, and ten thousand other possible hits in the national database."

"Okay. Let that go for now. I've got a name I want you to run, a Navajo man in his forties or early fifties—Caleb Frank. I want everything you can get me on this guy."

"Everything?" Tache repeated. "If that's the case, you may be better off letting me pass this on to someone who can search data banks I'll never be able to access."

Ella was surprised to hear Teeny's voice in the background asking for the phone. A moment later he got on. "I'll get you what you need," Teeny assured her. "I got the name from Tache and I'm on it."

"But your computers . . ."

"The ones in my office are trashed, but I've got last year's technology in my Farmington office, and next year's at home."

"Go for it then. Let me know what you come up with as soon as you can."

"Will do."

It was ten-thirty by the time they pulled up in front of the church, but the lights were still on in the preacher's office. "Maybe we should have called, but I didn't want to give him time to prepare. Once people are on their guard, it's difficult to get anything useful out of them."

"Looks like he's still working, or someone else is," she said, pointing to the back office.

Ella and Justine walked down the side of the building and knocked on the back door to the office. Ella identified herself in a clear, loud voice for the benefit of anyone inside.

Moments later Reverend Curtis came to let them in. "I'm surprised to see you two here so late."

"We work long hours, as do you from the looks of it," Ella answered.

"I've been working on Sunday's sermon," he said and led them to his office. "By the way, I'm glad to see you two are safe. I heard on the radio about that fire at the government offices." He made himself comfortable in his chair and waved them to two others. "So tell me, what can I do for you?"

"We need to ask you about a man by the name of Caleb Frank. I understand he was part of this church during my father's time."

"Caleb . . ." he repeated, then shook his head. "I don't remember."

"Let me jog your memory. He and my father had some serious differences of opinion. I've gathered that he was very charismatic and liked to use Scripture to justify the need for retribution in the here and now."

He nodded slowly. "Yes, now I remember. He's the man I told you about earlier—*natzee*. There's a file on him somewhere, I think. Or it might be with the records you took."

"Unfortunately, the files we took are all gone, Reverend," Ella admitted reluctantly. "They were destroyed in the fire."

"Is that why someone crashed the truck through the wall? That would have made perfect sense if they hadn't wanted you to look at them," he said.

"What made you jump to that conclusion?" Ella asked instantly.

The preacher grew serious, then took a deep breath. "I've received a few phone calls from a man who refused to identify himself but warned me that I'd pay if I continued to cooperate with you," he said wearily. "In view of what happened at the Good Shepherd, I have to admit, it concerned me."

"I know the group who was responsible for what happened there. The threats you've received don't fit with their MO. Can you tell me more about these calls you've gotten?"

"There've been two, and both were quick and to the point. He doesn't want me, or this church, to cooperate with you in any way."

"Did you hear any background noises when you spoke to him?" Ella pressed.

He thought about it. "Not that I could tell."

"When did you get the first call?"

"A few hours after I gave you the paperwork, and I told him, he was too late. Then I got one more call after that, warning me that I shouldn't give you anything else."

Ella and Justine exchanged glances.

"The man the other day, the one across the ditch. Could he have been the same man who made those calls to you?" Ella asked. "And do you think that man might have been Caleb Frank?"

"You know, the voice was a good match to that of the man we spoke to across the ditch. But I haven't seen *natzee* since I was a kid. I wouldn't know him even if I ran into him," he said then paused. "Caleb Frank . . ." he repeated thoughtfully. "You know, I think I've seen that name recently." He glanced around the office, lost in thought.

As Justine shifted in her seat, her elbow collided with the file cabinet.

The reverend's gaze shifted and suddenly he smiled. "I remember now. Your father started our heretical prophets file. That's still in this office. I came across it the other day when I was shifting files around."

"The what file?" Ella asked.

"It's a file with the names of people who are a threat to this church or the Scriptures. I should warn you that some of the people included in it are preachers from other churches, so it's not like a criminal file. Over the years we've added names to it but, overall, it's a very small file." He went to a file cabinet near the corner of the room then, after a brief search, pulled out a manila folder and handed it to Ella. "I will make one request. Considering what happened to the ones you borrowed before, could you look at this here?"

Ella nodded. "That's not a bad idea, Reverend."

Ella studied the contents of the folder. Toward the back, she found several handwritten letters made out to her father and signed by Caleb Frank.

"Our former church secretary mentions in there that the police came here after your father was murdered. They apparently saw that file but, at the time, they already had a suspect in mind."

Ella nodded, remembering that her brother Clifford had been their prime suspect. Working quickly, Ella searched all the papers in the file for any mention of Stan Brewster, but there was nothing there on him.

"Thanks," she said, handing the file back. "Is there anything else my father might have left behind?"

Reverend Curtis thought about it. "The burial records for his time here, maybe?"

"Can I see them?"

"It's just a list of everyone who was buried in our cemetery and what plot they occupy."

"I'd still like to see it," Ella insisted.

He nodded, then stepped over to a large walk-in closet. "We access these records from time to time though they go back fifteen years or more. But what earthly good could they possibly do you?"

"I'm not sure," Ella said. "Give me a chance to study them."

Ella and Justine examined the lists carefully, but there was nothing that caught their attention. Then Ella saw Dorothy Yabeny's name, read the small annotation beside it, and then pointed it out to Justine. "Apparently her family brought her body back and requested she be buried here," Ella said. "I didn't see that in the police reports." She glanced at the Reverend. "Do you know where we can reach the victim's mother?"

He nodded. "I'll get you her address. She lives north of Shiprock, about halfway to the Colorado state line."

After they left, Justine glanced at her. "It's close to midnight, boss," Justine said, "and we shouldn't go waking up people this time of night to ask them about their dead daughter. What do you say we get some sleep first?"

Before Ella could answer, their radio came alive. "SI One, you're needed at the new power plant's construction site. Backup's on the way."

"Ten-four, Dispatch. What's going down?"

"The night watchman needs help. His call was garbled, but we think he said something about skinwalkers."

"We're on our way."

"Skinwalkers?" Justine spun the unit around and headed for the turnoff to the site. "We haven't had any problems with that kind of stuff in ages—not that I've heard about anyway."

"We're going in silent. I don't want to scare the troublemakers off," Ella said. "I wonder if this is a new angle the protesters have come up with to scare off the crew."

When they arrived at the guardhouse, a big metal shed hauled in since their last visit, a portly Navajo man came out running, clearly spooked. "You got a *jish* with you?"

"A medicine bag?" Ella studied the man's face. The illumination from the two floodlights attached to the building was minimal, but she could tell he was terrified just from the sound of his voice. Ella pointed down to her belt and the small leather bag that hung from it.

"Good. It may help." He looked at her holster and added, "But that probably won't."

"Why don't you tell us what happened?" she said, perceiving that there was no immediate threat.

"It's *them*. They're cursing the place. The other Navajos in the crew, even the modernists, once they find out . . ."

Justine's gaze took in the area around them, and Ella noted that she was still keeping her hand close to her weapon.

"Over there," he said pointing, Navajo style, by pursing his lips. "Where the forms are going in for the footings and foundation."

"Are we still talking skinwalkers?" Justine asked him, not seeing anyone.

"Don't say the word out loud," he said, stepping away from her. "You call them to you that way."

"Sorry," Justine said quickly. "Wasn't thinking."

"Yeah, no kidding," he muttered.

Ella walked in the direction he'd pointed, then stopped at the edge of the fenced perimeter. It was still locked and the openings in the chain link fencing were too small to give anyone a climbing foothold. Beyond, was a deep, dark pit, and the vague outline of a vast network of metal forms and stacks of rebar. Closer, on the ground beside the first stack of reinforcing rods, she saw what appeared to be a very small severed hand.

"Oh, crap," Justine muttered almost simultaneously.

"We need to get in there. Key?" Ella asked the night watchman.

He fished it out his pocket and tossed it at her, remaining well back. "Stay away from the pit. You fall in there, you're dead."

Ella passed through the gate, breathing through her mouth as she drew closer. The flesh was shriveled and decomposed, and there were bugs on it now, feeding or laying eggs. "This isn't from someone who died recently," she said crouching by the body part, "but we'll need to get an ID. This is the hand of a young child. Get our people out here," she added, suppressing a shudder.

"The construction crew won't report to work if they find out about this, so my boss asked that you try and keep a lid on what's happened," he called out, cell phone still in hand.

"Stuff like this doesn't stay under wraps long," Ella warned.

Justine called the crime scene team, then joined Ella, who was already searching the ground with a powerful flashlight. "There's got to be half a million boot prints around here, not to mention all kinds of heavy equipment tracks," Justine said.

"Yeah," Ella said, refusing to be discouraged. "And a hundred discarded soda cans and food wrappers. But stay at it. I'm going to try and get more details from the night watchman." Ella turned her head and noticed that he was staying as far back as he could without getting out of earshot.

"So tell me what happened?" Ella asked, going over to join the man, whose name tag identified him as Albert Benally.

"I heard some really weird chanting, so I went to the window and looked outside. I saw a shadow—just darkness moving in darkness, really—and then, in an instant, it vanished. Just like that," he said, snapping his fingers. "I'm not superstitious," he added, "but this creeps me out. Particularly that," he said, gesturing toward the hand. "Even those dudes in the Anglo world who say they aren't afraid of nuttin' would get a little crazy around body parts, you know?"

"Sure," Ella said. She was willing to bet that it wouldn't take much to get Mr. Benally to quit his job altogether now.

"They give you a Taser or a nightstick?" Ella asked, glad he wasn't carrying a pistol. His training was obviously nonexistent.

"Naw, just that spray," he pointed to a cannister of pepper spray on the windowsill. "Probably only works on roaches. Besides, who wants to get close enough to use it? My job was just to watch the place and call for help if I saw anything." He avoided looking in the direction of the severed hand. "I called."

Officer Tache and Sergeant Neskahi arrived shortly thereafter. Joe was in jeans and a Chieftains sweatshirt—the local high school team—and Tache in khaki pants and a long-sleeved T-shirt. He had to be cold, but he'd shrugged out of his jacket so he could work without being encumbered. Navajos seldom needed a shave, so even at the late hour, their faces were smooth.

"I've cordoned off a perimeter and I've called the ME," Justine said. "She told me that one of us would have to deliver the severed hand to the morgue once we get enough photos. She's working on something else right now."

It didn't surprise her to hear Carolyn was still at the hospital. Carolyn was as dedicated to her job as they were to theirs. When your passion and what you did for a living were one and the same, they often combined forces and took over your life. She wasn't sure if that was good or bad, just that it was so.

"This entire area is fenced off, so we need to find his point of entry," Ella said.

Justine glanced over at Neskahi, who was setting up flood-lights to illuminate the perimeter defined by the yellow crime scene tape. As usual, Tache would be photographing the scene. "I walked all the way around the pit, and I didn't see anything but more work site refuse," Justine said. "If you want us to pick up every soda can or wrapper, we'll need some trash bags, too."

"How far down is the hole?" Ella asked.

"I shined my flashlight down there and it looks like fifty feet or more. The reactor vessel is supposed to be pretty small, if I recall the details from the newspaper, and they'll install it using a crane," Justine said, then in a softer voice added, "If anyone fell in, they're probably dead."

"How about if we hook up a searchlight to the generator and search below as far as we can—after we check at ground level. There was supposedly only one intruder," Ella said.

The search around the perimeter continued and they left anything that looked like trash in place for the moment. Ella contacted Dispatch to see if there had been any reports of grave robbing in the county, but the answer came back negative. Of course it was after midnight, and that just meant it probably hadn't been discovered yet. Seconds later, her cell phone rang. It was Big Ed.

"Shorty, we have a report of a grave broken into at Good Shepherd cemetery. The bad news is that Reverend Campbell closed the casket and covered it up again before he even thought of calling us. According to what he said, the body was that of a girl of six."

"When did she die?" Ella asked.

"Ten months ago in a car accident. The family's moved away since then and no one knows how to contact them. Officer Cloud filed the report but, basically, all we have is that the caretaker heard someone outside. Unfortunately, he was drunk at the time and passed out shortly thereafter. By the time he woke up it was over. Officer Cloud said the man was totally useless as a witness," Big Ed added.

"I'll look into it and give you a full report once I have more," Ella said, then hung up. Ella was about to go back and finish questioning the night watchman when her cell phone rang again. It was Teeny.

"I've got some bits of information for you. Come by whenever you can."

"I can drop by later, but it'll be closer to morning by then."

"I don't sleep much," he said. "Come by whenever."

Ella still wasn't sure how he did it, but the big man didn't seem to need as much rest as most people did. On the other hand, when he wasn't working, Teeny was known to hole up and sleep for days. She'd teased him about being part bear.

At Justine's request, Ella helped her team search for a point of entry, walking slowly around the fence line, looking over the chain link carefully. "It's possible we're dealing with someone with very tiny feet," Ella said after they'd gone around once.

"You'd have to be a size four or smaller to get it into these ultrasmall holes on the wire mesh," Justine said. "I'm a size five and I couldn't manage it."

"Well, the intruder didn't just materialize in there, so let's keep looking," Ella said.

As she moved around the fence line, the flashlight beam fell on a droopy-looking section leading into a corner. It immediately caught Ella's eye and she moved in closer, holding the flashlight, and studied the fenced section. It had been cut all the way down, then fastened back into position with wire hooks, undoubtedly after the intruder had stepped back outside the enclosure. "Guys, over here."

Neskahi crouched next to her. "Smart guy. All he needed were wire cutters, a pair of pliers, and a dozen or so ready-made wire hooks. He hung the fence back up again after he left. That's why we didn't see it before. A lot of places in this fence are droopy."

"He crept in and out," Justine noted, "and this was far enough away from the guardhouse that the snip of wire cutters probably wasn't heard at all. But how did the watchman spot the skinwalker? It's pretty dark out here, and this must be two hundred yards from his little building."

"Good question. While you guys keep working here, he and I are going to have another little talk."

Ella found Albert Benally on the front stoop of his temporary building. He had a cup of steaming coffee in his hands, and she noticed that they were shaking.

"It's cold tonight," he said, following her gaze. "Want a cup?"

"No, thanks," Ella answered, noting how nervous the man was.

"How long have you been working here?" Ella asked.

"Not long. I hired on just after that last protest. One of the old guys quit after having to chase some people around for a half hour."

Ella nodded. "We found how the intruder got inside the fence. He cut the wire way down at the other end, then slipped through. Which brings up a question. How did you discover he was in there? The glare of the lights hide everything beyond the fence."

He seemed uncomfortable and shifted from side to side. "Actually, he found me," he admitted grudgingly. "I was listening to a Lakers home game on the radio—gone into overtime, great game—and something hit the roof and rolled down. I turned off the radio then and listened. That's when I heard the chanting. At first I thought it was my fool of a cousin playing a joke on me, so I went outside."

"It was very dark. How did you manage to see anything at all?"

"I didn't—at first. I didn't have my flashlight, I'd left it in my truck, so I didn't go beyond the range of the floodlights. Then I heard someone laughing. That, the chanting and running around in the dark, well, that's a skinwalker thing. I went back and got my flashlight and when I aimed it through the fence, I saw the hand," he said and swallowed. "I ran back here double time."

"You a traditionalist?" she asked.

"No, but you don't have to be a rocket scientist to know that messing around with the dead is a real bad idea."

He had a point. Some crossed themselves, others backed off, but nobody wanted to hang around something death had contaminated.

Ella contacted Justine on the radio. "This might just be another attempt by the protesters to halt work on the plant, but just in case, keep a watch for ashes, bone ammunition, corpse powder, and anything else associated with skinwalkers," she said, then focused her attention on Albert once more. "Tell me something. Once you found the hand, that's when you called us? Or was it before that?"

Albert looked decidedly uncomfortable. "When I saw the hand I ran back here and locked myself in. I picked up the night vision binoculars, turned off the lights, and watched out the window trying to figure out who—or what—was out there. But what I managed to see didn't make much sense."

"Explain."

"The guy was inside the enclosure, closer to this end of the fence. I couldn't figure out how he'd gotten over the eight-foot wire, because it was still up." He shifted uncomfortably and rubbed the back of his neck with one hand. "Then I saw him open a pouch of something, throw it up into the air, and scatter it all over the place. Right after that, he stretched his hand to the sky and twirled something."

"What was he wearing?"

"A jacket with a hood and pants. No animal skin. I would have expected that. With that green image in the night scope, everything looks a little distorted, though."

"Then you stopped watching him and called us?" Ella asked.

"Yeah. But by the time I dialed, he was gone."

"How did you know he was gone?"

"I heard a car or truck driving off. Probably a truck, now that I think about it."

"In what direction?" Ella said. Maybe they'd be able to find tire tracks.

"To the south, *not* toward the highway. I remember because I thought it was strange. I mean there's nothing out there."

Ella got Albert's home address and telephone number in case she had to talk to him again. "We'll want to talk to you again so don't leave the area without telling us," she added.

"Leave? Where to? I can't go nowhere. Don't have the bucks. That's why I took this job. But I'm quitting as soon as the sun comes up."

"We'll be in touch," Ella said, then went back outside.

Justine met her. "I've got some kind of ashes, bone fragments, and other stuff besides the hand. And we haven't been able to lift any prints from the fence posts."

"I'm going to check out the area where Albert says he heard a vehicle driving off."

Ella walked out in a line directly toward the mesa to the south. Hogback was to the west but beyond was open desert with dirt roads between some low-production oil wells and a few remote houses. Finally she discovered a set of fresh-looking tire tracks, probably from a pickup or SUV judging from the size. She continued walking, but the tracks simply stopped. Ella crouched by the ground. This didn't make sense.

The breeze was picking up. Wind whispered secrets but

right now she could hear nothing, except the threat of evidence disappearing. She walked a little farther and something on the ground caught her eye. It looked familiar and as she crouched down for a closer look, she immediately understood why. It was her shirt—or the right sleeve of her shirt to be precise—bundled up in bailing wire. She'd discarded it in the outside trash at Justine's after the fire at the office complex. Someone had retrieved it, cut the sleeve off, bundled it up, then covered it with grayish ashes of some kind.

It was a clear threat. A skinwalker used personal items to work evil. But obviously the person didn't know her very well. This didn't frighten her—it just pissed her off.

She called Justine and Tache over. As they worked the evidence, Justine glanced up at her. "Let me guess. This is a piece of the shirt you were wearing earlier at Teeny's?"

"Yeah. I'd placed it outside in your trash barrel. But what worries me now is that this proves he knows where I'm staying—which means you and Emily are in danger, too."

"Let him take us on. It'll be fun," Justine answered with a lethal smile.

Ella understood. Emily would undoubtedly react the same way. None of them were the kind to back away from trouble. For the first time since she'd started working the case, she was glad she wasn't at home and that Dawn wasn't with her.

EIGHTEEN

✖ ✖ ✖

Anyone look familiar?"
Dwayne Blalock whispered, looking down from their perch inside the cab of a big yellow loader at the group of construction workers gathered about fifty feet away. Both were disguised in coveralls and wearing hard hats.

Ella yawned, having slept less than three hours before Blalock had called, suggesting they stake out Clifford's purification ceremony. FB-Eyes wanted to be there in case Leroy, Caleb Frank, or whoever had caused last night's trouble decided to return for another round.

She knew, in spite of the cliché, that perps, especially vandals, often *did* return to the scene of the crime to survey their handiwork. But it was barely sunrise, and if not for the coffee Blalock had provided, she'd have been half asleep right now.

"Looks like just the workers showed up. I recognize several faces," she finally answered. "But the one they called Leroy isn't here."

"He's gotta be Caleb Frank. Wish you'd let me use my camera."

Ella shook her head. "My brother consented to let us watch, but he's serious about his profession, and he needs us to show the proper respect for this Navajo ceremony."

"What was the stuff in the little pouches he handed out

when the workmen arrived?" Blalock whispered.

"It's gall medicine, which provides protection, especially against witchcraft. The medicine is made from the gall of an animal, like a bear, deer, skunk, mountain lion, or, less likely these days, an eagle. I think there's corn or pollen in it, too."

"And only a Navajo skinwalker would be messing with body parts, like that girl's hand, right?" Blalock replied.

"Yeah, or someone pretending to be one," Ella replied, looking down and taking a sip of coffee.

As Clifford had begun to chant, she kept her eyes on the workers, trying to spot any potential sources of trouble.

She wasn't a traditionalist, but Ella always enjoyed the complicated rhythmic and tonal patterns of a Navajo Sing. The prayer had to be perfect, and Clifford's voice was clear and strong. It was a Singer's knowledge that gave him power to call down the aid of the gods. The result would be certain if the prayers that compelled the gods were done just right. Clifford's skill as a *hataalii* would insure protection for those who intended to remain and work here. Ella noted that even the few Anglo workers present were watching and listening intently. She felt the power inherent in the Sing, and knew the Navajo workers standing around in their work clothes and hard hats were similarly affected. A few clutched medicine pouches in their hands.

A half hour later, after the final blessing and scattering of corn pollen, Clifford nodded to one of the Anglo workers, who climbed up into a loader identical to the one Ella and Blalock were in.

The engine started, and after warming up a moment, the loader lurched forward. Clifford pointed to a spot, and the big scoop came down, taking a big bite out of the ground. The loader turned, moved a hundred feet over to a dump truck, and dropped the collected dirt inside.

"That's where the hand was found, right?" Blalock asked, speaking normally to be heard above the noise.

She nodded. "Contaminated ground to some. Even though

it's been cleansed by the *hataalii*, the earth is going to be taken off the Rez by non-Navajos," Ella replied.

Clifford then turned to the gathered crowd, assuring them in Navajo and English that it was now safe to work there.

As the gathering dispersed, Ella glanced at Blalock. "It's finished. Time for us to move on, too."

Ella returned to Justine's place to find Emily and Justine both in the kitchen. A pot of freshly brewed coffee between them, they looked as if they'd been talking for a while.

"Well, FB-Eyes and I didn't find any bad guys at the construction site. But it was worth a shot. What's up here?" Ella asked, though she already suspected the answer.

"I told Emily about the shirt and ashes," Justine said. "I thought she should know. Though I haven't had a chance to analyze the ashes and determine their origin, the threat was clear."

"So what have you decided? Do you want me to move out?" Ella asked.

"Are you nuts?" Emily countered instantly. "You're staying. If three officers can't handle one sicko, then we might as well turn in our badges and take up needlepoint."

Justine laughed. "I don't know about the needlepoint thing, but I'm with her. We just have to play it smart and come up with a plan so we don't get ambushed at night."

"Agreed," Ella said, "but we can't expect our PD to be much help on this. We have a serious manpower shortage and I already have officers on my daughter and my mother."

"I know. That's why we were thinking of accepting Teeny's offer," Justine said.

"Teeny? What's he got to do with this?" Ella asked, joining them at the table.

"He called while you were out," Justine answered. "He's worried about you. He'd heard about the shirt."

"How . . . ?" She shook her head. "Never mind. So what was his offer?"

"He wants to put some of his own employees on the job and have them watch this place at night. He also wants to update our locks and put in the kind of alarm that'll alert his system. That way if there's a break-in, he'll know instantly."

"I don't know if we can afford . . ."

Before Ella could finish, Justine said. "Big Ed has approved the funding already, and the locks will appear as a short-term rental on the books."

"He was up early. What time is it?" Ella looked at the clock. It was a quarter to eight. "Did *you* guys get any sleep?"

Justine shrugged. "I can't speak for Em, but I figure I got three hours tops. I just couldn't get the image of that little girl's hand out of my mind," she added softly.

"So what's with this skinwalker creep?" Emily asked Ella. "Did he think you'd fall apart or something?"

"If I'm right, his goal was just to sidetrack our murder investigation. I can't prove it yet, but I think the guy was Caleb Frank pretending to be a skinwalker."

Justine gave her an owlish blink. "So this had nothing to do with the power plant issue?"

"No. The guy across the ditch all but admitted he was the one who threw the clod at me and tried to get a fight started at the last demonstration. His problem is related to me, my father, and the Divine Word Church. That all points to Caleb Frank," Ella answered. "I just wish I had a photo of that guy."

"Me, too. But when it comes to Valerie Tso's murder, my money's still on Stan Brewster." Justine stood, having finished breakfast. "Ready to go whenever you are."

Ella grabbed one of the breakfast bars from the table. "What's your schedule today, Emily?"

"I'm working the swing shift," she said. "I'll be here if Teeny or his people come by."

Ella and Justine were underway moments later. "Teeny's working from home because it's closer to Shiprock, so head there," Ella said.

"That place of his really creeps me out," Justine answered

as they hit the main highway. "I feel like I'm going to step on a land mine or something."

Ella shook her head. "If there's one place in the planet where you and I are totally safe, it's at Teeny's."

When they reached the fenced perimeter just outside Teeny's home, Justine glanced around. "Wow. He's added more security," she said, pointing to the cameras.

"Ladies, the fence will open up in a second for you." Teeny's voice came from a speaker.

They went inside Teeny's home moments later. Sophisticated computer equipment on sturdy wooden tables covered much of the floor space in the living room. A lot of the hardware wasn't at all familiar to Ella.

"Word about what happened last night is spreading like wildfire," Teeny said. "The skinwalker issue complicates everything. People are afraid that the ground has been contaminated and if the power plant is built there, it'll only bring evil."

Ella nodded. "Before the protestors tried to claim it was holy ground. Now they'll say it's cursed. What's worse is that this all took place right next to where the reactor vessel is going to be installed."

"What concerns me most is the threat—using your shirt and the ashes. That was directed at *you*, personally," Teeny said, never making eye contact with her. "So, skinwalker or not, his days of freedom are numbered. You've got a lot of friends, and we'll be there to watch your back."

Ella knew that not looking directly at her was a Navajo sign of respect, and his words and gesture touched her. "Thanks. It's good to have buddies I can count on when the going gets rough."

"Don't give it another thought. You're covered," he said gruffly, and then turned his attention back to the computer. "I've been trying to get something on Caleb Frank for you. But here's the thing. I've got zero—no driver's license, no birth record, nothing. So either that's not his real name, or he's existed under the radar all his life. Mind you, that's not uncommon among Navajos who were born at home and grew up on the Rez. And people can change their Anglo names."

"So what now? Any suggestions?" Ella asked.

"We move on until we get something new. I'll be sending some people over to your house today," he added, glancing at Justine. "By the time we're through, the guy will have to be invisible to get anywhere near you three."

"Thanks. We appreciate it," Justine answered.

Soon they were on their way to the station. "Partner, I'm going to need you to find out where those ashes came from," Ella said. "Specifically, I want to know if they have a biological origin."

"You're thinking corpse powder?" Justine asked somberly.

Ella nodded. They were both seasoned police officers able to take most crimes in stride, but things like these were in a category all their own. They'd encountered skinwalkers— Navajo witches—on other occasions, and experience warned them not to dismiss the power of rituals just because science didn't sanction them.

"I'll get on it immediately. But skinwalkers are also known to use ashes taken from a killed hogan. Pine ashes are pine ashes, and we wouldn't know the source," Justine said.

Ella nodded. A killed hogan was one where a death had taken place. They were usually easy to spot because of the hole on the side of the structure. "I'm just trying to determine how dedicated to the ritual he really was." Anything directly connected to the dead had more power than something that was merely associated with it.

After they reached the station, Justine went directly to her lab and Ella to her office. They'd been working for a little over an hour when Big Ed called for a meeting.

Less than twenty minutes later, Ella and Justine entered the chief's office. The rest of their team was already assembled there, waiting.

Big Ed gestured for them to take a seat, then leaned back. "I want a full report on the Special Investigations Team's progress. Go," he said, giving Ella a nod.

Ella filled him in on everything she'd learned so far. "But Teeny can't find anything on Caleb Frank."

"If he can't find it, it's not there," Big Ed said.

"We're still trying to pin down Brewster's alibi. Marco Pete said that the man might have been at Valerie's apartment that night."

Big Ed nodded. "So what's your next step?"

"I'm going to talk to Dorothy Yabeny's relatives. I want to find out if they remember anything that might help us. In particular, I want to find out if she was seeing Caleb Frank, or anyone who matches his description."

"What else have you got on the truck that was used to torch the office building?" Big Ed asked, looking at Justine.

"The perp stole it from a locked construction area reserved for vehicles of all kinds," Justine answered.

"A locked area . . ." Ella repeated, an idea forming in her head.

Tache sat up. "I bet we're dealing with a construction worker with access to keys, like one of the foremen?"

Ella nodded. "I just had the same thought. Get me that list," she said to Tache.

Big Ed looked at Justine. "What specifics have you got on the little package the skinwalker left for Shorty?"

Ella looked at Justine, eager for answers as well.

"The ashes on the shirt, as well as what he scattered beside the foundation pit, were from cured lumber, not cottonwood or peeled pine logs like those used to construct hogan walls. Traces of green dye, the kind used to mark grades of lumber, were found in the analysis."

"That suggests we're probably not dealing with a skinwalker at all. Just someone who wanted to create that impression, and cause more trouble at the work site," Big Ed said thoughtfully.

"Chief, the last two instances seem to have been instigated by the same individual, and not Benjamin Harvey. The guy with the camera that nobody seems able to identify is definitely out to create problems and might be our bogus skinwalker as well."

"The guy with the hat and sunglasses—maybe the same guy who was at the church. Right, Ella?" Justine asked.

She nodded. "I have a feeling that his real goal is to slow down the murder investigation by making sure he keeps us running in circles."

"Which suggests he's either the killer, or someone trying to protect him." Big Ed was about to say more when his phone rang. His expression darkened as he listened to the caller. "She'll be there," he said, then hung up.

"We have a potential situation at the construction site," Big Ed continued, looking at Ella. "I thought your brother did a protection ceremony there this morning."

"Blalock and I were there, and it seemed to go fine. What's up now?"

"That was Benjamin Harvey, the spokesman for the demonstrators. He needs to know what we've learned about last night—if it's a real skinwalker or just some sick guy trying to pit the demonstrators against the workers again. Benjamin apparently got a call from the same guy, John, who tried to start a riot last time, the guy we were just discussing, who was more than willing to fill him in. He apparently called others, too. Benjamin doesn't trust him so he's going to hold off talking to the workers until he meets with you, Shorty."

"If Benjamin had been there this morning, he'd already know what is going on. But I'll brief him on things, and see if he can get his people calmed down. Whoever's behind this knows how powerful fear can be in creating disharmony—and in keeping the department tied up," Ella said.

"Go ahead, Ella, and see if we can finally put a stop to this nonsense," Big Ed said.

Ella glanced at Justine. "You're coming with me this time.

Bring a copy of your report on the evidence this wannabe skin-walker left behind," Ella said.

"You gonna need backup?" Joe Neskahi asked.

"If we're lucky, only the *hataalii* kind," Ella answered. "Would you get hold of my brother and ask him to come back to the site?"

"Good thinking, Shorty. If he can't convince the skeptics that it's safe, a lot of Navajos are going to be giving up their jobs. And those who stay might be in danger. Frenzy Medicine, you know," Big Ed said. "There's a rumor about that starting up."

"Frenzy Medicine. That's bad," Ralph Tache whispered.

Ella nodded somberly.

NINETEEN
✖ ✖ ✖

Ella and Justine left for the construction site immediately while the team remained at the station, processing evidence but ready to back them up, if necessary.

"Okay, spill it," Justine said. "I've heard the term before but what exactly is Frenzy Medicine?"

Ella expelled her breath in a hiss. "My mother told me about this once. Frenzy Medicine is part witchcraft and part science. It's said to be brought on by a mixture of plants, one being Datura, that's sprinkled on people's food, or on their bodies, to make them act crazy. The suggestion that a skinwalker might use it on the workers who stay is going to heighten fear and complicate things even more."

"And there'll be some who'll say that anyone who shows up for work anyplace a skinwalker cursed is already crazy or bewitched—a victim of Frenzy Medicine. Am I close?"

"Yeah, this kind of things feeds off itself. I need to let everyone who wasn't there earlier know that my brother did a Shield Prayer, and that insures no one there's going to be bewitched."

When they arrived at the turnoff leading to the construction site, Ella was relieved to see Benjamin Harvey standing by his pickup, alone. From the dust in the distance, work was continuing, at least for the moment.

She climbed out of the department vehicle, along with Justine, who'd brought a clipboard with copies of her paperwork.

"*Yáat'ééh,*" Benjamin said to Ella, then nodded to Justine, who nodded back.

"Since you showed respect for our concerns, the people here trust you. I need you to tell me exactly what we're up against. What was a you-know-what doing here? What's the construction got to do with their kind? I've already been told that a *hataalii* was here at sunrise, but the workers who came later missed out on that. I need someone who doesn't sign their paychecks to reassure them with some straight answers. Give me something to tell them they can believe."

Ella noted that Benjamin was being careful. Just saying the word "skinwalker" was believed to call them to you. She turned to Justine. "Tell him, in nontechnical terms, what we found out."

Justine nodded. "I have the results of the chemical analysis we ran on the ashes found here the other night. They came from wood, as in the type that comes from a lumber yard, not from a hogan, killed or otherwise, and certainly not from any person or animal. The security guard here last night speaks our language, too, and after questioning, was able to confirm that the chanting he heard was nonsense, made-up sounds mostly, not Navajo songs."

"How do you know what sounds a real you-know-what makes during a ritual?" Benjamin asked.

"I've heard them myself, and they're distinctive," Ella admitted softly. "You never forget something like that, believe me."

Benjamin nodded somberly. "I see you're wearing a *jish.*" He glanced down at the medicine bag she'd attached to her belt.

"Do you have one?" Ella asked.

"In my pocket," he answered. "I have one more question about last night. What about that . . . hand? That was for real, wasn't it? Has the site really been cleansed of the contamination?"

Ella answered him. "Here are the facts. The hand was stolen from a grave and placed here. It's gone now, and will be returned to the cemetery later. But a *hataalii*, my brother, was here at daybreak, gave everyone gall medicine for protection, and conducted a Shield Prayer. Under his counsel, even the contaminated soil was removed with a piece of heavy equipment, and buried in a mined-out area off the Navajo Nation. The company brought in an Anglo crew to do the work. The equipment was blessed and also removed. There should be no danger now."

Benjamin said nothing, but he still looked worried.

"I've asked my brother to come back, talk to the men, and provide extra protection to anyone who feels they need it," Ella added, "especially those who weren't here when he sang the prayer. But what happened here was mostly staged—like it was with the fake pottery. Someone, possibly the same man who called you and others hoping to stir things up, wants people to be afraid. He might have been the one pretending to be—an evil one," she said at last. "But pretend magic can't harm anyone."

Ella had just sat down at her desk when her phone rang. Teeny's deep voice reverberated through the wire. "I've got some news for you. Once I hacked into the New Mexico Bureau of Revenue and Taxation gross receipts records—whoops, forget I said that—I discovered that our man had a print shop in Farmington eleven years ago. Caleb Frank would do notices and things like that for the church, giving them a discount in exchange for free advertising. But he shut his business down six months after it opened, and then dropped off the face of the earth. He stiffed a lot of people when he bailed, too, including the state of New Mexico."

"If he disappeared like that, then chances are he probably changed his name and took on an entirely new identity," Ella said.

"Yeah, that's what I thought, too, so I've got my people asking around about him. Maybe someone will remember something that'll give us a lead to his current whereabouts."

"I need you to check on something else for me. Look into the backgrounds of the victims in L.A. and Kayenta. See if either woman had children, and if they did, I want their addresses."

"What are you after?"

"A link between those two women and Valerie."

"So you're thinking that they might have had kids who went to the same reservation school, something like that?"

"Yeah. Like that. It's a long shot, I know, but give it a shot."

"You've got it."

Ella had just hung up when her phone rang and Big Ed called her to his office.

Ella joined him moments later, and took the chair by his desk.

"Anything new to report?" he asked her.

She told him about her conversation with Teeny. "I'm just playing a hunch."

"It sounds worth pursuing," he said with a nod. He regarded her for a moment then continued in a somber voice. "You need to go pay your brother a visit."

Ella sat up abruptly. "Has something happened?"

"He's safe, so breathe easy," Big Ed said quickly, "but while he was at the construction site talking to the workers, someone trashed his medicine hogan."

"That's got to be the work of that wannabe skinwalker. I'd bet on it," Ella said firmly. "No normal Navajo would hassle a *hataalii,* particularly one of my brother's stature."

"He filed a report, and a patrolman who went over said that there wasn't much by way of evidence. It went down as vandalism."

"Footprints?"

"Rubbed out with a branch. But go take a look."

It was a cloudless afternoon as she drove to her brother's place. The high plateau seemed to stretch out in all directions, and seeing the vastness helped her relax. She'd always been uncomfortable in the city, where views were restricted by masses of buildings. There'd been a time when she'd told herself that she was a new-generation Navajo, and she needed to experience urban life. Yet, in the long run, there hadn't been enough on the outside to keep her away from the sacred mountains. This was the land of her people—the *Diné Tah*. Now that she had a daughter, she wanted Dawn to find and claim a place for herself here, too.

Ella passed Rose's home, still under construction, but she didn't linger. There was more pressing business to take care of now. A short distance down the road she could see a pickup with four or five men standing around while two more were working on a tire. As she got closer, she could see carpentry tools in the bed of the vehicle.

Passing by at a crawl to prevent stirring up dust, she noticed the left rear tire had been changed, and lug nuts were being tightened. The men seemed to have everything under control and obviously didn't need any help. Recognizing a few faces, she waved but continued on.

Five minutes later, as Ella pulled up to her brother's place, her body stiffened behind the wheel. She'd expected to find things in disarray, but nothing had prepared her for this.

There was a gaping hole in the side of her brother's hogan. If it was supposed to look like a killed hogan—one where a death had occurred—the vandal had made a mistake. The hole was on the wrong side, maybe the result of someone not wanting to be seen by someone coming up the road.

The gaping hole hadn't been made by chopping out logs with an axe, or pulling them loose with help from a team of horses. From the precise cuts in the pine logs and sawdust scattered everywhere, whoever had done this had used a chain saw and had taken the evidence with him. This was no ritual act—it was pure vandalism.

As Ella climbed out of the cruiser, her brother appeared at the entrance to the hogan. "I was wondering if you'd stop by."

"Do you have any idea who did this?" she asked, her voice taut with anger.

"No. It could be someone who's trying to get back at me,

maybe because I keep neutralizing his efforts to halt work on the new power plant," he said in a very controlled voice.

She could tell he was fighting hard to stay calm and not give in to the anger he felt. "It's okay if you want to go punch something," she said quietly.

Clifford looked up at her and smiled thinly. "I may do that," he said. "Someone, not something, though."

"Can you afford to repair the hogan?"

"My services aren't in high demand now, since quite a few people feel I should oppose the power plant. But the construction company has already paid me for my services as a *hataalii*, so I'll be able to make repairs. I won't be able to hire any help though, so it's going to take some time."

Hearing an approaching vehicle honking, Ella turned. "I think you're underestimating your friends," she said and pointed. The pickup she'd passed on the way was now coming up the road. The men were shouting and waving.

"It seems that not everyone disapproves of your efforts, brother," she said.

Clifford smiled at her and went to greet the men. Ella watched for a moment, then returned back to her patrol car. It was time to go. Things here were as they should be.

Before she'd gotten a mile, Joe Neskahi contacted her.

"I've been running the names of all the workers at the construction site, anyone who might have had access to the fuel trucks, like the one used to destroy the office building," he said. "One by one, I've eliminated most of the crew. But there's one name that doesn't check out. I've got an address from the construction company's records, but the man has no driver's license or anything on record that I could find. He's a part-time worker who fits the description of the man at the demonstration, the one with the camera. And even more important, maybe, he fits the description of that man you saw at the Divine Word. The one who helped you go for a swim."

Ella grumbled something unintelligible. "He has a scar across his face right above his eyes?"

"That's him. He wears big sunglasses sometimes to hide it, according to people he's worked around."

"What's his name? Not Caleb Frank?"

"No, he's listed as a Leroy Atso," Joe said, and read off directions to the man's home. "Do you want me to send backup?"

"Too much attention might scare him off. Let me take a look first. I'm in that general area right now."

Ella drove to the highway, went farther south, then took another side road, and headed east. In this area, a location well away from any good water source, there were only a few NHA built homes. After driving two or three miles, Ella noticed the hollowed-out shell of what had once been a small wood-framed house. She recalled hearing about a fire out here that had claimed a life, so it surprised her to see recent vehicle tracks leading toward it.

She slowed down, looking in that direction as she drove past, but no vehicle was parked there now, not in front or back. This was Leroy Atso's address—obviously, nothing more than smoke and mirrors.

There was another house about a half mile away, so Ella decided to keep driving. Maybe the address was wrong or, if not, maybe the neighbor could tell her who'd been driving up to the burnt-out house.

Seeing a young Navajo woman hanging out laundry, Ella stopped and parked. The house was clean and pleasant looking, and had a small garden protected from rabbits by chicken wire. The residence even had a well.

Ella saw the woman was dressed like a traditionalist. She had on a long skirt, conservative green velveteen blouse, and her hair was styled in the traditional *tsiiyeel*, a bun that was knotted and tied with a long piece of yarn. It was said to wrap a woman's thoughts securely, near her mind, so good thoughts and wisdom could stay close to her.

Having seen Ella drive up, the woman placed her basket on the ground, then came over. "*Yáat'ééh*, officer," she greeted.

Ella returned the greeting. Clearly, the woman must have noted the extra aerial and the tribal plate, or had seen her before at a chapter house meeting.

"Please, come inside," she invited, motioning toward the front door. "I had a feeling the police would eventually come by to talk to me," she said, offering Ella a seat on the couch.

"I'm not sure what you're referring to," Ella said, surprised.

"You're here about that man, the crazy one, aren't you? The one who went to that burnt-out house?"

"As a matter of fact, I am. Tell me what you know about him."

"I first saw him a few days ago. He drove his truck right up there. I thought that maybe he didn't know the history of the place so I went over to warn him. I got as close as I dared, but he was busy ripping out what was left of some wood planks on the side of the house and either didn't hear me, or didn't care. So I came back home. I saw him build a fire from the boards, and he let it burn for a long time while he was hammering around back. Then it got dark and, a few hours later, I saw headlights as he drove away. I haven't see him since."

"Do you know what he was hammering?" Ella asked.

"No. I won't go near that place for anything," she said simply.

"Thanks for your help," Ella said walking to the door.

"Walk in beauty," the woman said.

Curious, Ella drove toward the house, parked about a hundred yards from the ruins, then circled the house on foot, giving it a wide berth. Something didn't feel right. In the shadows on the north wall, she could make out something shaped like a big X.

Ella advanced toward it, keeping her hand near her holster. She was out in the open, and the ruined house could still provide cover for someone hiding inside. Fifty feet away, able to see clearly into the burnt shell of a house for the first time, she verified that no one was inside.

She studied the X, moving in for a closer look. It was a

cross constructed from two lengths of two-by-four lumber that appeared to have been burnt in the original fire. It had been placed on the ground, leaning to one side. In the center, the letters *E* and *C* had been painted in red. She stepped closer to get a look at a strangely shaped object on the ground right in front of the cross. It was a *jish*, a Navajo's medicine bag.

Ella didn't want to draw her entire team to this remote spot and waste time, but she needed Justine now. Looking around as she spoke to her on the phone, Ella described the scene. "I don't see any discernible footprints, and the wood's just lumber taken from the frame of the house. But maybe the *jish* will tell us something."

"I'll be there in, what, say a half hour?" Justine said.

Ella took a quick look through what had been the front door. There was one footprint. It was almost obscured by the rubble around it, but it was there. She studied it for a moment then unable to shake the feeling that she was being watched, she went back to the cruiser. At least there, she wouldn't present an easy target.

Ella brought out her rifle, fed a round into the chamber, then placed it on the seat next to her. Minutes ticked by slowly. After about ten minutes, Ella heard a coyote howl. Coyote, in Navajo legends, was a trickster—uncertain as either an ally or an enemy. Bringing out her binoculars, she studied the surrounding area, looking for movement, or someone watching back. It was calm and she could see nothing out of the ordinary.

Justine arrived within twenty-five minutes, having made good time from the station. While Ella examined the scorched ground where the man had made the fire, Justine photographed the footprints and the scene. She then processed the cross for fingerprints. It was a futile gesture. Apparently, the crazy man hadn't been too crazy. He'd obviously worn gloves.

"I found tool marks over by the fire where he burned some of the wood he'd salvaged from the house. He also scooped up some of the ashes with what looks to have been a shovel."

"That's probably the source of the ashes we've been finding recently," Justine said. "I'll take some photos, and samples of the remaining ashes. If this stuff matches what we've already got, it'll tell us something, at least."

Justine looked at the cross and the *jish*. "This is the killer's signature—some Christian symbolism and some Navajo—like what we found at the murder scene."

"It's a message within a message and we're just not getting it," Ella said under her breath.

As Ella helped Justine gather and bag samples of ash, her phone rang. It was Big Ed.

"Shorty, I need you two back here at the station *pronto*. Teeny found something interesting."

"On our way," she said, then updated Justine. "We better go see what Teeny's got for us."

Ella drove back to the station, Justine in the vehicle behind her. Once there, Justine went to the lab to drop off the evidence while Ella went directly to Big Ed's office. Finding it empty, she looked up and down the hall. That's when one of the department's secretaries spotted her.

"Are you looking for the chief?" she asked.

"Yeah. Have you seen him?"

She nodded. "He, Mr. Little, and Agent Blalock are down the hall in the high-tech computer room Mr. Little set up."

Ella hurried down the long corridor and found them crowded into the eight-by-ten room. Teeny was sitting in front of an extra-large LCD computer monitor, typing at breakneck speed.

"Good, glad you're here," Teeny said, glancing up at her. "Turns out that the victim killed in L.A. and the one in Arizona both had children who were also killed later."

"How did they die and were their deaths staged as well?" Ella asked.

"No staging," Teeny answered. "Shot in the back of their heads, execution style."

"Were the kids the same sex?" Ella asked, searching for commonalities.

"No. The Kayenta woman's daughter was killed a month after her mom. The kid had been living in New Mexico with her grandmother. The woman in Los Angeles had two children who stayed with the victim's sister during the day. Someone broke in one afternoon while the sister was at the store. The son was killed almost immediately, but the daughter survived. She ran and hid in the closet. Interesting thing is that, according to the report, the killer knew the kid was there. That murder took place in 1996, about five weeks after the mother was killed."

"Why was the daughter killed in one instance and spared in the other?" Ella mused.

"You're assuming the crimes are connected, and we don't know that yet," Big Ed said.

"Sounds like the same killer, though. It would help if we could figure out how he chooses his victims. That could lead back to the motive—if there's one that makes any sense," Ella added.

"The daughter who was spared and her father both live outside Shiprock now, northwest from the Hogback. Why don't you pay them a visit and see what you can find out?" Big Ed said.

"On my way," Ella said, and jotted down the address and directions Teeny gave her.

"Take backup," Big Ed said.

"Justine's in the lab—"

"*Get backup.* From now on you don't travel solo."

Ella saw the expression on his face and knew no argument would change his mind.

TWENTY

—— ✖ ✖ ✖ ——

Twenty minutes later, Justine and Ella set out from the station.

"Were you able to get anything from the evidence we picked up at the scene earlier?"

"From the one footprint, I figure we're looking for someone of medium height and about one hundred and fifty pounds. The *jish* looped around the cross looks to be nearly identical to the one left with the murder victim. Pollen and soil, nothing more."

"So there's a high probability that this was the work of the same man who killed Valerie Tso . . . and who continues to try to misdirect and, basically, piss us off. If we'd only known back then that the guy wearing the sunglasses and baseball cap eating his lunch by Mrs. Barela's pickup was the stuff nightmares are made of. The guy has got a lot of guts and, worse, he's cold. It'll take a lot to rattle this nut."

"So the footprint . . . you think there's any way he might have just overlooked it?" Justine asked.

"Not a chance. I think this is one of those instances where the perp wants to rub our noses in it to show how superior he is. He's getting cocky," Ella said. "That means he'll do something else soon to prove how clever he is and how stupid we are. And maybe that's how we'll end up catching him." She paused for a moment, then continued. "I want this guy, even if it turns out he's just muddying the waters and has no connection to the killer—but, at this point, I'd say that's pretty unlikely."

"When it comes to Valerie's murder, I still say Brewster's our man," Justine said, her voice firm. "He likes having power over women and that often leads to trouble. I don't really think he would have purposely set out to kill Valerie, but accidents happen. The rest of the staging could have just been window dressing to throw us off."

"But how could he have made the details of the crime scene at Valerie's match L.A.'s and Kayenta's—unless he's somehow linked to those crimes, too?" She shook her head. "No, Justine. In my mind, that's reaching."

They drove east, then north. None of the roads in this direction were paved, and they left a trail of dust behind them that rose into the air like a giant rooster tail. Houses were farther apart as they drove north, away from the river valley. To their right lay the northernmost section of the Hogback, and beyond that were the coal mines and a second power plant. When the nuclear facility went into operation, there would be no plume of particulates or the constant roar of drag lines. A helium-cooled reactor would also keep more precious water from going up in smoke. At least that was the plan.

Finally, within view of Chimney Rock to the north, in a field dotted with natural gas wells, they saw a solitary gray, cinder block house with a peeled log corral that held two horses. The house, despite its isolation, had electricity, thanks to the relative proximity of two major sources of electricity.

Jackrabbits darted away and disappeared over the crest as they drove up the twin ruts serving as a road. Ella had expected to see a traditionalist living there, and was surprised when a girl in her late teens or early twenties came out wearing jeans and a sweatshirt, a huge German shepherd–cross mutt at her side.

She waved at them and came over to the vehicle. "Nothing but well roads out here. You lost?"

Ella nearly answered, "No, are you?" but resisted the temptation. "I think we're on the right track. We came here to speak with Roseann Yabeny," Ella said, getting out of the car.

"That's me, all right" the woman answered. "What's this all about?"

"We need to ask you a few questions about your brother's murder," Ella said gently, holding up her badge. "We're with the tribal police."

The young woman's face suddenly tightened. "Whoever killed him—and my mother before that—got away with it. That's all I know. What else could I possible tell you that isn't already on record? I was just five years old."

"We just need to ask you a few more questions," Ella pressed.

Roseann gestured to the house and Ella followed her in. A laptop computer sat on a table along with a printer and stack of paper. A bookshelf above the desk held dictionaries and other reference materials. Ella wondered if she was a student at the college in Shiprock.

"Look, Detective . . ." she said, then paused, searching Ella's shirt for a name tag.

"Clah. Ella Clah."

"Detective Clah, I don't remember much of anything. I was way too young. All I know is what people have told me I said at the time. But that's all on record back in Los Angeles with the police or sheriff's department."

"I understand you were present when your brother was killed."

Roseann sighed and dropped down into the closest chair. "Yes, I was, but I ran into the closet and hid, so I didn't see much of anything, apparently." She paused. "But *he* knew I was in there. I was crying and he heard me. He banged on the door and told me to shut up. But that's according to what my aunt says I told the police. It's third- or fourthhand now."

"Think hard. Is there anything else at all you can recall about your brother's death?"

"You don't get it. I haven't had nightmares for years and that's because I've refused to dwell on that anymore. I don't *want* to remember. It's too late to do anything about it now anyway," she added in an unsteady voice.

Ella picked up on the edge of fear that tainted her words. "It could be extremely important."

"You think it's my fault that he wasn't caught, that I held back on purpose?" Tears spilled down her cheeks.

Ella caught the last two words of her questions, and pressed, following her instincts. "As a child you did what you had to in order to protect yourself. But you're an adult now and in no danger."

Roseann's eyes grew wide and a shudder ripped through her. She took a deep, unsteady breath. "I peeked through a gap in the door . . . and I've regretted doing that every single day of my life," she added in a whisper thin voice.

"What did you see?" Ella asked.

"He was wearing a devil's mask. And it wasn't Halloween," she said, her voice unsteady. "Henry, my brother, came wheeling around the corner on his trike and ran into the man in the mask. That's when the man grabbed him," she managed, choking back a sob. "I know I should have tried to pull Henry into the closet with me right then, but I was too scared."

A back door opened and closed and a Navajo man in his early sixties came into the room. As he looked at her, Ella brought out her badge and introduced herself.

"None of you ever did a thing to catch the man who killed my wife and son," he said angrily, glaring at Ella. "We've rebuilt our lives and gone on, but no thanks to the police. You're not welcome here."

Ella heard the pain in his voice. He'd lived through the injustice and horrors of those murders as much as his daughter had. But his memory of those events would undoubtedly be much clearer than Roseann's and much more useful to her.

"I'm not investigating the past, but the present, uncle," Ella said, using the term of respect. "We've had some trouble here on our land that may be linked to what happened to your family."

He sat down as Roseann hurried out to answer the phone in the kitchen.

"If you have more questions, ask me now while she's busy. My daughter deserves the chance to put the past behind her," he said.

"I'm trying to figure out how this killer thinks, uncle. For example, why would he kill your son and let your daughter live?" Ella replied, trying not to draw things out.

"My daughter hid and he couldn't get to her."

"If he'd really wanted her, he could have found a way to get the closet door open," she answered.

He shrugged. "I don't know what I can tell you. There was no difference between them," he said firmly. "Not to their mother and not to me."

"But to other people?" Ella asked immediately, picking up on what he hadn't said.

He hesitated, then reluctantly answered. "Others were bothered by it a lot more than I ever was."

Ella waited, sensing he had more to tell her but he needed to do this at his own time.

Justine, aware of the breakthrough Ella had just made, slipped silently out of the room. Moments later, Ella glanced out the open window and saw her partner walking to the horse corral with Roseann.

"We're alone now, uncle, so you can speak freely," Ella encouraged.

"It's nothing she doesn't know, but she doesn't need to hear it again," he said, gazing at her through the window.

Ella waited, watching a moth caught on a spiderweb in the corner of the room struggle to get free. The more it struggled, the more entangled it became. A part of her brain registered the lesson it taught.

"Dorothy and I had some trouble at the beginning of our

marriage. I was barely making a living, running the movie projectors at the old Big Chief Drive-In. Then one night she caught me with one of her friends. But she never threw my stuff out of the house so I knew it wasn't over between us."

Ella waited. When a woman threw a man's possessions out of the house that signaled a divorce. Anything less than that meant that there was still hope.

"A few months later, she began seeing someone else, just like I had. I didn't like it much, but it's our way. I knew that would put us both on the same footing again so I didn't say anything. But then she got pregnant. I never knew for sure if Henry was mine or not, but I wanted to think he was, so I did," he said without any resentment.

To those raised Christian, affairs and children out of wedlock often carried severe social penalties. But things worked differently here. The People's perspective was rooted in concepts like harmony, order, and symmetry.

"Who did she have an affair with?" Ella asked.

"I don't know. I never tried to find out. Once it was over, we put it behind us. But there were other things we couldn't work out. She wanted to leave the Rez and go to California—Hollywood—and see if she could break into movies or TV. But my home was here, on the Navajo Nation, so we split up," he said. "At the time we both figured it would only be temporary. We didn't divorce or anything."

Ella had no time to consider what she'd learned. A moment later, Roseann returned, leading Justine back into the room.

They were underway in a matter of minutes, driving south toward the main highway. Ella called Teeny and told him what she'd learned. "Find out about the Kayenta woman's daughter. I particularly want to know if there's a father on record. We may be on to something."

"I can try, but to Navajo thinking, children belong to their mothers and that's that. So there may not be anything on record about the father unless the mother chose to list his name."

"See what you can get," Ella said. "Also ask Blalock to check VICAP and find out if there are any known felons who use masks, particularly ones of the devil, as part of their MO."

"I'll pass it along."

"Have you got anything new for me?" Ella asked.

"Just one thing. Leroy Atso—the name used by the part-time construction guy, and the social security number he listed—belong to a kid who died ten years ago in an auto accident. That kid was a member of your father's church."

There was that connection again, but there was still nothing solid to tack onto it. It was like trying to nail Jell-O to the wall. Frustration tore at her.

As Ella hung up, Justine glanced over at her. "Where to now?"

"We know that Caleb Frank owned a business in Farmington some time ago. Let's go talk to people who also have businesses in that area. Maybe someone will remember something. I know Teeny already covered this ground, but I think we might have better luck if we try a low-key, official, approach."

"It's out of our jurisdiction. We should call Emily and bring in the sheriff's department."

After getting clearance from her captain, Emily met with them at the Farmington strip mall where Caleb's print shop had once been.

Emily walked up and down the small mall with them, but it seemed no one remembered Caleb Frank. The clerical staffs were all more recent employees, and the owners were no help either. They were about to call it quits when a sign across the street caught Ella's eye—LELAND'S ICE CREAM PARLOR. "That place looks like it's been there forever," Ella said. "The sign by the door says 'family owned for twenty-five years.' Maybe they'll remember Caleb Frank."

"Let's go," Emily said.

One glance at the girl behind the counter told them that ten years ago she would have been in grade school. Deciding to take a break, Ella ordered hand-packed pistachio with chocolate sprinkles. As the girl worked to fill the order, Ella spotted the manager, a woman in her thirties, coming out of the back.

When Ella asked her about Caleb, the woman shook her head. "I've never heard of him, but you might have better luck talking to my mother, Fran Leland. She and Dad opened and closed up every day for twenty years, and she did it alone for another two years after Dad died. But after Mom's stroke last year, she decided to retire. I manage the business now and she sticks close to home."

Emily glanced at the address the woman handed them and thanked her. "This isn't far from here," Emily told Ella as they stepped back out onto the sidewalk. "Just follow me in your car."

They arrived at a small split-level home in a residential area just five blocks north of Main Street. The Leland house was wood-framed with white sideboard, and had a huge locus tree in the center of a nearly perfect green lawn. The yard was well tended, and yellow daffodils grew in profusion in flower beds beneath the windows.

Emily knocked, and moments later they were ushered in by a well-proportioned woman in her late sixties wearing loose-fitting jeans and a long smock. "Sit down, officers, please," she said in the halting speech of someone who'd had to relearn to speak.

"Mrs. Leland, your daughter told us you might remember Caleb Frank, the man who owned the print shop across the way from the ice cream parlor."

She scowled and nodded. "That was years ago but, yes, I still remember him," she said, looking over her thick glasses. "Caleb was a two-faced troublemaker."

"Why do you say that?" Ella pressed.

"He was a good-looking man and, in public, he was very personable. Most people were taken in by him, but beneath all the charm, he was a violent man. I once saw him severely beating a kid who'd painted something on the outside wall of his shop. The second he saw me, he let the kid go, but I was never fooled by him after that."

"I know it's been a long time, but he seems to have disappeared after his print shop closed down. Do you have any idea where he moved to, or where we might be able to find him now?"

Mrs. Leland hesitated before answering. "I don't know for sure where he went, but maybe I can help you find him. Will you give me a minute to remember a few things?"

Ella smiled and nodded. Anglos often apologized when they didn't have an instant answer or for allowing a pause in the conversation stretch out. Navajos, in contrast, believed it was extremely rude not to allow people time to think and reflect at leisure.

"Back then my husband and I were having a problem with another merchant who kept tossing boxes and such into our Dumpster and leaving us with no place for our own trash. Bob, my late husband, and I took turns watching, hoping we'd catch whoever it was. Then one evening, just after dark, I saw someone who looked like Caleb come up and stuff two large trash bags into our bin. I wanted to be positive—my eyesight's never been great—so I opened one of the bags, intending to wave some proof under his nose if I was right. But most of what I saw were copies of documents with the name Caleb Lujan on them. Several pages appeared to have been failed attempts to print out a phony New Mexico driver's license. The picture was Caleb Frank's, but the name was always Caleb Lujan. The name stuck with me because it's my daughter-in-law's maiden name."

"Did you confront him with that?" Ella asked, curious to learn what the man's reaction had been.

"Bob and I decided to go talk to him the following morning but Caleb's shop had closed down for good and we never saw him again. The owner of the property came by a few days later, wondering where Caleb had gone. Caleb had stiffed him out of two months' rent."

After thanking her, they walked outside and stopped by Emily's sheriff department's vehicle.

"Lujan's a pretty common name around here," Justine said, "but Caleb's is a little more rare in this day and age. Maybe we'll get a fast hit and be able to track the guy down."

"An amateur changing his identity often keeps his first name so he won't be as likely to slip up. But Caleb *is* distinctive. Good luck to you both," Emily said as a call came over her radio. "I'll see you later tonight."

Once inside the tribal cruiser, Ella contacted Teeny at the station while Justine headed back to the Rez. "I want you to get me everything you can on Caleb Lujan or anyone else in the area with that first name. Then cross-reference against the construction company's records and see if anyone using that first name is employed there."

"Consider it done," Teeny said. "I'll get back to you as soon as possible."

"This Caleb Lujan must be the same guy who's calling himself Leroy Atso," Justine said. "We already know he's using a phony identity."

"It's a good bet." As Ella placed the cell phone on her lap, she glanced over at Justine. "I've been considering all the conflicting details associated with these crimes. Like the skinwalker angle versus the passages of Scripture. Philosophically, those things are poles apart."

"Totally incompatible, unless you're right about the skinwalker angle being a red herring the killer threw in there just to confuse us."

"Or maybe the reason it doesn't make sense is because we're dealing with two killers," Ella said. "We need to hit the computers and concentrate on that possibility now." It was her least favorite thing, but would save time in the long run.

Twenty minutes later they sat in the crowded office. Blalock was still accessing VICAP and no one had found any information revealing the father of the Kayenta woman's baby.

"But I do have something for you," Teeny said, glancing back at Ella from where he sat at the keyboard. "I've been following a trail that started at Shiprock. Caleb Lujan appeared there suddenly after Caleb Frank sold his business and slipped off the radar. But he didn't stick around. A nationwide search revealed that a Caleb Lujan—listed as a Navajo—served nine years for burglary in the state pen in California after a former partner ratted him out. The authorities had a tough time establishing his identity because he had no birth certificate and no previous fingerprint records anywhere. His sentence started in late 1996. He got out on parole eight years later, failed to report to his parole officer, and just disappeared."

"Prison records carry photos," Ella said, standing up.

"Already on it. There it is," Teeny said, clicking the mouse, then leaning back.

"That's him, the same guy who was taunting me from across the ditch, scar and all," Ella said. "I should have nabbed the psycho right then."

Big Ed came into the room while she was still speaking and looked over her shoulder at the photo. "Make that available to everyone in the department."

Ella stared at the photo, lost in thought. "His parole officer has no clue where he is and that was over two years ago. The Kayenta woman was killed last year. . . ."

"What do you think links him to those women and Valerie?" he asked.

"He probably knew the women," Ella answered. "They attended the same church at the same time. If he's a ladies' man, he may have had affairs with all of them. Those affairs may have produced children. Some of the victims' children were killed later on," Ella said slowly. "These younger victims must have been singled out for some reason, then erased, along with their mothers. This killer is organized, with a plan in mind."

"Wait a minute," Big Ed said. "The kid angle . . . it doesn't really add up. I mean where would Valerie fit in with all that? She lived on her own and there's no child in the picture."

A cold chill wrapped around Ella. "Valerie had a daughter, Jennifer Clani—Boots. She's with my own daughter right now."

TWENTY-ONE

——— ✖ ✖ ✖ ———

Ella was out of her chair in a flash. "Alert the officer who's over there," she called back at the chief.

"Shorty, you may be overreacting," Big Ed warned, hurrying to catch up to her. "There's supporting evidence, I know, and the arrows seem to be pointing to Caleb. But all we have right now is a good theory."

"A theory is enough when my kid's involved," Ella said, already halfway down the hall. "What if Caleb's on some sick crusade, making up for past sins? He was preaching to me across the ditch at the church, talking about the sins of the father, and how he was going to be the instrument of justice. The ones he killed may have been his own kids, and the crimes, a sacrifice of atonement before God, righting some perceived wrong, or some such nonsense. Zealots have killed hundreds using weaker logic than that. Prison may have just interrupted his disturbed agenda. He's been sending out signals, and now I think I know what he's been trying to tell us."

Ella hurried out the lobby door to their patrol car, but Justine raced past her and dove behind the wheel before Ella could reach it. "I'm driving," she said.

"Don't take your time getting there, got it?" Ella snapped.

Justine turned on the sirens, and seconds later they were on the highway.

Ella tried to phone ahead, but all she got was the answering machine at Kevin's place. Her heart was pounding inside her, but she said nothing and tried desperately to hang on to one thought—her daughter wasn't the killer's target. But if Caleb harmed Boots, there wouldn't be a hole deep enough for him to crawl into. She'd make sure of that.

"We *could* be wrong about all this," Justine said. "It *is* just a theory at this point."

"Yeah, but it *feels* right, you know?" She wasn't sure if it was mother's instinct, or something more, but she *knew* that Boots was in danger . . . and so was her child as long as Boots was with her.

Ella checked her watch. "Dawn got out of school a short while ago. Boots may be outside waiting for the bus," she said.

"Do you know anything at all about Boots's father?"

Ella tried to think back, but if she'd ever heard anything on the subject, she couldn't remember it. Her cell phone rang and she picked it up in mid-tone. Ella recognized Teeny's voice instantly.

"We got the report from VICAP but we hit nothing there. I called my friend at the LAPD and he checked for us. A devil's mask was found across the street from the crime scene in a public park. Kids were playing with it, but they said they'd taken it from atop a trash can. Nobody saw who put it there. The detectives kept the mask along with the other evidence because the girl who'd survived the attack had mentioned seeing one. But they were never able to prove, one way or another, if it was the one used by the killer."

"Any DNA on it?"

"It had been thrown in the trash and handled by a half dozen kids. And, at the time, DNA samples weren't being taken automatically. All the officers got were a few hairs, and those were traced to one of the kids at the park who'd put on the mask."

"Check the DNA that belonged to the dead children. Caleb Frank's DNA is bound to be on record because he served time. If there's a paternal match, then my theory that he's killing his own children and their mothers is right on target."

"We don't have Boots's DNA, so don't jump to conclusions," Teeny warned. "But I'll stay on this and call you the minute I've got something."

Teeny spoke to someone beside him, then to Ella. "Blalock is going to Farmington to begin a search for Caleb using FPD and other county resources. If he's off the Rez, Dwayne will find him."

"Good." Ella hung up. They were approaching a school bus, and Justine was automatically slowing down. The flashers on the bus came on a moment later, and the little stop sign swung out from the driver's side.

Justine stopped about fifty feet away from the rear of the bus. "That's the right bus and stop, correct?"

Ella nodded. "And there's Boots." She pointed to Jennifer Clani, who was standing beside a pickup talking to one of the moms waiting for her kids.

Ella inhaled sharply, suddenly aware that she'd been holding her breath. "There. Dawn just got off."

"I see her," Justine said, just as Ella jumped out the passenger side.

Ella ran over, scooped Dawn up in her arms, and hugged her tightly.

"Mooooom!" Dawn squealed, drawing the word out in horror.

Ella laughed. "Sorry, kiddo. I'm just glad to see you." Boots was smiling, obviously surprised to see her, too.

"We need to talk," Ella said, looking over at Boots.

"Right now?" she asked. "It's fine, of course," she added quickly. "What do you need—" She stopped abruptly as Ella held up one hand.

"Not here. Let's all go to her father's house first," Ella said, glancing down at Dawn. "I'll call my mother and see if she can come over while you come with us to the station. I'll explain then."

"Nothing's happened to my grandmother, has it?" Boots asked, suddenly alarmed.

"No. This isn't about her. But let's wait until we have more privacy," Ella glanced over at Dawn.

Boots nodded.

Less than a half hour later—which considering the distance Rose had traveled meant she'd wasted no precious seconds—Rose showed up at Kevin's house. They'd all been sitting on the porch, waiting, and as Rose stepped out of the pickup, Dawn hurried to greet her.

"*Shimasání*, I'm glad you're here! I've wanted to show you Dad's new horse!"

Rose glanced over at Ella. "Go and take as much time as you need. I'll stay with my granddaughter."

"Thanks, Mom," Ella said, relieved. She knew Rose would remain with Dawn whether it took an hour or a month. After saying good-bye, Ella walked to the squad car, Boots between them.

They'd just pulled away from the house when Boots spoke. "Have I done something wrong? I'm not being arrested, am I? These doors don't have handles back here."

"No, it's nothing like that," Ella reassured her quickly. "We think you're in immediate danger, Boots, and we need to take you somewhere you'll be safe."

"Is my grandmother in danger as well?"

"No, I don't believe so. This is a matter that centers on your mother . . . and you. Do you know who your father was, Boots?" she asked directly, hoping her theory was wrong.

"My mom had many friends," she said slowly. "That's what she called them. I don't think she ever really knew who my dad was. She left home and lived on her own from the time she was fifteen."

Boots paused for several moments, then continued in a thoughtful voice. "When I was younger I used to be curious about my father and who he might be. But then as I got older, I realized it didn't matter. As Navajos, we inherit the things that matter most, like our clans, through our mothers. My own mother wasn't around much but *Shimasání* and I had each other and that was enough," she said, then after a long pause, added, "But why is knowing who my father is so important to you?"

Ella wondered how much to tell her. "It's possible he might know why your mother was murdered." Ella paused for a moment then continued. "There is one way you can help us right now. Would you consent to a DNA test?"

Her eyes widened. "What do I have to do?"

"Just let Justine swab the side of your mouth. It won't hurt at all. How about it?"

Boots considered it for a moment, then nodded. "Okay, if you really need it."

The sample was taken as soon as they reached the station, and Ella went with Justine to her lab while Boots remained in Ella's office. "How long?" she asked Justine, knowing no further explanation was needed.

"I'll get it to Farmington, and from there it'll be flown to the state lab in Santa Fe. They're going to expedite it, but it'll still be at least one day before we have the results, maybe two."

Ella returned to her office and met with Boots. "I'd like you to stay in a safe house tonight. A police officer will guard you," Ella said.

"Where is this safe house, and which police officer is going to stay with me?" she asked.

Reasonable questions, but Ella had yet to work that part out. "Give me a few minutes to make all the arrangements. I just wanted to run my plan past you first."

"You mean I don't have to accept?" she asked, reading between the lines.

"That's right, but I'd strongly recommend that you do. If we're wrong, then no harm will be done, but if we're right, it might save your life."

"Do you think my father is trying to kill me?" she asked directly. "And that he was the one who killed my mother?"

Ella knew she couldn't avoid the details anymore. Boots was a bright young woman who deserved an explanation.

As Ella told her what she knew, Boots seemed to pull back into herself, her dark eyes flat and hooded. Then, with the self-possession of a woman twice her age, she finally spoke in an even tone. "My grandmother will be worried if I don't come home tonight unless I can talk to her first. I need to let her know what's going on."

With a wave of her hand, Ella invited Boots to use her phone. "Tell her you're under my care, Boots."

"May I speak to her alone?"

Ella nodded. "Dial nine first for an outside line," she said, then walked out of the office. Seeing Big Ed, Ella explained her plan to him.

"I think that's sound thinking. But who'll be guarding Boots?"

"I was going to ask Philip or Michael Cloud. They're always looking for overtime work," she said.

He nodded. "Sound choices. If they aren't able to take the job, then come back to me and we'll try to come up with some other possibilities. She's going to need round-the-clock protection until this is settled."

Ella went to Dispatch to get a twenty on the Cloud brothers. "Are they out on patrol?"

"Yes. Shall I bring them in?"

"Not both. Just Officer Philip Cloud. I'll brief Michael later."

It took another twenty minutes for Philip to arrive, and during that time Ella worked hard to find a suitable safe house. She needed someplace no one would ever think of looking for Boots. After rejecting a half dozen locations, a new idea formed in her mind. Ella made the arrangements from Justine's office, then went to meet with Boots.

Ella had to give her credit. Boots looked far more composed than she would have been under similar circumstances.

260 ✳ AIMÉE & DAVID THURLO

"How long will I have to be in hiding?" she asked as Ella took a seat behind her desk.

"I'm not sure," Ella answered, "but my daughter needs you, so the second I think you'll be safe, you'll be back on the job," she added with a comforting smile.

Another half hour passed before Ella was able to finalize the plans. Philip Cloud was briefed and given directions to the safe house, but before he could set out with Boots, Lena Clani arrived.

Ella heard her voice down the hall at the same time Boots did. As they exchanged glances, Boots added, "I should have realized she'd come to the station."

Lena burst into Ella's office moments later. She gave Boots a loving, gentle smile, then glared at Ella.

"Who will be keeping my granddaughter safe?"

"My relatives," Ella answered, knowing that it was the only answer Lena would accept. The Cloud brothers were Herman's nephews and, sooner or later, Lena would undoubtedly find out they'd been chosen for the job.

Philip came in just then and, as Boots went off with him, Lena turned to Ella, her gaze hard again. "This is about Caleb Frank . . . Lujan now, right?"

It took Ella a beat to process what Lena had said. It was no secret that Lena was well connected, but the way she managed to keep up with their police investigation was deeply unsettling. "Who leaked you that information?" she demanded.

Lena simply stared at her. "This is the reservation, not one of your *bilagáana* police departments."

"This is a strange time to be criticizing the police department, considering that an officer was the source of your information—information the Fierce Ones were *unable* to give you, by the way. Knowing you were able to get one of our officers to violate a trust doesn't impress me—it just lowers my opinion of you. You've already behaved shamefully, nearly costing a man his life just a few days ago. Who else have you told about Caleb? Don't you realize how sensitive this case is? Do you want him to get away, then come back and strike next year or the year after that when our guard is down?" Ella argued, tired of Lena's meddling and afraid of the price it would ultimately exact.

Lena's jaw dropped, not used to having people stand up to her. Suddenly she looked tired and ancient.

"Have *you* seen Caleb Lujan?" Ella asked, hoping she'd finally managed to drive some sense into her.

"No, but I've contacted some friends, and they're looking for him."

"The Fierce Ones?" Ella asked, her gut tightening. Vigilante groups, no matter how well meaning, always left a bad taste in her mouth.

"Just know that you'll have help—people who can go down avenues you can't."

"Or who'll make it possible for him to slip through our grasp. Amateurs and professionals don't mix." She was about to say more when Lena continued.

"I have some other news for you. The white man who owns the diner was there on the night my daughter was killed. A local truck driver saw the white man's red Ford truck parked outside his diner around seven-thirty. He knows it was the owner's, because it's got a small dent on one fender—one that the truck driver's kid accidentally put there."

"Who's this witness?" Ella asked quickly.

"He'll be coming here this morning to make his statement," Lena replied.

"Is Brewster being watched by the Fierce Ones?" Ella pressed her.

"They're keeping an eye on things for the police," Lena said, sidestepping the question. "But you'll be the first to know if they learn anything."

"I know you think they're helping us, but to stand up in a court of law, evidence has to be gathered in a certain way. If we don't follow certain procedures, your daughter's killer could walk. It's not enough to *know*. We also have to *prove* it."

Lena's gaze hardened. "They might let him go, but he won't get far."

"And then what? They'll go to prison for killing someone they inadvertently helped escape justice," Ella said. "Let us do the work we're trained for. By interfering, all you're really doing is helping your daughter's killer."

Lena shook her head slowly. "You've had to take my granddaughter from me so you can keep her safe. If you'd really handled the situation, this wouldn't have been necessary. Those who are looking for this man—Caleb—won't rest until he's found. He thinks he can hide on our land. But he's one of ours and we'll find him."

Ella noticed that Lena had deliberately used Caleb's name. It was her way of taking power away from him.

"I miss my granddaughter. She's all I've got left." Her voice cracked, and before Ella could say anything, Lena hurried out of the office.

Justine, who'd had to sidestep to avoid crashing into Lena, came in next. "She's in so much pain, anger is all she's got to hold on to. When that's gone, she's going to fall completely apart," she said gently. "Don't let her get to you."

"She could end up costing lives if she keeps pushing this, and end up in a jail cell herself," Ella answered, her lips pursed. "But that's not why you're here. What's up?"

"I have some new information for you. Caleb Lujan was working using his Leroy Atso identity. He was caught on the construction company's security video. Teeny wants you to come take a look."

Ella hurried into the back room that Teeny and Blalock now shared. Looking over Teeny's massive shoulder, she saw Caleb clearly. "Is he at work now?"

"No. He hasn't reported to work for two days now. The foreman said that, as far as he's concerned, the guy's fired."

Big Ed came in a moment later and motioned for Ella to

follow him. When they entered his office, he waved her to a seat and shut the door.

"Okay, update me. What arrangements did you make for Boots and why haven't you filed a report?"

Ella hesitated. What she had to say was bound to make the chief furious. "Lena Clani came in and let me know that the Fierce Ones are hot on Caleb's trail. One of our people compromised themselves, accidentally or not, and now the Fierce Ones know the details of our case. I suspect that they've got a member among us, so I'm playing things close my chest."

Big Ed's hands curled into massive fists and his hardened expression mirrored his struggle to curb his temper. Ella knew it wouldn't take much to push him over that precarious edge now.

"A Fierce One here . . . right under our noses," he said in a taut voice. "I'll find him. And after I'm through with him he'll be lucky to get a job serving french fries," he muttered, then, after a pause, continued. "Okay, Shorty, moving on. I understand why you're going slow with the paper trail, but I still need to know where Boots is staying and what arrangements you've made."

"She's with Reverend Tome at his home over in Waterflow," Ella answered. "He's got a bear of a dog that'll give them plenty of warning if there's a stranger in the immediate area. Also, one of the Clouds, in plainclothes, will be there to keep an eye on things."

"Did you contact the sheriff's department? The deputy who patrols that sector needs to know."

"Haven't had time yet."

"I'll do that and ask them to increase their patrols, too." He gave her an approving nod. "Putting her at Reverend Tome's was good thinking, Shorty. No one will think of looking for her outside our borders or in the company of a Christian preacher."

"That's if Caleb's really after her," Ella added cautiously. "I wish we could hurry that DNA test."

"I'll see what I can do for you. But keep in mind that Caleb has no way of knowing for sure if Boots is his kid or not. All that may matter in the long run is who he *thinks* is his child. Now tell me what you're doing to follow up the lead you got on Brewster."

"I'm going to have Sergeant Neskahi keep an eye on Brewster and have Tache go talk to his wife once she's alone. I have a feeling Donna's the key. If Brewster's guilty, something tells me she'd know."

"If you don't want to file a report, keep me updated verbally, but I want to be kept current on what's going on. Clear?"

"Yes, sir."

Ella walked out of his office, then headed for the room where Teeny was working. Catching him alone, she gave him an update. "If you have any manpower you can spare, I'd appreciate having someone on the outside, keeping an eye on Ford's house. Just let Ford and the inside officer know. We don't want them stalking each other."

"Right. I'll let you know when things are in place. Anything else?"

"Keep trying to get a location on Caleb. I won't breathe easy until that guy is in lockup."

As she heard the words coming out of her own mouth, she realized that Caleb had pushed her buttons and, somewhere along the way, she'd made it personal. Looking at it dispassionately, Brewster was still a prime suspect. Maybe the murder in L.A. and Kayenta weren't related to what had happened to Valerie. Or maybe Brewster had preempted Caleb . . .

Until she knew for sure, making sure Boots stayed safe would remain her top priority.

TWENTY-TWO
———— ✖ ✖ ✖ ————

Ella went to Ford's house that evening dressed in simple brown slacks and a turquoise silk blouse—just as if she were making a social visit. She'd checked often to see if she'd been followed, but with only one major road in the area, tracking her from a distance would have been a relatively easy thing to do.

Ella checked with Officer Philip Cloud, who was standing by the window in a darkened back room and watching the open land behind the house. The night vision binoculars would allow him to remain watchful as long as necessary.

Ella filled him in about the extra patrols, and Philip nodded. "Good. Word has a funny way of getting out on this case, but if this place is somehow compromised, it'll still be well protected by people you can trust."

Ella couldn't ask for more. Confident Philip and his brother Michael were the right men for the job, she left him to his work.

Boots was in the study—a converted bedroom—seated at a large desk and reading from a textbook. She looked up as Ella arrived in the doorway.

"How you holding up, Boots?" Ella asked, noting with satisfaction that the shades were drawn and, from Boot's position, it was doubtful that any silhouette of her could be seen from outside.

"I'm okay. This is a good chance to catch up on my studies. But I'm worried about missing classes if this lasts beyond the weekend."

"I'll talk to your professors, if necessary. Just make sure you don't make any phone calls or do anything to give away your location."

"I understand. I'm forbidden to even stand in front of a window. Just catch the man who killed my mom, okay?"

"We're getting close," Ella replied, reluctant to say more. If Caleb took off, it might take weeks, or months, to track him down. "Stay safe."

Ella joined Ford in the kitchen moments later, regrets and second thoughts filling her mind as she considered his situation. She'd placed him in danger by getting him involved and, although he'd readily agreed, she now wondered if she'd been wrong to ask.

Ford brought her a cup of coffee. "I'm glad you called me," he said, as if reading her mind. "There's no safer place for Boots than here at my house. I'll be gone during the day of course, but I'm here at night, and Abednego will hear and start barking at anyone who tries to creep up," he said, glancing down at the dog and giving him an affectionate pat. "He's a pussycat around people he knows, but no stranger would dare make a move on this property."

Ella took a sip of the scalding liquid. "I've recruited you into something that may turn nasty," she said softly.

He chuckled. "Believe me, I can handle this. I won't lead anyone here. And you were smart wearing something other than your normal work clothes. Since people know you and I are seeing each other, no one will think twice about it. And Abednego is quite a sight when he gets riled up. He knows a few tricks, just as I do," he added with a grin.

"You two are filled with mystery," she said with a tiny

smile. "Wanna play twenty questions, Reverend?" she asked only half jokingly.

"You know more about me than most people," he said in a serious voice. "Relax and trust your instincts. They're more reliable than a long list of facts any day."

Ella looked at the man before her, more intrigued than ever. "When I look at you I see . . . a maze of government firewalls," she said, laughing.

He smiled. "Good. At least I'm not boring." He cocked his head toward his office. "Come on. I've dug up some information for you."

They entered his office, Abednego close to Ford's side. "You asked me to see what I could get on Caleb," he said, then pulled out a small vinyl-covered notebook from the desk drawer and glanced at his notes.

"Caleb Frank had his own take on retribution. He believed that it was God's will that man clean up his own messes here and now. He'd cite passages from the Old Testament to lend support, and made a very convincing case for that notion. But his philosophy went completely counter to the doctrine and practices of the Divine Word Church. That's why he and your father had to part ways."

"I have a theory that the murders are his way of cleaning up his own past sins," she said, and explained. "What do you think?"

He considered her theory, then nodded. "If you're right about that, then there's someone else you should talk to soon. She used to be in your father's church, though these days she and her husband come to ours. Her name is Martha Etcitty, and I was told she'd had an affair with Caleb Frank back in the days when he was a deacon at your father's church. The reason I didn't say anything to you before is that my source is far from reliable. She's an elderly woman who's known to be a gossip. The only reason she told me is because she dislikes Martha and didn't want her to become a member of our church."

Ella called Justine up immediately and passed the name on to her. "Find out whatever you can about her. We'll be paying her a visit later."

She'd just hung up when her phone rang. It was Big Ed and from the tone of his voice, she knew he was furious. "Have you looked at the *Diné Times*?"

"No, why?"

"They ran an article linking Brewster to Valerie Tso's murder. Lea Garner, the waitress, claims that Valerie had intended on taking Brewster to court for sexual harassment. She said that Brewster was desperate to stop Valerie and tried buying her silence, but she blew him off."

"I'll check it out."

Ella called the Navajo-owned newspaper next and asked for the editor, her friend, Jaime Beyale.

Moments later a familiar voice answered. "I thought I'd be hearing from you," Jaime said.

"Did you write the article?" Ella asked.

"Guilty," she answered. "We had no way of verifying Valerie's intentions, of course, but the rest of the story checked out. Lea called me and said she wasn't afraid of Brewster anymore, that she wanted to go public and expose the scumbag."

"Any reason for this sudden burst of bravery on Lea's part?" Ella asked.

Jaime hesitated. "I can answer that, but it wouldn't be based on fact, just my own opinion."

"Understood."

"I was interviewing her at her home when her brother Wallace came in. He had on that shoestring-size leather band around his wrist."

Ella waited, but Jaime didn't elaborate. "You've lost me."

"Word has it that when a member of the Fierce Ones wants to be recognized, he wears that as a sign of his affiliation."

"I hadn't heard about that." It made sense that the Fierce Ones would want to push Brewster's buttons. Since he was married to a Navajo woman, the Fierce Ones had multiple reasons for wanting him to go down. "Thanks for the tip, Jaime."

She was still sorting things out in her mind when Justine called. "New lead. I spoke to a couple of Jayne's friends about Martha Etcitty, and I guess she heard about it, because she just called me. She told me that she'd hooked up with Caleb many years ago, but it hadn't amounted to much more than a one-night stand. She said that if we needed to talk to her about it, we should stop by tonight, because her husband would be out till late."

"I'll meet you at her house," Ella said.

After saying good-bye to Ford and assuring Boots she'd be well taken care of, Ella hurried out to her car. It was already 9 P.M. It was going to be another long night.

Ten minutes later, she arrived at a house on the hillside behind the Good Shepherd Church where Ford preached. The neighborhood of wood-framed houses was relatively new and each residence stood on a one-acre lot. Justine was already there waiting as she pulled up and parked.

"Hey, cuz. Shall we go see what the lady has to say, or do we wait in case she's a traditionalist?"

Ella glanced around. One car, a late-model sedan, was parked near the side of the house. She could hear the TV all the way from the street. "Let's go up and knock," Ella said. "With that much noise inside, I doubt she heard us coming."

They were almost at the door, when Ella stopped. "Hang on. Something doesn't feel right." Over the years, she'd learned not to dismiss feelings she couldn't explain. Ella placed her hand on the badger fetish she always wore around her neck. It felt warm, but not hot.

"Stay sharp," she warned Justine and continued to the door. Nothing seemed out of place, yet the odd feeling persisted. When she knocked loudly, identifying herself, there was no response.

Ella stood rock still and listened. The raucous laughter of a television sitcom echoed across the yard, landscaped with colored gravel and a few hardy bushes. Aware of the slight part in the curtains to her right, Ella moved to the window, and, staying to one side, peered in. The interior was encased in darkness except for the glow of the TV set somewhere down the hall. From what she could see, everything looked neat and orderly.

"That's her vehicle. I already checked," Justine answered gesturing to the sedan.

"Go around the house and see if any other windows are open, or the curtains drawn back," Ella said.

"What if she's in bed, and she's not alone?"

"Then somebody is going to be embarrassed. It's worth the risk."

Justine went around to the left, and Ella covered the right. As she reached what she assumed was a bedroom window, Ella glanced inside. The muted light coming from the bathroom covered the bedroom in a pale yellow glow. She could see what appeared to be a bullet hole in the middle of the back wall, and dark stains on the carpet. A lamp lay on its side near the headboard, the shade askew. In contrast to the chaos surrounding the bed, some clothes had been neatly folded and placed at the foot of the bed.

"Something bad went down here, partner. We're going in," Ella said, using her handheld radio.

"Back door," Justine responded. "It's not locked."

Ella met her partner, and weapons out, they moved into the kitchen. Once again they identified themselves, but no one answered. After clearing every room they passed, they entered the master bedroom and followed the trail of blood into the bathroom.

The dead woman was dressed in her Sunday best—a yellow, flowery dress, low heels, and a matching scarf. She'd been propped next to the bathtub in a kneeling position. Her hair was still dripping wet. The cuts and bruises that covered her face, arms, and legs said she hadn't gone down without a fight.

Ella holstered her weapon. "There was a pair of slacks and

a sweater folded on the bed," Ella said. "This was staged after she died."

"Same MO," Justine answered quietly.

They went back to collect their gloves, two pairs each, and called Neskahi and Tache.

"Can you positively ID the victim?" Ella asked Justine.

She nodded. "It's the woman we were searching for. I know her face from her driver's license."

The full moon pushed back the darkness, and Ella's gaze took in the hillside above them. "While you begin processing the scene, I'm going to take a look outside and see if I can spot anyone watching us. This guy goes to a lot of trouble to stage things just right and he likes *signing* his work, so I've got a feeling he's not far. We may have interrupted him."

Leaving Justine to take photos and gather evidence, Ella walked out the back door and moved toward high ground, listening every step of the way. As she neared the summit of the small hillside she heard the sound of low laughter. Then, in a heartbeat, it was gone. Except for the distant rumble of a truck on the highway below, it was silent.

"Come out and avoid getting shot," she said firmly, peering into the darkness. She couldn't see him, but she could sense someone out there. For a moment Ella considered using her flashlight, but if the killer was armed—and the bullet hole in the wall suggested that was the case—she'd just make herself a target.

Another gust of wind swirled around her, but this time she heard nothing at all. Ella slipped noiselessly through the brush, a skill she'd learned as a kid growing up on the Rez. She also knew how to spot a trail, no matter how faint. Yet, as she searched the ground directly ahead, she found absolutely nothing.

Ella stopped and listened. Sound had returned to the desert, and that rhythm of life told her that the danger was now past.

TWENTY-THREE

————— ✖ ✖ ✖ —————

Ella began searching with her flashlight, and found a vague trail leading away from the graveled yard but it quickly petered out. By the time she returned to the crime scene, she found Carolyn, the tribe's ME, already at work, crouched by the body and speaking into her small cassette recorder. Tache, Neskahi, and Justine were going over every inch of the bedroom. They would move into the hall and beyond later.

"The victim fought like a wildcat," Tache said, snapping photos. "There was a .38 Blackhawk revolver under the bed, fired recently, and a partial box of ammo in the nightstand. Looks like she got off a round."

"I'll check for residue and let you know. She's got all kinds of defensive wounds," Carolyn added, glancing up at Ella. "There's also a deep gash across the palm of her hand. Like she grabbed the blade of her attacker's knife and took it away for a moment. Some of the blood here may not be hers."

"I hope you're right," Justine said. "I'll run the serial number on the pistol. Anyone locate the knife?"

Tache shook his head. "No," Joe responded. "Her assailant may have taken it with him."

"We'll need to search outside where I found some footprints and look for drops of blood." As Ella studied the scene empathy filled her. She would have done exactly as Martha had—fight to the bitter end. "Justine, have you contacted her husband?"

"There's a note on the calendar in the kitchen that mentions he's at a club meeting tonight, but it doesn't say which club. Without that, we have no quick way of tracking him down."

"The killer was interrupted," Ella said in a slow, thoughtful voice. "He didn't expect us to arrive when we did. That's why her hair wasn't combed like the last victim's and why there's no Bible or medicine bundle." She paused thoughtfully, then added, "It's the killer's use of those two things that confused me at first. But in terms of Caleb, it fits. Maybe he's trying to say that retribution is fitting no matter which path you choose—a return to harmony by death as well as peace with God."

"Nothing here suggests Brewster's involvement," Justine said, disappointed. "This wasn't a crime of passion. This was premeditated."

"He's not off our radar yet, partner," Ella said. Hearing a vehicle driving up, she glanced out the window. "I'd better get out there. It could be the woman's husband."

Ella stood by the front door in the glow of the porch light as a stocky Navajo man in his mid-fifties stepped out of a dark colored pickup. "Where's Martha?" he asked, giving Ella a puzzled look. "Was there an accident?"

"Are you her husband?" Ella asked.

He nodded. "I'm Leland Etcitty. Who are you?"

Ella introduced herself, then broke the news. As she watched, shock, then unbelief traveled across his features.

"No, this is a mistake. She's not dead. She can't be," he said in a strangled voice, and tried to go around Ella.

"You'll have a chance to go in later, Mr. Etcitty, but right now we need to keep the crime scene from being contaminated," she said, blocking him. "We need every clue we can find to catch whoever did this."

He stopped by the open front door and took a deep, unsteady breath. "What's that sick, sweet smell? Blood?" he whispered, horror coiling around his words. "If my wife died in the house, I can't go inside."

Ella waited. A New Traditionalist married to a Christian? Stranger things had happened.

There was a noise, then a bump, as Carolyn and Neskahi came out onto the porch, maneuvering a gurney with the black body bag containing Martha's body. Asking them to stop, Ella unzipped the body bag just enough to reveal Martha's face. As Leland saw his wife, he groaned. The sound, soft and deep, was ripped straight from his soul.

Ella zipped up the body bag and gestured for them to take the body away. "Do you need to sit down?" she asked Leland gently.

He shook his head, but shakily reached out and grabbed one of the porch supports. "Who did this?" Leland demanded, oblivious to his own tears.

Ella kept her voice as calm as possible. "We'd hoped you could give us some idea. A motive, perhaps?"

He gave her a bewildered look. "Martha had no enemies. I don't know anyone who *didn't* like her. She was the best wife and mother anyone could ever ask for."

Ella had hoped for the opening and, recognizing the opportunity, took it immediately. "How many children do you have?"

"Three boys. They're all grown, but they still live on the Rez."

"Are all three yours, or do any of them come from a previous marriage?" she asked without any particular inflection.

"They're *our* kids," he said, giving her a totally perplexed look.

"What I'm asking, is did your wife have any children from a previous marriage?"

"No," Leland answered, then shook his head. "Yes."

"Which is it?" Ella pressed, using a soft voice in hopes of

keeping him calm. She could read the confusion, the pain, and the outrage burning in his eyes.

"What possible difference does all that make now?" he yelled. "That was ages ago, before I even met her. And that child's dead. He died at birth. Back then, my wife didn't believe in prenatal care."

"She was a traditionalist?"

"More like a New Traditionalist with a stubborn streak," he answered, his voice breaking. He ran a hand through his hair, still struggling to understand. "This isn't happening."

"Have any strangers been around here lately?" Ella pressed. "Or did your wife mention being in contact with someone she hadn't seen in a long time? There was a .38 revolver under the bed and it has been fired recently. Is it yours?"

"We . . . I own a Blackhawk .38. I keep it loaded in the nightstand. She didn't like guns, but I taught her how to use it. I hope she hit the bastard."

Leland's eyes narrowed. "You think this was an old boyfriend, or something like that? You came here thinking she might be in danger, was that it? Then you discovered the body."

"Yes. Now we're trying to find the person who did this to her."

"But you're too late . . . too late to save her," he said, rubbing his forehead. "I've got to talk to my boys before they hear it from someone else. I need to go. Now," he added quickly.

"Maybe you shouldn't be driving," she said slowly.

"There are things I have to do," he said, as if he hadn't heard her. "Am I free to go?"

"Where can I reach you?"

"I'll be at the Trail Inn. This house and the contents will go to charity."

A few minutes later, all she could see were the taillights of his truck as it disappeared in the distance.

Justine was checking the front room as Ella came back into the house. "There's no sign of a burglary, boss. There are too many valuables around the house, including the revolver, and the place wasn't tossed like Valerie's apartment," Justine said. "Dr. Roanhorse believes that the victim has been dead less than an hour, so we got here just as he was leaving."

"He left because he heard us come up, and that's why he didn't have time to stage everything. I heard someone outside, but couldn't catch up to him or find out where he went," Ella replied.

"The message I left on her answering machine has been played. It's possible that both victim and killer heard me."

"If he was already here, the call probably had little or no effect on the outcome. My guess is the only thing it did was force him to race the clock. That, and fear that the noise from the gunshot would lead to a visit from an officer. At least we don't have to worry about any children. Martha had one child before she married Leland. He was stillborn."

"Caleb's child?"

"That's the way I see it," Ella answered.

As Justine went back inside, Joe Neskahi came up to her. "We found a scribbled note beneath the lamp with part of what may be a Bible quote. I'm not very familiar with Scripture so I can't say for sure."

"What did it say?"

" 'If thy right eye offend thee pluck it,' " he answered. "The starting vowel *o* was next, but he obviously never finished writing it."

She wasn't familiar with the passage, but she knew someone who would be.

"Do you think this guy has more people he considers an offense?" Neskahi asked her. "Someone else he needs to kill?"

"I sure hope not," Ella answered, getting the point he was making.

She was about to go back inside when her cell phone rang. It was Teeny. "I've got an address for Caleb Lujan. Turns out he rented an apartment in Farmington. He was behind on the rent, so the landlord locked him out. His stuff's still there."

"And Caleb?"

"Hasn't shown up. I told the apartment manager you'd be stopping by, even though he insisted that he doesn't know where Caleb went."

Ella took down the address. "I'm on my way."

"One more thing, Ella. I tracked down a former cellmate of Caleb's who's still serving time. The warden agreed to set up an Internet interview for us. I'll let you know when we're ready to go with that."

"Good work! You can reach me on my cell. I'm on my way to Farmington right now."

Ella went inside to update Justine. "Do you want me to go with you?" Justine asked.

"I need you to help Ralph and Joe finish up here. Check the neighbors and see if anyone saw or heard anything. Get me something we can hang this guy with, and remember to check for a blood trail outside, even if you have to wait till morning."

"Big Ed won't like you traveling alone," Justine warned.

"It'll be on my head," Ella answered. "But I'll need someone with jurisdiction. I'll call Blalock and have him meet me there."

Ella drove to Farmington, the biggest city in that corner of the state. The road was good, traffic light, and that made up somewhat for her lack of patience tonight. She had a feeling that the Fierce Ones would be half a step behind her once they learned about Martha Etcitty—if they didn't know already. Unless she collared Caleb Frank soon, they'd harass everyone who might have seen him, probably beginning with Reverend Curtis and his congregation.

After notifying the Farmington police via radio of her presence, she arrived at the northeast neighborhood. She had made good time, so Blalock hadn't caught up with her yet. The building had been divided into five apartments, side by side. Ella parked right outside the middle door marked MANAGER.

Just as she got out an Anglo man in his late fifties opened the door, a mug of something hot in his hand.

"You detectives always work this late?" he grumbled, stepping out onto the narrow sidewalk.

"Not when we can help it," Ella replied. She could smell the dark, rich roast of his coffee and found herself wishing he'd offer her a cup.

Instead, he held out the key. "It's the last one at the end, number five. You can take whatever you want. I was going to haul everything out of there anyway and drop it by the homeless shelter. I'm not a storage facility."

"Have you had any recent contact with Mr. Lujan?" Ella asked, taking the key.

"Recent?" He shrugged. "Not since I kicked him out, almost a week ago. I give the tenants two weeks' grace period with their checks, and that's it. Otherwise, people take advantage."

"What happened?"

"I went to see him the evening before to ask him for the rent one last time, and he put me off. So the next morning, after he was gone, I let myself and the locksmith in, and he changed the locks. When Lujan came back he was madder than a wet hen, but there wasn't much he could do about it. I had my cousin here, and he works for the Farmington Police."

"Who's your cousin?"

"Brad Whitacre. He's a sergeant."

"Okay, so what happened next?" Ella asked, taking note of the name.

"Lujan did a lot of yelling, but I wouldn't budge, so he lost it and slammed his fist against the door. Big mistake, considering it's a solid core door. Then Brad whipped out his can of Mace, and Caleb got the message. He left in a hurry after damning us both to the hellfire, or something like that. Haven't seen Caleb since, though he said he'd be coming back for his things."

"Be extremely careful. That man is dangerous," Ella warned.

"I figured that," he said, pointing to his door. "He racked up his fist pretty bad and bloodied up the door. Took me a while to wipe up the mess."

"A lab tech will be coming by and checking for any remaining traces of blood on that door, so don't clean anymore. In the meantime, I'd like to take a look around his apartment."

"Sure. Knock yourself out," he said.

As he walked away grumbling, Ella called Blalock, who was in the area now, and filled him in and what she'd learned so far.

"I'll get the Farmington PD in on this. Hang tight," Blalock said. "They'll be there in a few minutes and so will I."

Cooperation between the departments had always been strong. Sergeant John Vasquez of the FPD showed up seconds before Agent Blalock arrived.

Ella updated Vasquez quickly. "I need to process the manager's door, and Caleb Lujan's room and possessions for evidence. I've already been given permission by the manager."

"I'll notify our crime team," he said.

Ella entered the apartment, Blalock at her side, while Vasquez waited outside for the others. The photo on Caleb's desk immediately caught Ella's eye. It was over fifteen years old and showed her father and Caleb on the steps in front of the Divine Word Church. Her father's face had been sliced down the middle with a razor, and below that was the note EXODUS 20:5.

Blalock followed her gaze, then looked back at her and shrugged. "Any idea what's in Exodus 20:5?"

"No, but maybe the Bible on the dining table will tell us," Ella said.

Ella didn't even have to search. The page was marked, and the passage highlighted read, "I the Lord thy God am a jealous God, visiting the iniquity of the fathers upon the children until the third and fourth generation."

"Think he's referring to you?" Blalock asked, coming up behind Ella.

"I hope so. Nothing I'd like more than the chance to meet up with this guy," Ella said, her voice hard. "Then we'll see how well he does against someone who knows how to fight back."

Wearing gloves, Ella and Blalock studied the dog-eared pages and underlined passages in the concordance, and the various editions of the Bible stacked on the table, paying particular attention to the handwritten comments scribbled in the margins. "If there's an underlying theme to his favorite passages, it's hate," Blalock said.

"From what I see on the side margins, his handwriting is very close, or a match, to what we've found on the notes left at the crime scenes," she said. "But we'll need a handwriting expert to verify that."

An inexpensive laptop computer was plugged into a telephone jack and Ella switched it on and began to search the files. Although he'd used an on-screen name, Caleb was an active member of several radical religious groups.

"I believe he's looking for redemption by eradicating the women he slept with and the kids he fathered out of wedlock," Ella said after a moment. "Slaughtering my mom's sheep was his way of warning me innocents would die."

"We're going to have to come up with a way to force him out into the open," Blalock said. "But for right now, let the techs handle the scene. We'll start again in the morning after we get some sleep."

"You're right. It's time to recharge."

Ella slept soundly, too tired to even dream, and woke up when the alarm clock on the nightstand rang at seven-thirty. Twenty minutes later, Ella met with Justine in the kitchen.

"Good morning," Ella said, pouring herself a cup of coffee from the pot on the counter. "Anything new come in yet?"

"Word's out about Caleb and his apartment. The Fierce Ones have people driving all over the county trying to track him down."

"So they can turn him over to us?" Ella smiled wryly. "Why do I doubt that?"

"One last thing. The Internet interview Teeny arranged for

us is set for this morning. I understand the prisoner shared a jail cell with Caleb for five years."

"Let's go," Ella said, eager to get started.

When they arrived at the station a short time later, Blalock was already there waiting. "The interview is ready to happen," he said. "The prisoner is currently serving time in the California State Prison at Lancaster, and is ready to talk. He cut a deal in exchange for the testimony he's going to give us—a transfer to another less crowded lockup closer to his family. We've got a Bureau agent on-site to help smooth the process. Ready?"

"Whenever you are."

Ella entered the small room that Blalock and Teeny had made over into temporary offices.

"Almost ready," Teeny said, glancing over at them. "Just waiting for them to come online."

"Who's the prisoner we're questioning?" Ella asked him.

"His name's John Devlin. He was Caleb's cellmate."

"He's in for . . . ?"

"Auto theft, aggravated assault, bank robbery," Teeny answered. "The list goes on. He's a three-time loser."

A moment later a man in a suit and tie appeared on the monitor in front of Teeny. Behind him, a green-eyed, blond Anglo man in a bright prison jumpsuit sat on a chair by a simple wooden table. "I'm Agent Riley. We're ready here whenever you are," the man in the suit and tie said.

Ella sat in front of the computer as the camera shifted to the prisoner. His forearms were covered with colorful tattoos, and he was looking across the room, not at the camera. "Mr. Devlin, I understand you have something you want to tell us about Mr. Frank."

Devlin turned to the camera. If he was smiling, it came across as a sneer. "Who?" His voice was higher than she expected, then she noticed an ugly scar on his windpipe.

"Caleb Lujan," she said, correcting herself. "I think that's the name he used when you knew him."

"Yeah. His nickname was Righteous Dude. The man was a Jesus freak, crazy as they come. RD kept to himself, real clean and straight—unless you happened to start talking religion. Preachers drove him nuts."

"Could you give me an example?"

"RD said that preachers these days were too soft on sinners. He claimed that they'd become nothing more than the devil's helpers. There was one man he kept ragging on from back on the reservation, a Navajo preacher by the name of Raymond."

"Last name?" Ella asked, not really needing one, but wanting verification.

"Don't remember," he answered with a shrug. "It was the same preacher who got RD thrown out of the church there. RD said that Raymond was a hypocrite who'd led his congregation away from God's real message. The thing with RD was that he felt he was on a mission for God. He really believed he'd seen the light. He told me he had to make his peace with God and that the atonement of sins required a blood sacrifice. Righteous wasn't the kind to kill himself, so I sorta figured he had someone else in mind."

"But to what end? I mean, after they were dead, then what?" Ella asked.

"RD claimed that once he'd atoned, he'd be able to start a new life."

The interview continued a while longer with Ella probing for anything Devlin remembered that would help them locate Caleb Frank/Lujan. But the inmate couldn't remember anything specific to Shiprock.

After the interview ended, Justine glanced over at Ella. "Boots is out of his reach, so that's going to put a major speed bump on his road to sinlessness," Justine said.

"Yeah, but as long as he keeps looking, he'll stay within *our* reach, and that's how we're going to catch him," Ella said, an idea forming in her mind.

TWENTY-FOUR
—— ✖ ✖ ✖ ——

Directly afterward, they walked down the hall to Big Ed's office. Justine, Joe Neskahi, and Ralph Tache were there along with Blalock, who now looked as if he hadn't slept in a week.

"An initial examination by our handwriting people tells us that the samples we found in Caleb Lujan's apartment are consistent with the handwriting on the notes at the crime scenes," Blalock said. "I also verified Brewster's whereabouts for the time of the second murder and it checks out. He was at a strip joint in Farmington. The bartender remembers seeing him because he tried to pick up one of the girls—actually, he offered her a job working for him."

"What a surprise," Ella said acerbically.

"We've got another problem," Neskahi said. "Looks like the Fierce Ones are turning up the heat on Caleb. A cousin of mine who's with the Many Devils street gang let me know that the Fierce Ones want the eyes and ears of the gangs—but they're not asking nicely, if you get my meaning?"

"They want to regain their standing as protectors of the tribe," Ella said. "Anyone have a friend in the Fierce Ones?" she added.

Tache shrugged. "I know someone. He doesn't advertise the fact, but I'm pretty sure he's with them," he said.

The absence of a name suggested to Ella that Ralph was speaking of a family member. She wondered for a second if Ralph could be the source of the leak, then rejected the thought immediately. He'd been on her team from the beginning, and had never done anything to betray her trust. She avoided looking at Big Ed, but couldn't help but wonder what he was thinking right now.

"Try to send word to the Fierce Ones through him. If we happen to come across Caleb's dead body, or find out he had an accident and drowned in his bathtub, or even that lightning struck him, we're going to be focusing all our energy on them." Ella said.

She glanced over now, and Big Ed was nodding.

Once the meeting ended, Ella went to her office to check for messages. There was one from Carolyn with a request for a call back. Ella tried calling, but got no answer. Experience told her that it would be easier to go over in person than to get Carolyn to answer a ringing phone if she was busy with an autopsy.

Ella arrived at the hospital a short time later, and found Carolyn working on the late Martha Etcitty. Ella glanced in long enough to see more than she'd wanted, then took a seat by Carolyn's desk. Carolyn had seen her, so Ella knew she'd come out as soon as she could.

Less than ten minutes later, Carolyn stepped out. "I'm starving. Did you pick up anything for breakfast today?"

Ella cursed herself. "Sorry. I should have gotten something on the way. I haven't eaten either. It's been *that* kind of morning," she said.

"I wasn't hinting. In fact, I was hoping you hadn't eaten. I made some breakfast burritos with homemade chile sauce. Want to try one?"

Ella nodded, never one to turn down Carolyn's cooking. "I'd love one, if you've got extra."

"I brought plenty since I figured you'd be dropping by."

Carolyn placed the superthick breakfast burritos on two

paper plates, then set them on the desk. Coffee was on the table behind them next to the fax machine.

Ella took a bite, suddenly aware that she was famished. "You never cease to amaze me. You work magic in the kitchen." The egg and sausage mixture was laced with melted cheese and smothered in a salsa that was just right—tangy and hot, but not enough to take a layer of skin off.

"Every once in a while I like them made the Mexican way, with a touch of green chile and salsa."

Ella nodded. "Me, too." She took another bite, swallowed, then looked at Carolyn. "So what have you got for me?"

"You've got two murders with slightly different MOs. Valerie was beaten, then suffered massive cuts that killed her. She was already dead when her head was placed under the water. Martha, on the other hand, was drowned."

Ella considered the information, trying to come to grips with it. "It just doesn't make sense. Serial killers, by and large, don't change their MOs very much at all."

"What about the victims' kids? I understand they were also killed?"

"Shot, execution style, no beatings. No scriptural or other evidence of that nature found at the scene either," Ella replied, pouring Carolyn and herself a cup of coffee.

"You're pretty sure that you're after the same suspect for all these crimes?" Carolyn asked.

"The passages of Scripture left at the crime scenes were written longhand, and they all match Caleb Lujan's handwriting. But there are inconsistencies I can't account for. For example, there was no evidence of burglary at the murder scenes in L.A. and Kayenta or at Martha's, but Valerie's place was ransacked. Yet the note links Valerie's killer to the other murders." She was about to say more when Carolyn's phone rang.

Carolyn picked it up, then handed the receiver to Ella. "Big Ed. He knew you'd be here and that your phone would have to be turned off."

"Chief?" Ella asked.

"The Fierce Ones have found Caleb's hideout. Officer Talk was in the area and will be the first one on the scene. Blalock and your team are in transit and will meet you at the site." Big Ed gave her the location.

"On my way," Ella said, already on her feet and handing the phone back to Carolyn. "Don't have time to explain. We'll talk later."

Ella hit the highway a few minutes later, sirens wailing, and reached for her radio to contact Officer Talk. After three tries without a response, she tried to get word through Dispatch. With no luck still, she contacted Justine.

"Can't get through to Marianna Talk. You have any info on the scene?" Ella clipped.

"Last I heard, the Many Devils spotted Caleb inside a killed hogan they use to rank in new members and called the Fierce Ones. They went over to verify it and then we got called in."

"How long has it been?" Ella asked, wondering if Caleb had already taken off by now.

"Less than a half hour, total."

Ella drove up the dirt road and spotted two pickups beside a hogan about a hundred yards beyond a large arroyo. She continued into the arroyo, then noticed Officer Talk's unit to her right, hidden from above. She parked beside the empty vehicle, and climbed out, rifle in hand.

Blalock came down the road just then and pulled over opposite the dirt track to her left. Justine, Tache, and Neskahi were right behind the Bureau car in a department SUV, which stopped in the center, angling to one side and blocking the trail.

As they were climbing out of their vehicles, Marianna Talk appeared from around a bend in the arroyo, pistol in hand, and hurried over to meet them. "Did you see anyone coming this way?" she asked, trying to catch her breath.

"No. Give me a sit-rep, Officer Talk," Ella said, asking for a situation report as the others armed themselves while keeping watch.

"Two Fierce Ones drove right up to the hogan to check it out. I've verified that one of the pickups belongs to Danny Joe. Robert Pete was with him, but he looks dead. His body is lying beside the hogan."

"Where's Danny?" Ella asked.

"I don't know. He yelled to me when I came up out of the arroyo, then the suspect started shooting. I had to duck back into the arroyo. When I looked up again, he was gone. So I disabled the pickups and headed back in this direction."

Just then they heard several shots fired in rapid succession coming from their left beyond Blalock's vehicle. "Ralph, Joe. Take the left flank above the arroyo. Marianne, Dwayne, the right high ground. Justine and I'll go up the arroyo in the center. Watch your open flanks, and don't walk into an ambush."

Everyone moved out, keeping low and covering one another. Ella took the lead moving up the arroyo, with Justine several steps behind and to her left. They'd gone about fifty feet when Ella saw movement behind a mound of windblown tumbleweeds.

Pointing silently, Ella circled to her right, knowing Blalock and Officer Talk were covering her from that direction. "Tribal police, don't move," she said, sighting in on the man, who had a lever-action rifle pointing farther down the wash.

"It's me, Danny Joe. I got shot."

Ella saw fresh blood on the sand, then noticed a dark stain on his shirt. "Was it you shooting just now?"

"Yeah, at that crazy man. He ambushed us from inside the hogan, then ran off in this direction. He doubled back to finish me off but I saw him coming, so I cut loose."

Danny had been shot through the shoulder, and though the wound was bleeding badly, he'd probably make it, providing the bleeding could be stopped.

Justine came up, cell phone at her ear. "I'm calling for the

EMTs, but I'll make sure they hold back until we give the all clear."

Ella nodded, her eyes still looking ahead. "Where's Caleb now?" she asked Danny.

"He was right in front of me, less than fifty yards, but backed away when I fired. He may have seen or heard your vehicles coming."

"Think you hit him?" Ella asked.

"I doubt it. He was moving, and I was shaking too bad."

"What kind of weapon is he carrying?" Ella asked.

"He took Robert's assault rife and two ten-round magazines. And he has some kind of auto loader, a Glock, maybe. That's what he used to shoot me and Robert."

Ella picked up her handheld and contacted the others, who'd continued to advance, updating them about Caleb's weapons. Neskahi called her back immediately.

"We found a spot where it appears Caleb climbed out of the arroyo and headed east. Blalock and Officer Talk are trying to pick up the trail. Want us to help them out?"

"No, my guess is he's going to circle around behind all of us and, if he can't get to our vehicles, he'll make for the highway. We need to keep Caleb from carjacking anyone. Take Ralph and hightail it back to the main road. I'm going after him," Ella said.

Ella glanced down at Danny. "You'll have help, but I have to leave."

"Get him. He killed Robert."

Justine came up. "Want me here with him or with you?"

"Here, but stay behind cover and maintain contact."

Ella climbed out of the arroyo, then moved forward in an intercept course with Caleb. There was hilly ground to her right, a good place to sit and watch for movement as long as she was careful not to show herself against the skyline. As quietly as possible, she moved from juniper to juniper, selecting the biggest of the low-standing trees and using them more for cover than protection.

As she approached the rocky slope of the first rounded hill, she hesitated. The ground between her current cover, a stand of sagebrush, and a cluster of trees at the top, was wide open.

To her left, she saw two people moving slowly through the trees perhaps two hundred yards away, coming in her general direction. One was wearing a tan uniform—Marianna. To her right, halfway down another hill, Ella saw something blue just beyond the dark green of a juniper. It moved, disappearing from sight.

She picked up her radio. "Dwayne, the perp is on the second hill south of your current location, moving southeast. I'm southwest of you, beside the first hill," Ella whispered into the radio.

"Ten-four, Ella. We'll take the high ground and the eastern slopes. You parallel the hills and continue south. We'll try to drive him in your direction."

"Copy that."

Ella continued south, knowing that Caleb wouldn't be able to move uphill now without being seen. She advanced another hundred yards and stopped beside a wide juniper, listening, and looking for a patch of blue in the undergrowth. She used the scope on her rifle to check out a likely hiding place, and a face appeared just for a second, right in the cross-hair, startling her. The juniper branch to one side of her head suddenly shattered into splinters and a bullet whizzed by her face, stinging her cheek.

Four more shots from behind her rang out—covering fire from Blalock and Marianna. Ella, taking full advantage of it and hoping Caleb was being pinned down, raced ahead, zigzagging, rifle ready.

Their quarry had given away his position, and she hoped to cut him off by getting behind him. As she moved farther up a gentle slope, she saw the top of a small house just beyond, and a whiff of smoke coming from a stovepipe near one end of the corrugated metal roof.

Her stomach fell as she realized that Caleb would now have the opportunity to take a hostage. With no time to hesitate, not if she was going to prevent it, she circled around to the south, intending on approaching the building from that direction.

As she climbed up a small slope, Ella heard a strangled cry of pain, then a woman's panicked voice calling for help. She hurried to the top and as she arrived on a level surface, saw a faded white wood-frame house fifty feet away. On the ground just in front of the open door was a woman, her arm bent in an unnatural angle, her face bloodied.

An engine roared and a pickup suddenly raced into view from around the far corner of the house. It was Caleb, and he looked right at her. Ella raised her rifle and he swerved away, using the house to screen himself from her line of fire.

Hoping to get a shot at a tire, Ella ran to the house, but the road curved around the hill behind some trees and, now, nothing but dust remained. Furious, all she could do was use her radio. Caleb Frank had slipped right through their fingers.

Hours later, Ella was working alongside her crime scene team processing the hogan where Caleb had hid. The trash alone, based on the empty food containers in a pile outside, revealed that the man had spent several days there.

"There's DNA, footprints, everything we need—except Caleb," Justine muttered, gesturing toward a sleeping bag and small foam mattress pad.

Marianna Talk drove up, then approached Ella. "We've got officers stopping every vehicle within thirty miles of this place, but we've got nothing so far." She stared at the ground before her feet and shook her head. "I'm sorry I couldn't take him out when he fired at you," she said, noting the bandage on Ella's cheek where the bullet had grazed her. "I *should* have been able to hit him."

Ella gave her a surprised look. "You were at least one hundred yards away, firing through brush with a handgun. You and Blalock kept him from getting off a second shot, and that saved my butt. You have nothing to blame yourself for."

She nodded, unconvinced, and walked off as Justine came up. "What's eating her?" she asked Ella.

Ella gave her the highlights, then added, "It happens with rookies sometimes. Everything—or nothing—is their fault."

Hearing her cell phone ring, Ella reached into her pocket and brought it out. From Big Ed's somber tone as he identified himself she knew something major had happened even before he gave her the news.

"You can cross another suspect off the list," he said. "Brewster was found in the trash bin of an east Main Street bar by the Farmington police. He'd been shot in the head, execution style."

"Like the children we believe Caleb killed?" Ella asked, verifying the surprising news.

"Precisely. And his wife has an ironclad alibi. FPD is handling it, but they've assured me they'll cooperate and share information with us."

"Have them interview Lynn Bidtah. She was in love with Stan," Ella said, then added, "On second thought, I should do that. She's on our land, way out in the Chuska foothills."

"What's going down?" Blalock asked, joining Ella.

She updated him. "I need to go to Lynn Bidtah's."

"I'll drive, let's go."

Ten minutes later, passing through Shiprock, Blalock glanced over at her. "So what are we looking at here, a jealous lover exacting revenge?"

"I don't think so. Lynn wanted Brewster. It would have made more sense for her to shoot Brewster's wife."

"Could be Brewster dumped Lynn."

"Yeah, maybe," Ella conceded, "but that execution-style thing points to our most likely suspect, Caleb Frank."

Blalock nodded but remained silent, lost in his own thoughts.

The trip to Lynn's place took only about thirty-five minutes, easier this time because they'd made the trip before, and it was day instead of night. Lynn was in front of her sturdy little house, cleaning the windows of her dark blue pickup using a sponge and bucket of sudsy water. She'd probably seen them coming uphill for ten minutes or more, and came over to meet them when they pulled up in front of her house.

"How come you drove all the way out here again?" she asked, making it clear that neither Ella nor her companion was welcome.

Ella studied her face. Lynn hadn't heard yet, if the absence of tears meant anything. "I have some bad news. Do you want to go inside?"

She stared at Ella for a moment then nodded once, and led the way inside. She sat there in the center of the small living room, not offering them a seat. "It's that crazy man, right, the Bible thumper? I *told* Stan that he had to report it, but he said he'd handle things himself. So let me guess. Stan got arrested for beating him up?"

"What are you talking about?" Ella asked.

"That guy Caleb . . . something. He was trying to rattle Stan, leaving notes on his windshield, at the café, and just about everywhere, telling him to make his peace with God, and to beware of the Lord's retribution. The nut job's a real pain. He just doesn't quit. I told Stan to call you guys, but he didn't want anything to do with the police." She glanced at them with a worried frown. "So what happened? Stan lost it and started swinging?"

"Stan's dead," Ella said.

Lynn rocked back on her feet, her face turning pale. "No, that can't be. No, not Stan."

Ella nodded. "I'm sorry."

Lynn took two steps back and dropped onto the sofa. Her mouth was slightly open and her dark eyes registered nothing.

"Tell me more about the man you said was after Stan," Ella pressed, hoping to gather information before Lynn became guarded again.

"I don't know much more," she answered in a whisper. "At first he was just a pain, but then he started getting under Stan's skin. I really think the guy had something on him. I never did buy the reason he gave me for not calling the cops."

"Any idea what that could have been?"

She shook her head, then looked directly at Ella. "Are you sure Stan's dead?"

"Yes." Ella had seen this before. Right now her mind was refusing to process the information and that protected her. But in a few hours when the reality hit her, she'd fall apart.

"Do you remember hearing anything, anything at all, that might help us in our search for Caleb?" Ella pressed.

"Stan told me that Caleb was hassling you, too. The guy told him that you were standing between him and his mission. From what I put together, I think Caleb wanted to baptize everyone. He'd told Stan it was never too late and that baptism marked a soul as God's."

As the words sank in, her thoughts suddenly crystalized. She knew why Caleb had killed Brewster. He'd ruined Caleb's preconceived plan. The reason Caleb's MO at Valerie's had differed from the rest was because he hadn't been the first to arrive. Brewster had been there first, and it was Stan who'd beaten and killed Valerie, then torn up the place to make it look like a robbery. By the time Caleb arrived, he'd been forced to perform his baptism on a corpse, clean up some of the mess, then stage his little ceremony. Stan Brewster had prevented Caleb from fulfilling his mission to save Valerie, and that had carried the death penalty.

"Ella, Caleb killed Brewster because the man interfered with his plans for Valerie, right?" Blalock said. "That's why the scene was so confusing. Two men had been there that night."

"Yes, and Caleb isn't going to leave until he gets rid of all his children. And the only person still alive that might be one of his offspring is . . ." She clamped her mouth shut, unwilling to say anything else in front of Lynn.

Blalock looked over at Lynn, who was zoned out, and

shook his head. "The one we're having protected now," he finished, understanding precisely who Ella had meant.

"We've got to get going. Caleb's too close to succeeding. All he needs now is leverage," Ella said. To complete the tasks he'd set out to do in order to restore his own harmony and make peace with his god, Caleb needed to find Boots—and to find Boots, he'd find a way to get some leverage.

"Wait!" Lynn stood. "Take the shortcut."

"Where, how?" Blalock asked.

Lynn gave them directions, and they hurried out to Blalock's sedan. They drove away in a cloud of dust, this time heading almost due south over a barely traveled path.

"Ella, you thinking Caleb's going after your family?"

"Yes, or Lena Clani. Or anyone else he thinks will buy him Boot's location," she answered, bringing out her phone.

Wanting to warn her family that danger was imminent, Ella called Rose, but couldn't get an answer. A cold chill swept over her and she dialed Kevin next.

"Is my mom there?" Ella asked when Kevin picked up the phone.

"No, Rose left a while ago. She's going to her old house and look over some tile samples the contractor wanted her to choose from."

Ella told Kevin about Caleb and warned him to watch over Dawn carefully. She then called the house, but nobody picked up the phone. Ella tried the contractor last of all, but was unable to reach him.

A cold, mind-numbing fear swept through her. Something was very wrong. She could feel it with every breath she took and with each beat of her heart. Caleb was closing in on her and where Caleb went, death followed.

TWENTY-FIVE
——— ✖ ✖ ✖ ———

After confirming a search was underway for her mother, and an officer on his way to Lena Clani's, Ella called Clifford. In a short, staccato burst, she updated him on the danger.

"You think Mom was lured to our old home?" Without waiting for an answer, he added. "I can be there in five minutes."

"Brother, *think*. Don't go charging in there. For all we know, Mom had a flat tire, and is fine. What you do best—what I want from you—is stealth."

There was a pause and he added, "What exactly do you need from me?"

"Go over without letting anyone see you. Don't *do* anything. Just see if anything is out of place, or just looks wrong, then report back to me."

"Okay. But on foot, it'll take twenty minutes unless I run."

"Go, but don't get spotted," she added. "And if everything's okay, use Mom's phone and let me know right away."

They finally reached the highway. "Lynn's shortcut sucks, Ella. We must have wasted ten minutes just getting around that wash," Blalock complained.

Accelerating rapidly, Blalock was finally able to put the hammer down. He switched the siren on, and the fence posts beside the road started flashing by. It would be another fifteen minutes at this speed.

Finally they reached the turnoff. Another few miles by graveled road at forty-five tops, and they'd be here. Ella, on the lookout for anything out of place, noticed a blue pickup coming up fast behind them.

"A truck's following us. Stay sharp."

"Caleb?" He checked out the rearview mirror.

"Or maybe just one of the guys who've been helping my brother repair his hogan. But I'll keep a watch on it just in case."

Clifford called Ella as they reached the last turn leading to her mother's home. "I'm here in the kitchen. I sneaked in though an open window. Nobody's in the old part of the house, but Mom's truck is outside at the end of the driveway. She's got a flat rear tire."

"Where is she?"

"I don't know yet."

"I sure wish you had a cell phone. Is anyone else there?"

"No, not that I can see. It's after five. The construction workers are gone," he said. "But there's another pickup behind the horse's barn. I'll call you back when I know more."

Ella turned to Blalock, who'd been looking ahead. "My brother is inside the house, but can't find Mom. There's an unidentified pickup behind the barn."

"I'll slow down so we won't leave a dust trail," Blalock said.

"I'll let backup know to make a silent approach." Ella said, then called Dispatch, asking the station to advise those on the way. She had a plan, and would be too busy during the next few minutes to be tied down to the radio.

Ella knew every inch of this route, and she saw the place she had in mind coming up. "Stop and let me out here, Dwayne, then just drive by Mom's like you're heading for my brother's house. Once you get out of sight, double back on foot and approach from the north."

Blalock, already driving at a crawl, halted the vehicle quietly. Ella jumped out and grabbed her rifle, which she'd left in the backseat. She looked back but the blue pickup wasn't there anymore. It must have turned down another side road.

"I'll take my radio, but try to reach me on the cell phone instead," she said, setting the device on vibrate.

"Be careful," Blalock said.

"You too," Ella said, then ran toward the familiar arroyo. The deep wash went right past their corral, and she'd be able to get close without being seen.

She was less than a hundred yards from the house when her cell phone vibrated. "Blalock?"

"No. It's me, your brother. I'm still at the house," he said in a whisper-soft voice. "Mom's in trouble, and I can't help her because Caleb's between us. But the good news is that Caleb can't reach her either. She's up on the roof of the old house. Mom must have pulled the ladder up with her. I heard her moving around and that aluminum ladder makes a distinctive noise."

Ella smiled. Way to go, Mom! "She's out of his line of fire?"

"Absolutely. He knows she's up there, but just can't get to her at the moment. But keep in mind that if he'd wanted to shoot her, he could have done that from the outside. I'm sure he's trying to come up with a plan to get her back down. By the way, was it you who just drove by in that green car?"

"That was Blalock. He'll be moving in on foot from the direction of your house. I'm in the arroyo behind the old corral. I've got a rifle. Could I get into position to pick off Caleb?" Ella asked. She was standing in the arroyo at the spot where Dawn and her friends always climbed in and out of the arroyo. A trail led to the corral from there.

"I doubt it. All I've seen is his shadow. He's currently hugging the wall in that little courtyard between the old house and the new rooms. He doesn't have that many options, though. If he leaves to look for something to climb up with, he's risking Mom coming back down and making a run for it. But she can't make a move without him knowing it either, cause she needs to position the ladder first," Clifford said. "I've been trying to find a way to get to him, but there's only one way into that courtyard. We'd have to come in through the gap between the buildings where the wall and gate are going to go, and he's got that covered. He's armed, I'm sure."

"Caleb has an assault rifle and a handgun. What about you?"

"I've got my thirty-thirty."

Ella maneuvered to an angle where she could see her mother. Looking through the rifle scope, Ella could see that Rose was trapped. Her mom was on a section of roof that was in the process of being removed to make room for the installation of a new furnace and air conditioner, and she'd have to walk across a narrow roof beam to go in any other direction other than the courtyard. The aluminum ladder was on the roof beside her, but she'd have to lower it back into the courtyard to climb down and that's where Caleb was.

Then Ella had a sudden burst of inspiration. The ladder could be a bridge as well. Turning to look around at her resources, Ella noted, along with Blalock and the women officers on the way, there was a big yellow loader that had been used during a previous construction phase. Her idea was jelling now. All she needed was a heavy equipment operator.

Ella called her brother.

"Sure I can operate a loader," Clifford answered. "You remember that I worked construction for two years while I was still learning my profession?"

"And you can start it up without a key, right?" Ella replied.

"Yeah, how'd you know?"

"Hey, back in high school you picked up some moves that we never told Mom about. I covered for you a few times, if you recall."

"Oh, yeah. You gotta admit, sometimes, like when you've misplaced your keys, it's good to know someone who can get around vehicle ignition systems. What do you want me to do with the loader?"

Ella explained, and he agreed immediately.

"Okay, then we're all set," she answered. "Stay where you are, and be ready in case he makes a run for it. You're the only one currently in position to stop him if he tries to leave that courtyard. And turn the ringer down on Mom's phone."

"Already done."

Ella saw two police cars coming up the road—Marianna Talk and Justine. After briefing everyone quickly, Ella ran around to the back of the house and climbed in through the window. "It's me, brother," she said softly, not wanting to get shot by Clifford.

She moved into the kitchen and found him by the window, looking toward the entrance of the new courtyard. The phone—Rose still used an old-style corded phone—was on the counter, and his rifle was up and ready.

"I'll take over here. Go back out and around. Officer Talk and Justine know the plan and once Blalock returns, we can set things in motion." She set her rifle down, and brought out her pistol.

"You can see his shadow, but he's never stepped forward far enough for me to take a shot," Clifford said, indicating with a nod in the direction his rifle was aiming.

Ella took his place, and Clifford stepped away.

"Don't expose yourself any more than necessary, brother."

"Right," Clifford said, then left the kitchen.

Ella took out her cell phone and punched Blalock's number. "I'm keeping watch on Caleb from our kitchen, Dwayne. Run back and get your car, then park outside the bedroom window on the south side of the house. Then you can walk around and get set up with Justine. Once you two are in position to pin down Caleb, Clifford will move in with the loader. Officer Talk will ride with him to provide cover fire. The second everyone's in position I'm going up on the roof to get Mom."

"You'll have plenty of cover fire and I'm giving Clifford a vest," Blalock said. "One with added armor plates. Caleb has an assault rifle. And there'll be one waiting for you on the hood of my car."

"Good. How much tear gas do you have?"

"Three grenades. And two smoke grenades. Wanna use them, too?"

"Yeah. The less he can see, the better."

Five minutes went by, and she only caught a brief glimpse of Caleb. He took a quick peek to see what was going on, and a blast from somebody's pistol struck the wall, just missing him. Ella held off firing, the movement was so fast she would have had no chance of hitting him anyway. But the coverage told her that Justine and Blalock were outside the courtyard now, behind the walls on either side. Once Blalock called her on the phone, it was time.

Ella moved back through the house and exited out the front door. Circling around, she found Blalock's car parked in just the right spot. She put on the vest, checked her pistol, and then noticed a plastic drop cloth rolled up beside the house. It was normally used for covering floors when painting, but she had a better use for it now.

She set the roll atop the car, then climbed up onto the hood. Blalock's vehicle, always freshly waxed, was slippery, so she moved carefully as she stepped up onto the car's roof. The edge of the house was right there, just above waist height. She placed the drop cloth on the roof, then climbed up beside it. The additional weight of the heavy ballistic vest she now wore made her movements cumbersome.

With the drop cloth under her arm, she stepped across the fiberglass shingles of the old part of the house, came up to the crown, and stopped for a look. Beyond and below she could see Rose, sitting on a single sheet of old roofing plywood scheduled for removal. It had already been stripped of shingles and felt paper. The piece had been left till last because there was a light fixture just below it still in use, and wiring to be rerouted. Beside her mom lay the aluminum ladder, and beyond in every direction, nothing but bare rafters for at least twenty feet. Below, Ella could see the dirt floor of the courtyard. From her angle, she couldn't see Caleb, whom she knew to be beneath the overhang of the roof.

The sound of heavy equipment got Ella's attention and she looked away at the loader, which was coming into view around the corner of the house, moving in the direction of the open end of the courtyard. Down at the far end of the driveway, she also noticed the blue pickup she'd seen following them earlier. Hopefully, the visitor would have enough sense to keep away.

When Ella turned back, her mom was looking right at her. Despite the distraction of everything going on down below, Rose had somehow known her daughter was there.

Ella held a finger to her lips, then told Rose what to do next with gestures only, since speaking would alert Caleb. His strategy up to now had suggested he'd wanted to take Rose alive, but now that he was trapped, all bets were off.

Finally Rose nodded.

Ella untied the rolled up drop cloth, moved it into position, then stood and waved at Clifford, who'd been sitting at the controls of the loader, waiting. She gave him a thumbs-up, and he gunned the engine, raised the big scoop on the machine just off the ground, and began to inch forward.

Seconds later, Ella heard two small explosions. Detecting traces of tear gas in the air, she tossed out the drop cloth to cover as much of the open area of the roof as possible. That would conceal their actions from below and help keep the tear gas and smoke concentrated down in the courtyard.

Rose slid the end of the ladder toward Ella next, creating a metal bridge. When it got close, Ella maneuvered her end of it to connect with a solid area of the roof. Pistol in hand, Ella looked down into the courtyard area not hidden by the drop cloth, then waved to her mom to come over.

Rose crawled out onto the ladder but stopped as gunfire

erupted and bullet holes appeared on the plywood behind her, kicking up dust and splinters. Caleb was firing blind at the sound. Ella returned fire, hoping to drive Caleb back under cover until Rose reached the solid section of the roof.

Although Rose's eyes were watering, she arrived safe and unharmed. Ella gave her a quick hug, then peered down into the smoke, trying to see what was going on. The shooting had stopped. Then Clifford turned off the loader's engine. For a moment, all she could hear was coughing.

"Don't shoot! I'm coming out!" Caleb yelled coughing

"Throw out your weapons first!" Blalock yelled. "Then come out slowly with your hands up over your head."

Ella stepped around the solid part of the roof, looking for a good angle and, finally, through the haze of tear gas, saw Caleb. His hands were up as he stepped out into the open. Blalock was at the entrance to the courtyard, motioning him forward while covering him with a pistol.

Ella pulled away the drop cloth, then turned to her mother, who was now standing, brushing off her dress.

"You okay, Mom?"

"Of course, daughter. What took you so long? I've been on this roof for over an hour."

"Feel free to step off anytime," Ella joked. "Or maybe we should just use the ladder."

Suddenly there were two loud pops, followed by shouting below. Ella crouched and aimed her pistol into the courtyard. Lynn Bidtah was on her knees, sobbing, and Justine was placing handcuffs on her none too gently. Then she saw Caleb on his back. His chest was oozing blood, and Blalock was trying to stem the flow with some kind of cloth, maybe a handkerchief.

Marianna looked up. "You two okay?" Her voice was shaky.

"Yes. Lynn shot Caleb, am I right?" Ella verified. She recalled seeing the blue pickup, but had lost track of it when the action started.

"I'd warned her to stay in the pickup, but she came up

right behind me," Justine said, looking up, but keeping one hand on her prisoner. "Nobody even noticed her until she started shooting."

Ella and her mom climbed down from the roof into the courtyard. Rose looked bewildered, but remained steady as a rock. Rose squeezed Ella's hand tightly, then turned and headed into the house.

Ella then went to join her team, whose voices were being drowned out by the siren from the EMTs' truck as it raced up the road. Seconds later, the emergency vehicle came to a stop. As the medical team worked, Marianna and Justine led Lynn past Ella.

Lynn's eyes were wild, her face flushed with anger. "Is he dead? Is he dead?" Lynn kept repeating all the way to the Marianna's squad car.

Ella looked over at the EMTs working on Caleb, then back to Lynn, being placed in the backseat, a prisoner now. Neither would escape justice.

Two days later, Ella and Justine sat across from the chief's desk. Big Ed looked somber. "What's the word from the hospital on Caleb Frank?" he asked.

"Caleb will live, if you want to call it that, but he'll never be able to walk again, or even feed himself. His spine was pretty much severed. He's lucid, despite the pain, so maybe he'll discover firsthand that hell he's been preaching about," Ella said.

"Why did Lynn Bidtah follow you there? I still don't get that," Big Ed said.

"Lynn loved Stan Brewster," Ella answered. "She wanted his killer dead. I just never realized what price she'd be willing to pay to make it happen."

"I spoke to Caleb briefly at the hospital," Justine said. "He was eager to confess, and proud of what he'd done, if you can imagine. Turns out Brewster killed Valerie, just like I'd thought. Caleb saw Stan leaving the apartment. When he went inside, Caleb found the body. Brewster's wife confirmed it. She opened up to me yesterday and showed me her bruises. Donna said that Stan had been getting increasingly violent. My guess is that he went too far with Valerie."

"Dr. Roanhorse matched some of the DNA collected at Valerie's crime scene to Stan Brewster," Ella said. "The evidence supports the conclusions."

"With all the players either dead or in custody, our case is closed," Big Ed said. Then he lowered his voice. "Except for the Fierce One still employed in this department. He or she is working on borrowed time."

Ella nodded, recalling Ralph Tache's contacts with the group and hoping against hope he wasn't the one. She wouldn't want to be in his shoes for anything if it was true.

"Okay, enough shoptalk," he said with a shrug. Standing up, he reached for a cardboard box he'd placed beside the wall. Inside was a hammer and other hand tools. "It's time for us to go. We don't want to be late."

Justine stood up. "I left my tools in my office."

Ella gave them a curious look. "What's up?"

Big Ed grinned at her. "Word got out about what happened at your home, and how your entire family worked to stop a killer. Church volunteers and some traditionalists and New Traditionalists are already there to finish the roof and make that courtyard something special."

Justine grinned at her. "Even the Fierce Ones showed up. They're going to put in benches and flagstone."

Big Ed looked back at Ella. "You've got friends."

Ella thought about the diverse group that was gathering to help her family. For the first time in a long time she saw herself differently. Being 'alní, part traditionalist and part modernist, had often meant being torn in half. But maybe along the way she'd become a balance point—an anchor of moderation between two extremes—understood by neither side, but respected by both. It was the place she was meant to fill.

As the words of the Navajo blessing said, *Hózonji háaz 'dlíí:* It was beautiful all around her.